THE CONFESSOR

A Jayne Robinson Thriller: Book 3

ANDREW TURPIN

The Write
Direction
Publishing

First published in the UK in 2022 by The Write Direction Publishing, St. Albans, UK.

The Confessor paperback edition

ISBN: 978-1-78875-041-7

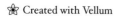 Created with Vellum

WELCOME TO THE JAYNE ROBINSON SERIES!

Thank you for purchasing ***The Confessor*** — I hope you enjoy it!

This is the third in the series of thrillers that features **Jayne Robinson**. Jayne is formerly of the British Secret Intelligence Service (the SIS, or as it is often known, MI6) and is now an independent investigator. She has strong connections with both the CIA and MI6 and finds herself conducting deniable operations on behalf of both services.

The **Jayne Robinson** thriller series is my second series and so far comprises the following:

1. ***The Kremlin's Vote***
2. ***The Dark Shah***
3. ***The Confessor***
4. ***The Queen's Pawn (due to be published late 2022)***

My first series, in which Jayne also appears regularly, features **Joe Johnson**, a former CIA officer and war crimes investigator. The Joe Johnson books so far comprise:

0. **Prequel:** ***The Afghan***
1. ***The Last Nazi***
2. ***The Old Bridge***
3. ***Bandit Country***
4. ***Stalin's Final Sting***
5. ***The Nazi's Son***
6. ***The Black Sea***

If you enjoy this book, I would like to keep in touch. This is not always easy, as I usually only publish a couple of books a year and there are many authors and books out there. So the best way is for you to be on my Readers Group email list. I can then send you updates on the next book, plus occasional special offers.

If you would like to join my Readers Group and receive the email updates, I will send you, **FREE** of charge, the ebook version of ***The Afghan***. It forms a prequel to this series and to the Joe Johnson series, and normally sells at $4.99/£3.99 (paperback $11.99/£9.99).

The Afghan is set in 1988 when Jayne was still with MI6 and Joe Johnson was still a CIA officer. Most of the action takes place in Pakistan, Afghanistan and Washington, DC.

To sign up for the Readers Group and get your free copy of ***The Afghan***, go to the following web page:

https://bookhip.com/RJGFPAW

If you only like paperbacks, you can still just sign up for the email list at the above link to get news of my books and forthcoming new releases. A paperback version of ***The Afghan*** and all my books is for sale at my website, where you will find large discounts on bundles of my books. I can currently ship to the US and UK:

https://www.andrewturpin.com/shop/

Or if you live outside the US and UK you can buy them at Amazon.

Andrew Turpin, St. Albans, UK.

DEDICATION

For my family

"Corruption is something that enters into us. It is like sugar: it is sweet, we like it, it's easy, but then, it ends badly. With so much easy sugar we end up diabetic, and so does our country. Every time we accept a bribe and put it in our pocket, we destroy our heart, we destroy our personality and we destroy our homeland. ... What you steal through corruption remains ... in the heart of the many men and women who have been harmed by your example of corruption. It remains in the lack of the good you should have done and did not do. It remains in sick and hungry children, because the money that was for them, through your corruption, you kept for yourself."

— Pope Francis, speaking at an audience with youth in Kasarani Stadium, Kenya, November 28, 2015

PROLOGUE

Wednesday, June 22, 2016
   Washington, DC

The flashes of bright red cassocks and skullcaps stood out against the pale sandstone building like flames in the night as the three cardinals and the archbishop filed out of the Apostolic Nunciature building. Above them, the gold-and-white Vatican City flag flapped in the breeze.

"There's no going back now," Cardinal Daniel Berg, the archbishop of Galveston-Houston, muttered as he paused at the bottom of the five steps that led to the driveway. He turned his neatly coiffured white head to his colleague Cardinal Lewis Brennan and caught his eye.

"Of course," Brennan said. "Nor should we. Our path is straight. This should have been done a long time ago."

Berg, a cardinal for the previous nine years, nodded and clasped his leather document case tighter beneath his left arm. Brennan was correct. As was often the case in the Catholic Church, they had dithered and delayed for too long, wary of triggering a direct confrontation. Procrastination seemed to have been wired into the DNA of too many of them.

The men turned as a black BMW sedan drove through the gate to their left and crawled around the neatly symmetrical semicircular drive before coming to a halt directly in front of them. The driver opened his door and got out.

"Your Excellence, Your Eminences," the driver said, nodding at the archbishop, then the three cardinals in turn. "Please do find yourselves a seat." He circled the car, opening the front passenger and rear doors.

Berg moved first. Easily the tallest of the group, he knew his aging knees, with their steadily worsening arthritis, wouldn't enjoy sitting three abreast squashed up in the rear.

"I hope you don't mind, gentlemen, but I'm just not going to fit in the back," he said, glancing behind him. He made straight for the front passenger seat without waiting for a response.

He pulled his cassock up behind him, lowered his angular frame, and slowly levered himself in.

"Don't worry about us," said Brennan, the archbishop of Chicago. "We know you only fly at the front of the plane."

The other two men gave a muted laugh. One of them, the somewhat rotund Cardinal Simon Kluwers, was archbishop of Detroit. The other, Antonio Delgado, who unlike the others wore a black cassock with a purple silk sash around his slim waist, was an archbishop and the *papal nuncio*, or ambassador, to the United States. This made him Pope Julius VI's representative in Washington, DC, as well as responsible for the Vatican's relationships with the Roman Catholic bishops in the US. He was a certainty to be elevated to the rank of cardinal once his term in the States had ended.

Delgado's office, staff, and living accommodation were in the elegant, historic nunciature at 3339 Massachusetts

Avenue, which the men had just left and which was within the Embassy Row neighborhood.

Berg glanced out the window at the three-story building, which dated back to 1893. He couldn't help envying the nuncio, who certainly lived and worked in style. The expansive reception rooms contained a wealth of ornate Roman furniture, artwork, tapestries, and other artifacts.

The driver made another circuit of the BMW, closing the doors as he went, before climbing into the driver's seat. "Next stop 1600 Pennsylvania Avenue," he said as he turned the ignition key.

Indeed, the White House was where they were headed.

Normally, such meetings were informal and were held in a meeting room in the Situation Room suite, down in the basement of the West Wing. In most cases, the only attendee on the White House side was President Stephen Ferguson's personal aide, Charles Deacon, an academic-looking man with black glasses and a hook nose. Delgado represented the Vatican, although Berg had accompanied him on a couple of occasions. The meetings, held every three months or so, had become a very useful way for Delgado to communicate the pope's views to the White House.

Today, however, the agenda was going to be somewhat different.

Delgado had been instructed by Pope Julius VI to communicate two key pieces of highly confidential, and rather controversial, information to the president.

The first, which Berg knew would be controversial, was that the Vatican was intending very shortly to officially recognize, and sign a treaty with, the State of Palestine, the mortal enemy of the US's ally Israel.

This was guaranteed to go down extremely badly with President Ferguson but far worse with Israel, which had fought long and hard over the years against such recognition.

The Israeli prime minister, Yitzhak Katz, was due to be officially informed later that day.

The second piece of information, designed to directly offset the impact of the first and to soften the blow for both the Israelis and the Americans, was that the Vatican was to open its Secret Archive and release its hugely controversial papers relating to the Second World War. These papers would shed light on the failure of Pius XII, who was pope from 1939 to 1958, to speak out against the Holocaust and the murder of six million Jews by Hitler's Nazi Germany. Nor did he speak out against Hitler's invasion of Poland, a strongly Catholic country, or other European states. It was something for which Pius had been widely condemned ever since.

Because Delgado had clearly indicated to Deacon exactly how contentious the agenda for their meeting would be, the list of attendees on the White House side had been expanded at a very senior level.

The secretary of state, Paul Farrar, was now due to attend, along with one of his aides. Because of the sensitivities surrounding the Israelis and Palestinians and the potential for a backlash against the Vatican, Delgado had also requested that someone senior from the Central Intelligence Agency be there. As a result, the CIA's deputy director for operations, Vic Walter, had been added to the list.

However, there was a third piece of information the four men wanted to disclose to and discuss with the officials at the White House. It was not something directed by the pope, but rather a somewhat incendiary issue that had caused them increasing alarm over recent months after it came to light. In fact, Berg had been the one who first became aware of it.

The details of the disclosure, which would also come as a bombshell, were recorded in documents tucked inside Berg's leather case, which he now placed on the car floor between his feet.

Berg fastened his seat belt and settled back for the drive to the White House, about two and a half miles to the southeast. The driver pushed down on the accelerator, and the car slipped quietly forward around the driveway, separated from the street only by a low fence of black metal railings and a row of ancient American linden trees, which Berg had discovered were more than a hundred years old.

The electric gates, which matched the fence, were already open, and very quickly, the car was heading south on Massachusetts Avenue NW toward the city center.

The street, with two lanes in each direction, was quiet for a change, with few other vehicles. They headed swiftly past the sprawling redbrick British embassy complex on the right, and the smaller but more elegant South African embassy on the left, with its outside statue of Nelson Mandela giving a clenched fist salute.

Then, as they passed the old Iranian embassy and approached the junction with 30th Street NW on the left, the lights at a crosswalk flicked to red. The BMW rolled to a gentle halt in the right lane, just a long stone's throw from the Italian embassy to the right.

A couple, hand in hand, stepped off the sidewalk and headed across, while the driver next to Berg tipped his head back against the headrest in a moment of relaxation.

Berg heard a guttural roar from a motorcycle as it pulled up next to the BMW in the left lane.

He glanced sideways at the bike, a powerful-looking silver Yamaha. The rider and passenger wore black leather and black helmets with gray tinted visors. Both were staring hard at the BMW and its occupants. Berg wasn't surprised. He had gotten used to such attention whenever he appeared in public in his red cassock and skullcap.

As he watched, the passenger unzipped his jacket and put his hand inside, his head still turned toward the car. The man took out a large handgun, and Berg's stomach flipped over.

A jolt of electricity shot right through him as the next couple of seconds unfolded in what felt like slow motion.

The man pointed the gun at the rear window of the BMW and, without hesitating, rapidly fired one shot, then another, and another, and another, and another.

The window glass exploded, and splatters of blood spurted all over the inside of the car, specking the windshield, the seats, and everything else with splashes of red, perfectly matching the color of the cardinals' cassocks.

Berg felt the urge to scream, but the noise stuck in his throat and he couldn't, his eyes fixed on the gunman.

Then the gunman turned his head toward the front of the car.

Berg knew that behind his visor, he was staring straight at him.

Instinctively, he tried to duck his head as low as he could and to get his body down. But the sudden movement tightened the seat belt across his chest.

It locked rigid.

Berg turned his head back to the window just as the gunman pulled the trigger.

There was another tremendous bang, a flash, and the glass next to his head erupted. Then came darkness.

PART ONE

CHAPTER ONE

Wednesday, June 22, 2016
Washington, DC

The main conference room in the White House Situation Room center was deathly quiet.

Vic Walter glanced around the long, polished wooden table. The men present were staring at a large monitor screen on the wall where the Washington, DC, police chief, Stuart Cobb, was describing what he knew so far of the horrific multiple murder that had taken place a couple of hours earlier on Massachusetts Avenue NW.

Over a secure video conference link, Cobb told them how the hit had lasted only a few seconds. It had involved two persons on a motorcycle, one of whom had fired a series of powerful 10mm Auto rounds through the windows of the clergymen's car. Two cartridges had been recovered from inside the vehicle, and ballistic tests were already underway to identify the gun used to fire them.

Three cardinals from Galveston-Houston, Chicago, and

Detroit, an archbishop who was the Vatican's apostolic nuncio in the United States, and their driver had all been killed instantly by head shots. It was a highly professional assassination.

There had been a handful of witnesses in other cars and on foot, but based on the initial interviews, there was little information of use. The gunman and his partner had roared off quickly and had so far not been traced. Nobody appeared to have taken note of the bike's license number.

There was a long pause when Cobb finished speaking.

The secretary of state, Paul Farrar, was ashen-faced, his arms tightly folded. He sat in the black leather chair normally occupied by the president, at the head of the table beneath the presidential seal on the wall behind him. To Farrar's right was the tall, lank-haired figure of Phil Anstee, the national security advisor who had not been scheduled to attend their original meeting but had since been called to the building.

Another monitor on the opposite wall was tuned to one of the rolling TV news channels and silently showed a reporter standing farther down Massachusetts Avenue NW with an array of emergency vehicles, their blue and red lights flashing, acting as the backdrop for his report. The media juggernaut was already gearing itself up. The evening news bulletins and the next morning's headlines would be messy, that was for certain. CNN, Fox, and other major news channels were already leading with the story.

Vic had a sick feeling at the base of his stomach. The impact of the assassinations on all the group had been so much greater given that the clergymen had been on their way to the White House to meet them.

When they failed to arrive on time, someone in the Situation Room had put a call through to the nunciature building, where an official then tried to call the cardinals' cell phones, only to get no response. It was then obvious that something was seriously wrong.

A few minutes later, an urgent call had come in to the Situation Room from the police department with news of the disaster.

"I'm assuming we have no idea why this happened," Vic said.

"The reason why is an issue for you, Vic, and for Paul," Cobb said, staring straight into his camera. His face appeared more lined and his neatly parted hair grayer than they had when Vic had last seen him. "It makes sense for us to focus on tracking down the killers and collecting the evidence right now, not figure out why they were there. We've sealed the area. CSI is there, and we're well underway with full interviews of the few witnesses. The Feds are fully involved now, as you'd expect."

All agencies involved had immediately categorized the killings as a terrorist incident, which meant the FBI would work alongside the DC police on the case.

Vic turned to Charles Deacon and raised his eyebrows. "Were the clergymen going to tell us anything that might have triggered this?"

Deacon, who had beads of sweat visible on his forehead despite the cool temperature in the room, shrugged. "God knows. No pun intended."

Nobody smiled.

"Listen, I've told you all I know," Deacon said. "Delgado hinted that Palestine and Israel would be on the agenda, but said I wasn't to put that down on paper. My guess is that the Vatican is about to announce it is recognizing the State of Palestine, although we've had no previous sign of that. The Israel bit was likely to involve more detail around the planned opening of the Secret Archive and the Nazi documents— we're in the loop on that one. That was it."

Deacon adjusted his glasses and pursed his lips. "Of course, I don't need to remind you all that the president is due to visit the Vatican in less than three weeks—Monday the eleventh—followed by meetings with the Italian prime minister. He has an audience with the pope, and the plan is that they will jointly announce the initiative on the Secret Archive —in public, in St. Peter's Square. The president is not eager to be associated with the recognition of Palestine, although he can see the argument. But the Secret Archive is a different matter. He sees plenty of upsides there among the Jewish lobby, and so he's on board with it. However, these killings are going to provide an awful backdrop for that visit."

The president's adviser caught Vic's eye and raised his eyebrows. Vic, who was only too well aware of President Ferguson's impending visit, said nothing but slowly shook his head to convey his dismay.

Farrar clasped his hands behind his head. "I'll speak to the Vatican and see if they can shed any more light on it," he said. "The Secret Service team working at the Vatican ahead of the visit there might also pick up some information."

Vic knew that a Secret Service team had traveled to the Vatican to put security arrangements and protocols in place ahead of President Ferguson's visit.

Farrar turned to Cobb on the monitor screen. "Do you have any CCTV of the incident, Stuart? And what do the Feds think?"

Farrar had only returned to work the previous week following a spell in the hospital after being badly injured in a terrorist attack on an offshore gas platform he had been visiting in Israel. Now this. Vic knew it was the last thing the secretary of state needed.

"We're gathering video from surveillance cameras," Cobb said. "The team is already going through what we have so far. We might get the bike license plate from the video. And I'm waiting to get a proper view from the Feds. I have a call arranged with Bonfield when we're done here."

Robert Bonfield was the FBI's director, responsible for national security and intelligence gathering at the domestic level.

Farrar exhaled heavily. "I'm trying to brace myself for what's coming. Are we talking isolated Islamic fundamentalists? Is it something like the Boston Marathon attack, some lone individuals? Or is it driven by one of the bigger organizations?"

There had been a series of isolated attacks by Muslim extremists in various parts of the United States over recent years, all carried out by individuals working on their own initiative rather than as part of some larger coordinated master plan. Apart from the Boston Marathon bombing, which killed three and injured hundreds, Vic recalled a hatchet attack on policemen on a New York subway and shootings at two military bases in Chattanooga, Tennessee, among many others.

"We've had nothing on our radar about a coordinated attack," Vic said. "Let's wait and hear from Bonfield, but as far as I know from my regular conversations with him, the Feds haven't either. I would have bet it's another isolated incident if it weren't for the fact that those guys were on their way to the White House to discuss some highly sensitive issues with us. It might just be coincidence, but that's unlikely. The clue is in the timing. My guess would be it's based on inside information. A leak."

Farrar pressed his lips together. "This is a big step too far, though. We are going to be pummeled by the media and the Republicans over this. Social media will go berserk. If we can't keep our church leaders safe, who can feel safe?"

Nobody spoke.

Vic knew the secretary of state was correct. The climate

of fear amid the general population of the United States had risen markedly with each successive attack. With a presidential election on the horizon, President Ferguson had better brace himself for an onslaught from his Republican opponents, led by their candidate for the White House, Nicholas McAllister, all of whom had law and order at the top of their agendas. Without a doubt, they would make huge political capital out of this.

Vic and his boss, the Director of the CIA Arthur Veltman, did their level best to stay out of politics and just do their job. But it wasn't always that easy, because the politicians of both major parties often crossed the line by trying to persuade their various intelligence and security agencies to take certain actions that were bound to yield political benefits.

But in this case, there was no such issue. The killers had to be caught. As soon as the meeting was over, Vic planned to get on the phone with Bonfield.

Surely it was impossible that two assassins could carry out the cold-blooded murder of four high-ranking Vatican churchmen and a driver in the middle of the nation's capital and just disappear without a trace. They'd find them.

* * *

Wednesday, June 22, 2016
   Washington, DC

The moon was glinting through Vic Walter's seventh-floor office window and the digital clock on the wall read 11:19 p.m. when he finally turned off his computer and his desk lamp and pulled on his jacket.

After returning to the CIA's headquarters building at

Langley, the rest of the day had been predictably chaotic. An endless stream of calls, video conferences, and internal meetings, all of them concerning the assassinations earlier, had left him no time for dinner. Instead, the remains of a chicken sandwich lay on a plate on his new oak desk, next to a cold, half-drunk cup of coffee.

As he expected, the evening news bulletins led with a mixture of gory details, shots of emergency vehicles and crime scene vans, and scathing criticism of the United States' security and intelligence services for allowing such a deadly attack to take place in the nation's capital with no warning.

He walked out the door and was about to lock it behind him when his cell phone rang yet again. He pulled it out of his pocket. It was Robert Bonfield. He pressed the green button.

"Are you still in the office, Vic?" Bonfield said without preamble.

Vic paused. "Do you have any idea what time it is? I was about to leave, finally."

"We're in for an all-nighter here. I've just come off a long call with Stuart Cobb. They're handing most of this over to us now. Are you sitting down?"

"I've just shut my office door."

"Turn around. Best take a seat. Switch your PC back on. I need you to look at a video, and there's something in it you won't like."

Vic swore out loud but did as instructed. He returned to his desk, flicked on his PC, logged in, and turned on the desk lamp, which left him illuminated by an eerie half circle of light in the gloomy interior.

A couple of minutes later, he was hunched over his monitor screen as he loaded a short segment of footage from a police surveillance camera that Bonfield had sent to his secure download site.

He hit play.

The somewhat grainy footage showed a black BMW sedan approaching traffic lights on Massachusetts Avenue NW and then braking to a halt as the traffic light turned red.

A couple, hand in hand, were crossing the street.

A few seconds later, a silver motorcycle carrying two people dressed in black leather came to a halt in the lane next to the BMW.

The passenger, partially concealed from the camera by the rider, unzipped his jacket and removed a handgun, which he then immediately used to pepper the BMW next to him, firing multiple shots first through the rear windows, then the front.

The shooter then got off the bike, walked to the front passenger door of the BMW, bent down, and peered in. Next, he opened the door and took out what looked like a brown leather document case.

He then shut the door, calmly walked back to the bike, climbed back on, and tucked the document case inside his jacket.

The motorcycle then roared off through the traffic lights, which were still red.

The brief video clip ended at that point.

"Shit," Vic said. He leaned back in his chair, feeling stunned. It was one of the ugliest assassinations he had seen in his entire CIA career, dating back to the 1980s, and he had witnessed a number. "What was in that case? Documents for the meeting, presumably."

"Good question," Bonfield said. "Police have been trying to trace the bike, but it had false plates. Stuart's guys followed it via CCTV for another half mile or so to Sheridan Circle Park, but it turned off there, and we lost it in the back streets north of Dupont Circle. It probably stopped somewhere prearranged so they could change the plates again and disappear. Police have alerts out for them, but no sign of them so far."

Vic sat silent for a moment, thinking, his tiredness forgotten. "You said you were going to tell me something I wouldn't like."

"It was the manner in which this was carried out. Very clinical and professional. Certainly different from your usual hit. Did the style ring any bells?"

"A professional hit is a professional hit. So not especially."

"All right. Take another look at that video. Go to the bit where the gunman on the bike takes out his weapon, and play it in slow motion. Tell me what you see."

Vic sighed. Using his mouse, he pushed the slider on the video clip slowly back to the point where the motorcycle pulled up next to the BMW. Then he selected slow motion and clicked the play button.

"I'm seeing him take out his gun and blitz the hell out of the car, Robert. That's all."

"Play it again. This time, don't look at the gun. Concentrate on the other side of the bike, farthest away from the BMW."

Vic did as instructed.

"I see what looks like a small piece of paper fall to the ground next to the bike," he said. "Is that what I'm looking for?"

"Indeed. The CSI guys spotted it first. They also found it. White on one side, brown on the other. There was no wind this afternoon, and it was still there."

"And?"

"The brown side had a picture of a cow on it and a kind of multicolored flower logo."

Vic nearly growled in frustration. "Cut the crap, Robert. Get to the point. I'm tired."

"One of the techs recognized it," Bonfield said. "It was part of a chocolate bar wrapper. Guess where from?"

Vic remained stubbornly silent.

"Parra chocolate. Often called 'cow chocolate' because of the logo. Made by a company called Strauss."

"Okay. And?"

"It's Israeli."

Vic let out a long breath. "Holy shit."

CHAPTER TWO

Thursday, June 23, 2016
  Washington, DC

"If those Mossad bastards have done this, I'll fly to Jerusalem myself, personally pin that damned prime minister of theirs up against the Wailing Wall, and give him a kicking he won't forget," President Ferguson said.

An image flickered across Vic's mind of President Ferguson's imposing six-foot two-inch frame shoving the diminutive figure of Prime Minister Yitzhak Katz backward against the ancient stone structure of Jerusalem's Western Wall and handing out a beating.

Vic blinked as the president rose from his chair and did a lap of the Oval Office, both hands on his hips, his face as black as a thunderstorm. "Why the hell would they do this?"

It was quarter past eight in the morning, and Vic, the CIA Director Arthur Veltman, and Robert Bonfield had just finished giving their update to the president on events of the previous day. The disclosure about the piece of evidence that appeared to link the killings to the Israelis had been the final straw for Ferguson.

"We don't know they did it, sir," Veltman said. "But if they did, then the upcoming Vatican announcement about Palestine might have something to do with it. We know how that would go down in Jerusalem and Tel Aviv."

"No, Arthur—I don't like the pope recognizing Palestine either," Ferguson snapped. "In fact, I detest the idea. But that doesn't mean I'm going to gun down a group of cardinals on Massachusetts Avenue, does it?"

"Of course not, sir," Veltman responded, sticking his barrel chest out. "Personally, I can't see the Mossad going down this route." He glanced sideways at Vic, who could see his boss was looking for some reinforcing comments.

"Agreed," Vic said, sitting up straight. "I really don't believe they would. If there's any Israeli involvement, it's most likely to be a lone operator. Some kind of hawkish, right-wing extremist who has a special reason for hating the idea of recognition of a Palestinian state." He stifled a yawn as he spoke. He'd only managed about three hours' sleep.

"I also can't see it," Bonfield added. "But . . . " He let his voice trail away.

"But what?" the president demanded. "This is bad, but we all know they've done far worse."

Nobody spoke.

The president continued. "Are you really ruling the Mossad out? Are you saying they're not capable of assassinating those clergy and stealing a document case from a dead man's hands?"

Nobody wanted to answer that question, but eventually Bonfield leaned forward. "We all know the only certainty in our business is uncertainty. There must be an explanation for that chocolate bar wrapper. We have forensics on it now.

They'll do a thorough analysis, see what they can get off it. Prints, DNA, whatever."

"That would be a start," Ferguson said. "I need to know. And it's your job to find out. I can't go and ask Katz myself, that's for sure."

The president picked up a sheaf of newspapers from his desk and walked back to the twin sofas where his three intelligence chiefs were sitting. Veltman and Vic were on one sofa and Bonfield on the other. The president threw the newspapers on the coffee table between them.

"Look at those," Ferguson said. "We've only got four months until the election. If this isn't resolved quickly, I'm dead."

He sat in one of the two armchairs that faced the sofas, the ornate white marble mantelpiece that dominated the northern end of his office looming above his head, topped by a large portrait of George Washington.

He was correct about the election, Vic thought to himself. The headlines were almost universally condemning of the government's grip on the security situation. But at the same time, he felt irritated by the president's apparent thought that his intelligence services should win the election for him. It happened too frequently for his liking and was definitely unhealthy.

"Can't you go and talk to your friends in the Mossad?" Ferguson asked. He flicked a hand across his neatly trimmed iron-gray hair, eyeballing Vic as he did so.

Vic creased his brow. "If you mean Avi Shiloah, I'm in a similar situation to you and Prime Minister Katz, Mr. President. It's not a question I can ask with any expectation of getting a proper answer. Whether they've done it or not, he's certain to say it's not them with exactly the same degree of conviction. And he's a very good poker player, so we'll never know the truth."

Avi Shiloah was the newly appointed *ramsad*, or head of the Mossad. Previously a deputy director, he had been elevated to the top job less than three months ago after his predecessor, Eli Elazar, had been killed by the same drone attack on an Israeli offshore gas platform that killed the Israeli foreign minister Moshe Cohen and badly injured Paul Farrar. They had all been on an official visit when the attack took place.

Shiloah had been a long-standing friend of Vic's. The two men knew each other from the late 1980s in Islamabad and Afghanistan, when they, Jayne Robinson, and Joe Johnson had first become acquainted as they operated for their respective services to help the Afghan mujahideen against the occupying Soviet forces.

Vic and Shiloah had remained friends, but as they rose up the ladders of their services, politics had gotten in the way, as had the tendency for both the CIA and the Mossad to mount surveillance operations on each other's officers in both countries. There had been wiretaps, illegal room searches, and bugs planted on both sides. It had led to a few tough conversations over the years and, as a result, a certain cooling of relations.

Bonfield's phone pinged loudly in his pocket.

"Excuse me, sir," he said to the president. "I've been waiting for an update on a few things relating to this issue. Do you mind?"

The president indicated his assent with a wave of his hand.

Bonfield took his phone out and scrutinized the screen, then suddenly sat upright and cleared his throat. He looked directly at Veltman first, then Vic.

"You're not going to like this, in view of the conversation we've just had," Bonfield said.

"Go on," Veltman said. He pushed his wire-framed glasses

back up his nose, giving him a donnish look that contrasted with his muscular chest.

"Customs and Border Protection has just reported back. They've pinpointed two Israeli men who flew separately but on the same flight into Dulles on Saturday on El Al and who flew back to Tel Aviv last night. Their passports appeared clean, but we'll check further. Interestingly, there were no other pairs of men flying in and out in the window we're interested in."

"Israelis do tend to fly to and from DC on El Al, Robert," Veltman said in a dry tone.

Bonfield ignored him, looked at the president, and shrugged. "Doesn't necessarily mean anything, but on the other hand . . ."

Ferguson stroked his chin. "It might. Get them checked out."

"We'll get Tel Aviv station onto it too," Veltman said. "There is one other thing. Our research people reminded me that Cardinal Brennan caused something of a stir in Chicago a couple of years ago when he accused the Jews of trying to divert attention away from the Palestinian-Israeli conflict by influencing the media to focus on sexual abuse by Catholic priests. Might not be relevant to this incident, but we can't rule out a link."

"Is that right?" Ferguson asked. Veltman nodded.

The president switched his gaze between Veltman and Vic. "Listen, I hear what you're saying about Avi Shiloah, but I would still like you two to touch base with him, check him out. You're closest to him, despite the issues I know you've had. I don't care how you do it. Use a back channel if you have to. But I want to know what the vibe is like in Tel Aviv about the Vatican and the Palestinian recognition issue, if nothing else at this stage. That might give us something of a steer as to whether we're on track. And I need it done well before my visit to Rome."

"Yes, sir," Veltman said. "We'll get on it."

Vic was struck by how massive a blow it would be if it turned out it was the Israelis who'd assassinated the clergymen. Was this how they were going to repay the Agency after the hugely complex and dangerous work recently done by Jayne Robinson to track down the plotters who blew up the Israelis' gas platform?

"And I also want to know the view from the Vatican," Ferguson went on. "Have they had threats, direct or implicit, from the Israelis about them recognizing the Palestinian state?"

"We've already had a few conversations about that, and so has Paul's team at the State Department," Vic said. "The Vatican is completely in the dark, so they tell us."

"Has the Secret Service team in Rome picked up any useful information?" Ferguson asked.

"No, nothing," Bonfield said.

"Find another way of getting the information, then," the president said. "Somebody must know something. These things don't happen without a good reason, usually."

The president stood up and returned to his desk, signaling that the meeting was over.

"We'll get it done, sir," Veltman said.

Like many politicians, Ferguson had a knack for speaking the blindingly obvious, but making it sound as though he was coming up with a completely fresh idea that nobody else had ever thought of.

But there was one suggestion the president had casually thrown out that had given Vic an idea—that of a backchannel to Avi Shiloah.

CHAPTER THREE

Thursday, June 23, 2016
   Vatican City, Rome

Cardinal Michael Gray hurried along the corridor, pushed open the paneled oak door, which was slightly ajar, and entered the pope's private study as instructed. There was only one man in the room, Cardinal Alfredo Saraceni, archbishop of Turin, who was standing in front of the ancient wooden desk, holding a small wooden crucifix set into a white base. It was identical to those for sale to tourists in the Vatican souvenir shop. Saraceni turned his head as Gray entered, swiftly crossed himself, then replaced the crucifix on the desktop, where the pope always kept it.

Saraceni was the Vatican's secretary of state. That made him effectively the prime minister of the Holy See, the sovereign entity that includes the Vatican city-state, and the second most powerful man in it after the pope himself.

"Hello, Eminence," Gray said as he closed the door behind him. "Has the Holy Father seen the video yet?"

A computer monitor screen that stood on one corner of the desk, next to a larger carved wooden crucifix, had a frozen frame of the video in question displayed on it.

Saraceni shook his head. "No, Eminence, he hasn't. He's on his way right now, and I'm not looking forward to this at all."

Gray, the archbishop of Westminster in London, could feel the knot in his stomach. This was going to be a difficult meeting.

Saraceni moved to take one of the seats in front of the desk, and Gray followed suit. The two men waited in silence, the lack of air-conditioning in the room adding to the discomfort that Gray was feeling.

Sunlight streamed into the room through the third-floor window, from which the pope spoke every Sunday at noon to the crowds in St. Peter's Square below, when he invariably delivered a brief speech, then the traditional Angelus Prayer, and finally a blessing.

It was the first time Gray had been in the study without the presence of the Holy Father, and normally he would have taken the opportunity to scan the bookshelves or look out the window over St. Peter's Square. Today, however, his mind was elsewhere.

After a minute or two, the door opened again and three men entered. One of them was Pope Julius VI, his aged pink face looking purposeful and the whiteness of his cassock matched perfectly by the color of his neatly combed hair. He walked to his chair behind the desk and sat down in front of a messy bookcase that was full of disordered volumes and papers.

The other men were the pope's personal secretary, Christophe Despierre, bishop of Avignon, and Carlo Galli, titular bishop of Capri and the prefect in charge of the Vatican's Secret Archive. The two men, who had been appointed by the pope, sat in the other vacant chairs next to Gray and Saraceni.

"Can we play the video?" the pope asked immediately and with an unusually abrupt note in his voice. It was an instruction, phrased as a question.

"Yes, Holiness," said Despierre. He picked up a remote-control unit, clicked a button, and the video clip, which Gray knew had been emailed to Saraceni by the FBI, began to roll.

The pope leaned forward and used both hands to cup his chin, his forearms propped on the work surface, his eyes fixed on the gory drama that unfolded on the screen. He murmured something to himself in his native Italian and made the sign of the cross in front of his chest halfway through.

When the video finished, the pope made a circling motion with his hand. "Play it again, please."

Despierre pressed play again.

Gray scratched his mainly white hair, which he knew needed a trim, pushed his black glasses up his nose, and forced himself to concentrate on the monitor screen. He was the pope's closest adviser and confidant, alongside Despierre. Although both of them had a long history with the Holy Father, Gray still dreaded crises such as this, when he was expected to provide advice and solutions even when there was no obvious way forward.

There had been many dramas and crises over the years—there was always something in the Vatican. They ranged from sexual abuse committed by priests in many countries to corruption and fraud within the Roman Curia, the central governmental body that administered the Holy See and the Catholic Church. The Holy Father had seemed to value his counsel on all such issues over the years. That was why he had been appointed to his current role as coordinator of Pope

Julius's Council of Cardinals, or C9, so called because it had nine members.

When the film clip finished, Pope Julius tapped the table with the flat of his hand, as he often did when irritated, and looked at each of his colleagues in turn. "Has the FBI identified the man who killed our brothers and took the documents?" he said in his accented but fluent English, the language he normally used when speaking to Gray or to a mixed group such as this one.

"The FBI has not done so yet, Holiness," Saraceni said. "As you can see, it's not possible to make out his face, so they haven't been able to identify him, at least, not so far."

"You have spoken to them?" the pope asked.

Saraceni's face, smoother than his sixty-eight years might suggest, was as impassive as always. "Yes, Holiness. I took a call from the FBI director, Robert Bonfield, in Washington. He wanted to know our views and whether there was any obvious reason for the attack. We discussed the Palestinian issue and the papers relating to Pius XII and the Holocaust, but beyond that, I was unable to help him. He said they were making slow progress but had a couple of leads. The Secret Service team working here ahead of the president's visit are also taking a close interest, of course."

Gray knew that several Secret Service agents had been at the Vatican, working with the Swiss Guard on security arrangements to prepare for President Ferguson's scheduled visit on July 11.

The pope leaned back in his chair and looked at Galli, who, as prefect of the Secret Archives, had been leading the project to release the Pius XII papers. "You have had many discussions about Pius and the wartime files, Excellence," the pope said. "Have you seen anything that might have incited this tragedy?"

Galli shook his head, causing his somewhat unruly silver

hair to flop from one side to the other. "There is much controversy surrounding our project, but nothing has surfaced that might have caused this, to my knowledge."

The pope looked up at the ceiling, as if seeking inspiration. "And what *are* your views?" he asked, glancing at the other men. "Between us, inside these four walls, why did this happen?"

The pope glanced over his shoulder at the door, which Gray assumed was to ensure it really was shut properly. In the corridor behind it, as usual, would be one of the Swiss Guard who were responsible for the safety of the pope and the Apostolic Palace in which they sat.

Despierre, a small, slim man and the youngest of the five men in the room at fifty-two, shook his head. "Within these walls, Holiness, we know why our brothers were going to the White House, and we know roughly what they were going to say. We also know what the impact of the imminent announcement about Palestine would have inside Israel. That may be one potential cause." He shrugged.

"But who are we to accuse—without evidence?" Pope Julius asked, looking down at his blotter, which was patched with ink stains. "No, we cannot, and we will not, speculate."

He looked up again, this time at Saraceni. "And you, Eminence. What are your thoughts?"

"The enemies of the Vatican, of the Church, are plentiful," Saraceni said.

That was for certain, Gray thought. Saraceni, as the leading figure in the Roman Curia, the governing body that effectively ran the Vatican and the wider Catholic Church, would know that better than anybody.

"It makes it impossible to know from which direction this attack might have originated," Saraceni continued. "I think we are in the hands of the American criminal investigators, the FBI, to a large degree."

Pope Julius's eyes narrowed. Gray knew he preferred to take control of proceedings whenever it was feasible to do so.

Gray shifted in his seat and fixed his gaze on Saraceni. "With respect, Eminence, while that may be true, I believe we should work proactively to give whatever assistance to the FBI that we can. They will be working in the dark. They will need leads and help. I suggest we pool our thoughts and comments, and take soundings from a wider pool than this room and feed that back to your contact at the FBI."

The pope nodded. "I believe that is a sensible suggestion. Michael, are you able to coordinate those responses, and then Alfredo, will you communicate them to the FBI, please?"

"Of course, Holiness," Gray said.

"Yes, Holiness," Saraceni said. "I agree it is a very sound suggestion."

The pope glanced at them all. "We will need to convene again tomorrow to discuss funeral arrangements for our brothers, and Alfredo, we will at some point also need to discuss a replacement for Archbishop Delgado as papal nuncio in Washington. But that can wait for a few days."

He paused for a moment. "Now, let me pray for you all."

After he had finished, the pope stood and walked around his desk to signify the end of the meeting. Saraceni, followed by Despierre and Galli, rose and filed out the door.

Gray moved to do likewise and was halfway through the door when the pope spoke behind him.

"One moment, Eminence. Could I have a quick word with you?"

Gray turned. "Of course, Holiness."

"Privately, I mean. Shut the door, please."

The pope waited until Gray had done so, then beckoned him nearer. Both men remained standing.

"There is something that's troubling me," the pope said, lowering his voice a little. "The afternoon before our brothers were so brutally attacked, I had a telephone conversation with one of them—Cardinal Berg. We discussed how he should position the disclosures to the White House and the others about Palestine and the Secret Archives. We agreed on the approach, but then the cardinal told me there was something else he needed to disclose to them, and also to me as soon as it was feasible to do so face-to-face."

"Face-to-face? Did he give you any sign what it was, Holiness?"

"No."

"Or about whom? Did he give names?" Gray asked.

"No details at all. It was all very mysterious. He said that because of the nature of the conversation, it must be had in person. He didn't want to discuss it over the phone, so he planned to fly here directly after the White House meeting and give me a briefing."

"It sounds serious, Holiness," Gray said. "Did you suggest that he should approach it the other way around and speak to you first and the White House afterward?"

"I did, but although he apologized, he said it was vital that he also passed the information to the White House as soon as possible. As the meeting there was already arranged, he said it was essential that he take the opportunity to brief them first. He said he felt he had no choice." Pope Julius shrugged. "He nonetheless asked me for my blessing with the course of action. I felt a little uncomfortable about it, but I gave it. I would have preferred to discuss it with him first, but I must also trust he had sincere reasons for his actions."

"I see. Did he say if he had confided in the other cardinals who were going to the White House?"

"Yes, I asked him that, and he said he had fully discussed the matter with them in private and they were all four agreed that the disclosure needed to be made but that they were working hard to keep it confidential for reasons that would become obvious. He said they had told nobody here at the Vatican."

"And had he told the White House people that he had this issue to discuss during the meeting?" Gray asked.

Pope Julius shook his head. "No. He said he hadn't forewarned them. He'd only hinted in advance about the Palestinian and Secret Archive topics, but not this other matter."

Gray nodded. "Yes, I noticed that this confidential item was not mentioned in our meeting just now."

The pope's slightly rheumy pale blue eyes, oozing intelligence and energy despite his eighty years, were fixed on Gray's face. He played with the plain wooden cross that hung over his chest. He was a few inches shorter than Gray, and his upward gaze, as always, had a beseeching quality to it.

"Holiness, do you have any feeling, any instinct, about what it could be that he needed to discuss?" Gray asked.

The pope shook his head. "I assume it was something to do with the Church in the United States. But that is just my assumption. I know nothing."

There was a short silence. "I need to ask you to do something for me, Eminence," the pope continued.

Gray knew what was coming next.

"Of course, Holiness."

"I need you to find out what our brothers were going to communicate to the White House. I suspect that may not be a straightforward task. You will need to use your own methods and take guidance from the Holy Spirit as you do so."

May not be a straightforward task. Gray fought back the urge to make a slightly sarcastic, but humorous, comment. This was no time for humor of any kind.

"Of course," he said. "I will try."

"I have prayed on this," the pope said. "And you are one of my most trusted advisers, Michael. Until I know exactly how sensitive this matter of Cardinal Berg's was, it must be you alone whom I trust with it. Is that understood?"

Gray inclined his head in agreement.

The pope glanced at the clock on the wall. "I need to go now, Eminence. There may be expenses attached to what I am asking you to do. I suggest you draw on your C9 expenses account if required. I will ensure there are no awkward questions."

"Thank you, Holiness. That makes sense."

The pope nodded at Gray to indicate he had nothing further to add.

Gray turned, made his way to the office door, and went out, closing the door behind him.

He stood still in the corridor for a few moments, pondering the conversation he had just had.

Gray had worked with the pope for several years, and the old man sometimes made the oddest of requests, but the slight subterfuge was something new—and unexpected.

He had traveled to more than sixty countries at the Holy Father's direction. He had made speeches to the United Nations and the European Parliament, and he had helped in negotiations with the World Bank.

But he had never been involved in a murder investigation. And certainly not one where several of his colleagues were the victims.

* * *

Thursday, June 23, 2016
    Vatican City, Rome

Gray made his way along the corridor past the pope's private chapel, out the door of the papal apartments, and past the armed Swiss Guard in his magnificent blue, red, orange, and yellow uniform. The guard was deep in conversation with his boss, the commander of the Pontifical Swiss Guard, Heinrich Altishofen, a tall, straight-backed man in his fifties who ran his service with an iron hand.

Altishofen turned to Gray as he passed. "Good day, Eminence."

"And to you too," Gray said. He was on good terms with Altishofen. The commander was regarded by some as arrogant and aloof, but he had never behaved in that way toward Gray.

Gray walked toward the elevators along the ornate *loggia*, a sixty-five-meter arched corridor with intricate fresco artworks on one side and open on the other side with views through glass over the Vatican.

His phone vibrated in his pocket, and he paused to fish out the device.

The message was short and to the point and came from a number he didn't recognize. However, scrolling down, he found it was signed by a man he hadn't seen at the Vatican for a while but with whom he had a long-standing friendship: Cardinal Kamal Baltrami, the archbishop of Ramallah, in the West Bank, just north of Jerusalem.

I need to speak to you urgently re. Washington. Have received important information. Can come to Rome or London to discuss in person. Phones not secure here. Do not discuss this with anyone yet. May need to involve our intelligence friend. Great care is vital. Kamal B.

Gray stared at the screen.

Baltrami was one of the most streetwise churchmen he knew, and as a fellow member of the Council of Cardinals, he had proved himself a sage counsel on all matters relating to the Middle East and the wider Arab community. He wasn't someone who overstated his position, so Gray took his warnings at face value.

The gravity of whatever Baltrami had learned was underlined by his suggestion of involving their "intelligence friend." Gray knew precisely who he meant by that: Enrico Rossellini, a deputy director at Italy's foreign intelligence service, the AISE, or Agenzia Informazioni e Sicurezza Esterna. The two men had gotten to know him when AISE had carried out a quiet investigation into corruption at the Vatican a couple of years earlier.

"Eminence, excuse me, are you leaving?" came a voice from over his shoulder.

It was the Swiss Guard. Gray knew the meaning behind the ostensibly polite inquiry. The guards didn't like anyone loitering in the *loggia*, especially outside the pope's third-floor private apartments.

Gray nodded and resumed his walk toward the elevators at the far end of the corridor, now feeling very distracted.

What had Baltrami discovered that had triggered this message? The two men had a good rapport, and for the past couple of years Baltrami had acted as Gray's preferred confessor—the person to whom he often made his confessions and asked for absolution.

Once he was out of the Apostolic Palace, Gray stopped again, and instead of walking the short distance to the Vatican's St. Martha's House guesthouse where he had a two-room apartment on the second floor, he headed into the Vatican Gardens. The gardens were open to the public, but bookings were required, and access was heavily regulated.

After a few minutes of searching he was able to find a quiet bench. There he spent a short time thinking, checked his calendar, then tapped out a short reply to Baltrami.

Very good to hear from you again, Eminence. Please travel as soon as possible. I would be delighted to see you again. I am in Rome for a few weeks before returning to London. We can meet outside the Vatican. Keep me informed.

Despite the summer heat, Gray felt a shiver go through him. This situation was stretching him well outside his comfort zone. He could do with some advice here, but he wasn't sure who he could confide in about this right now. None would be able to help with this type of scenario.

He glanced once more at the message Baltrami had sent. There was the option of talking to Rossellini, certainly. Both Gray and Baltrami had liked him. However, they did not know the man that well, and Gray had no real sense if he was someone they could completely trust.

Then he had a sudden thought.

There was one person he could talk to with whom he went way back, and much further with her father before that. She was far better equipped than he was to steer through this situation. Someone whom he definitely *could* trust and who would give wise, unbiased counsel. And she wasn't in the Church, which right now was a big plus point as far as he was concerned.

CHAPTER FOUR

Thursday, June 23, 2016
 Portland, Maine

The whitecaps were skimming swiftly across Casco Bay from south to north, and the gulls were squawking as they soared around the imposing structure of Portland Head Light. The historic lighthouse, built on a rocky outcrop, stood guard over the coastline south of the city. Beyond the bay, the Atlantic Ocean glittered in the late-afternoon sun.

It had become one of Jayne Robinson's favorite places to visit since her move from London to Portland to live with Joe Johnson two years earlier. They often took a walk along the cliff paths and open spaces in Fort Williams Park, in the coastal area around the lighthouse. Invariably, as today, they then found a bench with a view out over the bay toward Cushing Island where they could sit, talk, and enjoy the view.

On the grassy area behind them, kids were flying kites. When a couple of dogs began barking, Joe's chocolate Labrador, Cocoa, who had been lying peacefully on the ground next to the bench, suddenly jumped to his feet, arched his tail upward, and added his deep voice to the cacophony.

Jayne laughed, reached over, and fondled the dog's ear. "Can't help himself, can he?"

"Compulsive behavior," Joe said. "Bit like us in some ways. Half the time we do things and I struggle to explain why. It's no different."

"Like me moving to Maine, you mean?" She had often thought hat her move across the Atlantic from her London apartment near Tower Bridge, had happened almost without her having any say in the matter. But it had been an instinctive move and she was happy she had done it.

Joe reached out and squeezed her thigh. "That was a purely primal decision. Only one explanation for that." He turned his head and winked at her.

They had been enjoying the past couple of months following Jayne's previous operation, a particularly arduous one. It had ended with her tracking down the man responsible for killing her father in a bombing twenty-two years earlier in London.

It had been nice to do nothing except wander around Portland and explore the coast north and south of the city for a while. Together with Joe's son, Peter, who had recently graduated from high school, they had also been to visit Joe's daughter, Carrie, before her semester at Boston University ended for the summer. She was now back at home and looking for a summer job. Jayne got along with both of them, and they each had opened up a little about how they missed their mother, Kathy, who had died from cancer in 2005 at the age of only forty-six.

The reversion to a period of relative domestic normalcy had recharged Jayne's batteries, which sometimes seemed to deplete a little faster now that she was into her fifties.

Such a period of recuperation, quite doable as a freelance operative, would not have been possible in her previous role with Britain's Secret Intelligence Service, otherwise known as MI6. She had worked for MI6 since leaving university in her early twenties until Joe, a onetime CIA officer, persuaded her to join him on several war crimes investigations.

"Come on, let's walk," Joe said. He grabbed Jayne's hand and stood. "This boy needs some exercise." He patted Cocoa's head with his other hand.

Jayne also stood and squeezed Joe's hand. "I've already had a four-mile run today. So make it a short walk, then the wine bar on the way home. How does that sound?"

"Done."

They strolled hand in hand along the path, the ocean to their right. The site, popular with tourists, included several disused and dilapidated batteries that comprised the former US Army base, Fort Williams, which was operational during the First and Second World Wars. At that time, the fort had been heavily armed with large caliber guns of various types, including anti-aircraft variants, and later housed a radar station.

They had just walked past Battery Hobart at the northern end of the site when Jayne's phone rang.

She took it from her pocket and studied the screen.

"Michael Gray," she said, turning to Joe. "This is the old school friend of my father's who became a cardinal. He gave Dad the last rites in the hospital. I haven't spoken to him for a long time."

Joe's face fell. She could see what he was thinking. This wasn't going to be a quick call.

"Call him back in the morning, or else he'll ruin your evening," Joe said. "I'm looking forward to a glass of wine."

She nodded and punched the red button. The constant access that cell phones provided could be invasive at times.

Less than a minute later, the phone trilled once again.

She looked at Joe, who raised his eyebrows but said nothing. She shrugged and this time tapped the green button.

"Michael. How are you?"

"Hello, Jayne. I'm fine, thank you. I apologize if you're busy, but something very urgent has come up."

"What's that?"

"It's about those cardinals who were murdered in Washington yesterday. You see, I think I need some help."

CHAPTER FIVE

Friday, June 24, 2016
Portland, Maine

It had taken only a few seconds for Jayne to realize that Michael Gray intended to tell her something that should not be said over an open phone line.

Because it had been almost midnight in Rome, she persuaded him to wait until the morning, when she could more easily talk him through installing a special voice and message encryption app on his phone and instruct him how to use the public and private keys that went with it.

Now, though, at just after breakfast time in Portland, Jayne was sitting in the small home office she shared with Joe at the rear of the house. It was away from the kitchen, which could be noisy if Joe's children were around. There were two desks, one at each side of the room, an old whiteboard on the wall, where Joe sometimes scribbled his to-do list in red marker pen, and a couple of bookshelves. A printer and scanner stood on a table next to Joe's desk.

Jayne had her phone pressed to her ear. Gray was at the other end of the line, in his apartment in the Vatican. He was at last bringing her up to speed on a sequence of events that had clearly left him out of his depth.

She listened carefully as he read out a message he had received from Cardinal Baltrami. The sense of urgency in it was clear, but Jayne didn't need to read between the lines to pick up a clear note of fear, too.

. . . Can come to Rome or London to discuss in person. Phones not secure here. Do not discuss this with anyone yet. May need to involve our intelligence friend. Great care is vital.

"Who's the intelligence friend he's referring to?" she asked. It obviously wasn't her, as she had never met him.

"A deputy director at the AISE named Enrico Rossellini. We had dealings with him a few years ago when he got involved in a corruption investigation at the Vatican. He's helpful, but I'm not at all sure I can trust him. That's why I got in touch with you. Have you come across him?"

Actually, Jayne did know Rossellini. She explained to Gray that she had been in contact with him several years earlier during a joint MI6 operation with the AISE and had found him cooperative. They hadn't remained in touch, however, and she certainly couldn't claim to know him well.

"I'm flattered you approached me instead," Jayne said. "But do you think Baltrami might have spoken to Rossellini or contacted him separately?"

Gray shook his head. "I am certain he would not have contacted Rossellini without me. I dealt with the man more than he did. But it shows how worried he is that he suggested it."

"Okay, continue."

Gray then told her about the request made of him by Pope Julius VI.

The assassination of the three cardinals and the archbishop in Washington, DC, she knew all about, because it had of course been plastered all over every newspaper front page and every TV and radio news bulletin.

But the rest came as something of a surprise.

Gray had been one of her father's closest school friends. As their very different careers progressed—Gray in the Church, Ken Robinson in the police—they had remained in touch, albeit intermittently. As her father lay dying in 1994 in the hospital following serious injuries in a terrorist bomb blast outside the Israeli embassy, Gray had joined her at his bedside and read the last rites.

"This meeting with your friend from the West Bank," Jayne said. "He wants to tell you something that's too sensitive to say on the phone, and it's coming after four of your colleagues have been shot dead. And after the pope has asked you to find out what the dead men were planning to communicate to the White House. Can I ask, do you trust Cardinal Baltrami?"

There was a slight pause at the other end of the line.

"Of course I trust him," Gray said. "We've worked together for years. I've got one hundred percent confidence in him. I'm sure many other cardinals would do too. We'd all vouch for him."

Gray hesitated, then continued. "This is going to sound bad, and please don't tell anyone I'm saying this, but it's the truth: there are many people here who I unfortunately do not trust. But he's definitely not one of them."

"It's obvious to me he's worried, frightened even," Jayne said. Her gut instinct was that Baltrami was seeing danger signals, and her alert system was now on red, too. "Are you planning to take any precautions for the meeting?"

Gray paused before answering. "I plan to meet somewhere quiet and confidential outside Vatican territory in

Rome. But I'm not sure if that's enough. What do you think?"

"I agree with you. Somewhere away from the Vatican is a start. But you need to do more, possibly a lot more. What about surveillance? What do you do to make sure you're not being followed, recorded, filmed, and so on—or worse?" Jayne asked.

Another pause. "That's not something in my skill set, Jayne. I'm an archbishop, not a spy. That's the reason I've called you."

"Based on what you've told me, and the message you've received, I think you need to be extremely careful, and so does Cardinal Baltrami," Jayne said. "Would you like some help?"

"If you can offer, yes, that would be exceptionally helpful. As you can doubtless tell, I'm a little out of my depth. And I can cover your costs, don't worry."

"Are you sure?" Jayne asked.

"Well, we are in pursuing truth and justice here."

"All right. Tell me about this cardinal. What's his background?"

Gray told her. Baltrami was the archbishop of Ramallah, was aged seventy-three, and had been a priest since the age of twenty-eight. He had been appointed as bishop of Caesarea some eighteen years later, at forty-six.

Baltrami's elevation to cardinal came in 2003, and he had taken part in the conclave that elected Pope Julius a couple of years later. He then joined the Council of Cardinals in 2009 at Pope Julius's request. Baltrami had gotten to know Gray in the 1990s, but their friendship had become stronger once both were spending significant amounts of time at the Vatican.

"He's a man of God but also a man of the people," Gray said. "He's got an unbelievable number of contacts littered through the Middle East. Political and military and church people, not just in the West Bank and Gaza, but Syria and Lebanon too. I can tell you he has the ear of some of the Hamas and Hezbollah leaders too. People who wouldn't know a Bible if it hit them on the head. Not sure how he's done that."

"He sounds like something of a character," Jayne said. "It can't be easy doing his job in that region. There can't be many Catholic priests there, and certainly not cardinals, or am I wrong?"

"Very few cardinals in that region," Gray said. "There's one in Beirut—Cardinal Filippo Martelli, who's the Maronite Catholic Patriarch of Antioch and heads up the Maronite Church. I don't know him so well; he's not very sociable when in the Vatican."

"Do Baltrami and Martelli get on well, support each other?" Jayne asked.

Gray cleared his throat. "I don't think they're very close, as far as I know. Not sure, actually. But I know they are both very enmeshed in their local communities and support the people in them."

Gray paused. "That region around Israel is a highly dangerous melting pot for clergymen. But Baltrami's survived and thrived for several decades—despite being regularly threatened, harassed, and put under surveillance by the government and others, including having his phone and emails tapped."

"Did he take precautions when contacting you?" Jayne asked.

"He used what I think you call a burner phone, not his regular device," Gray said. "And he said he could only discuss this face-to-face."

"I assume few of your colleagues at the Vatican use burner phones?"

Gray gave a short, sharp laugh. "Some of the older ones don't even know how to use cell phones at all."

Jayne smiled. "All right. And what about his credibility? I mean, when he tells you he has received some information and needs to speak to you urgently, you can be sure he's not overstating his case?"

"I can tell you for certain, he'll be understating, not over-stating. Not his style."

There seemed almost no decision to make. "Would you like me to fly to Rome to join you for this meeting, to do my best to make sure it goes smoothly, and to advise as best I can on how to both deal with whatever comes out of it and carry out the pope's request?"

"Does the sun rise in the east?"

Jayne chuckled at Gray's use of the old quip. "Very good, Michael. Tell Baltrami he can meet you in Rome, then. Warn him I'll be there too. We don't want any surprises. But don't see him, speak to him, or arrange a venue until I'm there. We'll find somewhere secure and then let him know. All being well, I'll get there in the next three days, so we could meet him on Tuesday."

"Thank you so much, Jayne. You're very much like your dad. He always did what he could to help if someone needed it."

The two finished the conversation with a few reminiscences about Ken Robinson, then Jayne ended the call.

She slipped her phone into her pocket and walked through the living room, where Joe was sitting in an armchair, reading a copy of *The Economist*. He glanced up and lowered his magazine.

"How did it go?" he asked.

Jayne sat in an armchair opposite Joe and folded her arms. "Something's going to crawl out of the woodwork regarding these cardinals. I can feel it. Michael wants me to go to Rome —to meet another cardinal. From Ramallah."

"They have cardinals in Ramallah?"

She ran through the details of the call she had just had with Gray.

There was a pause after she finished. Joe placed his hands behind his mainly bald head and rocked back in his chair.

Jayne looked at him. "Do you want to join me for this one?" she asked.

Following a job that had nearly killed him and had involved the kidnapping of his kids and sister by the Russians, Joe had taken a break from operational work. He had needed to be around for his family. But Carrie and Peter were now technically adults and much more independent.

Joe threw her a glance and a half smile. "Tempted. But probably not this time," he said.

"Maybe soon?" she asked.

"We'll see."

"All right. So, any thoughts on this?"

"I think you should call Vic before you do anything," Joe said. "He's going to be up to his eyeballs in this cardinals case. He won't appreciate you doing anything without running it past him."

Joe was right, as usual. It was good advice.

"He might be of use, actually," Jayne said. "I'm thinking I might need a few resources from his Rome station for this meeting."

* * *

Friday, June 24, 2016
    Portland, Maine

. . .

"You want to borrow a safe house in Rome?" Vic said. "Can I ask why?"

Jayne, the phone against her ear and using a secure encrypted connection, had just gotten through explaining the background to the call she'd had with Michael Gray, including his links to her father. Vic, who was well aware of Ken Robinson's story, listened carefully with just an occasional question.

"Gray wants to meet with Cardinal Baltrami in Rome and has asked me to help him," Jayne said. "I strongly think, given the circumstances, we should do it somewhere secure. That's why I would like to use a safe house, if possible."

She paused. "I'm assuming you're already engaged with this case yourself?"

"You could say that," Vic said, his gravelly tones as dry as usual. "There's a lot going on, as you'd expect. The Feds have made some significant progress that's not in the public domain."

"Am I allowed to ask who the suspects are?"

"You might be surprised at the answer. I certainly was."

"Try me."

"The evidence is so far circumstantial, but unfortunately, it fits with the highly professional way the assassinations were carried out," Vic said. "However, given the close connections you made in a certain quarter of the eastern Mediterranean on your recent operation, you might not like to hear it."

Jayne was silent for a beat or two.

Surely not.

"I hope you're not trying to tell me what I think you are," she said.

"It wouldn't be the first time they've done something like this, would it?"

"I think it would," Jayne said. "I can't think of any previous instance of clergymen being targeted like that. We all know there's not a lot of love lost between Israel and the

Vatican for historical reasons, but there's a world of differ-ence between that and the operation carried out in DC. How much credibility are you giving to this? What is this circum-stantial evidence?"

Jayne knew she was sounding a little defensive, given her recent operational links to the Mossad.

"Keep an open mind about this, Jayne," Vic said. "I know you're close to them."

"All right, I will. Tell me what you know."

Vic quickly ran through the evidence he was referring to, specifically the chocolate wrapping found at the scene and the flight bookings under Israeli passports.

"Forensics are doing tests on the wrapper as we speak," Vic said. "And Tel Aviv station is chasing the passports. We'll know a little more soon."

"Interesting. I'm guessing the Ramallah cardinal might help to put a few more pieces into the puzzle," Jayne said.

"Yes, I agree. I'll speak to Constanzo in Rome and get this arranged for you."

Jayne knew that Donald Constanzo, the CIA's chief of Rome station, currently had a cloud over his head after a rendition operation that involved snatching a Muslim cleric from the streets of Milan had gone spectacularly wrong. The CIA was not the flavor of the month in Italy.

Vic paused momentarily. "But I will probably need you to do something else for me once we have all our ducks in a row in terms of the evidence."

"What?"

"You know it will not be possible for anyone with any kind of official Agency role to talk to Avi about the cardinals. As I told Ferguson, whether or not they've done it, he'll deny it. But if I was going to try to feel them out via a back chan-nel, I thought you might just fit the bill, Jayne. I'll need someone not directly connected to the Agency but who knows the game and has a good enough relationship with Avi and his people in Tel Aviv. I can't think of anyone better than you."

Jayne glanced up at the ceiling.

Is he serious?

"Right," she said. "So you want me to go and casually ask Avi over a quiet dinner if his boys shot the cardinals?"

"What I want you to do is go there, as someone he will trust implicitly, look into his eyes, and ask him who's done it," Vic said. "Then report back what's in those eyes. You'll know."

"Not necessarily, Vic. Avi's a poker player." Jayne exhaled heavily. "And what do you think?"

Vic pressed his lips together. "It will depend on the forensics we get back and what Tel Aviv station finds on the passports. My gut feeling, for what it's worth, is that if this has been done by Israeli hands, it's likely to be a lone wolf, some fanatic, not Avi's team. You don't need me to tell you this, but I think the aim would be more to make subtle inquiries about whether he knows who might have done it, not accuse him or ask him if his service has done it."

"I'd say that's the best approach, yes. And this is in return for allowing me use of a safe house in Rome?"

"No, it's not a trade. We need to do both. As you say, Cardinal Baltrami's input could be important. We need to find out what he's got to say."

Jayne rocked back in her chair and closed her eyes, thinking. What Vic was saying made complete sense. Never in her wildest thoughts had she imagined that her rather tenuous friendship with Michael Gray, born out of one tragedy, would lead to her investigating another awful killing twenty-two years later.

"All right, let's do it," she said. "I'll get myself to Rome as quickly as I can for the meeting with Michael and Baltrami.

We'll need to do it properly and set up countersurveillance for that with Constanzo. Then, depending on the outcome of that meeting and the forensic tests the Feds are doing, I'll go on to Tel Aviv to see Avi."

There was a moment's silence at the other end of the line.

"Yes, that's a good plan," Vic said eventually. "But I'm also thinking I need to visit Rome station again soon. Constanzo's still trying to rebuild his team after that rendition disaster. Let me come with you. We'll travel tomorrow."

CHAPTER SIX

Monday, June 27, 2016
  Rome

Jayne paused as she and Michael Gray followed Vic and Donald Constanzo through a set of lofty glass doors into the lobby of the Palazzo Margherita, the magnificent old Renaissance-style palace that now housed the United States embassy in Rome.

The two CIA men walked straight toward the sweeping stone staircase that wound its way upward to their right, heading for the CIA station on the top floor. But Jayne stopped dead, as did Gray.

Ahead of them was an exquisite white marble statue of a woman emerging naked from a bath, one towel draped around her torso and using another to dry her left breast.

"What's this?" Jayne asked.

Constanzo stopped at the bottom of the staircase and turned. "That's our Venus, by Giambologna. You didn't know she was here, I can see."

"I've heard of Giambologna," Jayne said. "But I didn't know you had one here, no."

Gray, a tall, upright figure, was also looking with interest. It was the first time Jayne had seen him for more than ten years. Now aged eighty-two, his hair remained in the slightly unruly state she remembered, but its salt-and-pepper color had faded to mostly white and contrasted with his black glasses.

Constanzo explained that the legendary sculptor, originally from Flanders, had created the Venus in the 1580s. The sculpture had come with the building when the United States acquired it in 1946, but the Venus had not been restored and placed in her current location until 1993.

Constanzo, Vic, and Jayne had picked up Gray earlier in an anonymous unmarked CIA station wagon with heavily tinted windows from outside a café in Trastevere, Rome's 13th *rione*, or district, that lay to the south of the Vatican, next to the River Tiber. After a half-hour surveillance detection route, they had headed into the US embassy compound.

Jayne finally followed them up the staircase, with Gray close behind. He had declined Constanzo's offer of the elevator and had insisted on using the stairs, saying it was the only exercise he got. Dressed in a simple black shirt, white Roman collar, and black trousers, he climbed the first of the four flights of stairs slowly but without stopping.

As they reached the landing, Jayne asked Gray again if he was certain he didn't want to switch to the elevator, and he declined a little testily.

"I need to be fit to stand on my feet and preach, you know," he said.

Jayne was impressed. She paused and glanced down at the Venus from above. The statue, mounted on a pink marble base, was one of many artworks and statues scattered throughout the building, Constanzo explained.

Constanzo turned to Gray. "As you may know, Eminence, this site was originally owned by a cardinal."

Gray inclined his head. "I had heard that."

"Who?" Jayne asked. "Surely not recently?"

"Cardinal Ludovisi in the seventeenth century," Constanzo said.

Jayne couldn't help a faint smile. The site must be worth an enormous fortune now. "Some cardinals have always liked their luxuries," she said, glancing at Gray as she spoke. "Present company excepted, of course."

Gray smiled, now somewhat out of breath. Jayne knew he was not at all materialistic, although as part of his role as the Roman Catholic archbishop of Westminster, he was living for the duration of his tenure in the very grand Archbishop's House. The property, a redbrick mansion behind Westminster Cathedral, was a long stone's throw from Victoria Station in London.

"Everything I have is on loan, including my house, which is admittedly very luxurious, as archbishop," Gray said. "But frankly, I prefer the two-room apartment I have at the Vatican when I'm here."

"That's good to hear, Eminence," Constanzo said.

Jayne found Constanzo's use of the title "Eminence" an endearing habit. Clearly in Rome, everyone, even CIA veterans, adopted the correct way of addressing senior Vatican clergymen—*Eminence* for cardinals, *Excellency* for archbishops who weren't cardinals. Jayne had done likewise with Gray until he told her to use his first name if they were together in private, as her father had always done, and to only use the title when in company.

When they reached the top landing, Constanzo took out his CIA passcard, tapped it against an electronic keypad, and entered a number. The gray steel security door to the CIA station, the electronic complexity of which stood in contrast to the historic stone staircase next to it, clicked open.

The sprawling CIA station covered perhaps a quarter of the top floor of the embassy building and consisted of a mix of open-plan and private offices. Jayne guessed that it probably employed about fifty people out of a total embassy staff that Constanzo had told her totaled about three hundred expatriate Americans and another five hundred locals. As was normal for intelligence operatives, the CIA contingent was employed under cover in other supposedly genuine roles, ranging from political analysts to cultural attachés.

Jayne recalled from her days at the Secret Intelligence Service that the CIA's Rome station also included a significant telecommunications base. On their way in, she had spotted a cubed white structure on the roof of the building that she knew housed signals intelligence collection equipment capable of picking up cell phone, radio, and other communications signals across the city.

Both Jayne and Vic were staying in a two-bedroom annex at Constanzo's expansive rented villa on the eastern side of Rome and had traveled to the embassy with him that morning.

Constanzo led the way to a small meeting room with a circular table and six chairs next to his office. He told them to take a seat and asked an assistant to bring coffee.

"Thank you, Donald," Vic said. He rubbed his hands together, glanced at Gray, and got right to business. "I have an idea about what security measures and precautions we need to take for this meeting with your colleague, Cardinal Baltrami, but first, Michael, I mean Eminence, tell us how you and others at the Vatican see the security situation given what happened in Washington."

Gray nodded. "I'll be honest with you. It has frightened

all of us, from Pope Julius downward. Nobody I speak to knows why this has happened."

"But somebody does," Jayne said.

"Yes, certainly," Gray said.

"And it sounds as though Cardinal Baltrami is going to tell us more."

Gray shrugged. "That's what we need to find out. I also need to find out what my four deceased brothers were going to communicate to the White House, as requested by His Holiness. The two are obviously linked, but I won't make any headway without your help." He glanced around the table at each of them. "I thank you for getting involved."

"It's in all our interests to get answers," Vic said. "I've heard from the FBI that forensics on the chocolate bar wrapper from Massachusetts Avenue is coming up with nothing. It's clean. No DNA, no prints. So let's hope Baltrami can help us instead."

He turned to Constanzo. "Donald, tell us your plan."

The station chief leaned forward.

"We've got a safe house in Trastevere." He glanced at Gray. "It's near to where we picked you up. An anonymous four-story house on a quiet street. It's already set up for precisely this kind of meeting, with surveillance cameras outside, monitor screens, communications gear. Should be perfect. Oh, and it's only a few hundred meters from the local Carabinieri headquarters. Perfect location. They'll never look there. Too close."

He was probably correct about that, Jayne thought.

Constanzo went on to outline the arrangements, which included three of his team on countersurveillance duties. They would tail Baltrami en route to the safe house, checking that he wasn't under surveillance or under threat, and getting him to his destination safely. As part of the security protocols, the apartment was being swept regularly to ensure it had no bugging devices.

He tapped his fingers on the table. "Just to let you know, I'm not involving the Secret Service team in this. Best we just keep it to as small and tight a circle of people as possible. They don't need to know. Agreed?" Constanzo looked around the table for confirmation. The approach made sense to Jayne, who nodded her assent.

"Agreed," Vic said. There were nods from the others.

"What's the latest update from Cardinal Baltrami?" Jayne asked.

"I've kept communications to a minimum, but he seems ready to go," Gray said. He said he had received a confirmatory message via Baltrami's burner phone saying that he had arrived safely in Rome. Rather than staying at St. Martha's House within the Vatican grounds, as did Gray and most other visiting cardinals, he had checked into a one-bedroomed apartment he had rented online. The apartment, in Via Glorioso, was in the southern part of Trastevere, only a fifteen-minute walk from the safe house.

Gray looked at Jayne. "I've told him the arrangements and that you're involved as an old friend of mine, together with the rest of you. He's happy to deal with you rather than the AISE contact of ours he originally suggested."

"You're absolutely sure he's okay with it?" Vic asked. "He's not going to be freaked out by all of this—safe houses and security measures, run by the Americans?"

"He actually seemed a little relieved," Gray said. "He said there was no way he and I could handle this. I mean, he's better equipped and more street-smart than I am, given his background working in the Middle East where there are constant threats and surveillance. He's very used to this sort of thing. But nevertheless, he's nothing like as skilled as all of you, and anyway, we don't have the resources to carry out investigations and so on. He clearly has some big disclosure to make, and he'll be happy with the precautions."

"And he's shared nothing more about what he wants to say?" Jayne asked.

"Nothing."

Staying outside the Vatican seemed like a sensible precaution to Jayne. It was already obvious to her that Baltrami was a breed apart from most of his cardinal colleagues, and this explained how he had functioned and survived so well as a Catholic clergyman in a highly dangerous part of the Middle East.

"All right, Eminence," Constanzo said, "tell him two o'clock tomorrow afternoon for the meeting, then. The city will be quieter. Most shops will be closed for our long Rome lunches. It'll be easier to spot any surveillance. Will he be able to walk to the safe house, or do we need to arrange a car? If we use the car, I'd like to drop him at the end of the street, so he walks to the house. It's less noticeable that way—neighbors will remember a car dropping someone off, but a man on foot, slipping through a front door, is unlikely to register on anybody's radar."

"He's a sprightly seventy-three-year-old who's as fit as a butcher's dog," Gray said. "My guess is he'll walk the whole way. It's not far." He reached into his pocket for his cell phone. "I'll tell him two p.m."

"Walking is better," Constanzo said. "Our countersurveillance people will then be able to flush out any tail that he has. They'll be there from the moment he leaves his apartment, although he won't see them. And tell him he must leave his Roman collar behind. A nonclerical shirt will do. Tell him to look like a tourist." He turned to Gray. "The same applies to you, Eminence. I want to keep you both as anonymous as possible. A priest will be noticeable."

Constanzo rose. "I'm going to fetch my countersurveillance team and introduce them. Give me two minutes." He exited the room.

CHAPTER SEVEN

Monday, June 27, 2016
   Rome

When the two pensioner look-alikes and the twentysomething blonde woman appeared outside the door of the meeting room, Jayne's first thought was that they were a group of tourists who had somehow taken a wrong turn at the embassy.

The gray-haired woman and her partner, both bespectacled, a little hunch-shouldered, and dressed in anonymous beige, blue, and black clothing, looked like any retired married couple. The younger woman looked like a student in her jeans and navy T-shirt, with a dark ponytail, and a bag slung over her shoulder.

All of them were instantly unmemorable.

Constanzo ushered the three of them into the room and introduced them.

"These three are world class on the street because they

look anything but that," he said. "We call them the Forgotten Family. Once seen, never remembered."

It emerged that the older pair, Roberto Flamini and Gina Cavallaro, were both retired CIA officers with mixed American Italian backgrounds. They worked freelance for the Agency on a variety of tasks, chiefly surveillance or countersurveillance roles. Their specialty was to follow targets on the street without being detected. Those skills served the pair, both in their late sixties, equally well when they were keeping watch for any sign of surveillance on their own people, as was the case here.

The younger woman, Teresa Berlanti, was a current CIA case officer, although if anyone had bothered to check her employment contract, they would have found it stated that she was a mere political analyst in the embassy, Constanzo said.

The trio listened carefully as Constanzo took charge of the meeting, while Jayne and Vic sat back and listened for most of the time, apart from asking the occasional question or making a few suggestions. Gray sat in silence, a slightly bemused expression on his face.

Constanzo unfolded a large-scale map of the Trastevere district onto the table and explained the operation to his surveillance experts. He used a red pencil to mark the map with the route that was to be given to Baltrami for the following afternoon, taking him from his rented apartment to the safe house on Via dei Panieri.

Although Constanzo explained to his countersurveillance team that Baltrami, codenamed PHOENIX for the operation, was a cardinal, at no point did he tell them why the meeting with him was happening. None of the surveillance trio asked. They all knew there was no need for that detail to be supplied—these teams operated almost invariably on a need-to-know basis when it came to sharing information.

The two pensioners, Roberto and Gina, possessed encrypted communications devices disguised as standard hearing aids, while Teresa had a similar device designed to look like a set of Bluetooth earphones. These units would enable them to keep contact with the team at the safe house. Constanzo insisted on spending a few minutes testing them with his own secure headset to ensure they were working as intended.

After a brief discussion, it was agreed that Roberto and Gina would follow Baltrami from his apartment. Both would be carrying shopping bags, as if they were en route home from the supermarket. That would give them a ready-made excuse to stop if needed, ostensibly for a rest.

Meanwhile, Teresa would operate as a kind of advance guard, positioning herself a hundred meters or so ahead of Baltrami, although that would vary from time to time.

Based on recommendations made by the trio, they also agreed on a few changes to the route to incorporate certain pinch points that would enable them to flush out any surveillance. These included a small square that had only one route in and out.

Meanwhile, the CIA team would go to the safe house in the morning, arriving individually at different times in order to avoid generating any interest from other residents on the street. The safe house was equipped with two high-definition remote-control cameras mounted above the front door, concealed inside an outdoor light unit, and would give those inside an excellent view of the street in both directions. The cameras would feed into a sophisticated communications and video monitoring room at the rear of the house, where the team would be based.

Another microcamera built into the peak of a cap worn by Roberto would provide a further feed as he walked. Constanzo explained it was the first time the Rome station had deployed the device, so it was something of an experiment.

He passed around a series of photographs.

"This is Via dei Panieri," Constanza said. "The safe house is that one." He stabbed a fleshy forefinger at one of the photographs.

The photograph showed a straight, narrow street that was more than a hundred meters long. This would enable them to spot any surveillance as Baltrami approached his final destination, which was about two-thirds of the way down the street, Constanzo said.

If there was anything that caused concern, Baltrami would be told to simply continue past the safe house and abort the visit until the surveillance had been lost. If necessary, they would have to try again the following day.

One side of Via dei Panieri was lined by several ancient four-story stone houses, one of which was the safe house, together with a disused industrial building, also built from stone.

On the other side of the street stood a row of mainly two- and three-story houses, all of similar vintage and all joined to their neighboring properties. There was also a car garage with a steel roller shutter door opposite the safe house.

This was an old quarter of an old district. The street ran in a northwesterly direction from Vicolo del Cedro and, typical of the streets in Trastevere, was lined almost all the way down by a row of tightly parked cars and motorcycles on the western side, where the safe house stood.

Finally, it was agreed that Roberto would visit Baltrami at his rented apartment later that afternoon to brief him on the details of the plan and ensure he was clear on the route. He would also give him a communications device, identical to the fake hearing aids that the others were using and which had been carefully tested. The apartment was tucked away inside a small building with a high security gate and fence at the front, so it would be safe for Roberto to go there without it being obvious from the street who he was visiting.

Roberto was to give Baltrami strict instructions to use the device in listen-only mode unless there was an absolute emergency. They did not want to risk him trying to speak to the safe house team without proper training in how to do so in an undetectable manner. He was to use the talk mode only if something unexpected occurred.

After nearly an hour of intense discussions about the fine details of the operation, Constanzo pronounced himself satisfied. He turned to Vic and Jayne.

"Are you happy with this arrangement?" he asked.

Both nodded.

Jayne could not think of any detail he hadn't covered. "In many ways, all this seems way over the top for a meeting with a clergyman," she said, "but given the backdrop to this, it's far better to take a cautious approach."

She glanced at Gray, realizing that he had been little more than an interested spectator for most of the session and had hardly spoken. "What do you think, Eminence?"

Gray smiled at her use of his title. "Frankly, it's been an eye-opener. I'm astonished at the precautions you take and the detail you go into, but I have to say, it's reassuring. I had been extremely nervous about arranging this meeting, and I feel less so now. I'll just pray for the safety of all our journeys tomorrow and that it will help us all understand what's happened."

CHAPTER EIGHT

Tuesday, June 28, 2016
Rome

A brown-and-white terrier lay motionless in the shade on a doorstep, and two cats loitered near the heavily graffitied entrance to the car garage across the street as Jayne walked across the cobblestones toward the safe house. Otherwise, there were no signs of life.

She ran her hand across her brow and it came away glistening with sweat. The morning sun had left Rome under a heat haze that more than once had caused her to blink and try in vain to refocus on some distant blurred landmark as she walked.

Jayne squeezed through the gap between two parked cars directly in front of the house and, after a glance in both directions to finally check she still had no coverage, pushed a discreet silver buzzer to the right of the doorframe.

The facade of the house was badly in need of maintenance. An ancient layer of stained, rotten cement cladding was flaking away, and chunks had fallen off in several places, revealing the stonework beneath. Electrical cables emerged from a plastic junction box attached to the front of the building and snaked across the surface on long makeshift supports, mostly rusty nails that had been driven into the mortar.

But most of the other buildings in the street were in a similar state of disrepair. Some even had graffiti sprayed on their doors, and the safe house therefore fit perfectly and unobtrusively into its surroundings.

The solid security door, the only modern part of the facade, clicked silently open and Vic's face appeared. Jayne was the last of the group to arrive. Vic beckoned her inside and shut the door as she entered.

"Ops room is upstairs at the rear," he said, as he led the way across a red-tiled hallway, up a short flight of wooden stairs, and along a corridor with a threadbare beige carpet to a white door that was half open.

Inside, Constanzo sat at a desk with a laptop computer and a bank of four video monitors in front of him. There was also a microphone on a stand and a speaker, from which a few muffled squelch breaks could be heard as his countersurveillance team clicked in and out of the secure network. At the rear of the room, Gray stood looking somewhat self-conscious, with a bottle of water in one hand and a sandwich in the other.

The CIA station chief turned his head. "All going to plan. Roberto, Gina, and Teresa are in place already." He glanced at his watch. "Twenty minutes to go. Baltrami's comms device is working well. We've had a quick chat with him."

"Good," Jayne said. "How does he sound?"

"Seems relaxed and chill with everything following Roberto's briefing. He said he felt bad putting us through so much trouble, but he found it reassuring given what happened in DC and added it would be worth our time."

Jayne nodded. "Let's hope so." She too hoped privately that it would be worth all the effort. If not, and if Baltrami's information proved worthless, she knew her credibility bank would be depleted as far as Vic and Constanzo were concerned. Moreover, it would put their fledgling investigation back to square one.

She moved to the back of the room, took a bottle of chilled water from the fridge, and quickly toured the house. It was her usual routine in a new environment, enabling her to note entry and exit points as she went.

Next door to the ops room was a living room with two long sofas, two armchairs, a television set, and a dining table with chairs. That was where they would debrief Baltrami.

On the floor above, there were two bedrooms, a bathroom and a storage room. None of them appeared to have been used for some time. The entire house was sparsely and cheaply furnished. It was designed for functionality, not comfort, and was similar to scores of other safe houses Jayne had used during her long career with MI6 and beyond.

Jayne continued up the next flight of stairs to the top floor of the house, but it was simply being used for storage space, and the two rooms there were undecorated and unfurnished.

She returned to the ops room and stood next to Vic, sipping her water and watching the screens.

A few minutes later, there came the low tones of Roberto's voice through the speaker.

"PHOENIX is on the move."

There was a sudden movement from one of the monitors as Roberto presumably swiveled his head, rose to his feet from what looked like a bench beneath a tree, and began to walk down the street. Once the image stabilized, in the distance a figure in a navy collared shirt and dark trousers could be seen crossing from one side of the street to the other. At least Baltrami had gotten his dress code right.

Jayne took a couple of steps toward the desk, just as Constanzo stood.

"Good work. Thanks, Roberto," he said into the microphone. "I assume that's him in the blue shirt on your camera feed?"

"Affirmative."

"Thanks. Keep us updated."

He turned to Jayne and Vic. "I have to say, this will be the first time we've had a cardinal, let alone two, in this safe house."

For the next several minutes, Jayne stood close to Vic and Gray, saying little but listening to the occasional update that came over the communications radio link from Roberto, Gina, and Teresa. They all kept a close eye on the monitor screens that showed the various feeds coming in.

Two of the feeds were from the cameras concealed in the lamp over the door to the house. One showed Via dei Panieri in a southeasterly direction, which was a long stretch of perhaps eighty meters that led to the junction from which Baltrami would come. The other camera, looking northwest, covered the shorter stretch of about twenty meters to where the street joined the busier Via Garibaldi, which, as Constanza had said, housed the Carabinieri headquarters.

There was no action in either direction. Even the dog and two cats had disappeared. The residents were all having a quiet afternoon.

The third feed showed footage from the microcamera built into Roberto's cap, and the fourth displayed similar footage from a hidden camera in Gina's shoulder bag. Teresa was not carrying a camera.

For much of the time, Baltrami was too far away from the cameras to be clearly visible, but occasionally Roberto or Gina closed the gap. At those times, the cardinal could been seen walking at a steady pace along the route given to him, mainly narrow cobbled streets typical of the type seen all over Trastevere.

Finally there came the whispered tones of Gina from the speaker on the desk. "PHOENIX will be on the street in approximately three minutes—that's my best estimate. No sign of surveillance. He's good to go. Staying calm."

Teresa, who was walking well ahead of Baltrami, gave a short confirmation that there were no obvious problems or issues looming. "Target street is clear," she said. "I'm moving into it."

Indeed, Teresa was now visible on the feed from the camera outside the safe house as she walked briskly toward it. The arrangement was that rather than entering the house, she would continue past it and exit the other end of the street to double-check that there were no looming threats there.

Meanwhile, the video feed from Gina's bag camera showed Baltrami perhaps fifty meters ahead, moving along Vicolo del Cedro, a street similar in architecture to the one they were on.

Almost exactly three minutes later, he disappeared from view on the feed from the bag camera and reappeared on the surveillance camera positioned outside the safe house. His dark clothing made him appear like a distant silhouette as he turned the corner and made his way down the center of the street, outlined clearly against the gray cobblestones. By that stage, Teresa had exited the street and disappeared from view.

"He looks like Clint Eastwood arriving in town," Constanzo said, deadpan, as he watched the screen.

Vic chuckled. "Could be a scene from *Pale Rider*."

The cardinal moved steadily along Via dei Panieri, a lone, upright figure on a deserted stretch of pavement. He made his way past the heavily shuttered houses at the far end of the street, with their iron security bars across windows and doors, and the tall ivy-covered wall of the disused industrial unit halfway along.

Behind him, Gina appeared at the end of the street and followed Baltrami toward the safe house, her bag swinging slightly over her shoulder. The video feed from her bag, displaying on one of the monitors in front of Constanzo, showed Baltrami fifty meters ahead of her.

The cardinal drew near to the safe house, his hair still neatly combed back flat against his skull, looking alert, his eyes searching for the door number that he needed.

Gina stopped and appeared to take a pack of cigarettes from her bag.

"I'll let Baltrami join you inside, then follow," she said, her voice emanating tinnily from the speaker as she took out a cigarette, placed it between her lips, and clicked a lighter. "Someone should meet him at the door."

"Yes, they should," Constanzo said.

Constanzo turned to Jayne and Gray. "Do you two want to go downstairs and form the reception committee? I think he'd be reassured to see you, Eminence."

"Of course," Gray said.

Jayne nodded and headed for the stairs. When they reached the front door, she turned to Gray, close behind her. "I know it's your face he'll want to see, but for safety, I'll bring him in."

Gray inclined his head in agreement.

She opened the front door and stood in the center of the

frame, watching Baltrami as he approached. She raised a hand in greeting, and the cardinal smiled.

As he drew nearer, Jayne noticed that behind Gina, a motorcycle had turned into Via dei Panieri from the far end. It accelerated hard toward her along the street. Two people were visible on the machine, both wearing black helmets and black leathers.

Gina turned, presumably alerted by the bike's engine noise, and stepped back from the middle of the street into the gap between a couple of cars to allow it to pass safely.

All Jayne's instincts screamed at her as the motorcycle barreled past Gina.

Too fast for this little street.

She shot a look at Baltrami, who now drew level with the safe house entrance. He glanced over his shoulder, presumably also alerted by the loud noise of the motorcycle, which was speeding ever closer. Then he carefully squeezed through the narrow gap between the two parked cars right outside the front door, just five meters away from Jayne.

Jayne stepped out of the doorway just as the rider braked hard, skillfully corrected a slight skid, and then slowed to a crawl outside the safe house entrance.

She felt her chest tighten as the passenger, tucked snugly behind the rider, lifted an arm and pointed a black pistol directly at Baltrami.

"*No!*" Jayne screamed.

Baltrami, who had been concentrating on maneuvering himself between the cars, turned belatedly. He must have instantly realized what was about to happen for—in a vain attempt to stop the inevitable—he raised both arms over his face, trying to protect himself.

Jayne dove toward Baltrami's thighs, arms wide, in a purely instinctive attempt to push or drag him to the ground behind the cars and out of harm's way.

But it was too late.

The gunman had fired a couple of shots and loosed off a couple more just milliseconds before Jayne wrapped her arms around Baltrami's lower body, just as the clergyman was already falling backward. She ended up diving on top of him instead as he tumbled, arms spread wide, in the gap between the cars.

Instantly, the motorcycle's engine roared as it accelerated again, and Jayne heard more gunshots from Gina's direction, farther up the street. She realized Gina was trying to take down the motorcyclist.

But the sound of the motorcycle's engine faded as it rounded the sharp corner at the end of the street.

Jayne found herself lying on top of Baltrami's chest.

She placed her palms on the cobblestones, pushed herself up, and gazed down at him. The cardinal's eyes were half closed. There were two small bullet wounds in his face, one near the left eye, and two more in his chest, blood bubbling out from both.

Jayne grabbed Baltrami's wrist and searched for a pulse. "Shit," she yelled as she frantically tried different spots. "Get a bloody ambulance. Quick!"

She felt a hand on her shoulder and looked up to see Gray, who crouched next to her. Gina was standing behind him, her face crumpled and distorted and clearly in shock.

"I need to give him the last rites, right now," Gray said, his voice cracked and broken.

But she knew it was too late for that. Her probing fingers had found nothing, confirming what she could see. Death must have been almost instantaneous.

Jayne caught Gray's eye and dumbly shook her head. "He's gone," she said. "The bastards have *killed* him."

Gray bowed his head, crossed himself, and closed his eyes. He placed a hand on Baltrami's wounded chest and prayed.

As he did, two tears trickled down each of his cheeks, followed by another, and another.

The sight of Gray crying made Jayne well up too, not something that happened often.

Who did this?

In that moment, she vowed to herself she would find out.

CHAPTER NINE

Tuesday, June 28, 2016
  Rome

To Jayne's relief, Vic took instant charge of events. Although now rarely involved at such a hands-on level given his seniority, he had been caught in such catastrophic ends to operations on foreign soil before. Jayne had too, but she never relished leading the cleanup.

Within what seemed like seconds, the rest of the team had gathered outside the safe house door. Roberto and Teresa arrived swiftly, and working under Vic's instructions, they all lifted Baltrami's lifeless body and carried it inside and into the hallway, where they placed it on a rug.

Vic closed the front door behind them and leaned back against it, hands clasped behind his head, surveying the scene. He shut his eyes momentarily. Constanzo stood at the bottom of the staircase, looking equally distraught, while Gray, one hand clasping each of his tear-stained cheeks, remained next to the body of his friend.

There was going to be no easy way out of this mess—that was obvious to Jayne. Sentiment and emotion would have to be put to one side right now. Coming on top of the assassinations in Washington, this killing, much closer to home, would send seismic shock waves through the Vatican and indeed the whole of Italy and beyond. They needed to go straight into damage-limitation mode.

"We'll have to involve the authorities here, the police," Vic said, as if reading her mind. He looked at Constanzo. "It's best if we all disappear apart from you, Donald. I'm sorry, but you and the embassy will have to manage this one. The rest of us can't afford to get caught up in it, for obvious reasons. We can't get outed as Agency people, especially in connection with another cardinal's murder."

The look of dismay that crossed Constanzo's face was palpable. But he nodded slowly. "I know the Carabinieri vice commander general for Italy now. Tommaso Porpora's his name. He's the number two in the force. I'll give him a call in a few minutes. We'll need to work out our story first, though."

"Thanks," Vic said. "But this Porpora. Can we trust him?"

"I dealt with him most recently over the Muslim cleric case in Milan," Constanzo said. "He's been helpful. A tough guy, I get the impression, but down-to-earth. He did his best not to fuel the rendition crap in the Italian press, and I appreciated that. I trusted him after that."

"He wasn't buying favors off you by being so helpful?" Vic asked, a skeptical look on his face.

Constanzo shook his head. "I think not."

"All right. If you're sure about him, go ahead. Contact him," Vic said. "Sorry again to drop this into your lap so soon after the rendition."

Constanzo didn't look happy but shrugged. "It's okay. Comes with the territory."

"What about Michael?" Jayne asked. "He can't afford to get caught up in this mess."

Her concern was that Gray might now become somehow implicated in his fellow cardinal's death. It was a certainty that if the media, especially the voracious and scandal-hungry Italian and British tabloids, got wind of what had happened, they would trash his reputation, even though he had nothing to do with the murder.

She glanced at Gray, who was standing with hands on hips.

"I'm playing no part in any cover-up," Gray said. "That would be worse. It goes against everything I stand for."

"I know that. We're not talking about a cover-up," Vic said. "We're talking about protecting the innocent—which is you—and doing what's necessary to enable us to pursue our own investigation and find out who did this, and who did the DC killings, and why. If we all get entangled in an Italian police investigation now, that'll be the end. You'll be all over the newspapers and the TV news. We could even end up spending the next day or two in police cells for starters, knowing how they operate here. It will put us back by weeks. In the meantime, the perpetrators will be long gone, their tracks will be covered, and they win. And all our covers will be blown too, because you can guarantee our photos will be on the front pages worldwide."

Jayne knew that Vic, as ever, had summed the situation up precisely. They had no choice.

"He's right, Michael," she said. "We need to get out of here. Donald will take care of things. We can't afford to be associated with this—it's not our fault this happened. But we need to be free to find out what's behind it. We can't afford to end up in a massive tangle of Italian red tape. You, more than any of us, must know what that's like."

Gray visibly gritted his teeth. "I see what you are saying."

Teresa took a step forward. "I found this," she said. She took a tissue from one pocket and used it to remove a pistol from another pocket. "After I heard the shots from round the corner I kind of guessed what was going on. A few seconds later, the bike came flying around the corner and straight past me. As it went around the corner, this clattered onto the cobbles. Must have fallen from a pocket or a hand. They weren't stopping to pick it up. Just kept going. Maybe they didn't realize they'd dropped it."

She held out the gun. Jayne recognized it immediately as a Beretta 71, a compact weapon with a nine-centimeter barrel, designed to fire .22-caliber Long Rifle ammunition. She had used that type of gun herself frequently, although she preferred the Walther PPS.

"I also got the license plate of the bike," Teresa said.

"Well done," Vic said. "Although my guess is they'll be false plates."

The switch of topic to evidence triggered a thought in Jayne. She moved toward the door. "I'll take a look outside, see if any of the cases are on the ground." The gunman had fired multiple shots, so she knew the spent cartridge cases from the Beretta must be lying out there somewhere. The gunman certainly hadn't stopped to pick them up.

Vic nodded. "Good thought." He moved away from the door to allow Jayne out.

She opened the door and glanced up and down the street. There was still no sign of anyone. The gunshots hadn't been particularly loud, with none of the crack that comes with high-powered supersonic rounds, which might account for the absence of local residents coming out into the street to see what was going on. But equally, she hadn't seen a silencer on the gun, so it crossed her mind that he must have been using subsonic cartridges.

Jayne squeezed between the parked cars and started looking around. She expected any minute to hear the wail of sirens and see flashing lights. Surely someone must have seen what had occurred. But all was calm. Maybe the few residents on the street were taking an afternoon nap.

A few seconds later she found two spent brass .22 cartridges lying a few meters away. She took out a handkerchief, used it to pick up the cartridges, and slipped them into her pocket. She continued looking and quickly found another two but couldn't see any more. By her count, there had been four shots, five at most, fired by someone who was a highly accurate shot, based on the two strikes to the head and two to the chest. Forensics could probably match the cases to the gun, although there seemed no doubt about that.

She returned to the safe house to find Constanzo on the phone, talking animatedly to someone at the CIA station, judging by the tone of the conversation. He was issuing instructions for someone to pick the team up from the safe house as soon as possible and for the ambassador to call him back. Jayne was relieved she wasn't in Constanzo's shoes.

Meanwhile, Vic was also on the phone. It took her only a few seconds to pick up that he was speaking to Arthur Veltman at Langley, forewarning him that another crisis had just begun.

It was at times like this that Jayne was grateful she was no longer a senior employee at an international intelligence agency but a freelancer who didn't have to deal daily with the knife-wielding internal politics that often made Vic's life so difficult. She just wanted to get on with her investigation, not engage in organizing high-level cover-ups or be weighed down in managing expectations at the White House level.

Jayne turned to Gray, who stood next to the body of his fallen fellow cardinal, his face drooping. He seemed to have developed some kind of twitch in his left eye, which kept blinking, seemingly involuntarily. He removed his glasses, wiped a hand over the eye, looked up, and met Jayne's gaze.

"He was my friend," Gray said as he replaced his glasses. "One of the few I really trusted in the Vatican. I could be completely honest about things with him. I can't say that about many of the others. This is a disaster. His family is going to be inconsolable—his brother and sister, Sami and Laila." He shook his head. "They were a tight unit. They were all he had apart from the people at his church. Now God's taken him home before his time."

Jayne found herself not knowing what to say to Gray. In the end, since this was her father's friend, she decided it would be best to do what her father always taught her to do— look forward, seeking solutions to problems. She put a hand on Gray's shoulder. "Listen, Michael, I am telling you now, we are going to find whoever has done this. We're going to find the truth. I promise you that. But for now, I think we need to get out of here."

Constanzo finished his phone call and turned to the others in the room. "The car will be here in one minute. You all need to go. I'll take care of things here."

Vic had also finished his call, so Jayne showed him and Constanzo the spent cartridge cases she had found, again taking care to use a handkerchief.

Constanzo carefully tipped the cases into a plastic bag, into which he had already placed the Beretta. "We'll have to hand this over to the police team. They'll have to run them through forensics for DNA and prints, much as I would like to keep them and have our own tests done."

Vic watched him thoughtfully. "I doubt they'll get anything useful from them, frankly. This was a highly professional hit." He paused and fingered his chin. "Of course, you don't need me to tell you who has historically used the Beretta 71 as their go-to weapon?"

Immediately Jayne knew to whom he was alluding. She didn't say anything, but Constanzo did.

"Very careless, if it was them," he said.

Vic shrugged and caught Jayne's eye. "When you go to see Avi Shiloah, you can let him know that his colleagues need to up their game."

Jayne just nodded and pursed her lips.

What Vic had said was true. She knew the Mossad often favored the Beretta 71 because of its superb accuracy and reliability as well as its lightweight design, which meant it was easy to rack the slide to load the chamber and get it into firing position at lightning speed.

Despite its small caliber, the 71 was an excellent weapon in a gunfight, but only if the user was skilled and capable of hitting a small, vital target—like a human head or heart—while on the move. For less-skilled operatives, the reduced stopping power of the .22 Long Rifle rounds used in the 71 compared to a larger 9mm round meant it was not such a good choice. That wasn't an issue for highly capable Mossad agents.

Jayne's first thought was that if she threw the Beretta into her chat with Shiloah in connection with the killing here, it was going to be a conversation stopper.

From outside, she heard a car engine and a slight squeal of brakes.

Constanzo opened the door and looked out. "The car's here. Off you go. This will take you back to the embassy. You can disperse from there. I'm going to tell my police contact Porpora I was here alone to meet Baltrami to receive some information about an ongoing issue in Ramallah involving Hamas, and that I suspect they are behind the killing. I've thought it all through quite carefully, don't worry."

"Good luck with that," Jayne said. She guessed, knowing how the Italians operated, that money would likely change hands at some point, but she didn't want to mention that in front of Gray. He was uncomfortable enough with the situation already.

Constanzo inclined his head to one side as if to say he had no choice. "You and Vic will need to find somewhere else to stay, and immediately," he said. "My wife will take you to a hotel. You can guarantee the police will be at my house at some point, no matter how good my explanation is for Porpora. Might not be advisable for them to find you there."

That also made sense. Jayne could see why Vic rated Constanzo highly. He was thinking fast on his feet.

Jayne turned, took Gray by the arm, and steered the aging cardinal toward the door. His face crumpled once again as he took a last look at Baltrami's body on the rug before stepping outside.

As they went through the door, Gray stopped and looked her in the eye. "Jayne, I need you to know that Cardinal Baltrami was my friend, but more than that, he was a friend to the Palestinian people. He changed many lives. He deserves to have the truth known about this, and justice done, just as you had justice done for your father's killing all those years ago. Your father would want you to do this."

Jayne folded her arms. "You're spot-on about that. We'll do it."

"And we must remember the pope's instruction too. I'm still no nearer to finding out what the cardinals in DC were going to tell the White House. I'm now thinking that's why Cardinal Baltrami was killed—because he was going to tell me. And someone knew it."

Jayne had been thinking precisely the same thing. She could see Gray was feeling under pressure. "We'll find out. Don't you worry."

* * *

Tuesday, June 28, 2016
    Rome

The late-afternoon shadows were lengthening by the time the
cab dropped Gray off near the Vatican. He had the driver
stop on Borgio Pio, a cobbled street a few hundred meters
east of St. Peter's Square.

There he stood for a few minutes, trying to collect his
thoughts. His mind felt foggy, his head numb. It was difficult
to believe what had just happened to his friend Kamal
Baltrami. But he knew he needed to carry on as normal,
somehow. He couldn't give away to anyone what he had
witnessed; otherwise he would end any chance Jayne and her
colleagues had of discovering the truth behind what had
happened.

Eventually, he crossed the street and entered Fratelli
Zeffirelli, a tailor shop owned by the Zeffirelli brothers, in a
slightly run-down terracotta-colored building, sandwiched
between a fruit seller and a tobacconist. It was an old-fashioned outlet with a front counter from where he needed to
pick up his new bespoke red cardinal's cassock, which he had
ordered two weeks earlier.

This wasn't the official Vatican tailor, which had supplied
papal outfits to the Holy See since the 1700s and was located
nearer to the Vatican in the barracks of the Swiss Guard. But
like some of his colleagues, including Pope Julius, Gray had
tried a couple of smaller alternative suppliers and found he
preferred the fit and cut of garments from the store owned by
the effusive and popular Vincenzo Zeffirelli, who did the
tailoring work, and Luigi Zeffirelli, who did the accounts and
dealt with suppliers.

Gray still used the official tailor for some of his clothing, particularly the more ornate items worn on ceremonial occasions. But he found the lighter and cooler material used by the Zeffirellis suited him better for his day-to-day clothing, including his shirts, cassocks, and Roman collars, given that he was often traveling from the rain and cold of London to the heat of Rome.

As soon as Gray entered the store, Vincenzo emerged from behind his counter, walked over, and shook his hand with his usual crushing grip, which went on for several seconds longer than necessary. His hair was slicked back as always, and these days it was almost white. Like his brother, Vincenzo always had a roguish, conspiratorial air about him, and Gray always suspected it wouldn't be wise to ask too many questions about his background.

"Vincenzo, how are you? How is business? Have you sold up yet?" He tried to put the all-enveloping sadness flooding through him to one side and instead use a ritual joke between them to lift his mood. The Zeffirelli brothers, both in their late seventies, had continued to work hard well beyond normal retirement age, admittedly helped by their highly skilled team of tailors. The answer to Gray's question about selling the shop and retiring was always no.

The elderly tailor, several inches shorter than Gray, looked up at him. "I'm well, and you cardinals keep me living in the style I'm accustomed to." He glanced around the store. "However, the answer to your question, just privately between us, is yes, I have sold."

Gray looked at him. "What do you mean you've sold?"

Vincenzo nodded. "It's true. Luigi and I have told the staff but not anyone else yet, apart from the pope when I was in his office a few days ago. Please keep it to yourself for now. The time has come. We're both getting old. Our wives need us around more."

Gray felt more than surprised. "Who have you sold to? Will they keep the business going as it is?"

"We haven't announced the buyer yet. But yes, they're in the clothing business, so it will continue. I won't be here for much longer."

"Well, congratulations. You've certainly earned your retirement."

One of Vincenzo's senior lieutenants, his long-serving chief tailor Massimo Valli, walked by and greeted Gray as he went. Valli had fitted him and many other cardinals, including the pope, with cassocks in the past and was one of the best in the business.

Gray struggled his way through a conversation about more inconsequential matters, including prospects for the coming season for Vincenzo's beloved A.S. Roma football team. He then shook hands once again and, to his relief, said goodbye.

He paid his bill, picked up the cassock encased in a protective plastic bag, draped it over his arm, and headed toward the Vatican's Santa Anna Gate. This was the low-key commercial entrance into Vatican City located north of the busy St. Peter's Square, which was always swarming with tourists, especially in summer.

He stopped to check his phone. Many at the Vatican knew of his friendship with Baltrami, and it seemed news of his demise was already spreading. There were two text messages about it from other cardinals and a missed call.

Gray walked through Santa Anna Gate, with its ornate black ironwork flanked by twin eagles mounted on stone pillars. He inclined his head toward the Swiss Guard on duty, who was keeping a close watch on the cars and vans passing through.

Normally a serene character, Gray was feeling somewhat off balance and fidgety. He felt uneasy not just because of what had happened to Baltrami, but also because of the cover-up, of sorts, that was being implemented by the CIA team and Jayne, although he knew it was all for the right reasons. He could entirely see the argument that being tied up in a long police investigation would torpedo any chance of progress in their own inquiry.

But it didn't feel right. He liked to have truth on his side and to do things in a correct, orderly way.

Gray made his way westward along Via Santa Anna, past the Vatican Bank and Apostolic Palace, then cut past the Sistine Chapel toward the gardens. His thought was to do a short circuit around the gardens and find a bench where he could sit, think, and pray for a while.

But outside the Sistine Chapel came a voice from his left.

"Eminence, there you are. At last."

He turned to see the pope's personal secretary, Christophe Despierre, striding toward him.

"We've been looking for you," Despierre said. Next to him was Cardinal Saraceni, and trailing a couple of paces behind was the Vatican's financial chief, officially known as the prefect of the secretariat for the economy, Cardinal Louis Sweeney, the archbishop of New Orleans. Gray knew that Sweeney, who looked pale and as if he had lost a few pounds, had just returned from a short visit to various parts of southern Africa.

The three men came to a halt in front of Gray.

"Have you heard what happened?" Saraceni asked, his eyes, small and dark, fixed on Gray.

Gray pressed his lips together. "Cardinal Baltrami? Terrible. I really can't believe it. There is something awful going on. First Washington, now this. We need to get to the bottom of it. How is His Holiness?"

"I've just come from him," Despierre said. "He has taken

it very badly. He is going to issue a statement soon. He's been asking for you. Where have you been?"

There was an interrogative note to Despierre's question, and Gray hesitated for a beat, then immediately regretted doing so. "I've been out, visiting a friend, and then to the tailor to pick up my cassock." He held up the garment bag. "It's bizarre. Five deaths. No explanation. Why is this happening?"

Saraceni shook his head and folded his arms tight across his chest. "No idea. At least we have highly capable law enforcement agencies to investigate this, both here and in the United States. I am sure they will get to the bottom of it." He paused, looking slightly down his nose at Gray. "As you said yourself in our meeting with His Holiness the other day, we should assist the FBI however we can. The same now applies to the Italian state police, given what has happened to Cardinal Baltrami. And as we agreed with His Holiness, I will collate our thoughts and comments. It's my job to feed the Vatican's position to the FBI and to the state police."

There was a slightly arrogant note in his voice, but that was nothing new. Saraceni was clearly trying to warn him not to interfere in what he viewed as his own domain.

Gray looked at him. "Of course. Let's hope they resolve it quickly."

"Good," Saraceni said. "So, if you have anything else you want to contribute that you think may be of help, please feed it through me, and I will pass it on to them."

Saraceni glanced at his watch, then at his two compan- ions. "Let's get to our meeting, shall we? We're already late."

The three men walked on. Sweeney, still trailing the other two, caught Gray's eye as he passed by.

"Are you okay?" Gray asked.

"Not really," Sweeney said. "Awful what's going on here."

Then he continued walking after the others.

Gray exhaled, partly in relief that they hadn't prolonged the conversation.

Although in his view the vast majority of cardinals and others who worked at the Vatican were extremely decent, godly men with their hearts in the right place, there were a few whom he found difficult to tolerate. Most of them were the more politically-minded, the ambitious ones, who held senior positions in the Roman Curia. In some cases, it was the cultural and language differences that were to blame for misunderstandings between them, but not all.

The various scandals that had enveloped the Vatican and the global Catholic Church, particularly the numerous sexual abuse cases and ensuing cover-ups, also made it impossible to know whom to trust. So many people spoke in code, wary that they might say the wrong thing to the wrong person, and by so doing upset someone in a position to wreck their careers.

This felt like dangerous territory.

Gray knew the pope would now likely want him to find out what he could about Baltrami's death and whether there was a connection to whatever the four brothers in Washington were intending to disclose to the White House. It felt like an impossible situation and meant he would have to be extremely economical with the truth with almost everyone. He knew he wasn't going to be able to confide fully in others until this was resolved, and that was not a position he felt comfortable with.

Gray glanced up to his left at the soaring 136-meter dome of St. Peter's Basilica, a sight that never failed to spur him onward. That and his faith sometimes seemed to be the only constants in his life.

The FBI and Italian state police would do what they could, he told himself. But the person he felt instinctively he could trust to do whatever was necessary to find out what he needed to know was the daughter of his old friend Ken Robinson.

He just hoped she found some answers quickly. With five of his brothers gone, and not the slightest clue why, Gray felt it was quite possible more could follow—and he couldn't help wondering whether he himself was in danger.

CHAPTER TEN

Wednesday, June 29, 2016
Rome

Rather than check Jayne and Vic into a large hotel, where there would be an instant digital footprint of their whereabouts, Constanzo's wife, Maria, had come up with a better solution the previous evening: one of her friends had a couple of empty spare bedrooms at their home. The two had quickly agreed to stay there instead.

Maria, a diminutive, busy, raven-haired woman, seemed completely unfazed by the situation and appeared to know exactly what to do. Clearly she had found herself in similar situations before. Jayne noticed her checking her tail as she drove them to their destination.

In any case, it was only a one-night stay. Jayne had a flight out of Rome to Tel Aviv that evening, while Vic was flying at about the same time to Paris, where he had meetings with the acting chief of station scheduled for the next day. Jayne was secretly glad he was remaining in Europe, just in case she needed support on the ground if her investigation progressed further.

Jayne and Vic had finished a late breakfast and were packing their bags when Constanzo called Vic on his secure line. Vic summoned Jayne from her room to join the call and put his phone onto speaker so she could hear.

"I have some good news and bad news," Constanzo said, once they were all set up. "The good is that Tommaso Porpora over at police HQ appears to be in helpful mode. He says he'll do his best not to generate any more media coverage than there is already, and to keep us out of it."

"He'd struggle to generate any more," Jayne said.

That morning's newspapers were plastered with wall-to-wall coverage about the demise of another cardinal, this time in a Trastevere side street. That the victim was based in the West Bank added to the sense of drama and mystique that had obviously seized the imagination of Rome's newspaper editors and TV news producers.

Jayne had seen Porpora in some of the TV bulletins. He was a bristling man with short blond hair, thick eyebrows, and hard gray eyes and wore a white shirt with black epaulets that had three white stars bordered in red. The police chief was trying to deflect questions that reporters shouted at him.

Porpora was going to have his work cut out for him. The ingredients were all laid out on a silver platter for the media. Speculation about the identity of the perpetrators was rife, and potential explanations for the shooting included some kind of conflict between Hamas, to whom Baltrami was rumored to be close, and their rivals Fatah. An alternative theory was that it was an attempted robbery or it might have been an Italian mafia hit that had simply taken out the wrong man, given that Baltrami was not wearing his Roman collar.

There was also some bewilderment at the Vatican, it seemed. Some journalists there had got extensive quotes from unnamed cardinals stating that Baltrami had not been staying at the St. Martha's House guesthouse, as he normally did. Indeed, nobody even seemed aware he was in Rome, and there was no obvious explanation for the anomaly.

An official statement from the Vatican press office, published via the Vatican News website, included a message from Pope Julius. "On learning with sorrow of the terrible and sudden death of our brother Cardinal Kamal Baltrami, I wish to express my shock and offer my condolences and my union in prayer with the College of Cardinals, the family and friends of the deceased, and all those who mourn him," the pope said. "Coming so soon after the deaths of our four other brothers in the United States, this represents another blow, but one from which we will recover, with God's grace."

There was an additional quote in the statement from Cardinal Alfredo Saraceni, the Vatican's secretary of state, stating that "Cardinal Baltrami left an unforgettable mark on the Church and on the social and political life of Ramallah over a long period."

Thankfully, however, despite the pages of coverage, none of the reports mentioned Constanzo or even referred to a CIA connection, as far as Jayne could see. They stated only that Baltrami was believed to have been going to a meeting over coffee with an unnamed friend and that police were grappling to come up with an explanation for the killing. So Constanzo's dealings had spared them that, at least.

"Well done, Don," Vic said. "I assume Porpora is continuing to investigate, though?"

"Yes, he is investigating who carried out the hit. Just not who Baltrami was going to meet."

"Good, but keep an eye on him," Vic said. "Otherwise, he will have his claws into you. You know how these things work. He'll want a payback at some point, guaranteed."

"He won't get any from me," Constanzo said.

For a few seconds, there was silence on the call.

Jayne broke it. "So, you said you also had bad news. What is it?"

"Well, I've just had some forensic results back from Porpora," Constanzo said.

"And?"

"There's nothing on the spent cartridges, but you'd expect that. However, the Beretta was another story. Although there were no prints, it did give us some DNA. There was a small piece of saliva on the barrel, which seems weird, but that's what he said. Apparently, it was enough to get a match."

"A match for who?" Jayne asked.

"I'm coming to that. I asked if there was a DNA match and how the original sample was obtained, and Porpora wasn't telling me. I pushed him, persuaded him, and he eventually let slip that the person involved paid a visit to AISE's headquarters a few years ago while engaged in a joint operation with them. While he was there, he was taken for a few meals at the cafeteria, and he had a few drinks in a bar with them too."

"So he was known to them?" Jayne asked.

"Yes."

"So they swabbed the person's glass or his cup or something?" Jayne asked.

"Precisely. Typical underhanded Italian methodology."

"Come on, then, tell us who it is," Jayne said.

"You're about to fly off to their head office. It's a Mossad *katsa*, name of Rafael Levy."

"*Rafael?*" Jayne was struggling to compute what she was hearing.

"Yes. That's the name. Rafael Levy. You know him?"

Jayne didn't speak for a couple of seconds, so Vic jumped in.

"Must be the same Rafael you worked with, Jayne?" Vic asked.

Jayne nodded. She had just worked alongside Rafael and his senior Mossad colleague David Zahavi for all of April that year, tracking down the terrorist Kourosh Navai—dubbed the Dark Shah.

Navai, who they eventually trapped in Mexico, had been responsible for the deaths of the Israeli foreign minister, Moshe Cohen, and the Mossad chief, Eli Elazar, in a brazen attack on an offshore gas platform. Far more personally significant for Jayne, Navai had also been responsible, together with his girlfriend, for the bomb attack that had killed her father. She had found Rafael to be a world-class operator and held him in the highest regard.

"This is bloody unbelievable," Jayne said. "It can't be. How certain are they? What's the match confidence score for the DNA? Did you get one?"

"Virtually a hundred percent," Constanzo said. "There's no doubt about it. It was his DNA on the gun."

"Bloody hell."

Jayne exhaled loudly. It was difficult to argue with DNA evidence. She also recalled that Rafael's weapon of choice, like many *katsas*, had been a Beretta 71. Indeed, he had used it, very expertly, to take down two Iranian Quds Force guards in a Vienna hotel during the operation they had only recently completed.

It still didn't sound quite right to her, though. Even if he was involved, Rafael wasn't the type to leave a trail of evidence, especially on an operation as sensitive as this one.

"What are the Italians going to do?" Vic asked. "Aren't they going to go public with it immediately and cause a massive international stink? I'm guessing they'll haul in the Israeli ambassador and give him a dressing down."

It was a good point, Jayne thought. If that happened, it

would make it very difficult for her to have the back-channel discussion with Avi Shiloah that she and Vic had been planning.

"I'm sure they will go public, yes," Constanzo said. "But Porpora said it won't be in the next day or so. He said before they make a serious allegation like that, they'll need to have discussions with the minister of the interior and the PM—those guys will handle it, of course. And they're both out of the country at the moment, in Norway."

"Gives us a little breathing space," Vic said. "That has to be a good thing." He looked at Jayne. "And allows you time to talk to Avi."

Jayne shrugged. It was true, it gave her a little time. But how on earth was she going to have a sensible discussion about this with Avi Shiloah?

CHAPTER ELEVEN

Thursday, June 30, 2016
Jerusalem

Jayne downshifted a gear as Highway 1 rose more steeply ahead of her into the Judaean Mountains east of Tel Aviv. She caught the scent of pine trees and lowered the window to allow it to permeate the rented Ford Focus sedan. It was one of her favorite smells and was particularly strong now beneath a late-afternoon sun as she drove eastward toward Jerusalem along the ribbon of black highway that ran through the white limestone hills.

At two and a half thousand feet above sea level, Jerusalem was at a greater altitude than she had expected before her first visit to the city, and the climb was a reminder of that.

Her destination was the house of Avi Shiloah, the Mossad chief. Jayne had messaged him from Rome the previous afternoon to say she was heading to Israel and would like an urgent meeting. He hadn't asked why, but to her relief he invited her to meet him at his home rather than at the Mossad's expansive headquarters complex next to Glilot Interchange, the highway junction a few kilometers north of central Tel Aviv. She was keen to keep as low a profile as possible, given the sensitivity of the questions she needed to ask Shiloah.

Jayne had certainly not been expecting to return to Tel Aviv so soon, just a couple of months after her previous visit. Out of habit she had taken the precaution of checking into a different hotel than the one she had stayed in before. The Renaissance was a few blocks north of the Sheraton, where she had stayed with Joe last time, but still had views over the beach.

Michael Gray had asked to accompany her, because after seeing Shiloah, her plan was to visit Cardinal Baltrami's brother and sister, Sami and Laila. Perhaps they might know something of what their brother had planned to tell Gray. They both lived in Ramallah, the Palestinian city in the West Bank located about ten kilometers north of Jerusalem and where Baltrami had served as archbishop.

She had declined Gray's request and told him he needed to maintain a normal routine in the Vatican. If he were to suddenly drop off the radar, it would instantly invite suspicion.

Apart from that, she needed someone she could trust on the ground at the Vatican who could feed her any useful information or new developments. And her gut told her that although Ramallah was probably safe, it was better that Gray didn't travel there. The reasons behind the deaths of the five clergymen were unknown so far, and the last thing she wanted was another casualty on her hands, particularly her father's old friend.

An update message from Vic that morning had confirmed that the FBI was making little progress identifying who had been behind the assassinations in Washington. They had interviewed families, colleagues, and friends of the three cardinals and the archbishop who had died but had received no useful leads.

Good luck with Avi and in Ramallah. We badly need a break, Vic wrote at the end of his message.

They certainly did.

Jayne flicked on the car radio and tuned to a news bulletin on the BBC World Service. The second story was about the assassination the previous evening in Tehran of Amir Rad, the head of the Atomic Energy Organization of Iran (AEOI), the government's main nuclear energy agency.

Feeling a little stunned, Jayne slowed down as she listened.

Rad's car had been blown up in a remotely controlled explosion on a busy city street, the reporter covering the story said. The death was being attributed to Mossad agents operating undercover in Tehran. As usual, the agency had declined to comment.

In response, the Iranian Supreme Leader, Ayatollah Ali Hashemi, had sworn revenge against Israel and the United States, whom he blamed for the attack. The reporter quoted from a statement issued by Hashemi that said the leaders of both countries would never be safe as long as he was governing Iran and called on his followers to exact revenge on both men. To Jayne, it sounded like a *fatwa* had been issued in Tehran.

Her mind flashed back a few weeks to the death of the AEOI's deputy director, Jafar Farsad, at a Vienna hotel just moments after he had been coerced into giving Jayne and David Zahavi details of his country's uranium enrichment operations. Farsad had jumped from his hotel room's balcony to his death while being pursued by a gunman from Iran's Quds Force security service. Jayne and Zahavi had just managed to escape the gunman, who had eventually been shot dead by Rafael Levy.

Jayne was surprised that the Mossad had moved to take down the AEOI chief so soon after the death of his deputy. Between them, the two men were responsible for Iran's weapons development program and for organizing the uranium enrichment process critical to that. She knew the Mossad had recently been having difficulties gaining access to Iran, so those issues had clearly been overcome. Maybe Shiloah would have something to say about that when she reached his house.

The satnav on her phone, mounted on the dashboard, ensured the seventy-kilometer journey was straightforward. Although there were parking spots near Shiloah's stone house on Negba Street, she found one beneath a shady oak tree a few hundred meters away and walked the rest of the way to give herself a chance to carry out final checks for any signs of surveillance. There was none.

The narrow lane, lined by a mixture of tall pines and oaks with vehicles parked down one side, seemed a peaceful area, but the steel fences and gates that separated the property from the street were a reminder of the troubles that continued to hang over the capital. Most properties had shutters or bars over the windows.

Jayne pushed the button on the intercom mounted next to the gate and waited. She could see a camera on the other side of the steel bars swiveling on its mount.

Then the gate clicked open and Shiloah's disembodied voice came from a hidden speaker. "Make sure you close it behind you."

He was standing at the heavy front door at the top of a short flight of stone steps when Jayne turned the corner into a small courtyard. He sucked heavily on one of his trademark

Camel cigarettes, dropped the butt to the ground, and crushed it beneath his foot.

"Good to see you again so soon," he said. He extended a hairy hand, shook Jayne's in a grip that was too tight for comfort, and kissed her on both cheeks. "Come in. I've got a Golan Heights sauvignon blanc on ice."

He led the way through the house, across a dark wooden-floored hallway, and up a flight of stairs to a landing, where he stopped outside a door.

"There's two people here who will be pleased to see you again," Shiloah said. "We've just been having a discreet cele-bration."

"Who?"

Shiloah didn't reply. He opened the door to a living room, in the center of which were two sofas and two armchairs posi-tioned around a large wooden coffee table.

Jayne stopped dead.

Sitting on the sofas, both wearing sunglasses, were two familiar figures: the shaven-headed David Zahavi, the Mossad's director of operations, and the more athletic figure of Rafael Levy.

Shit.

Jayne had been hoping for a quiet, confidential chat with Shiloah so that she could discuss the DNA test results that appeared to pin Rafael to the assassination of Cardinal Baltrami.

Clearly, that now wasn't going to be possible.

"Is there something wrong?" Shiloah asked.

Jayne shook her head. "No, not at all."

There was no need to ask what the three men were cele-brating. On the table was a copy of *The Times of Israel* newspa-per. The front-page splash story was all about the assassination of Amir Rad and included a photograph of the tangled wreck of his car after the explosion that killed him.

Jayne forced herself to put on a cheery, gregarious front as she greeted the two men, kissing them on their cheeks and exchanging banter while Shiloah poured her a glass of wine.

The room looked out eastward over an elevated stone terrace toward the Old City, a couple of kilometers away.

"You didn't waste any time," Jayne said as she sat in one of the vacant armchairs and indicated toward the newspaper.

"The PM wanted quick action," Shiloah said as he handed Jayne the glass and took a seat opposite her. "The threat is real."

"I understand that," she said. The Israel prime minister, Yitzhak Katz, was renowned for his hawkishness when it came to dealing with his country's enemies and for his speed of action—as well as his impatience when his subordinates failed to act as swiftly as he wanted them to. He had doubt-less spelled out his orders regarding Amir Rad in no uncertain terms to Shiloah.

There was a brief silence. Jayne sensed the three men wanted to change the subject. She wasn't going to ask for details of the Tehran operation or if any of them had been directly involved.

"Where are you staying?" Rafael asked.

She told him, adding that in her view, it was a nicer hotel than the Sheraton.

Rafael nodded. "I'd agree with that."

Another short silence.

"So, Jayne," Shiloah said, finally breaking it. "What brings you here? I'm assuming it's not to congratulate us on our opera-tional excellence in Tehran or to discuss hotels." He paused for a second, folding his arms tight across his chest, then added, "And I hope it's not to question us about any other operations we might or might not have been involved in either."

Jayne looked at him sharply. "What do you mean?"

Shiloah leaned forward, placed both hands on the table in front of him, and looked Jayne in the eye. "It wasn't us."

He knows why I'm here. Of course he does.

"What wasn't you?"

Shiloah rolled his eyes. "Rome, nor DC. I know you've just come from Rome, and that your friend from the Vatican got you involved."

Oh God. His tentacles reach everywhere. How did he know about Gray?

Jayne said nothing. She knew what was coming next. He had clearly been ready for this.

Shiloah tapped his index finger on the table for emphasis. "Whoever killed those cardinals, it wasn't us, I can tell you that."

Jayne looked him in the eye and injected a note of cynicism into her voice. "Are you sure?"

"The last thing we want to do is upset the Vatican or the pope. They are about to do Israel a long-overdue service and publish their records in the archives that should at last cast some light on why that disgusting man Pope Pius XII watched in silence while Hitler murdered six million of us in the gas chambers."

Jayne placed both hands behind her head and continued to eyeball Shiloah. "Yes, but at the same time, the pope is also about to recognize the State of Palestine. That's not going down too well here, is it? In fact, the archives release is being seen by some as a bribe from the pope to shut Israel up, to stop you criticizing the Vatican over the Palestine announcement."

"Bullshit."

That was an interesting response, Jayne thought, given she knew for a fact that Shiloah was lying, and he must know that she knew. He just wasn't going to admit it.

She glanced at Rafael, who had so far sat listening in silence.

"And you, Rafael," she said. "I know precisely where you were two days ago, on Wednesday afternoon."

He raised an eyebrow. "Do you really?" He lifted his glass and coolly took a sip of wine.

"Yes. On the back of a motorcycle in Rome." Jayne was doing her best to keep her voice low and under control, but she couldn't stop it from rising inexorably. "And from the back of that motorcycle, hidden behind your helmet, you gunned down Cardinal Baltrami, the archbishop of Ramallah, in a street in the middle of Trastevere. You bloody well shot him in cold blood with a Beretta. Right in front of me. What the hell was that all about? Why did you do it?"

She reached into her pocket and removed a printout of the report Constanzo had forwarded to her that confirmed Rafael's DNA had been found on the Beretta. She unfolded it and pushed it across the table to Rafael, who picked it up and read it.

When he had finished, Rafael turned his gaze back to Jayne, his face betraying no emotion.

"On Wednesday afternoon, I, along with a small group of colleagues, was involved in an operation that did require a man to be killed, it is true," Rafael said. "It went completely to plan, the target was taken down, and we exited the country without further drama or casualties to our team."

"Thank you," Jayne said. "Finally, the truth is spoken."

"However, we were not in Rome," Rafael said. "We were not even in Italy." He paused. "We were in Tehran."

He picked up the newspaper that was lying on the table and tossed it over to Jayne. "Here, you can read all about it in the *Times*. That's what I was doing on Wednesday. You're looking in the wrong direction, Jayne."

* * *

There was a silence that lasted several seconds as Jayne digested what Rafael had just said.

This had to be a complete fabrication. Or was it? Now she was feeling a slight sense of doubt. Her mind was buzzing.

"The DNA results put you firmly in Rome," Jayne said.

Rafael shrugged and glanced at Shiloah. "Italian DNA tests?" he said sarcastically, raising his eyebrows.

Jayne hesitated. "Are you trying to suggest you've been framed? This time, I have to say I'm not sure I believe you." She picked up the sheet of paper detailing the DNA test results and folded it carefully.

"We've been here before, Jayne," Shiloah said. "How many other operations do you think we've been blamed for or framed for when it had nothing to do with us? We never confirm or deny anything publicly. We can't afford to. You know that—if we start down that road, then every time we don't deny something, everyone will assume it's us. Sometimes, of course, we do give journalists or politicians a bit of guidance behind the scenes if they're kicking up a fuss. This Rome killing might be an example of that."

Indeed, Jayne did know the Mossad had a policy of not commenting on operations. It was the same at MI6 and the CIA.

"But it's easy to say you've been framed," Jayne said. "You're telling me Rafael was in Tehran on Wednesday, but are you going to prove it to me? Or if not Rafael, maybe it was one of your other operatives on the back of that motorcycle in Rome."

Shiloah stared at her. "I can prove it to you, no problem, if you insist. But I'm just telling you, it wasn't us. Not Rafael. Not anyone else from here."

"What about the DNA, then?" Jayne said, looking over at

Rafael. "Someone can't just manufacture that in the kitchen, or even the lab."

Rafael spread his hands wide. "It's easy enough to get a nice sample of someone's DNA, especially in saliva. How many bars do you think I drink in each week? How many coffee shops do I visit, or restaurants? It just takes a bit of persistence to acquire a beer glass or a drinking mug or a fork with a bit of saliva on it. Not difficult, let's be honest. We've all done the same ourselves. I bet MI6 has too."

Rafael was right, Jayne thought. If someone wanted to set up Rafael in that way, it probably wouldn't be that difficult. She scratched her head.

"If not you, then who?" she asked. "And why? How did they know Baltrami was going to speak to Michael Gray, and how did they know what he was going to say—because presumably they *did* know, otherwise why kill him before he could get there?"

Jayne just didn't feel she could trust what she was being told. She knew these people wouldn't hesitate to lie to her if it suited their purpose for whatever reason. On the other hand, her first instinct had been to doubt the DNA test result. It had just seemed too unprofessional of them to have left such an obvious trace.

Shiloah leaned back in his armchair, looking a little more relaxed. "It'll be the usual suspects," Shiloah said.

"Possibly Hamas," Zahavi said. "The pope is going to recognize the State of Palestine, but it's going to be Fatah and Mahmoud Abbas he's recognizing—not Hamas and Khaled Mashal. Their rivalry is a real issue. Or, of course, it could be Hezbollah."

Jayne knew there was a high level of hostility between Fatah, led by Abbas, and Hamas, whose leader was Mashal.

Fatah, the dominant party in the Palestine Liberation Organization and which controlled the West Bank, had a somewhat more diplomatic approach now than in the past toward achieving agreement with Israel to create a Palestinian state. Hamas, meanwhile, was a militant group that controlled Gaza and favored a more aggressive approach of armed resistance, rockets, and bombings against Israel to get to the same outcome.

"So you think Hamas might murder a few cardinals—including one from Fatah's West Bank territory—in order to make the pope change his mind and not get into bed with Fatah?" Jayne asked.

Zahavi nodded. "It's possible. They may be aiming to make him realize he can't take sides without causing a lot of trouble. Or maybe they're trying to stop him from cozying up to Israel as well—letting him know he can't do that without consequences."

Jayne inclined her head. Zahavi had a point. But to her mind, Hamas was less likely to have carried out a targeted assassination on US or Italian soil than the other fiercely anti-Israeli terrorist group, Hezbollah.

"I would say Hezbollah's the favorite," Jayne said. "More of a track record for this kind of thing. They would be against the pope building a relationship with Israel. And they wouldn't worry about disposing of a Catholic cardinal, even if he came from the West Bank."

"Yes, all that is true," Zahavi said.

Jayne wanted to accept their rationale and explanation. But she knew she needed some kind of verification from elsewhere. The only lead she currently had was in Ramallah.

"I want to go see Baltrami's family," Jayne said. "His brother and sister live in Ramallah, and he was apparently very close with them. They might know more."

Gray had given Jayne contact details for both of Baltrami's siblings, who had lived very near to their brother, and she had briefly considered giving them an advance call to arrange a meeting but had then thought better of it. It was quite possible that their phones might be tapped by whoever had killed their brother, or by the Palestinian authorities, or both. Better, perhaps, just to turn up on the doorstep unannounced and hope for the best.

Rafael sat up straight on the sofa. "I'll come with you. I know Ramallah. We need to get to the bottom of this."

Jayne looked at him. Was he trying too hard to prove her wrong over the DNA sample? Or was this just a *katsa* who had suddenly seen the possibility of landing a blow on one of Israel's main enemies?

Maybe a bit of both.

"You need to be careful in Ramallah. You'll need help," Rafael continued, clearly trying to clinch the deal. "If someone has taken out Baltrami, they're likely to keep an eye open for visitors who are investigating, especially from intelligence services."

Jayne inclined her head. He was probably correct about that. "All right," she said. "We'll go tomorrow morning."

CHAPTER TWELVE

Thursday, June 30, 2016
Vatican City

The Swiss Guard in his full red, dark blue, and yellow uniform remained as rigidly upright and motionless as a flagpole as Gray walked past him. He opened the dark wooden door, entered the papal apartments, and, after closing the door behind him paused for a second.

He wasn't looking forward to this. The pope had asked for an update, and Gray had little to tell him about progress, although plenty in terms of what was becoming a rapidly deepening mystery. He had received a message half an hour earlier from Jayne, telling him she and a friend from the Mossad planned to visit Baltrami's brother and sister in Ramallah the next day, and Gray had found himself in two minds about whether to tell the Holy Father about that.

The Vatican had been empty of tourists over the past couple of days. Following discussions with the Italian state police, the Swiss Guard, and the Vatican police, it had been decided to close all of Vatican City to visitors until the weekend while investigations and interviews continued.

A line of TV news trucks stood in the piazza just to the east of St. Peter's Square, and reporters were carrying out a seemingly endless series of live broadcasts with the basilica as the backdrop. However, despite ongoing speculation about why cardinals were apparently being systematically targeted, the journalists had so far reported nothing of substance, largely because the state police on whom they relied for information had nothing to go on themselves.

Gray continued along the red-carpeted corridor, the long wall of the pope's private chapel to his left. He turned the corner and passed the chapel entrance and another guard in the corridor, then paused outside the door of the study on the right.

He crossed himself, said a brief prayer asking the Holy Spirit for guidance, and knocked.

Several seconds later, the door opened, and there stood Pope Julius VI.

"Come in, Eminence," the pope said. Gray immediately noticed the pale purple bags that had developed beneath the pope's eyes and his face seemed gray rather than its usual pink.

The pope closed the door carefully, paced methodically back to his seat behind his desk, and indicated to Gray to take one of the three seats in front of it. The wooden chair creaked loudly as he sat, the sound amplified by the silence.

"So, Eminence, have you made any progress?" the pope began, folding his hands on the desk in front of him. "I am hearing from Cardinal Saraceni that there has been little headway in Washington, and our police chief here, Mr. Porpora, is also failing to discover much of value."

"I have set the wheels in motion, Holiness," Gray said.

"There has so far been no more progress than that. However, I have not had a chance to tell you this yet, but I have employed the services of someone who is well equipped to deal with this situation—the daughter of an old friend of mine."

He lowered his voice and told the pope about Jayne Robinson and the story of her father, and about her background in MI6 and as a freelance investigator.

"I may need to make a confession to you, Holiness," Gray continued. "I am unsure whether I have sinned or not, but there is something that I have not yet told anyone."

The pope shifted in his seat and fixed his gaze on Gray, his lips pressed together. "Go on," he said. "I'm listening."

Gray hesitated. "Cardinal Baltrami was on his way to meet Jayne and me when he was shot. He had something he urgently wanted to tell me."

The pope sat back in his chair and clasped a hand to each of his cheeks.

"I knew he was coming to meet you," the pope said. "He phoned me here in my office about something else concerning the wider church in the West Bank, a scheduled call, and he told me as part of the conversation. He said he needed to communicate something to you about the deaths of our four brothers in Washington. I asked him what it was, but he said it was too sensitive to discuss over the phone and that he would tell you, and you would tell me. He sounded quite worried about it."

Gray felt more than a little surprised and sat in silence for a couple of seconds. "Really?" he asked eventually. "He never told me he had informed you."

The pope shook his head. "They are shooting the servants of God," he said. "Shooting the messengers of Heaven. First in Washington, now here. But why?"

"I don't know," Gray said. "But it was certainly important

to someone to prevent him from telling me whatever it was he wanted to say."

He ran through the sequence of events outside the safe house.

"My logic, my mind, with its church training to follow rules and laws, tells me I should inform the state police about the ill-fated meeting with Baltrami," Gray said. "But my instinct says no. It tells me to let Jayne continue her work."

The pope looked uneasy about the suggestion, as Gray had guessed he probably would. "Hmm. I don't know. What does Ms. Robinson say, Eminence?"

"Jayne thinks if we get ourselves involved in a police investigation, we will be detained for many days of questioning," Gray said. "She believes we will get so bogged down and delayed that we'll make no progress. She is not in favor of that, Holiness, although she's aware it's what we should technically do. Also, she thinks they won't like us trying to do any kind of investigation ourselves and will do everything they can to obstruct it. You know what it's like here—this is Rome. The police have egos, and they like to protect their own interests."

"Some of them like to protect and enhance their bank balances too," the pope said. He crossed himself, clasped his hands in front of him, closed his eyes, and murmured to himself in his native Italian. Gray watched as he prayed for guidance.

After a short while, he opened them again. "If your instinct tells you to put your trust in Ms. Robinson, that is the spirit guiding you. Go with that, Eminence."

Gray nodded.

"But don't tell the state police I said that," the pope added. He tilted his face to one side and eyed Gray carefully. "I don't want to advise you down a course of deception—of course I don't. But this is a difficult situation. You know what I mean?"

"I do," Gray said.

"What is Ms. Robinson planning next?"

"She's going to Ramallah to visit Baltrami's brother and sister, Sami and Laila. She wants to know if they have any insight into what he was going to tell us, anything that might help."

The pope sucked in air from between tightly clenched teeth. "Ramallah is not always the safest place to be. I've been to the West Bank myself—I know what it's like."

"It's the best hope we have right now. Cardinal Baltrami clearly knew something important." Gray paused. "And Jayne has friends in Tel Aviv and Jerusalem. One of them will go with her."

"Friends? What kind of friends?"

Gray hesitated. "I believe intelligence service friends."

"I see. I assume I don't need to ask which intelligence service."

Gray said nothing.

"When is she going?" the pope asked.

"Tomorrow morning."

The pope creased his brow. He clearly wasn't comfortable with this.

"She knows how to handle herself in difficult situations, Holiness," Gray said. "That's why I asked her to get involved. She's good. Earlier this year she tracked down the terrorist who killed her father in 1994 in a bombing at the Israeli embassy in London. She doesn't give up. But if I could just make a request with Jayne's safety in mind, Holiness, I'd ask that you don't disclose her plans to anyone else."

"I have no intention of discussing it with anyone," the pope said. "Let's hope she can find out whoever is responsible here." His blue eyes flicked over Gray's face. "I have to say, Eminence, I'm well out of my depth with all this."

The pope stood, ambled to the window, and stared out for a few seconds before turning. "All I can say for now is this: continue with what you're doing and ask Ms. Robinson to do likewise. I just hope she will be careful."

PART TWO

CHAPTER THIRTEEN

Friday, July 1, 2016
Nablus, West Bank

The white Toyota Camry sedan had left the West Bank city of Nablus behind and had just turned onto Highway 60 toward Ramallah, about an hour and forty minutes to the south, when one of the two phones mounted on the dashboard rang.

The driver, Ghassan Nafi, leader of Hezbollah's Unit 133, glanced at the device. It wasn't his new iPhone, but rather a cheap throwaway burner that he used to communicate with his sources, usually for a maximum of three weeks before switching to another.

The caller was a highly valuable source whom he had code-named CIRRUS, largely because, like a cloud, he was hard to pin down.

Nafi jabbed at the green button with his thick, stubby index finger, then switched the device onto speaker and pulled onto the side of the highway so he could concentrate on the conversation.

"What's happening?" he asked without preamble or pleasantries as he switched off the car engine.

"I have an update for you," came the refined tones of CIRRUS in fluent though heavily accented English. "There is a new independent investigator working on the case. Not police—this one is a British woman. An intelligence operative."

"*British?* Do you know her name?" Nafi asked, a little abruptly. He needed to keep this call as short as possible. The Israelis were notorious for tracking and tracing cell phones, even anonymous burners.

"Jayne Robinson."

"Background?"

"Formerly of MI6 in London," CIRRUS said. "She has a reputation for being difficult to deal with."

Nafi paused, his mind now buzzing with adrenaline. "What's your source?"

"I can't tell you that."

"Do you know where this Robinson woman is?"

"That's why I am calling. She is apparently going to Ramallah today to see Baltrami's brother and sister. Their names are Sami and Laila. She may be accompanied by a friend who is also an operative, someone from Tel Aviv."

"*Ya ibn el sharmouta,*" Nafi muttered. "You sonofabitch. Sorry, but this is not good news."

There was silence at the other end of the line for a few seconds.

"I'm sure it's not good news," CIRRUS said. "But I'm just doing what you asked me to do."

He certainly had, Nafi thought. "Thank you. It's useful information. Just not welcome. Do you think Baltrami confided in his brother and sister? Are they close?"

"I believe so."

Nafi let out another Arabic curse and stared out the car windshield. "Do you have any idea what time this Robinson is going to Ramallah? What car she might be driving, if any? The name of her Mossad friend?"

"No."

Nafi calculated. He could get to Ramallah inside an hour and a half if he pushed it. There was an AK-47 assault rifle and a Heckler & Koch pistol with plenty of ammunition hidden in a specially designed long compartment behind the rear seat of the Toyota, together with a box of grenades.

"Thanks for the information," Nafi said. "I need to go. We've been on the phone long enough. I will be in contact."

He ended the call and sat thinking for a few moments. As leader of Unit 133, Hezbollah's special operations group responsible for orchestrating attacks inside Israel and the Israeli-occupied portion of the West Bank, Nafi was also tasked with trafficking drugs and weapons of all types. Most of the trafficking was carried out along the so-called Blue Line that separated Lebanon from Israel, where Unit 133 worked closely with a handful of crime families who had good connections on both sides of the border.

He knew he needed to move fast, but he decided first to send a quick, secure message to his boss, Talal Hassan, who headed Hezbollah's much larger elite Unit 910 foreign operations organization, also known as the External Security Organization.

The Beirut-based Unit 910 included Hezbollah's ruthless and highly lethal international special forces team and also its business affairs unit. The latter was responsible for fundraising through drug trafficking and other ventures and for laundering cash generated through those businesses.

Nafi and Hassan had built a close friendship over the years. They shared a vision of how they and Hezbollah could work against Iran's enemies, both in the Middle East and much farther afield, and how that vision could be funded. Financial wizardry was a key component of their plans—without money they could achieve nothing.

Nafi tapped out a message summarizing what he had learned from CIRRUS, of whom Hassan was well aware.

Had call from CIRRUS. Ex-MI6 operative Jayne Robinson investigating Rome/DC with Mossad. Visiting Baltrami sister/brother today in Ramallah. Am driving there now. Will terminate if possible, report back after. Pls advise any info on Robinson.

It was possible, given the breadth of Hassan's international expertise, particularly across Western Europe, that he had come across Jayne Robinson previously, and he might have some useful knowledge he could pass on.

Nafi would have preferred a phone conversation with Hassan, but he felt wary about making more calls while in this area. He knew the Israelis were particularly stringent in monitoring any communications in this part of the West Bank, especially along the Highway 60 corridor. Even though he had an encryption app on his phone, it would be better to wait and speak to Hassan after he had completed his hit on Robinson, when hopefully he would have good news to deliver.

Nafi turned the ignition key and gunned the engine. Within seconds he was back on Highway 60, this time traveling at a faster speed than before. There was no time to lose.

He considered picking up another Unit 133 colleague, his third in command, Abu Alami, to help him, given that he lived in Ramallah. But there was no time for that now, he decided. In any case, he'd had a furious row with Alami the previous day because he seemed lethargic and uncommitted, so the idea of involving him in an operation right now didn't seem a good one.

Nafi just hoped he could locate the British woman in

Ramallah. A few en route calls to contacts in his broad network, probably to those in the police or the Palestinian Authority, would enable him to find out precisely where the sister and brother of Cardinal Baltrami lived and whether they were alone or had family living with them.

Indeed, one of the reasons Nafi had been appointed as leader of Unit 133 two years earlier, at the age of forty-two, was because of his skill in forming good contacts among the Arab-Israeli and Palestinian communities.

In particular, he had proved adept at recruiting those who were not from Hezbollah's usual Shia Muslim background, including Sunni Muslims and Arab Christians, and were therefore not obvious allies of Hezbollah. That was important because it made it more difficult for the Israelis to identify and deal with operatives who were working for Unit 133 on Hezbollah's and Iran's behalf.

These abilities allowed Nafi to build an exceptional track record in setting up cells with the capability to strike hard and often against the main enemy, Israel.

If this operative Robinson was meeting Baltrami's relatives, it was clear to Nafi that the easiest course of action would be to take down all of them in one strike.

That would remove not just the investigator but also the others who might potentially be damaging to Hezbollah—and especially to Operation Prada, in which Nafi had been heavily involved.

CHAPTER FOURTEEN

Friday, July 1, 2016
    West Bank

The eight-meter solid gray concrete wall, topped with double layers of coiled barbed wire and sprayed with graffiti in many places, towered up to the right of the Ford Focus as Jayne and Rafael headed north from East Jerusalem up Highway 60.

It gave Jayne flashbacks to the Berlin Wall during her visits in the 1980s. Indeed, the Israeli West Bank barrier, built by Israel in phases from 2001 onward, and now comprising over seven hundred kilometers of wire fencing and solid concrete, was like the structure that used to divide East Germany from West Germany. Here, though, it separated Israel from the Palestinian West Bank.

Next to Jayne in the passenger's seat, Rafael craned his neck to peer up at the top of the wall. "Ugly monster, isn't it?"

"Awful," Jayne said. "Looks like a prison camp."

In many places, streetlights were mounted on top of the

walls and reminded Jayne of the searchlights she had seen in photographs of World War II concentration camps.

"Does its job, though," Rafael said. "Keeps most of the terrorists out."

"Maybe." Jayne said. "Or perhaps it incentivizes them. Certainly makes everyone miserable. You sound like you approve of it."

"I didn't say that," Rafael replied, his voice taking on a defensive tone.

Jayne had other things to focus her mind on right now, but she knew that the separation wall continued to be hugely controversial. It had, in effect, formed a new border some considerable distance east of the so-called Green Line established by international agreement as the division between Israel and the West Bank in 1949. Israel had then seized additional territory east of the line during the Six Day War in 1967. The Palestinians hated the wall, which made it very difficult for many of them to move around the area.

Eventually they came within sight of the checkpoint between west and east at the Qalandia refugee camp, near to a military airstrip.

Rafael directed Jayne to a side street, about half a kilometer from the crossing, where she parked. The plan was to go through the crossing on foot and to meet one of the Mossad's Palestinian agents on the other side who would act as their driver and also supply the weapons they had requested. Rafael didn't want to take an Israeli vehicle into Palestinian-controlled territories, explaining it would be too obvious, and in any case, car rental companies didn't allow it.

After walking to the barrier, Jayne showed her recently acquired false British passport in the name of Ashima Caire, supposedly a self-employed personal financial adviser, born in Mumbai, India, of British parents. The Caire identity, developed with the help of Vic's team at Langley, had been fully

backstopped, like her other two legends. It included a fully
working UK bank account, credit cards linked to an address
in London, and a British driver's license.

Rafael used his false British passport, in the name of
Martin Levitt, that he often deployed when traveling. Israelis
were barred from entering parts of the West Bank, including
Ramallah. They explained they were a couple on holiday from
London.

Both passed through the metal detectors, were waved
through the barrier, and walked past the Qalandia refugee
camp, set up in 1948 for Palestinians who were fleeing the
new Israel. They were now in the West Bank.

A short distance farther on, Rafael turned right and
headed toward a yellow taxi parked beneath a tree. "Here's
our man," he said.

The driver of the fake taxi, which was actually owned by
the Mossad, was Abdullah, a broad-faced Palestinian. He
greeted Rafael like an old friend, put him in the front
passenger seat, and chatted nonstop in fluent English for the
remaining seven kilometers of their journey into Ramallah.

Jayne looked out the window as they drove past a mixture
of new flat-roofed concrete apartment buildings, Arab shops,
and construction sites busy with cranes and bulldozers.

"Look at this idiot," Abdullah said, cursing heavily as a
badly driven, battered van pulled out sharply right in front of
the cab. Two minutes later an overloaded yellow minibus
service taxi, crammed with passengers, did exactly the same
thing.

A quick piece of research by the team at Mossad's headquarters had told them that Baltrami's sister and brother,
Laila and Sami, lived in adjoining houses on a street very near
the church where their late brother, Kamal, had his ministry,
the Holy Trinity Church, only a kilometer from the center of
Ramallah. As Gray had said, the family seemed tight-knit.

Once in Ramallah, they drove along Rukab Street, lined with shops and apartments, and found a stone archway that formed the entrance to the church, a convent, and an adjoining school next to a dry cleaner's shop. Abdullah headed through the arch to a large, secluded parking lot outside the church and opposite a stone rectory, where she presumed Baltrami had lived.

"I'm going to park here," Abdullah said. "You can walk. I'll wait here, out of sight of the street."

Abdullah then reached beneath his seat, opened a hidden compartment, and pulled out a leather pouch. From it he removed a Walther PPS and spare magazine, which he handed to Jayne, and two Beretta 71 pistols, one of which he gave to Rafael, together with an extra loaded magazine.

"In line with your request," Abdullah said with a smile. "Keep me updated and let me know if you need help."

Jayne assumed the other Beretta was for Abdullah's own use. She thanked him, pushed the Walther into her belt, and let her linen jacket drop loosely over it. She put the spare magazine into her jacket pocket and climbed out of the fake taxi.

She and Rafael left Abdullah in his car and walked across the parking lot toward the beautiful old stone church. Above the door was a colorful fresco that dated back more than a hundred years, according to a brief history on a noticeboard.

Jayne checked—there was nobody observing them.

"I want to take a quick look inside," she said.

Rafael nodded as she opened the door of the church and stepped over the threshold. He followed behind her.

The cavernous white stone interior was spotlessly clean, with rows of new wooden pews, large chandeliers, and a huge colorful fresco of Jesus in an arch-shaped alcove at the far end, behind the altar. Three elderly women, one of them a nun wearing a pale gray habit, were sitting separately in the pews, their heads bowed.

On a table near the door were bunches of flowers and cards of condolence from worshippers. They were all obviously there because of Baltrami. Jayne bent down to read them, a wave of sadness passing through her as she did so. Many carried handwritten messages of shock and sadness; word had spread quickly about their archbishop's death in Rome.

Eventually Jayne stood.

"Right, we'd better go find his family," she said. Baltrami had obviously been killed for a reason. Although the street outside the church appeared calm and they had faced no threats from local people, it was impossible to know whether his family might also be under threat or surveillance.

They exited the church and crossed the street, and before going farther, Jayne pulled out one of her favorite props: a pack of Camel cigarettes and a lighter. Although a virtual nonsmoker, she did use cigarettes on occasions when she wanted a pretext to pause in the street, check around her, and be certain there was no trailing coverage. Rafael also lit up, and between them, they casually surveyed the street in both directions.

There was nothing and nobody that merited any obvious concern, so they continued west down Rukab Street, then turned left past a rustic fruit and vegetable store onto St. Andrew Street, and walked down a hill.

The street was dusty and the pavement was potholed, with weeds growing from some of the many cracks in the sidewalk. A stone wall down one side of the street had been whitewashed many years ago but was now faded and peeling and covered in graffiti.

On the left, beyond a white-painted apartment building, stood two plain old semidetached cottages made of gray stone with red-tiled roofs and shutters over the windows. According to the directions from the Mossad, these were the houses occupied by Sami and Laila Baltrami.

There appeared to be only one street number for the two properties: a faded, peeling "2" painted on a white plaque next to the gate. Perhaps they had at one time been a single large house, Jayne surmised.

The houses were separated from the street by a two-meter gray steel fence with spikes on top and a matching pedestrian gate in the center. A scratched and dented white Honda Civic sedan was parked on the side of the street next to the gate.

Rafael glanced at her. "Shall we go in?"

She nodded, took a final look up and down the street, then grasped the gate handle and pulled it open.

They walked through to find a rough gravel path, strewn with weeds, that led beneath a dilapidated wooden pergola to the houses.

It was impossible to know who lived in which property, so Jayne pointed to the first house and got a confirmatory nod from Rafael. There was no bell, so she knocked firmly on the weather-beaten solid wood door, stained black in places and with more than a few chips and scratches near the bottom.

A few moments later the door squeaked open and there stood a thin, olive-skinned woman who looked about seventy, with shoulder-length gray hair, a bony nose, and dark eyes hooded by somewhat wrinkly crow's-feet beneath wire-rimmed glasses. She wore a neatly ironed white blouse and a long black skirt.

"Hello?" she said in Arabic with a questioning expression on her face.

"Are you Laila?" Jayne asked, also in Arabic.

The woman nodded. "Yes. Can I help you?"

Jayne held out her hand and shook Laila's. She decided to

use her proper identity. "I'm Jayne Robinson, and this is my colleague Martin Levitt. We're investigating the death of your brother, Kamal, which I am sure has been an awful time for you. I would like to offer my condolences. I am so sorry."

Laila's face crumpled, and Jayne thought for a second she was going to burst into tears, but then she gathered herself.

"Thank you," Laila said. She wiped a hand across her eyes and glanced first at Jayne, then at Rafael. There was a suspicious look in her eyes. "Yes, it's been awful, terrible. Can I ask who sent you here and why you're investigating?"

"We were sent here by Cardinal Michael Gray, an adviser to Pope Julius. He suggested we speak to you and Sami."

Laila scrutinized Jayne and Rafael from beneath lowered eyebrows. "Where are you from? You have identification?"

Jayne took out her British passport and held it open and Rafael did likewise. "We're both intelligence officers from the UK. We believe Kamal's death was linked to the murders of other cardinals in the United States and may therefore be part of something significant. Kamal was on his way to meet Cardinal Gray and me in Rome when he was shot. Cardinal Gray is an old friend of my father's from London."

Laila nodded. "I know he planned to meet Michael," she said, switching to English, which she spoke quite fluently but with a heavy accent. She glanced out toward the street, looked in both directions, and then held the door open. "Come in. I will fetch Sami."

Jayne and Rafael glanced at each other. Laila was obviously familiar with Gray, judging by her use of his first name.

The interior was dark and simply furnished. She led them to a living room at the rear of the house and seated them on a dark brown canvas sofa that had seen better days, then disappeared through a back door.

A few minutes later she reappeared with a man who was

just as thin as her, but who Jayne could see was a few years older. His skin had a yellowish tinge, and he didn't look well.

"This is Sami," she said, and went on to introduce her two visitors to him.

"I have coffee that I made only a few minutes ago," Laila said. "I'll fetch it." She disappeared through the door.

Sami shook their hands, exchanged pleasantries in English that was more heavily accented than his sister's, then walked with a slight limp to an armchair and sat down.

"So, you are investigating our brother's death?" Sami said.

Jayne repeated what she had told Laila. "I'm sorry for both of you," she said. "It must be terrible. I can see you're all close."

Sami nodded. "We only have each other. Laila and I both lost our spouses several years ago, and our children moved to New Zealand and Canada to find work."

Laila walked back into the room with a coffeepot and cups on a tray. She poured coffee for all of them and handed the cups around, then sat on a dining chair to Sami's right.

Sami sipped his coffee. "What have you discovered and what do you need to know?" he asked.

"We have discovered very little so far," Jayne said. "Kamal was going to tell us something important he had learned about the deaths of his four colleagues in Washington that was too sensitive to talk about on the phone."

She leaned forward and clasped her knees together. "Did Kamal confide in you at all about what he knew and what he was going to tell Michael?"

Sami shook his head slowly. "The only thing he told us was that he was flying to Rome to meet Michael. He was very upset about the shootings in the US and said he had heard things that were extremely worrying during a confession that had been made to him. He did a lot of confessions, and he was happy to do so for his fellow cardinals. The point is, he said nothing to us about confessions made to him, rightly, but this time he did. It was the first time he had ever done that. He said he faced a big dilemma."

A lightbulb went off inside Jayne's head. "A dilemma because confessions are confidential, right?"

"Completely. You've heard of the sacramental seal? A Catholic priest who hears confessions is bound to keep them utterly secret. If he broke that rule, well, he'd be excommunicated, for sure. Career over."

Jayne nodded. She knew about that. "But you think Kamal might have heard something in this confession that he felt he had no option but to disclose."

"I don't just think so, I know so, but I'm really not sure I can go into a lot of detail." Sami glanced at his sister and fingered his chin uncertainly as he spoke.

Jayne could see he was having some sort of internal debate about how much he should say. This was going to be tricky.

"Can I ask something?" Jayne began. "Did he indicate whether the things he heard could potentially mean someone's life was at risk?"

"That was the problem," Laila said. "He said he had heard that there was a plot being put together."

"A plot?"

Laila stared up at the ceiling momentarily. "He was horrified by it, actually."

"Why?" Jayne asked. "Who was the target of this plot?"

Laila exhaled. She was clearly finding it difficult to speak of what she had heard.

"It was a plot to kill more cardinals, if necessary," Laila said. She leaned back on her chair and folded her arms. "That's it. I've told you now."

Jayne felt a bolt of adrenaline kick through her. She looked at Rafael, who was leaning forward a little, visibly intrigued.

"You mean more cardinals besides those killed in Washington?" Rafael asked.

Laila nodded.

"Was this planned killing likely to be imminent?" Jayne asked.

"My brother thought possibly so, yes," Laila said.

"And did he indicate which cardinals might be at risk, apart from himself?" Rafael asked.

Laila shook her head. "He didn't say, and I didn't like to ask for that much detail. I assumed that my brother was going to deal with what he had learned his own way."

"And what did he mean by 'if necessary'?" Jayne asked.

Laila shrugged. "I really don't know. He was quite vague about it, and I really didn't want to keep asking questions."

Jayne hesitated. "Listen, both of you, you are doing the right thing by talking to us about this. It seems this threat to other cardinals may still exist if your brother has been killed to stop him from talking about it."

Sami gave a short nod. "I believe that may be correct. It is very worrying. I have been sleeping very badly just thinking about it."

"You both attend your brother's church, I assume?"

"We do," Sami said. He caught Jayne's eye. "Do you believe?" he asked.

Jayne paused. Over the years her faith had oscillated like a metronome. "That's a good question," she said. "In God I trust, but it's the church I usually struggle with—too many humans involved. So I mostly tend to plow my own furrow, I guess."

Sami pressed his lips together. "I know what you mean."

"Can I ask, and I know this is difficult," Jayne went on. "But do you know who the person is who made this confession to Kamal?"

Sami looked at Laila, who shrugged. "Can we say?" she asked him.

"I don't know. The confession wasn't made to us."

Laila stood, paced across the room, and stared out the window. "Sami, I think we have to say who the person is. Lives are at stake. More cardinals could be killed. Imagine other families going through what we've been through. We're not priests, so we're not bound by the sacramental seal. I think we should say."

She turned and faced her brother, hands on her hips. "I'm going to tell them."

Sami nodded. "All right. Tell them."

Laila returned to her seat and faced Jayne. "The person who he took confession from works for a terrorist organization. He is a high-ranking commander in Hezbollah's Unit 133, which you may or may not have heard of, but they organize attacks against Israeli targets, mainly."

Jayne was stunned. "So he works for Hezbollah, but he comes to a Catholic church for confession? That doesn't sound right."

Why would a Catholic work for a Shiite Muslim organization? she wondered.

"I know," Laila said. "But it's because Hezbollah has been recruiting all over the West Bank, including a lot of non-Shiites. They have Sunnis and a few Arab Christians working for them now."

"Well, how do they do that?"

"Money. They pay their recruits well."

Jayne leaned back on the sofa, her mind buzzing, and glanced at Rafael, who nodded his affirmation.

"It's true," Rafael said. "There are a lot of jobless people around here. The economy is terrible. People are prepared to take the money."

"Bloody hell," Jayne muttered. She turned back to Laila.

"So how did this guy hear about the potential attack on the cardinals?"

"Because he was in the Unit 133 office here in Ramallah and overheard his boss, the head of the unit, discussing it on a video call with another Hezbollah leader."

"And he confessed this?" Jayne asked.

"Yes," Laila nodded. "He found the idea of an attack on cardinals too much. He's a Catholic, remember. It was one step too far."

Jayne wasn't going to say so, but clearly Kamal Baltrami, by confiding in such detail to his siblings, had already gone well beyond the bounds of the sacramental seal even before he stepped on the plane for his fateful journey to Rome. But it was just as well he had done so, given the invaluable information now being handed over.

"What are the names of these Hezbollah leaders?" Rafael asked.

"The one who made the confession is Abu Alami and his boss, the head of Unit 133, is Ghassan Nafi," Sami said. "I've met Alami at the church, although we've only spoken a few times. To be honest, anyone who works for Hezbollah is not the sort of person I would want to get close to or have time for. I don't know Nafi, although I've heard a lot about him."

Jayne committed the names to memory and made a mental note to ask Rafael later if the Mossad had the two men on their radar, although she was certain he would check anyway.

"Had your brother discussed this with any of his other fellow cardinals?" Jayne asked. "For example, any of the others from this region? There's one in Beirut, isn't there? Cardinal Martelli. Do they talk?" Jayne had been told by Gray that Baltrami and Martelli weren't particularly close, but she thought she would check.

Sami shook his head. "They're not close, despite coming from the same region."

"Did your brother mention who Nafi was talking to on the call that Alami overheard?" Jayne asked.

Sami shook his head.

"How can we find out?" Jayne asked. It seemed like a critical piece of the jigsaw puzzle to her. If a major plot was being hatched against more cardinals, it was essential to know who the ringleaders were.

Sami shrugged. "We would have to ask Alami."

"Is that possible?"

"It's possible. He lives only two kilometers from here. I know his house. I dropped off a letter once for the church. But whether he would talk, I don't know. He might be extremely angry that his confidential confession has been betrayed."

"He might be angry," Jayne said. "But my gut feeling is that if he was motivated to make a confession like that, he's got a conscience. And not only has the person he made the confession to been killed, but more murders are being planned. So he might talk. Can you take us to his house?"

Sami looked at his sister.

"I guess we could do that," Laila said.

"Now?" Jayne asked. She was intensely aware that time was critical. If there was a plot, it was impossible to know when it might be executed, but clearly it could be imminent.

Laila nodded. "We'll take my car."

CHAPTER FIFTEEN

Friday, July 1, 2016
Ramallah

Jayne noticed that Rafael, who sat alongside her in the back seat of Laila's battered white Honda, grimaced as they drove past the Mukataa, the heavily guarded walled complex that housed the Palestine Liberation Organization and the Palestinian Authority, a short distance north of Ramallah's city center.

A black pickup truck was emerging from a side gate with a group of Palestinian National Security Forces soldiers sitting in the back, clad in red berets and camouflage battle fatigues.

"What's up?" she asked.

He shook his head. "Nothing," he murmured, so Laila and Sami, in the front seats, couldn't hear. "The PLO just reminds me of Black September, that's all. The Munich disaster. It was Fatah who controlled them, of course."

Jayne nodded but didn't reply. Rafael had spoken to her

a few times of the impact that the massacre of eleven Israeli athletes at the Munich Olympics in 1972 had had on him. The attack had been carried out by Black September, a terrorist group coordinated by Fatah, now the largest faction within the PLO. He had said that although he was only two years old when it happened, the incident later inspired him to become an Olympic track athlete himself. He ran in the 5,000 meters at the Barcelona Olympics in 1992 and in Atlanta in 1996. It also persuaded him to join the Mossad.

Laila drove past the security watchtowers, heavy steel gates, and guards of the Mukataa, which also housed the mausoleum of the PLO's former leader Yasser Arafat, who died in 2004. Indeed, the entire complex was known as Arafat's compound when he ruled the roost there, but was rebuilt after the Israeli military destroyed it in 2002.

Laila then turned right onto a residential street, cut another right past a car repair garage, and braked sharply to a halt outside a flat-roofed single-story house with green shutters.

"This is it," she said. "I think it would be too much for all four of us to go. I suggest that just Sami and Jayne go to the house. I can wait here with Rafael."

Laila went up in Jayne's estimation. She had been about to say exactly the same thing.

"Agreed. We will need to be quick, too," Jayne said. "This guy won't want a bunch of foreigners hanging out at his house if he's Hezbollah."

She glanced up and down the street, but the only traffic was a car pulling out of the repair garage.

"That makes sense," Sami said. He got out of the car, as did Jayne. They had agreed he would start the conversation, then hand it over to Jayne.

The house, made of sandstone blocks, sat behind a green

wrought-iron fence atop a stone wall. The gate was half open and an old BMW sedan stood in the driveway.

Sami led the way through the gate and up a gravel path to a door at the side of the property, which he knocked on firmly.

It was opened by a man wearing a black T-shirt. He had a long, thin scar down his left cheek and oily dark hair and appeared to be in his forties. There was a moment's silence as he seemingly struggled to place his visitor.

"Ah, Sami," he said eventually in Arabic, squinting a little through impenetrable black eyes. "A while since I have seen you. How are you?" He shook hands with Sami.

"Hello, Abu, I'm doing well, thanks. I'm not on church business this time, but I was just passing through here with a visitor, a friend of a friend from the United Kingdom. Jayne is her name. She's here for a short while, and we were hoping you could help us."

Abu Alami raised his eyebrows a fraction, took a step forward, looked Jayne in the eye, and switched to English. "From the UK? We don't have many British visitors here."

Jayne extended her hand, knowing Arab custom dictated the woman needed to initiate a handshake.

Abu took it with a softer grip than she expected and shook. "Come in. Would you like tea?"

"We'll come in, but we don't have time for tea, unfortunately," Sami said. "It's a very quick visit."

They followed Alami into a tiled hallway with an arched entrance at the far end. A wicker chair stood to the left, next to a dark wood table.

"So, what is this about?" Alami asked, standing with his legs apart and his arms folded.

"You heard about my brother, Kamal? His death in Rome?" Sami asked.

Alami nodded. "That was very sad. A great loss for the

church. In fact, a great loss for all Palestinians. He was a church leader we all looked up to. My condolences to you and your family."

"Yes, very sad. You used to go to confession with him, I believe?"

Alami said nothing for a second or two, but his eyes narrowed and he stared at Sami. "I did. Why do you ask?"

Sami looked at Jayne and gestured with his hand, indicating that she should take up the questioning. She felt grateful that Sami had engineered the conversation quite expertly so far.

"I would like to ask you something," Jayne said. "I believe that lives are at risk. Indeed, some lives have been lost already, but I am anxious to avoid losing more. Do you understand?"

Alami looked first at her, then at Sami, his face impassive. "Go on."

"We understand you might be able to help me—I'm carrying out an investigation into the death not just of Cardinal Baltrami but of others as well."

Alami's eyes were now reduced to slits.

"Do you mean the cardinals in Washington?" he asked in a low tone.

"I do," Jayne said.

"And who, exactly, are you?" His voice remained dead level.

She decided to be honest. "I work for the intelligence services. We believe there is some kind of international conspiracy against these cardinals, possibly with its origins in this part of the world, and we need to find out what."

"I thought so. Are you MI6 or CIA?"

"The United States is very concerned about what has happened," Jayne said. "And so are other cardinals in Rome and elsewhere."

"And how did you know to ask me? I told only one person —and that was in my confession. Obviously my confession has been betrayed." He turned and faced Sami. "You can imagine how that feels."

"My brother did something that he felt he had no choice over," Sami said. "He heard your confession and intended to keep it sacrosanct, but he felt he had to speak up because four of his fellow cardinals had died, and he thought more were going to follow. But instead, he himself was murdered in Rome—before he could tell the right person what he had heard."

"But he obviously did tell what he had heard. He told *you*."

"He told me a little," Sami said. "Not much, though. And that's why I am here. My brother is dead, and Jayne is trying to find out more so she can prevent more killings."

Jayne was starting to feel concerned that the conversation might not head in the direction she wanted it to. She took a small step forward, ignoring Alami's body language.

"Mr. Alami," she said. "I know you work for Hezbollah, but that is irrelevant here. I don't need to know about that— it stays confidential. Your name and identity will not leave this room. We do not need a lot of information, but we do need a few important details."

Jayne had half expected some kind of denial from Alami about his Hezbollah links, but there was none.

Instead, he removed a pack of cigarettes from his pocket, expertly eased one out with a fingertip, and placed it between his lips. He then searched for his lighter in another pocket, lit the cigarette, and took a deep drag.

"No. I'm not going to help you," he said, finally. "There's too much risk. They'll kill me. Now get out of my house."

He walked to the door, opened it, and indicated vigorously with his hand that they should leave.

Jayne remained rooted to the spot.

"Go on, go," Alami said, raising his voice and eyeballing first Jayne, then Sami. "Get out now."

* * *

Friday, July 1, 2016
Ramallah

Ghassan Nafi parked his Toyota around the corner from Laila and Sami Baltrami's houses, in a spot next to several other cars near a small fruit and vegetable store on Rukab Street. The street was busy, and he knew that neither he nor his car would attract any attention.

He had been given the address, as he had hoped, by one of his Unit 133 recruits within the Palestinian Authority who was a senior manager in the taxation department. The brother and sister lived alone in adjacent houses, he was told.

Nafi extracted his Heckler & Koch P7 pistol from behind his rear car seat, stuffed it into an inside jacket pocket that was designed for the purpose, and slipped a spare magazine into his pants pocket.

He took out his phone, logged onto his secure encrypted messaging service, and sent a brief message to his boss, Talal Hassan.

In Ramallah. Will report back when done.

Then he got out of the car.

He walked casually past the twin properties on St. Andrew Street. There were no cars parked outside and no signs of life. He decided to take a closer look and slid through a gray steel metal gate that was unlocked.

Nafi edged his way around the side of an old pergola, using a couple of large, unkempt bushes as cover, then moved down a path that ran along the right side of the building to the rear, where there was a small patio with a table and chairs.

There he took out his pistol, racked the slide, and flicked off the safety.

He could see rear doors to both houses, and a ground-floor window of the house nearest to him was ajar. That told him someone was probably at home because people in this area were normally scrupulous about locking their properties when out.

He edged closer to the window and glanced inside. It was a living room with a sofa, armchairs, and a couple of dining chairs. There were four coffee cups, two of them half full, on a table, together with a coffeepot.

But there was no sign of any occupants.

Nafi had been told that both Laila and Sami lived alone. So four coffee cups, two half empty, told their own story. Robinson and her Mossad companion had likely been here already and had seemingly gone.

But if nobody was here, why was the window ajar? Had they left in a hurry? Did they somehow know he was coming? He wouldn't be entirely surprised if that was the case, because the Mossad's reach and range of contacts in the West Bank was almost certainly even better than Unit 133's.

He moved farther along the path at the rear of the house, checking the windows as he went, and then did likewise with the adjoining house.

There was definitely no sign of anyone at home. Then he knocked at both rear doors as a final check that the properties were unoccupied. There was no response.

Where are they?

CHAPTER SIXTEEN

Friday, July 1, 2016
Ramallah

Jayne and Sami made their way back down the path and through the gate of Abu Alami's house, then stood on the sidewalk next to Laila's Honda.

Laila lowered the window. "Any luck?" she asked.

Jayne shook her head. "He's scared he'll be outed by his Hezbollah bosses. He refused to say anything. He wasn't happy about the confession details being revealed."

"Understandable, I guess."

"I suppose so."

There was a pause as they all stood in silence.

Laila looked up and down the street, an anxious expression on her face. "Are you giving up?" she asked.

Jayne gave her a sharp glance. "Giving up is not something I normally do in life, no."

"Can't you appeal to his conscience, as you said?" Laila asked.

She thought she had done that, Jayne reflected. But maybe she needed to be a little more direct about it. Another alternative was the blunt weapon of a threat to disclose to his Hezbollah boss he had been leaking details of their operations to others. Maybe they even knew already.

"I wonder if Hezbollah knows about the church link between Alami and Kamal," Jayne said.

"I doubt Hezbollah has the time to keep track of their employees' religious habits," Sami said. "Most people around here go to either the mosque or the church. It's nothing out of the ordinary."

Jayne paused. Despite their understandable nervousness about the situation, Kamal Baltrami's brother and sister were both impressing her with their lines of thinking. They were also keen that she get to the bottom of what had happened to their sibling—that was for certain. She made a decision.

"I'll go back to the house and give it one more try," Jayne said. She turned to Sami. "I'll go alone. I don't want to put you in that position again—I'm sure its uncomfortable for you. Wait here. I'll be quick."

She turned and walked back through the gate and up the path, then knocked on the door.

It opened a second later. Alami stood there, scowling at her.

"What *are* you doing?" he snarled. "Maybe my English isn't quite clear enough. Didn't you understand when I said 'no'?"

Jayne held up both hands in a gesture of surrender. "I'm really sorry, but there's something I just wanted to say. I know you made your confession because your conscience was speaking to you, and I admire you for that, truly I do. You did the right thing."

She paused for breath, hoping her words didn't sound too

condescending or too much like bullshit, although she feared they probably did.

"To disclose this," she continued, "even under the seal of confession, was a big step, and I recognize that. You knew what was happening was very wrong, and you said so. My belief is that you would like some good to come out of what is already a very tragic situation. We know that the lives of more cardinals are at risk. These men—most of them, anyway —are doing good in the world. Now, can I please ask, beg, implore you to help us?"

Alami stared at her, then exhaled noisily and muttered something under his breath in Arabic that she didn't understand. It was clearly a curse.

She braced herself for a verbal or physical assault, or possibly both.

But Alami took a step backward and beckoned her in. "Come in, out of sight. Don't stand there on my doorstep."

Jayne stepped smartly forward and closed the door behind her.

"You've got thirty seconds," Alami said. "What do you want?"

The words tumbled out. "Which other cardinals are in danger?"

"I don't know," Alami said. "Some of them. That's all I know."

"Who is organizing this operation against them?" Jayne asked.

"Hezbollah."

"I know that. But which units, which leaders?" she asked.

Alami closed his eyes for a second, as if in pain. "It's Unit 910. Their leader is Talal Hassan. You've probably heard of him."

Jayne had indeed heard of him, and she knew well that Unit 910 was Hezbollah's foreign operations division. Her next question was almost a reflexive one, born of old habits formed during years of undercover tracking and tracing activity.

"Do you have his phone number?" she asked.

Her thought was that if she had his number, the Mossad's signals intelligence division, Unit 8200, might run him down. Their specialty was tapping into phones, computers, and emails.

Alami reached into his pocket and took out his phone, then tapped on the screen a few times before rapping out a number.

"Wait," Jayne said. She quickly typed the number into her own phone. It had a +961 prefix, which Jayne knew was for Lebanon.

"Thank you," she said.

"I have another for him. A French one, which I never use. He may not know I have it."

"Good. What is it?" Jayne asked.

Alami read out another number.

"And his email?"

Alami shook his head. "No. I don't have that."

Jayne's mind was now whirring. "What about in your unit, 133?" she asked. "You overheard a conversation, I understand, but who did it involve? One of your bosses?"

Alami nodded tersely, a nervous expression across his face. "The unit leader, Ghassan Nafi. He's my boss and has been involved in the operation. Talal Hassan is his boss. The conversation I heard was between those two. Don't ask me exactly what they have been doing, because I don't know. He's not confided in me at all."

"Do you have his number, too?" Jayne asked.

Alami recited another number, which Jayne also typed into her phone.

She paused. "Another thing. About the cardinals who were

killed in Washington. Do you know why? I understand they were on the way to the White House with something crucial that they wanted to discuss. I would like to know what that was."

Alami shook his head. "I have no idea."

"Do you know when the next attack is? Will there be another?" Jayne asked.

Alami shrugged. "I don't know when or if there will even be another." His tone was emphatic, and he glanced at his watch as he spoke. "We are well past your thirty seconds. Anything else?"

Jayne had a whole ream of questions she felt she should ask, but the important information was in the bag, and she didn't want to stay any longer than she had to. Alami was undoubtedly correct that he was putting his life at risk by talking to her. "There is, but I understand your risks, and you've told me the important points."

"Go now, and this time don't come back," Alami said. "Go. Quickly."

Jayne nodded, turned, and opened the door.

She had taken two steps down the path when, from behind her, Alami's voice came again.

"He's not in Lebanon right now."

She turned. "Hassan?"

Alami nodded.

"Do you know where?"

"No idea," Alami said.

"Okay. Thank you."

Jayne turned again and strode through the gate to the car.

She climbed into the rear seat, next to Rafael, who was busy tapping on his phone.

Laila, in the driver's seat, already had the engine running.

"Let's go," Jayne said.

* * *

Friday, July 1, 2016
   Ramallah

Laila unlocked the front door of her house and led the way inside. Jayne followed, with Rafael and Sami bringing up the rear.

Thankfully, there had been no sign of any surveillance, no tail, no coverage, on the short journey back from Abu Alami's house. Jayne knew that what they had done had been risky, both for them and for him, but it had paid dividends.

"Would you like something to eat, or a coffee, before you leave?" Laila asked. She stood in front of the closed door that led from the hallway into the living room where they had been sitting earlier.

Jayne, in the hallway with the others, was feeling very hungry, and she also needed a coffee, but she shook her head.

"No, thank you, Laila, we need to go," she said. "I don't want to put you at risk any longer. We've been here long enough already." She glanced at Rafael, who was nodding in agreement.

"Yes, I agree," Rafael said. "We'll get on the—"

But he was interrupted by a loud squeak and a crash from behind Laila as the living room door was thrown open.

A man appeared suddenly from behind the doorframe, grabbed Laila across the throat with his forearm, pulled her backward against him, and pinned the barrel of a pistol against her temple.

The whole thing happened too quickly for either Jayne or Rafael to react.

Laila gave a short involuntary shriek, at which the man

yanked his forearm back hard against her throat, reducing the shriek to a strangled gurgle.

"Don't do that again," he said, speaking rapid Arabic in a booming baritone voice.

Sami, standing next to Jayne, took a step forward. "Leave my sister alone, you bastard," he swore, also in Arabic. "Who are you?"

"Shut up," the man said. "Stay right where you are."

He eyed first Jayne, then Rafael. "You won't be going anywhere," he said, now in halting, slower English. "You do what I tell you, or the lady is dead."

Jayne considered pulling out her Walther, which remained in her belt, but decided that would likely not result in a good outcome.

Instead, she decided to try to delay things briefly, to give herself and Rafael some thinking time.

"There's no need for this," Jayne said. "You're hurting the lady and she's old and frail. Who are you, and what is this about?"

The man grunted as he adjusted his grip on Laila. "First, you, Jayne Robinson, and second you, Mossad man. I'm guessing you have guns. Throw them on the floor nice and slowly and kick them here. Do it now—or this lady is finished."

Jayne cursed inwardly but didn't move immediately.

This had just been careless. She should have foreseen something like this happening, particularly in the West Bank. There hadn't even been any need for her and Rafael to come back to Laila's house other than to make sure she and her brother were comfortable and reassured.

Her best guess was that this guy had to be linked to the same Hezbollah group as Alami. Was this his boss, the man he had mentioned, Ghassan Nafi? Had Alami gotten on the phone with him as soon as they left his house and tipped this guy off? She was certain he hadn't, given the highly confidential information that he had given Jayne. There hadn't been enough time, anyway—the journey back from his house had taken only a few minutes.

"I said hand over the guns." The man moved the barrel of his pistol, which Jayne could now see was a Heckler & Koch P7, slightly away from Laila's temple. Then there came a deafening bang as he pulled the trigger.

A round hammered into a glass picture frame that was hanging on the wall, shattering it and sending shards of glass flying to the floor. The entire picture frame, now destroyed, with a large hole in the center, fell to the floor. Laila whimpered.

There was a second's silence.

"I'm not telling you again," the man said. "Now, throw your guns to me."

Jayne glanced at Rafael. "We had best do what he says."

"That's good advice," the man spat. "I suggest you all follow it."

Jayne eased her jacket to one side, pulled the Walther out of her belt by the butt, leaned forward, and threw it onto the tiled floor toward the man, where it landed with a clatter that echoed around the hallway.

A few seconds later, Rafael did likewise with his Beretta.

The man inched forward, still clasping Laila tight to him, until he could reach the Walther with his right foot. He used the sole of his shoe to flick the gun back behind him and into the doorway of the living room, making it skitter across the tiles, and repeated the procedure with the Beretta.

Then he retreated into the living room, still holding Laila, and squatted down next to the guns, forcing Laila to do likewise.

Jayne could see he was going to have to move his own pistol away from Laila's head in order to pick up the other two guns. For a moment, she considered using that opportunity to rush him, knowing that Rafael would do likewise.

She glanced at Rafael, but the Israeli must have read her thoughts and imperceptibly shook his head. He was correct—there probably wasn't enough time to guarantee overpowering the man before he killed Laila.

"Don't try anything," the man said. "You will regret it."

Sure enough, he moved with lightning speed. He transferred his own gun to his left hand, still clasped around Laila's neck, and used his right to scoop up both pistols from the floor.

He shoved one gun into his jacket pocket, the other into his trouser pocket, then switched his own gun back to his right hand, put the muzzle back against Laila's temple, and continued to reverse into the living room.

"Come in here and line up with your backs against the wall," the man commanded. "Right now, or else I will kill her. Walk slowly. Don't do anything to surprise me."

Jayne had only a single thought.

Shit. A firing squad.

CHAPTER SEVENTEEN

Friday, July 1, 2016
Ramallah

Rafael walked into the living room first, followed by Jayne, and Sami last. They stood in a row against the wall to the left of the door, facing into the room. The coffee cups and pot that they had been using earlier were still on a tray on the table.

The window at the rear of the living room, behind the gunman, was wide open. That must have been how he got in, Jayne realized.

Why had Laila left the window open?

It crossed Jayne's mind briefly that this was some kind of setup, but then she ruled that out when she saw the coffee cups and pot still standing on the table. The gunman must have seen it and put two and two together.

The man reversed a little farther, still holding Laila, and addressed Jayne directly.

"You," he said. "Tell me why you are here. What have these people, the Baltramis, told you?"

"They have told me very little," Jayne said. She decided to gamble with the truth, hoping the man knew nothing of their movements, although he clearly knew who she was and why she was there. "We have only just arrived here, as you can see. I was hoping to ask them about their brother, who was tragically murdered recently in Rome."

"That is bullshit. First, you have just arrived back with them from somewhere. It's obvious you have been talking with them somewhere else at length." He gestured toward the coffee cups. "And it looks like you've been sitting here drinking coffee and chatting, too."

Jayne cursed silently to herself.

"Now, let's try again," the man snarled. "What have they told you? If you lie to me or say nothing, this woman's brains will be decorating her wall."

"I'll be quite honest with you," she said. "We were coming here to have a conversation. However, you have stopped it from happening. It's true, we have an investigation under way because there had been several horrific murders, and I wanted to interview these two. They might know something helpful. But like everyone in this part of the world, they're cautious and so far have said very little. I don't know what your reason is for being here or why you want to stop us, but you might be better advised to let us get on with it."

"Don't give me all that crap. Your investigation ends right here." He waved the muzzle at Jayne. "Put your hands above your head."

As he spoke, Jayne caught sight of a shadow moving almost imperceptibly against the frame of the open window behind the gunman.

To her horror, a head covered in a black balaclava rose slowly above the level of the windowsill.

What the hell?

She felt like crying out, but somehow held back. Her guts turned over inside her as the figure, dressed all in black, rose a little farther and lifted a pistol above the sill.

She heard Sami take a sharp intake of breath, but the gunman holding his sister didn't appear to notice.

The next thing she knew, the head of the gunman holding Laila exploded like a melon in a shower of red, splattering blood, brains, and bone all over the room.

A chunk of flesh hit Jayne squarely in the chest, and she looked down to see red stains and drops all over her clothes.

The gunman's body was catapulted to the floor, his fingers still wrapped around his pistol.

Laila, whose face, arms, and white blouse were now covered in blood, screamed a loud, piercing squeal, and Sami also yelled out loud.

"Bloody hell," Jayne said, involuntarily.

The figure in black rose to full height, gun still held out in front.

Jayne braced herself.

But the figure reached up, grabbed the balaclava, and pulled it off.

There was a slight pause.

"Abdullah, you bastard," said Rafael, his slightly shaking voice betraying his relief. "What took you so long?"

"I heard a gunshot when I was coming up the path," Abdullah said. "I was fearing the worst."

Laila fell to her knees and prostrated herself, ignoring the dead body next to her and the mess of blood and gore, weeping uncontrollably. "Oh God, oh God, please help me," she wailed. "I'm sorry. It's my fault. I left the window open."

Sami rushed to her side and also burst into tears.

Abdullah began to climb over the windowsill and into the room. "Are there any more of them? Just this guy?"

"Just this guy, as far as I know," Rafael said.

Jayne exhaled, partly in relief, partly because she could see they now faced a different kind of crisis.

With the dead body of a Hezbollah terrorist on their hands, the consequences of being hauled in by the Palestinian police were probably unpredictable. Somebody almost certainly heard the gunshots, given there was a large apartment building right next door. Furthermore, they couldn't just leave Laila and Sami to clean up the mess and deal with the body.

Jayne walked over to the brother and sister and put a hand on each of their shoulders. "Come on, let's get you out of this room. It's best you wait in the kitchen while we clean up here. It's not your fault—it's mine. I'm so sorry. I should have seen this coming."

She escorted them to the kitchen and made them a coffee, by which time Laila had thankfully calmed down a little.

"We've seen death so many times here," Sami said. "But never in our own home."

"If it hadn't been him, it would have been us," Jayne said. "I didn't mean to put you through this. We'll fix this mess. You clean yourselves up."

She walked back to the living room, where Rafael and Abdullah had already placed the dead body on a plastic shower curtain they had taken from the bathroom.

"Shit. This is a bloody disaster," she said.

"Let's think this through—quickly," Rafael said. "First job, clean up the room. Second, dump the body somewhere. Abdullah will do that—he knows the routine."

Jayne nodded. "Good. Though I'm not sure what this churchgoing pair is going to make of that. Then we need to get out of here as quickly as possible. I'm worried that this guy will have backup nearby. Did he have any ID on him?"

Rafael nodded and handed her a credit card in the name of Ghassan Nafi, a green West Bank ID card in the same name, and a blue Israeli ID card in a different name, which Jayne assumed was fake or stolen.

"He's Hezbollah," Abdullah said. "Unit 133. I think he runs the unit in the West Bank, actually. We've asked the team at Glilot Interchange to check him out."

Rafael held up a phone. "He also had this. We'll get everything off it. I've turned off the security lock so we can now get into it when needed." He indicated toward Nafi's body on the floor. "It was fingerprint recognition. This one seems to work even when you're dead."

Jayne looked at him. "Lucky. It usually stops working shortly after someone dies. Let me look." Jayne took the phone and clicked onto the directory. She then searched through it until she found what she was looking for.

"Talal Hassan. Here we go," she said. "Two cell phone numbers, one Lebanese, one French. Both match the numbers Alami gave me. And there's a Gmail address here, too—which Alami obviously chose not to give me. Perfect."

She tapped and scrolled a little more. "They've got an end-to-end encrypted message chain between them, but all the messages have been deleted. There's nothing. They're careful."

Jayne tapped Hassan's email into her phone alongside the numbers she had already noted.

"Let's get these numbers triangulated," Jayne said. "We'll track him down."

Jayne took a small Faraday pouch from her back pocket and pushed the phone into it. The lead-lined pouch, which she normally used for her own phone, would prevent any signals being transmitted or received and would stop the device from being traced.

She handed the pouch to Rafael. "After you've uploaded

the contents of that to your techies, we might be able to make use of it."

Rafael nodded. "Especially if Hassan doesn't know this guy is dead."

She then grasped Abdullah's hand and shook it. "Thanks for doing what you did. Another few minutes and we'd all have been dead, not him. How did you know to come?"

Abdullah indicated with his thumb toward Rafael. "He messaged me a while ago to pick you both up from here."

"That was from outside Alami's house," Rafael said. "There was no problem at that stage, of course. I just thought it would save us walking back to the church."

Abdullah nodded. "After I heard the gunshot, I snuck around the back and saw what had happened. Good thing the window was open."

"That's how the bastard got into the house," Jayne said. "He ambushed us."

She paused for a second. "There is, of course, the bigger question of how Nafi knew we were here, given that we had mentioned it to nobody and neither had Sami nor Laila, because they didn't know we were coming. I'm certain Alami would not have told him."

"Highly unlikely, I agree," Rafael said. "He didn't have the time, anyway. But somebody knew."

"Yes. Anyway, let's get moving with this cleanup—before any more Unit 133 goons or police turn up."

An hour later, Ghassan Nafi's body, neatly wrapped in the shower curtain, was in the trunk of Abdullah's car, ready to be taken to a place where Abdullah seemed confident nobody would find it.

Thankfully, and to Jayne's surprise, there had been no visits from Palestinian police. "Clearly the sound of gunshots doesn't raise eyebrows in Ramallah," she said.

"Happens all the time," Abdullah said. "Nobody takes any notice."

Laila's living room had been restored to normal, apart from a few remaining blood stains on the walls and floor that she said she could get rid of.

Abdullah promised the Baltramis that he would arrange a round-the-clock guard and surveillance of their homes for the foreseeable future in case there were any reprisals.

"We are waiting for my brother's body to come back from Rome," Sami said as Jayne, Rafael, and Abdullah prepared to depart. "I would be honored if you all could come to the funeral at our church."

"I would like to," Jayne said. "But I have to follow this investigation. We have a lot of work to do now to find out why your brother and the others were killed, and exactly who did it. These things are unpredictable—I can't promise I'll make it."

Laila shook her head. "I can see that. I wish you good luck."

Jayne nodded. "Thank you. I suspect we'll need it."

CHAPTER EIGHTEEN

Saturday, July 2, 2016
   Tel Aviv

The huge golf ball–style white fiberglass radomes, which concealed a host of listening devices, radar, and satellite monitoring equipment, rose high into the blue sky on red-and-white steel supports. Together with an array of large white satellite dishes, they dominated the well-guarded military compound about a kilometer and a half east of the Mossad's Tel Aviv headquarters.

Jayne looked up at the radomes from the passenger seat as Rafael's car drew up outside the rambling site, operated by the Israel Defense Forces' Unit 8200. Although the facility was separated from the Mossad's offices by the busy Highway 20—the Ayalon Highway—and the spaghetti-like Glilot Interchange, the two organizations cooperated closely.

The creative two-meter-high UNIT 8200 sign outside the main security gate was fashioned from old circuit boards and other electrical components, neatly symbolizing the unit's chief role of collecting digital intelligence, often by hacking into or monitoring the output from computers, phones, and other devices.

While Rafael was completing the lengthy security process for entry, he explained that the bulk of the legwork within Unit 8200 was carried out at a huge signals intelligence receiving base at Urim, in the Negev Desert in southern Israel, about thirty kilometers west of Beersheba and a similar distance from the Gaza Strip. Data from there was passed for analysis to the compound they were about to enter.

The security process included extensive scrutiny of Jayne's credentials, a confirmatory phone call to Avi Shiloah's office, and passing through an airport-style scanner. Finally, they were waved through to the parking lot.

"If you want to find yourself a rich husband someday, this is the place to come," Rafael said in a dry tone. "Half of the people here will be high-tech millionaires inside the next decade. No exaggeration."

Jayne knew there was a lot of truth in what he said. Unit 8200 had a reputation for giving its recruits—Israel Defense Forces conscripts mainly aged between eighteen and twenty-one—the knowledge that enabled them to become technology entrepreneurs once they had left the service.

"I guess they learn a lot of skills that are impossible to acquire elsewhere," Jayne said as they walked into the reception area.

"That's one way of putting it," Rafael said.

Unit 8200, or *shmone matayim* in Hebrew, was the Israeli equivalent of the National Security Agency, the NSA, in the United States or Government Communications Headquarters, GCHQ, in the United Kingdom. Smaller than either of its two rivals, yet seen as more focused, it formed the engine room of Israel's defenses against its myriad enemies.

The entire contents of Ghassan Nafi's cell phone had been sent to the unit first thing that morning for analysis after being downloaded by the technical team at the Mossad's offices. Rafael had also submitted requests for traces on the phone numbers obtained for Talal Hassan.

Vic had agreed to let the Mossad handle it once he had been reassured by Jayne, on her return from Ramallah, that the cardinal killings were Hezbollah operations. The Israelis had clearly been framed, and the DNA evidence was the key element of that. Resolving that with the Italian police would be a matter for another day, however.

Vic's condition for allowing the Israelis to handle the phone analysis was that he also would receive copies of any significant data extracted from the device.

Rafael had insisted on a personal visit to Unit 8200 to get the results. It had been some time since he was last there and he wanted to maintain his contacts, particularly with the commander, Brigadier General Beny Arison. Jayne was equally anxious to accompany him—she too made a habit of forging high-level contacts in person whenever she could. On numerous occasions throughout her career, it had paid dividends.

They walked into the reception area at the front of the building to find a group of at least a dozen people in pale green military dress with sleeves neatly rolled up, talking animatedly. All were youngsters who looked no older than their early twenties.

They dispersed as Jayne and Rafael drew near to reveal a solitary older man standing behind them, his black hair brushed back, his mustache neatly clipped, and his back as straight as a length of steel. Next to him was a slim, younger woman with long dark hair tied in a ponytail, wearing a pale shirt and dark green slacks, a green beret tucked into her epaulet, and a matching green headband.

The man stepped forward and shook Rafael's hand.

"This is Brigadier General Beny Arison," Rafael said to Jayne. "We go back a long way."

Arison gave a thin-lipped smile as he shook Jayne's hand. "I have the misfortune of being commander of this unit." He indicated to his colleague. "This is Lieutenant Colonel Neta Rosenblum, my deputy. Avi Shiloah has told me all about you —your reputation precedes you."

Jayne smiled at the flattery, shook hands with Neta, and introduced herself.

Arison and Rafael then spent the next five minutes reminiscing and laughing about a couple of old operations against the Iranians and the Russians they had both worked on a few years earlier, before Arison glanced at his watch.

"I don't have a lot of time, unfortunately," Arison said. "I'm only here to say hello—I need to get to a meeting, so I'm going to leave you in Neta's capable hands. She's the telecommunications and cyber expert around here."

He made his apologies and left toward the elevators.

Neta stood, hands on hips, and surveyed her visitors. "We've just about finished the analysis on the phone download you sent us, and we've done the traces on the other numbers. If you come this way, we'll find the tech officer who's done the work and he can talk you through it."

She led them up two flights of stairs, chatting as she went. It turned out she was aged thirty-nine and had two children, aged ten and twelve. She had joined Unit 8200 at twenty and had stayed, unlike most recruits who left after their two- or three-year military service was over. She had worked initially in network intelligence, helping to track terrorists operating

in Jerusalem and other parts of Israel and the occupied territories. Jayne resisted the temptation to ask if she had worked
on Stuxnet, the computer worm devised by Unit 8200 that
had caused tremendous damage a few years earlier to Iran's
nuclear warhead development program.

Neta took them into a large room lined with a dozen long
rows of desks at which an army of youngsters dressed in
Israeli green military fatigues were busily and noisily working
away at computer terminals, most of which had at least two
monitors operating.

"This is our telecoms analysis room," Neta said. She
pointed to a young man sitting in the far corner against a
window that looked out over agricultural fields to the north
of the compound. "That's Daniel Shavit. He's an expert in
telecoms and computer systems penetration. One of our
rising stars, actually. A genius. He's been working on your jobs
and may have finished by now."

She led the way over to Daniel, a rake-thin youth with an
acne-ridden face.

"These are your clients, Rafael and Jayne," she said, and
introduced both of them. "Can you talk them through what
you've found?"

Daniel greeted his visitors, shook hands, then toggled his
computer screen to a brief report. "I've only just finished.
First, we have the download of the phone's contents. Unfortunately, there seemed to be very little of value on it. Typical
Hezbollah. They are very careful, mostly. No files saved on
the device, and no email set up. No social media, and no web
browsing either. However, I've got the call history. Again, not
many calls on it, but it does include one interesting incoming
call from a pay-as-you-go cell phone, a burner most likely,
using an Italian SIM card."

"Italy?" Jayne asked. A flash of adrenaline went through
her. "Where in Italy? Is it possible to trace the user?"

"I've tried that," Daniel said. "The SIM was on the TIM network—that's Telecom Italia. The call was made from the Rome area and lasted just over one minute. But the SIM it came from isn't active currently. Most likely, the card was used briefly, then thrown away. Usual story. But I've included all the details we have in my report."

He printed out a copy of the half-page report on a printer next to his desk and handed it to Rafael.

"And the phone numbers we need to trace?" Rafael asked. "The ones owned by Talal Hassan."

"That was interesting," Daniel said. "I got both of them. One is a standard French cell phone, the other a burner, Lebanese. Ghassan appears to have only ever called the Lebanese one, never the French, despite it being saved in his phone directory."

That was in line with what Alami, too, had said about only calling Hassan's Lebanese phone, not his French one, Jayne noted. Maybe Hassan used the French one only for certain other calls, she guessed.

Daniel paused, leaned back in his seat, and folded his arms. "It's been nice to do something other than tracking West Bank Palestinians."

"Are they your usual targets?" Jayne asked. She assumed that a lot of the activity at Unit 8200 would involve monitoring Israel's opponents in the neighboring Palestinian territories that had been occupied by Israel after the 1967 Six Day War: the West Bank, Gaza Strip, and Golan Heights. Such surveillance had provoked a fierce debate over privacy and intrusion into innocent Palestinian people's lives, and the controversial ways in which that information was used by the Israel Defense Forces, sometimes to coerce individuals.

"Ninety percent Palestinian, yes." He looked at Neta, a slightly uncomfortable look on his face, perhaps thinking he had said the wrong thing. She didn't comment.

"Anyway," Daniel continued, "both phones have been active in the past twenty-four hours."

"Where? I know he's not in Lebanon," Jayne asked.

"You're correct about that. Look, I'll show you."

Daniel turned to his computer, toggled to a different app, and clicked on a link.

A detailed street map in satellite mode appeared, with a blue dot flashing intermittently, positioned right in the center of the screen.

Jayne leaned over to look. It took her less than a second to realize where it was. The dot was a few hundred meters south of the River Seine and a similar distance east of the Hôtel des Invalides.

"Bloody hell. Paris," she said. "What's the leader of Hezbollah's Unit 910 doing there?"

Daniel shrugged.

"A very good question," Neta said. She folded her arms. "We will continue to monitor the phones for you and see what we can find out."

* * *

Saturday, July 2, 2016
    Tel Aviv

"So it may have been someone in Rome who leaked details of your visit to Ramallah?" Avi Shiloah said. "Who actually knew about it?"

Jayne watched as Shiloah pulled the wrapper off a new pack of Camels and flicked one out of the box.

His smoking habit hadn't changed since she had first met him in Islamabad in 1988, when he was working for the Mossad in the Pakistani capital and she was with MI6. Both had been covertly offering support to the Afghan mujahideen in their ongoing fight against the occupying Soviet military.

"It's a short list," Jayne said. "As you might expect." In a small meeting, she and Rafael had just given a briefing about the trip to Ramallah, the information sourced there, and the outcome of the phone-tracking process carried out by Unit 8200.

Apart from Shiloah and his deputy David Zahavi, the attendees also included Vic Walter, who had joined via a secure video link from the CIA station in Paris, where he was still working. Given the unexpected revelation that Talal Hassan also appeared to be in the French capital at the moment, Vic's contribution was going to be vital.

Shiloah picked up a lighter from the steel-and-glass desk in his second-floor office and lit the cigarette, despite the no-smoking policy inside the Mossad's headquarters building. Jayne felt like making a sarcastic comment but held herself back. This was, after all, Shiloah's own fiefdom. Since taking on the top job a couple of months earlier, he seemed to have made himself completely at home in the office suite reserved for the *ramsad*.

"So, who's on the list?" Shiloah asked as he took a deep drag, then tilted his head back and exhaled vigorously toward the ceiling, where the smoke particles danced beneath the fluorescent light.

Jayne and Rafael ran through the people who had known. Apart from them, Shiloah, and Zahavi, there was Abdullah in Ramallah, two Mossad officers who carried out the background checks on Laila and Sami Baltrami, and another two on the operations team who had helped work out the logistics. There was Joe Johnson, whom Jayne always informed when she was traveling somewhere potentially dangerous, but he was completely trustworthy. On the CIA side there was Vic and Neal Scales at Langley. Finally, there was Michael

Gray, who had told Jayne he had informed the pope during a confidential one-to-one meeting behind closed doors.

"There's no way Michael Gray or the pope would have leaked it—Michael has assured me of that," Jayne said. "And I can't see anyone else doing so. This call from a burner in Rome to Nafi's phone is odd. Maybe it's coincidental but—"

"Unlikely," Shiloah interrupted.

"Agreed," Jayne said. "Unlikely indeed. That's what I was about to say."

Shiloah took another drag from his cigarette and stubbed out the butt in an ashtray, which was already overflowing. He leaned back in his chair, over the back of which his black leather jacket was hanging. "We'll carry out a full audit on the people involved at the Mossad end, although I'd stake my house on it not being any of our team. First-class people, all of them."

"Likewise with my team," Vic said, his voice a little distorted over the video link from Paris. "Jayne, can you get Michael Gray to double-check with the pope that he's not inadvertently told anyone he shouldn't have? I don't like to say this, but the pope is in his eighties, correct?"

"Eighty. And will do," Jayne said. "Highly unlikely, though. I mean, the pope must deal with more confidential information than we do, and Michael tells me he's very switched on. And the church seems very good at keeping secrets—they're better at it than us."

"Let's hope he only told God about it, then," Shiloah said, running a hand through his wiry, graying black hair. "But before we decide on the next steps, let's see if we can summarize where we're at with this investigation," he said. "We've got five dead cardinals, and there's been a shitty, predictably unsuccessful attempt to frame the Mossad for all of them. And efforts to chase down the very thin leads we've got resulted in Hezbollah's West Bank thugs trying desperately to block us. So we can see what we're up against. We can deal with them. But the much bigger questions, to which I see no answers, are why is this happening, and where do we go next?"

"We've still only got one clear lead," Jayne said. "So we're not exactly flush with options, are we?"

"We're not," Vic agreed. "I had Charles Deacon at the White House on the phone this morning, wondering if there was any progress. He tells me, Avi, that the president is glad to hear it wasn't your team who gunned down those cardinals in DC, but he wants to know who did it before his Vatican visit. So I would suggest, Jayne, that you better get your ass over here to Paris. It might make sense for Rafael to accompany you, if he's happy to do that."

Jayne grinned. In these politically correct days, a man could only get away with talking like that to a woman when the woman knew he respected her. "I'd agree with that," she said.

Jayne glanced at Rafael, who nodded, as did Shiloah.

"Unit 8200 is keeping a twenty-four-hour watch on Hassan's phones," Rafael said. "If he so much as calls for a pizza, we'll know about it."

"Send me the details of the phones and I'll get the NSA to run the numbers through their system," Vic said. "They might have something Tel Aviv doesn't."

"That would be a first," Shiloah scowled. "You can try if you want."

The suggestion made sense to Jayne. The NSA, like GCHQ, maintained a global watch on phone and email traffic involving those on their watchlist. Anyone with a link to Hezbollah would be on that list.

"Also, I was just considering whether to suggest involving our friends at the DGSE," Vic said. "But that would complicate things hugely."

Even before he had finished speaking, Shiloah was shaking his head, as was Jayne. Strictly speaking, if they were to work in France, protocols would require them to inform or involve the Direction Générale de la Sécurité Extérieure, the DGSE, France's counterparts to the CIA or the Mossad. They were a highly skilled unit but notoriously difficult to deal with, as were the DGSI, the French internal security agency, similar to the FBI or MI5.

"That's a big fat no," Shiloah said. "Jayne can run this. Then we can deny we're operating on French soil. Simple."

Vic gave a slight chuckle. "Same here."

"And I'll just keep my head down," Rafael added.

Shiloah gave a witchlike cackle. "You've had plenty of practice at that the past twenty years."

Rafael had indeed. The vast majority of his covert operations against Israel's many enemies had been on European soil, mainly in Germany, France, and Switzerland.

* * *

Saturday, July 2, 2016
Tehran

The last time Nasser Khan had seen the small meeting room at the Office of the Supreme Leader in Tehran more than two months ago, it had been splattered with the blood, brains, and flesh of his onetime colleague, minister of intelligence and security, Abbas Taeb.

One of the bodyguards employed by the Supreme Leader, Ali Hashemi, had shot Taeb dead on the spot on his boss's instructions after Taeb had supposedly failed to do his job properly. Khan had been sitting right next to Taeb on the sofa and despite being a man who had dealt in death for most of his life, he still wasn't sleeping properly as a result of the flashbacks that continued to trouble him. The abrupt killing had been too close to home, too personal. In fact, it could very easily have been him.

Now the bloodstained sofa had been replaced with a new model, on which Khan, the head of Iran's Quds Force special operations group, was now seated. The rug on the floor had also been replaced, and the wall behind the sofa had been repainted.

Next to him sat another replacement—the man who had only a few days earlier been appointed as the new intelligence and security minister, Nader Vazhiri, a bespectacled character in his late forties.

There was no evidence that the atrocity—or any of the other executions of senior officials before it—had ever been committed there. Neither did Hashemi refer to it or to Taeb as he ran through his briefing for Khan and Vazhiri. The former minister was history: forgotten, replaced, and wiped from the accounts.

Ayatollah Hashemi sat motionless in his chair, studying his notes. A portrait of him, the only decorative element in the room, hung on the nearby wall.

The meeting room at the Office of the Supreme Leader was quite different from most of the ornate, highly decorated rooms within the complex of historic buildings off Azarbayejan Street in District 11, which many also referred to as the House of Leadership.

The entire site functioned not only as Hashemi's official residence and his place of work but also as offices for his administrative staff. It included an enormous Shia Muslim congregation hall, known as the Imam Khomeini Hussainia.

Despite Khan's grand title, he always felt that the Supreme Leader's decision to use this small, bland room for their meetings was designed to put him in his place. He knew he didn't matter in the scheme of things here. Like Taeb, he was dispensable and replaceable.

Finally, the Supreme Leader spoke. "My chief concern right now, of course, is Amir Rad. I particularly want to know how and why it happened."

Khan pressed his lips together and in his peripheral vision, he could see Vazhiri sitting absolutely still. The assassination two days earlier in Tehran of Rad, the head of the Atomic Energy Organization of Iran, had sent another shock wave through the government machine. Everyone knew it was the Mossad who had done it, and it represented yet another major setback dealt by the Israelis to Iran's covert nuclear weapons development program.

Hashemi turned his gaze toward Vazhiri and his voice dropped another level so that they had to strain to hear him. "Your predecessor paid a price for his failures to collect accurate and useful intelligence, as a result of which this country was dealt several damaging blows. Now we have been dealt another—the loss of Rad was also due to serious intelligence failures."

It was indeed an enormous embarrassment that another country's operatives had snuck into Iran, assassinated a senior nuclear official, and exited again without detection.

Now Khan could see the fear in Vazhiri's eyes.

Vazhiri sat up straight. "Sir, I have already begun an investigation into how the Israelis penetrated the country. I will report back to you as soon as it is complete. I must apologize for the—"

"I do not want apologies. It is too late for that," Hashemi said. "I accept that you have only been doing your job for a brief time and therefore cannot be held responsible—at least not this time. But that period of grace will expire quickly, as you will discover if this kind of thing happens again. Do you understand?"

Vazhiri's Adam's apple moved up and down as he visibly swallowed hard.

"Of course, sir. Yes, I understand." Vazhiri bowed his head toward the Supreme Leader, his gaze focused on the floor.

"I hope so."

The Supreme Leader stared at Khan. "As for you, I would like to see some revenge exacted when an opportunity arises for what happened to Amir Rad yesterday. That is your job."

"Yes, sir," Khan said. "I am in constant discussion with Hezbollah about this. I and they continue to look for ways to further our objectives internationally—to strike against Western infidels, to help Hezbollah raise the funds it needs to do that, and to protect our position."

The Supreme Leader nodded. "I saw your reports on the cardinals in Washington, which pleased me greatly."

"Thank you, sir," Khan said. "That is one example, sir. We had a good reason for doing that."

"Continue to take opportunities to inflict maximum damage on the Roman Catholic Church or any other Western institution or country. That goes without saying—especially their leaders. They are a threat to Islam, and they take every opportunity to criticize us. If Hezbollah can carry out those strikes rather than your Quds, all the better—it makes it easier for me to distance myself and to remain silent in public."

"I am noting your wishes, sir," Khan said.

Khan knew well that Hashemi had met the pope for the first time only a few months ago, following which his already intense dislike for the Catholic Church, and indeed for Christians generally, seemed to have deepened. More than 95 percent of Iranians were Shia Muslims, but there were still estimated to be more than three hundred thousand Christians in the country, mainly Catholics, who were relentlessly persecuted by Hashemi's government. Jail sentences of over ten years were common, along with beatings and the occasional death.

Hashemi folded his arms. "I need to stress the importance of Hezbollah increasing and protecting their own fundraising," he said. "As you know, international oil prices have dropped significantly, which reduces our ability to provide capital to them."

Khan knew of the impact that lower international oil prices were having on Iran's geopolitical maneuvering. Crude oil from Iran's massive production fields accounted for over three-quarters of the country's foreign currency earnings and exports, but prices had fallen this year to about $43 per barrel from more than $100 three years earlier. This was starving the country of revenues and having a real impact on its people. There was much less cash available to channel to Hezbollah now than previously.

"We know how crucial the fundraising operations are," Khan said. "Hezbollah's business affairs unit is very much in control of those. Don't worry."

The Supreme Leader stared at Khan. "I'll decide whether to worry or not. Now, tell me," he said. "Is it still Talal Hassan who is in charge of Unit 910 and the business affairs unit?"

Khan nodded. "Yes, sir."

"You can tell him I am keeping a close eye on his progress. And on yours. Is that understood?"

"Yes, sir. It is completely understood."

Hashemi placed his hands on the arms of his chair. "You both may go now. I would like to see you again soon for a follow-up report on these issues. My office will tell you when to come."

The Supreme Leader turned to his bodyguard who stood near the door. "Take our two visitors out."

Khan and Vazhiri stood, bowed in unison to the Supreme Leader, and followed the bodyguard to the exit.

Khan felt some relief that, once again, he had survived his meeting intact, but his levels of anxiety had risen sharply again. The Supreme Leader, as always, was intensely focused on results and extremely demanding.

Khan knew he needed to deliver, somehow. And therefore, so did Talal Hassan.

CHAPTER NINETEEN

Saturday, July 2, 2016
Paris

Yet again, the call went to voice mail.

It was the third time that morning that Talal Hassan had tried calling his longtime colleague and friend, Ghassan Nafi, but there had been no answer. Not even a ring tone.

The number you are trying to call is unavailable. Please try again or leave a message after the tone.

Hassan muttered a curse and glanced across the café table at the man sitting opposite him, who was quietly sipping an espresso.

"There's something wrong," he said. "Still no answer. It's not like Ghassan."

His companion, who had long ago been code-named VALENCIA by Hassan and whose real name was Pierre Fekkai, frowned a little in response but said nothing.

Now Hassan was fearing the worst. He had never known Nafi, a real professional, to stay out of communication for so long, particularly after an operation. Usually, he delivered precisely what he had said he would do, then invariably called with an update and a plan for the next move.

He glanced once again at the brief message received from Nafi the previous day.

In Ramallah. Will report back when done.

After sending it, Nafi had apparently disappeared off the face of the earth.

"Have you talked to Basheer?" Pierre asked. He fingered his scalp, which was bald apart from a short gray semicircle of hair around the edge.

Basheer Teebi was Nafi's deputy in Unit 133.

Hassan nodded. "Half an hour ago. He didn't even know Ghassan was going to Ramallah. I couldn't reach Abu Alami either. He's not answering his phone."

The phone belonging to Alami, who was Nafi's third in command, was not switched off but had consistently gone to voice mail.

Pierre stroked his chin. "If Ghassan has been compromised, trapped, or worse, then we have to assume they have his phone." He pointed at Hassan's phones. He had two on the table, one of them an old Nokia, the other a smartphone. "And we therefore have to assume they have your numbers and may even now be tracing you."

Hassan glanced at his companion. Pierre was undoubtedly correct. He had long held the view that although Unit 910 could not function without cell phones, they were also its biggest liability.

"It's that British bitch Robinson," Hassan said. "I'd better get another burner." He picked up the Nokia, switched it off, then picked up his coffee and took a sip.

"What about the other phone?" Pierre asked.

Hassan shook his head. "He only calls me on the burner. He doesn't have the French number. But I'll turn it off anyway." He picked up the phone and switched it off. "Call me paranoid, but we'd better move hotels again this afternoon. These people are not stupid. If they've got the phone number, they'll have our recent locations."

They had already moved from one cheap hotel to another twice in the past four days. It was Hassan's habit never to stay in the same place more than two nights, even when he was confident there was no threat of surveillance. It was part of an ingrained routine that had kept him alive and out of prison.

The content of the message from Nafi and the identity of the investigator, Jayne Robinson, had come as a surprise—and had caused Hassan's anger levels to spike sharply.

He didn't need to be reminded who Robinson was.

She had been part of a joint team of operatives along with people from the Mossad, notably Rafael Levy, who had done immeasurable damage to Iran's black market nuclear components supply chain only a few weeks earlier.

In the process, the head of Iran's nuclear weapons program, Jafar Farsad, had died in a Vienna hotel.

Furthermore, the financing for that program had been thrown into disarray after Robinson and her team had unmasked the two Swiss bankers who had been masterminding it.

And most damaging of all was a very personal blow. Robinson had been largely to blame for the recent death of Pierre's twin brother, Henri, code-named JAFFA, who had been shot dead by an MI5 sniper during an operation in London that had gone wrong. The operation had been handed to Henri by Hassan, with one objective being to eliminate Robinson.

Following that, the middleman who had coordinated supplies of components for centrifuges and other essential nuclear equipment, Kourosh Navai, had been captured by the

FBI at Toluca International Airport in Mexico and was now awaiting trial. A long prison term beckoned. Pierre, who had been acting as armed security for Navai at the time, had been the only one of his group who managed to evade capture. Robinson and the FBI team had also captured two US businessmen who had been assisting them.

The fallout from these multiple disasters had been significant.

The biggest impact had been the reaction from Tehran and the resultant increase in pressure on Hassan. His role as head of Hezbollah's Unit 910 was two-fold. First it was to run paramilitary operations against Iran's enemies worldwide, although in practice the bulk of these were against Israel and its allies in Europe and the Near East. Second, he needed to raise money through a variety of means, very few of them legal, to fund those operations and to make significant financial contributions to Hezbollah's general funds. This fundraising was a truly worldwide enterprise, conducted through Unit 910's business affairs unit, and projects were actively running in North America, Europe, Asia, and Australasia.

Within days of the disastrous series of events that had befallen the nuclear black market operation, Iran's leadership had acted. The Iranian Supreme Leader, Ayatollah Ali Hashemi, had ordered his team to significantly increase their capability to attack Israel and to step up fundraising. The order had been passed down the chain from Hashemi to the head of Iran's Quds Force special operations group, Nasser Khan. And then from Khan down to Hassan.

Hassan fingered his beard. His biggest fear was the consequences if an operation of this scale turned into a disaster. He had in the forefront of his mind the fate recently suffered by Iran's minister of intelligence and security, Abbas Taeb, who had been shot dead by a guard at point-blank range on a whim by the Supreme Leader after the last such failure.

A phone call Hassan had just received from Khan had added significantly to those fears. The Supreme Leader had Unit 910 under his microscope, Khan had told him. He wanted more operations against Western targets and leaders, not least in revenge for the killing of Amir Rad in Tehran. He also wanted Hezbollah to ensure the unit generated as much of its own funding as possible.

"We can't afford for this operation to go wrong. You know that," Hassan said.

Pierre gave a nod. "Let's make sure it doesn't."

"If Ghassan has been blown, though, I'm worried. What if he talked?" Hassan asked. "What if they squeezed him—or maybe they're squeezing him as we speak?"

"Then they're likely heading here."

Hassan's height, at about six feet five inches, and his sheer physical presence had helped build his legendary status within Hezbollah's military arm. That reputation stemmed from many years of personally carrying out deadly, incisive covert operations earlier in his career, and directing them in more recent years.

Those early operations included several attacks against US Marines based in Lebanon in the 1980s and a truck bomb attack at a Jewish community building in Buenos Aires in 1992. It killed twenty-eight people and injured more than two hundred others.

Now aged fifty-two, Hassan missed his old operational life. True, he occasionally ventured out into the field, but mainly he was stuck behind a dusty, dilapidated old desk in a basement in Beirut.

With all that in mind, Operation Prada, which had so far been highly complex to devise and deliver, had proved something of a lifeline, and not just financially. It had brought him out of his Beirut bunker and put him back on the street. Riding the motorcycles in Washington and Rome from which his passenger Pierre had carried out the hits on the cardinals had taken him back many years to his old operational days. Moreover, it promised to help protect the healthy revenues that his paymasters in Tehran were demanding.

However, the big challenge was to ensure that the operation remained confidential and to prevent any leaks that might threaten future cash flows.

Hassan drained his coffee and glanced up the street, first in one direction, then the other. It was a habit born of a survival instinct. They were sitting at a table beneath a canopy outside Le Gévaudan café in Rue du Bac, a short distance from the Rue du Bac metro station.

Hassan caught Pierre's eye. "What are you going to do with the shop?" he asked.

The shop in question was a tailoring business situated a block away to the west, in Rue de Saint-Simon, a quiet, quintessential Parisian street filled with shuttered apartment buildings, houses, a handful of shops, and the delightful Hôtel Duc de Saint-Simon. Pierre had originally operated the shop in partnership with his late twin brother, in addition to carrying out operations for Hezbollah under Hassan's guidance.

After Pierre had moved to the United States in 2006, Henri had continued running the business alone, and it had proved an ideal cover for the various Hezbollah operations Hassan gave him to carry out across Europe.

Pierre shrugged. "It's going to be far too much of a risk to restart work there. I'll be a sitting duck for just about every intelligence service in the West. I haven't even set foot in it since I came back."

"Sensible. I guess it's inevitable that they know your brother had the shop."

Pierre gave a thin smile. "I have to assume they found out after he was killed, even though it happened in the UK. They don't miss these things, although he would have covered his tracks, used his fake ID and so on. They could have put in cameras and bugs, although there's no sign of anyone there."

"True. So what will you do with it?"

Pierre shrugged. "We have had it on a long lease, which is due for renewal next year. Otherwise it expires. I was originally thinking I might just get a van and see if I can find a way to safely clear it out one night. There will be a lot of stock in there—rolls of cloth, finished suits, all the equipment. It's all worth a lot of money. I was thinking I could take it all down to Rome and sell it to Vincenzo and Luigi Zeffirelli. We've done them a lot of favors over the years—I could call in those favors."

"Hmm. I do have access to a van here," Hassan said. "One of my people has a Volkswagen. If you check out the shop first, and it's safe to do so, I'm sure I could get it for you if you want to empty the place. The Zeffirelli business is still thriving, I assume?"

"They do good business. He has a captive market at the Vatican. Doesn't make a fortune, but does well enough."

Although Pierre and Henri's tailor's shop on Rue de Saint-Simon was primarily focused on business suits for local customers, it also had a lucrative sideline producing clerical gowns, cassocks, hats, and other garments for the Catholic Church. The church-related side of their business, which Hassan had strongly encouraged despite the fact it went against the grain in terms of their Muslim beliefs, gave them excellent credibility and provided even denser cover for their Hezbollah activities. It certainly provided a useful layer of respectability in France.

Pierre and Henri had links with the Zeffirellis dating back many years and sometimes supplied them with finished items when required. If they were short of stock and demand was high—for example around a papal conclave when cardinals from all over the world congregated at the Vatican to elect a new pope—Henri and Pierre would help them out, including some fitting and measuring work at the Vatican on occasions.

"But if I were to clear out the shop, it would mean checking that nobody had been in there and hidden bugs or cameras," Pierre continued. "And then I'd need to clear it out at lightning speed in case the security people arrived. A real hassle and probably too risky. But on the other hand . . . " He let his words drift.

"On the other hand what?" Hassan asked.

"I've just had an idea," Pierre said as he stretched his muscled six-foot, two-inch frame. "If they do come after us, that shop might come in handy."

"What do you mean?"

"I know my brother kept stocks of ammonium nitrate in the cellar, along with other components. It would be a pity not to make use of it—and we could put your burner phone to some use at the same time rather than you throw it away." He paused, a grim expression on his face. "Robinson needs to pay for what happened to Henri."

Hassan knew that both Pierre and his brother had been experts in deploying improvised explosive devices, or IEDs, manufactured from ammonium nitrate granules, heating oil, a battery, a detonator, and a trigger linked to a cell phone. The ammonium nitrate was usually identical to the dry agricultural fertilizer variant used by farmers to feed their crops or to the granules used in single-use cold packs for treating sprains, bruises, and other sporting injuries.

In an initiative largely masterminded by Hassan, Hezbollah had built large caches of ammonium nitrate stashed in various corners of Europe, North America, and the Far East, as well as Beirut.

A faint flicker of a smile crossed Hassan's face. "I see what you're saying. But you really want to say goodbye to that tailor shop?"

Pierre shrugged. "It's no use to me anymore."

* * *

Saturday, July 2, 2016
   The Vatican

Michael Gray made his way across the gray cobblestones of the magnificent Belvedere Courtyard, the sixteenth-century enclosed space that was surrounded on all sides by tall, ornate, dun-colored brick buildings. He passed the enormous fountain in the center of the courtyard and picked his way between a handful of diagonally parked cars. His destination was the Vatican Secret Archive in the far northwest corner.

By now, the sun had descended behind the narrow terraced building that formed the western side of the courtyard. The usual visitors to the Vatican had gone and the area was quiet.

Gray was carrying a bundle of documents relating to Westminster diocesan business in London that he had just finished checking and needed to deposit in the archive. As it was a Saturday, the archive offices and those of the neighboring Vatican Library were closed, but he had arranged to meet one of the archivists who he knew was working on a research project that day.

Normally, if he wanted access to the archive building outside its normal working hours, he would use a trade entrance, comprising a nondescript set of green wooden doors at the rear of the building. The trade entrance emerged onto Stradone ai Giardini, the avenue that ran alongside the Vatican Gardens.

But now he noticed that the main door in the courtyard was open, so he decided he may as well use that.

The workings of the Secret Archive remained a complete mystery to him, as it did to almost all his fellow cardinals. Only qualified scholars from recognized universities with a specific and legitimate research objective were allowed to view a limited number of the millions of pages within.

Gray knew the secret documents, which dated back more than twelve centuries, included unknown treasures that had never seen the light of day since their storage and possibly never would for fear of the embarrassment they might cause the Catholic Church. Some of them were locked in vaults deep underground, known as the Bunker.

The known ones included transcripts from the trial of the Knights Templar from 1307 to 1310. There was a papal bull from Leo X, excommunicating Martin Luther in 1521, and the letter that arrived from a bunch of English peers in 1530 asking the pope to annul the marriage of King Henry VIII and Catherine of Aragon, which he refused to do.

Gray had once been shown a letter to the pope from President Abraham Lincoln in 1863, and another in the same year from the Confederate president Jefferson Davis defending the South as a victim of northern hostility in the American Civil War. Clearly, both men, on opposing sides in that war, had been trying to curry favor with the Vatican.

But there were also very recent documents that cataloged the affairs of the church, both anodyne and potentially explosive. Gray was well aware those relating to the sexual abuse scandals that had impacted the church in several countries were a time bomb waiting to go off. Although a lot of detail had already become public, there was much more that hadn't.

It wasn't going to happen anytime soon, though, as any document less than seventy-five years old was off-limits to anyone.

Thankfully, the documents under Gray's arm related to nothing more sinister than the financial records and property portfolio of his diocese in London.

In any case, the contents of the Secret Archive were not foremost in his mind right now. Earlier that day he'd had a phone conversation with Jayne Robinson, using the encrypted app she had loaded onto his phone. Although she reported progress from her visit to Ramallah the previous day and mentioned she was heading to Paris early on Monday to pursue a lead, the trip had also resulted in a deeply worrying outcome, including her life being threatened and the death of a Hezbollah leader. Any news of violence and death left Gray feeling a little destabilized.

The biggest question, to which he had no answer, was how details of her trip had leaked. One thing was for certain: it wasn't him, and he could hardly imagine it was the pope, who was the only other person with whom he had discussed Jayne's trip.

Gray had then spent almost an hour after lunch praying about what he should do next, but had received no guidance beyond the need to discuss it further with the pope at the next opportunity.

He passed through the stone archway and its intricately carved wooden door by sculptor Tommaso Gismondi that formed the entrance from the courtyard. He continued into the lobby through an internal set of glass-and-wood swinging doors into the lobby, greeted the porter, whom he knew well, and went through the ritual of showing his entry pass.

Then he stopped dead in his tracks.

Walking toward him across the tiled floor was Pope Julius, accompanied by Bishop Carlo Galli, prefect of the Secret

Archive. The pope was carrying a bundle of documents beneath his right arm.

That explained why the main entrance was open. But this was unusual. The pope had every right to visit the archive—after all, it was technically his and his predecessors' archive and had been for hundreds of years. But he wasn't often seen in the building.

"Good evening, Holiness," Gray said. "Are you doing some research?"

The pope nodded, a solemn expression across his face. "Good evening, Eminence. It's related to the events we have been discussing. I'm going back to my office to go through these papers." He tapped the bundle beneath his arm. "I have something in mind."

Gray knew better than to ask for more details in such a public space, and although he also wanted to speak to the pope urgently about events in Ramallah, he certainly wasn't going to do so here, especially with Galli present and a porter loitering.

"Perhaps we can meet again to discuss progress?" Gray said. "I too have made some headway, but there are other things we need to talk about as soon as possible."

He glanced at the papers the pope was holding. He couldn't see exactly what they were, but they were definitely modern documents, all closely typed, in a clear plastic folder, not one of the historical artifacts held inside the archives.

"Of course, we must," the pope said. "After the weekend. Give Christophe a call and arrange it. Has your old friend's daughter made any progress?"

Gray hesitated. He didn't really want to reply in front of Galli but felt he should say something minimalistic. "She has. She is going to Paris on Monday, but I will tell you more when we meet."

The pope nodded. "That's good." With that, he continued out the door, Galli two paces behind him.

Gray watched him go, then continued to the reception room, which always reminded him of a small somewhat old-fashioned hotel, and stepped into an ancient 1950s-style cage elevator, complete with metal mesh sides and a wooden frame.

The elevator creaked and groaned as it took him at a snail's pace up through the void at the center of a marble staircase to the so-called index room, lined floor to ceiling with leather-bound books several inches thick. These volumes provided a guide to at least some of the contents of the archive, but Gray had always found them completely unintuitive, unlike the computerized English national archives system he had used back home.

Sitting alone at one of the long wooden tables that ran in rows down the center of the room was the man he had come to see, Dr. Paolo Petrocchi, the secretary to the prefecture of the archives. He was surrounded by papers that he was inserting back into files.

Gray guessed roughly what he had been doing and for whom.

Petrocchi, who wore a navy blue suit and had dark hair cut trendily short at the sides and long on top, peered over the top of his black-rimmed glasses. The look on his face told its own story.

"Don't ask," he said. "Two hours to deal with all of this. I've done no work on my research project. Should have stayed at home."

"His Holiness operates to his own agenda," Gray said.

"How did you—"

"I bumped into him downstairs on his way out."

Petrocchi grunted, stood, and walked over to Gray. "You've brought your London files for me, I assume?"

Gray handed him the papers he was carrying. "Thanks for taking them. I know you're busy on other things right now."

Petrocchi took the file and inclined his head in acknowledgment. He paused for a moment, then sighed. "Any idea what His Holiness is doing? He's been in here twice in the past two days."

"Give me a clue. Which files did he want?" Gray asked. It was the usual type of cat-and-mouse conversation he often had with Petrocchi. Each of them knew they were unlikely to get a truthful response to their questions about the pope's activities and didn't expect one.

Petrocchi shook his head and stared down at the floor. "I would like to tell you."

"So would I."

Another shake of the head and this time Petrocchi looked Gray in the eye. "His Holiness would kill me."

CHAPTER TWENTY

Monday, July 4, 2016
   Paris

Pierre Fekkai drove the gray Volkswagen panel van along Rue Paul-Louis Courier with its elegant stone buildings and gray-painted shutters, past a couple of restaurants and fashion stores, and pulled onto the side of the street.

There, he checked his mirrors one last time to ensure he had no surveillance. As had been the case during the previous forty-five minutes of random driving around the Seventh Arrondissement, there was nobody that was giving him any concern.

Pierre then reversed slowly around the corner and down a short, narrow cobbled street to his left, passing a Pilates studio, and continued carefully until he reached the dead end. There he parked the van, borrowed from Hassan's Unit 910 contact, next to a black metal pedestrian gate.

He hopped out of the van, which was facing forward,

ready in case a sharp getaway was required. He took a key from his pocket and used it to unlock the gate, which he slipped through, clicking it shut behind him.

Now he was in an even narrower alley, less than a meter wide, which also provided access via gates to a house behind a wall to his left and a small office building to his right. At the far end of the alley was a tall wooden gate, which Pierre also opened with a key. He went through and found himself in the rear walled courtyard of the tailor shop that fronted onto Rue de Saint-Simon.

Only five meters long by ten meters wide, the cobbled yard still had the metal table and two chairs that he and Henri had used for their coffee and cigarette breaks while working in the shop or planning the next Unit 910 operation.

At the right-hand side of the yard, between the main shop building and an outbuilding that was used for storage, was yet another narrow alley that led out into Rue de Saint-Simon via a high metal gate secured with a numerical keypad lock. But Pierre hadn't wanted to enter that way in case he was seen from the front of the building, and he made sure he stayed out of sight of anyone passing in the street.

The early morning sun cast a long shadow from the building he had just walked past over the courtyard. It was not yet seven o'clock, but Pierre had moved early after Hassan had received a slightly vague message late the previous night from CIRRUS. One of CIRRUS's sources in Rome had told him that Jayne Robinson and her colleagues were traveling from Israel to Paris sometime on Monday morning. There was no further detail.

It had been ten years since Pierre had left Paris for Los Angeles and more than eighteen months since he had last been into the tailor shop while on one of his frequent visits. However, the hidden back way into the shop hadn't changed.

The route, designed primarily as an emergency escape option, had been put in place by him and Henri in the event of something dramatic happening, like a raid by police or French special forces, or retribution from some business associate they had crossed through their arms smuggling or money laundering activities for Hezbollah.

Pierre and Hassan had decided it would be better for Pierre to visit the shop alone rather than put both of them at risk. Hassan had a couple of other tasks to carry out and would remain in his room in a small hotel half a kilometer away, ready to act as backup if required.

Cut into the cobbles, right up against the wall, was a watertight steel trapdoor mounted on hinges and secured with a large padlock. There were no signs that the lock had been broken or disturbed, so Pierre unlocked it, pulled his Heckler & Koch semiautomatic from his belt, flicked off the safety, and then cautiously lifted the hatch door.

Although no longer living in Paris, Pierre had always kept a full set of spare keys for the shop, just in case. On a couple of occasions, after changing the locks, Henri had mailed a new set to him in Los Angeles. There was no burglar alarm because neither brother wanted to risk sirens sounding and police searching the property. They had preferred to rely on the best locks they could buy instead.

Pierre waited, holding the pistol ready and half expecting someone to point a gun at him from inside. But all was quiet.

Below was a short flight of wooden steps that led down into the dark cellar of the building.

Pierre paused. This was going to be difficult.

He and his brother had formed the tailoring business more than twenty years earlier, operating under the name Charles & Philippe Simenon. They both had false passports and French driver's licenses in those names, which had occasionally proved useful. With Henri now dead, this visit held a particular poignancy.

The two brothers, like many identical twins, thought alike and had been a formidable partnership. Their parents, Jamal and Mona, had instilled in them the principles of Shia Islamism from an early age. Both became followers of Ayatollah Ruhollah Khomeini, who led the revolution in Iran after 1979. Although they grew up in France, they both felt aligned to their parents' original homeland and tried to support Khomeini in small ways, mainly by distributing leaflets.

Their support for Hezbollah became something quite different after Jamal's sister Nadine, their aunt, died in April 1996 during Operation Grapes of Wrath, a massive sixteen-day Israeli bombing campaign against southern Lebanon. The Israelis were trying to stop Hezbollah rocket attacks on towns near Galilee in northern Israel. Nadine was among 170 civilians killed after her legs were blown off.

Within four years, both Henri and Pierre, while training as tailors by day, had swapped leaflet distribution for assassinations by night and in their spare time. Running their own business had given the flexibility they needed to carry out operations as required by Beirut. The two brothers weren't just business partners and operational colleagues, they were best friends. Losing Henri had been a huge blow.

Standing in the tailor store now, Pierre forced himself to push his memories to one side. He needed to focus on security.

Given Henri was no longer around, the only other person who might conceivably have a viable reason to enter the building was a property management man who lived nearby and whom Henri used to monitor the place occasionally if he had a long overseas trip planned. However, Henri had specifically mentioned prior to his ultimately fatal trip to London that he hadn't requested his services, as the trip was intended to last only a few days.

The real risk in Pierre's mind was that, as he had mentioned to Hassan, security services might have been in the building since Henri's demise and installed hidden cameras or microphones to monitor any activity. The last thing he wanted now was for his face to be captured on-screen by French intelligence.

Therefore, Pierre first pulled on a black balaclava before flicking on a light switch beneath the hatch, which turned on a single lightbulb. He then made his way cautiously down the wooden steps and closed the hatch softly behind him.

At the bottom, he glanced around, scrutinizing the walls, corners, shelves, and ceiling. There were no telltale winking LED lights in the recesses, no sign of unusual black boxes or wiring he didn't recognize. But there was something else he would also check.

In the corner stood three crates of wine bottles. Behind them was a rusty black square metal grate of the type used for ventilation.

Pierre moved the wine crates, then crouched and removed two loose screws before shifting the heavy grate to one side. He then flicked on his phone flashlight and shone it into the cavity.

To his relief, nothing had been disturbed, it seemed. He rummaged around in the cavity, checking everything. Henri's boxes were still there, containing scores of plastic sports injury cold packs from which ammonium nitrate granules could be extracted. There was a container of heating oil, a burlap bag containing old cell phones and chargers, a couple of black canvas bags with two pistols and ammunition, and a handful of detonators. There were enough components to swiftly manufacture several small but powerful explosive devices.

Pierre was fairly sure the items wouldn't still be there if police or special forces had searched the building. They would be in some forensics laboratory instead. So the chances were that there were no surveillance devices hidden in the building.

Had the shop somehow been overlooked by the security forces when they made the inevitable background checks following his brother's death? It seemed that might be the case. It wouldn't be the first time European intelligence and security services failed to cooperate efficiently and key information slipped through the net. Unit 910 had taken advantage of such lapses several times before, especially where it involved the notoriously inefficient French.

Nevertheless, he wasn't going to take that for granted.

Pierre switched on three of the old cell phones. They all still had a partial charge, so Henri had obviously kept them topped up. He plugged in the chargers and connected the phones to charge them fully.

All the phones had a pair of red and white wires protruding from adaptors at the bottom; Henri had already prepared them as the key element in an electrical circuit, designed to detonate a bomb.

Then Pierre walked to the front of the cellar and climbed a short staircase to a wooden door, which he unlocked carefully. He edged open the door and peered through the gap.

The interior of the store was gloomy and dark, mainly because the metal roller shutter that covered the entire front of the shop was down. But there was enough light for Pierre to tell that nothing had obviously changed.

His eyes flicked over all the walls, corners, shelving, and recesses, searching for any sign of unusual devices. There was nothing obvious, so he reached around the door and flicked a light switch on and checked again, which confirmed his impression.

However, if the message Hassan had received about Robinson heading to Paris was correct, and assuming he and Hassan had now been compromised by Ghassan's phone, that wouldn't last for long.

Still wearing the balaclava, he stepped into the store and began to evaluate the volume of stock: the suits, jackets, trousers, waistcoats, and other items. He then went to a back room and did likewise with the rolls of material stacked on racks.

His initial intention had been to load the contents of the shop into the van and take it. The stock was worth thousands of euros, if not tens of thousands.

But now he forced himself to think logically.

Simply being on the premises was a significant risk, and it would take him probably a couple of hours to load the stock into the van. It was tempting, but he knew it would take too long and could cost him dearly.

Pierre shook his head. He hadn't survived this long by being foolish. And he didn't want to end up the same way as his twin brother.

He reluctantly decided to forget the stock—he had more than enough in his bank account, and there were much more valuable issues at stake here.

Rather, he would focus on what was more important: setting the stage for a potentially devastating attack with a multiple purpose. First, if Allah willed it, it would exact revenge on the person he viewed as ultimately responsible for taking Henri's life. And second, it would protect a critical and highly lucrative activity that was helping to facilitate Hezbollah's work on Allah's behalf in the Near East.

But first Pierre spent a few more minutes checking that Henri hadn't left any potentially incriminating evidence relating to his Hezbollah activities in the shop. As he had expected, there was nothing obvious—Henri had always been very careful, given the constant presence of other people in the store. Although a monitor screen and cables stood on the countertop, there was no computer attached to it and no sign of any other electronic device, apart from the cash register. What Henri had done with his laptop, he had no idea, but it certainly wasn't here. There was a handful of paper invoices and business cards on a shelf beneath the counter, but nothing out of the ordinary.

Pierre returned to the cellar and began preparing three improvised explosive devices. He had had plenty of practice over the years, much of it in tandem with Henri.

First he went through the routine of extracting the dry ammonium nitrate granules from the cold packs by slitting them open with a knife. Once he had about two kilograms of the stuff, he mixed it with a small amount of fuel oil to form a combustible mixture, known as ANFO.

Then he placed a third of the ANFO in a small cardboard mailing box and added a detonator connected to a small nine-volt battery. The final element was to connect one of the old cell phones, which were by now well charged, to the circuit and to fasten all the components in place with gaffer tape. If the phone was called, the circuit would be completed, and the detonator would be fired. There was enough explosive to kill anyone in the vicinity and wreck the store, without a doubt.

Pierre repeated the exercise twice more, then switched on the three phones. All of their numbers were written on stickers on the rear of the devices, so Pierre carefully inputted all three into his own phone and then checked the phones were all getting a good signal.

Just as he was finishing, his phone rang. It was Hassan, asking for an update, which Pierre briefly gave, conscious that he needed to get out of the building as quickly as possible.

When Pierre had finished the call, he then placed one cardboard box and its explosive contents next to the front door of the shop, beneath a couple of other empty boxes. He put another next to the trapdoor at the rear of the building, and the third beneath an old newspaper next to the internal door that led from the cellar to the store.

Finally, Pierre slipped Hassan's old burner phone, which they believed was now almost certainly compromised, from his pocket. He switched it on, checked the signal, and placed it on a shelf beneath the countertop, near to the cash register.

That would act as the cheese in his mousetrap.

For a few moments he stood, considering whether to remove the external padlock that secured the shutter at the front of the shop and the one that fastened the trapdoor at the rear of the building in order to make it easy for his intended victims to enter. But he knew that if intelligence officers wanted to get into a property, they would do it, locks or no locks. And he didn't want to arouse any suspicions. Everything had to look normal.

Then Pierre returned to the cellar and headed for the trapdoor through which he had entered, his surprise reception party ready in case the place received a certain set of visitors.

The only remaining requirement was to position himself somewhere that gave him a vantage point over the tailor shop, so that if the opportunity arose, the explosions could be timed to perfection. He had specified what he needed to Hassan, who was making the arrangements.

* * *

Monday, July 4, 2016

Paris

Jayne waited as Vic Walter adjusted his metal-rimmed glasses, propped his elbows on the desk, and clasped his graying temples with his palms as he studied the printed report in front of him.

"The NSA has had a productive day or so, it seems," he said, his voice just as gravelly as ever. "Hassan's two numbers have opened up quite a useful network of other contacts."

He looked over his glasses at Jayne, who was sitting with Rafael in a small meeting room in the CIA station on the top floor of the stone four-story United States embassy on the corner of Avenue Gabriel and Rue Boissy d'Anglas, a long stone's throw southeast of the Élysée Palace. Through the window, Jayne could see the cobbled expanse of the Place de la Concorde beyond the clump of trees and the concrete bollards that lined the front of the embassy complex.

Vic had asked Jayne and Rafael to come to the CIA station on the grounds that it was easier for him, as deputy director, to get them in there than it was for Rafael to get him into the Israeli embassy on the other side of the palace.

"What have they found?" Jayne asked.

"In the past few months, Hassan has used his Lebanese number to call a phone that they believe is owned by a man who has until recently been living in Los Angeles and was in Toluca, Mexico, at precisely the same time as you two were two months ago."

Jayne tried to process what she was hearing. "What, they think he is linked to the Iranians?"

Vic nodded. "We think he is the guy who got away—the one you and the Feds didn't capture in Mexico. If we're correct, he headed back into the US from Mexico soon after that operation."

An unidentified gunman who was part of the captured group had somehow escaped the dragnet and fled Toluca International Airport.

"What's his name?" Jayne asked.

"The NSA say he's Pierre Fekkai."

"Fekkai? That's the same name as the guy MI5 shot dead in London when he tried to kill me and Navai's parents at the safe house. Henri Fekkai, wasn't it?"

During the hunt for Navai, a marksman from the British internal security service, MI5, had belatedly shot dead a bomber who pushed an explosive device through the mail slot of the front door of a safe house where Jayne was questioning Navai's parents. Two other MI5 officers had died in the blast.

"It's Henri's twin brother, they believe. He used to live here in France but then moved to the US in 2006, according to Homeland. The NSA says he's been living in Los Angeles, in Westwood. They've put together quite a jigsaw puzzle on him in the past twenty-four hours."

"So Henri had a twin brother? That's news to me."

"News to all of us," Vic said.

"How did we not know—"

"Wait, there's more," Vic interrupted as he continued to scan down the report in front of him.

He applied an index finger to the page and moved it down the sheet, then again looked over his glasses at Jayne, then at Rafael. "Take a guess where the NSA located Pierre Fekkai's phone on the afternoon of June 22?"

Jayne shook her head. "I'm not some kind of cell phone clairvoyant, Vic."

But then it dawned on her. She knew where she had been on the day after that, Thursday, June 23—visiting Portland Head Light with Joe, looking out over Casco Bay, when her phone had rung, with Michael Gray on the line.

"The twenty-second was the Wednesday. My God." She

stared at Vic for a couple of seconds. "DC. Massachusetts Avenue? Is that what you're telling me?"

Vic nodded slowly.

"Circumstantial. But obviously . . . " Her voice trailed off.

"Obviously," Vic said. "He must then have traveled to France using a false identity, because there are no flight or passport records under his own name. Possibly, even likely, he might have been responsible for Cardinal Baltrami's death in Rome."

Jayne looked at Rafael, who was looking as stunned as she felt.

"So where is he now?" Rafael asked. "Unit 8200 has found no signal from either of those phones for the past couple of days. I'm waiting for them to come up with something. Your people seem to have beaten them to it—for once." Rafael let a faint grin creep outward from the corner of his mouth.

"Don't worry," Vic said. "The NSA said exactly the same thing. It seems both phones have been turned off since Saturday. However, they pinpointed a latest location for them."

"Somewhere in Paris, in line with Unit 8200 findings, presumably?" Rafael asked.

"Of course. About a kilometer or so south of here on the other side of the Seine. A café called Le Gévaudan, in Rue du Bac, near to the metro station. There were quite a few other locations all in that same area, too." Vic peered down at the report again. "In fact, the NSA says here that nearly all of them are within two kilometers of a certain street, Rue de Saint-Simon. In fact, two of the pinpointed locations are on that street, which is in the Seventh Arrondissement. They spoke to MI5 and were told by them that Henri Fekkai was running a shop—a tailor's—on that street when he died in London. It's called Charles & Philippe Simenon, but presumably it was some sort of front business, a cover, for his Hezbollah activities. There can be little doubt that his twin brother was fully aware of the business and was probably involved in it before leaving Paris for the US."

Jayne and Rafael both sat and stared at Vic.

"Aren't you a little surprised that MI5 didn't inform you, or the French, about the tailor's shop previously?" Jayne asked eventually. "I mean, if that angle had been pursued by them, or by the French, and if a link had been made to a twin brother who had moved to the United States, then it's possible these cardinal deaths could have been avoided."

Vic spread his hands wide. "I'm not disagreeing with you. Someone's screwed up, I would say. That's assuming our perpetrator is this Pierre Fekkai."

"How could they miss it?"

"The person my NSA contact spoke to said it appeared to have slipped through the net. There seems to have been an assumption that given Henri Fekkai died in London, there was no need to pursue his affairs any further at the British end. So they left it to the French. But nobody passed any details to the French, and so it all went into someone's inbox at MI5 headquarters and stayed there. Of course, French intelligence never requested the information because they didn't know it existed."

"What a bloody mess," Jayne muttered.

She picked up her cup of coffee and took a sip. It had gone cold, so she put it back on the saucer. "So I'm guessing that French intelligence or the police won't have searched that shop?"

Vic gave a shake of the head. "My contact at the NSA asked MI5 the question. But obviously, if they didn't know about the shop, they couldn't search it."

As he spoke, Vic's phone beeped. He scrutinized the screen and tapped in a code to read the incoming message.

Vic leaned forward, hunching his shoulders. "Got an

update here from the NSA. They've just had a signal from Hassan's Lebanese phone."

"Bloody hell," Jayne said. "Where is it?"

"Same area again. They say it's on Rue de Saint-Simon." He looked up from his phone. "It's in the tailor shop."

"We'd better get down to that shop ourselves and look. The bastard must be in there right now."

CHAPTER TWENTY-ONE

Monday, July 4, 2016
   Paris

The discussion about whether to involve the French intelligence services or police in the operation to surveil and possibly enter the tailor shop on Rue de Saint-Simon had been a short one. It had ended with Vic walking out of the room, saying he needed a comfort break.

Jayne had watched him leave. She knew it was his way of telling the rest of them to just get on with the job and forget the usual diplomatic niceties and protocols involved with operating in another intelligence service's backyard.

An hour and a half later, she was glad he had done so. She, along with Rafael and the acting deputy chief of the CIA's Paris station, Francine Dutoit, were sitting in the rear of a soundproofed blue Citroën Relay van at the end of Rue de Saint-Simon on the corner of Rue de Grenelle.

The van had been converted from its usual commercial configuration. In the cargo space there were eight seats, and the steel bulkhead dividing the driver's cabin from the rear had been replaced by a one-way Perspex screen, so passengers could remain unseen from outside yet get a clear view out of the front windshield. There were also a series of fish-eye peepholes, variously disguised through the adroit use of magnetic signage stuck to the sides and rear of the van that gave it the appearance of a pharmacy delivery vehicle. A microphone and speaker system allowed passengers to speak to the driver, who in this case was another Paris CIA officer.

After some discussion, it had been decided that Vic and the acting chief of Paris station, Paul Wilkie, should remain out of sight two streets away in a Peugeot sedan, ensuring they were on hand in case they were needed.

An advance party of two surveillance officers who had been involved in planning at the CIA station, Patrick and Dominique, had already been up and down the street, posing as guests at the hotel near the Charles & Philippe Simenon tailor's shop. They had reported back via secure radio and via the secure group messaging facility set up by techs at the CIA station that the shop appeared deserted. The green front roller shutter was pulled down and covered the entire frontage, including the door and window. The shutter was secured with a large padlock. A gate immediately to the left of the shop that led into a narrow alley between the store and an outbuilding was locked, the officers added.

A third surveillance officer, Antonin, had been to the rear of the tailor shop, approaching via a narrow lane that led off Rue Paul-Louis Courier. On the pretext of visiting a neighboring house, he had got into an alley leading to a courtyard at the rear of the building but reported that there appeared to be nobody in the yard.

However, Antonin also reported that a man was working at the rear of the small store directly next door to the tailor's, Caves de Saint-Germain, which was a *cave à vins*, a wine merchant. The store, an old-fashioned place, was closed, but the man appeared to be repairing the catch on a window above the door that led onto a courtyard next to the tailor's yard. He wasn't visible from the front of the store.

Jayne, Rafael, and Dutoit sat in the van and listened to the surveillance reports coming in on Dutoit's secure radio.

They all felt slightly confused by the statements that there was no sign of occupancy, as an update from the NSA stated that Hassan's Lebanese cell phone was still showing up at the site. Was Hassan holed up inside, then? This might be a golden chance to take him by surprise, if so.

In a box on the floor of the van next to Jayne were two Berettas and a Walther 9mm pistol that Dutoit had procured from the station's weapons locker, together with spare magazines. They also had ski masks, rubber gloves, plus a handful of plastic cable ties and gaffer tape in case they needed to restrain Hassan, Pierre Fekkai, or anyone else they might find there.

Jayne also had her personal set of lock picks and rakes tucked safely in her pocket, in case it was required.

She knew that if they had gone down the official diplomatic channels and approached Alain Imbot, the recently appointed director of the Direction Générale de la Sécurité Extérieure, the DGSE, it was unlikely they would have gotten clearance to run the operation by this time tomorrow, nor possibly the day after, or at all. She knew Imbot from more than twelve years earlier, when he had been operating in Bosnia and Serbia at the same time as she was working there for MI6, and he had always been a prickly and highly political character.

The Mossad, the CIA, and MI6 had all been here before. There had been many hostile exchanges of views and threats between them and Imbot's predecessors over similar breaches of protocol in the past.

Dutoit, an elfin woman in her late thirties with a sharp nose, auburn hair that was cut a little shorter than Jayne's, and intelligent dark eyes, leaned forward in her seat on the driver's side of the van. She peered through the windshield and down the street.

"I suggest you and Rafael go to the store and see if you can speak to the man working in the *cave à vins*," Dutoit said. "He might have seen someone at the tailor's, or he just might know something. Knock on the front door, say you're a customer and were wondering if they are open. I'll stay here in the van and back you up."

Jayne nodded. That was a sensible suggestion. They would need a way to get into the tailor shop, either through the front, which seemed unlikely, or the rear. Perhaps the workman knew something that could help with that.

"While you're doing that, the surveillance team can go to the courtyard at the back," Dutoit said. "Perhaps they can find a way in that way and let you in. They have bolt-cutting equipment if needed."

Jayne was impressed by Dutoit. She made sensible suggestions rather than try to show off. Jayne looked at Rafael, who nodded.

Jayne picked up the Walther, pushed it into her belt, and put a spare magazine in her pocket. She then stuffed a mask, gloves, cable ties, and tape into the pocket of her jacket, which she zipped up, covering the handgun. Rafael took one of the Berettas.

"Let's go, then," Jayne said. "If Hassan's there, we should be able to flush him out of either the front or the back." She paused. "There is of course the possibility that this is some kind of a trap."

Dutoit looked at her. "True. But what are you going to do? Just back off and not go in?"

Jayne patted the handgun in her belt and shook her head. That wasn't an option and they all knew it.

She checked the van's mirrors and peepholes to ensure nobody was watching, then opened the side door of the van, and they both climbed out.

* * *

Monday, July 4, 2016
    Paris

The green door to Caves de Saint-Germain half opened, and a well-built man wearing paint-splattered coveralls and holding a wrench looked out. He nodded at Jayne and raised an inquiring eyebrow. "Bonjour?"

"Bonjour. I'm a customer of the Simenon tailor's next door," Jayne began in fluent French. "My father buys his suits there. This is my brother." She indicated toward Rafael. "I need to speak to the owner of the tailor's. Have you seen him, or has anyone else been there?"

The man, now wearing a slightly suspicious look, shook his head slightly. "I wish I had. Not for some time, a couple of months. The shutter's been down since April." He paused and put a hand to his graying temple. "Why do you need him?"

Jayne had prepared her lines and didn't hesitate. "As I said, my father's a customer. But also we needed to speak to him about a business matter. An unpaid debt, actually."

Her guess was that with the sudden fate suffered by Henri Fekkai, the shop had not been open for some time. There were highly likely to be creditors who were owed money, so this was hopefully a viable position to take.

The man snorted. "Pah. Another one. You can join me in the line."

Immediately, Jayne's mind began to whirr. "Ah, so we're not alone, then. There is quite a significant sum of money involved in our case. So I guess you have no idea where Monsieur Simenon is?"

The man shook his head. "Gone, probably run off somewhere. Abandoned his ship. Knowing the way he operated, I'm not surprised."

He doesn't know he's dead, then.

Jayne tried to put on a quizzical expression. "What do you mean by that? Has there been something going on I should know about?"

The man glanced a little furtively up and down the street, then at Jayne and Rafael. "I'm sorry, but I don't know you. I'm not going to discuss this. You'll need to go through the owner's attorney."

"Wait a moment," Jayne said. "Have you not seen anyone at all in the shop?"

"No. Not at all."

That was odd, she thought, given the phone signal reportedly coming from inside.

"I don't understand," Jayne said. "I thought there was someone around. Can we just—"

But the man just shook his head and shut the door before she could finish.

Jayne cursed inwardly.

She looked at Rafael and lowered her voice. "Shit. I had a feeling he was going to say something."

Rafael nodded. "Me too."

"Should have introduced ourselves. Didn't even get to that."

Rafael shrugged. "We didn't get a chance. We could try one more time. Tell him we have contacts who could help him and we're willing to share our information."

Jayne paused, then nodded. She turned and knocked

sharply twice on the door.

A few seconds later it opened again.

"What?" the man said. There was an irritated note in his voice. "I said speak to the owner's attorney, not me. I can't help you."

"No, but we may be able to help you," Jayne said. "We have good contacts who specialize in this type of situation. We're happy to share our contacts and our knowledge if you're willing to do likewise."

The man put his hands on his hips. Eventually he gave a short, curt nod. "Come in. I'll speak to you inside."

He held the door open while Jayne and Rafael walked in. Stepping into the wine merchant's was like going back in time, Jayne thought. There was a long chipped wooden counter, bottles standing haphazardly on shelves and on the tops of old wine barrels, and a chalkboard with the latest bargains scribbled in yellow. The whole place appeared dirty.

"I'm Sebastian Blondel," the man said as he closed the door. "And you?"

"Ashima Caire," Jayne said, using the new alias she had deployed on the West Bank.

"And I'm Michel," said Rafael in a perfect French accent.

"Come this way," Blondel said as he walked through a swinging door to the rear of the store, where he indicated to a circular table and chairs in a kitchen area. "Sit. I can tell you a few things about the business next door."

Jayne and Rafael sat and Blondel took a seat across from them. He placed both palms on the table and took a deep breath.

"First, a bit of background information. I run a property management and maintenance company," Blondel began. "I've been doing maintenance work for Monsieur Simenon for the past couple of years, when required, and likewise for this wine merchant, along with other businesses in this neighborhood. So I have gotten to know both businesses and their owners reasonably well. And I can tell you that the tailor's is not all that it seems. I've been spending a lot of time working here the past few weeks, and I've spoken to quite a few people who have come to the door of the store, asking for the owner and saying they are owed money. You're not the first."

"Who are they? His suppliers?" Jayne asked.

Blondel inclined his head. "Some are suppliers. But there have been others."

"Who else, then?" Jayne asked.

"Nobody gave their name, apart from one. But I got talking to a few of them, and they were making wild allegations about him. Some claimed that he was involved in activities that are on the wrong side of the law." Now there were a few beads of sweat visible on Blondel's creased forehead.

Jayne consciously raised both eyebrows and folded her arms. "Really? What type of activities?"

"I don't know, they didn't say precisely, but I have seen evidence that Simenon is not his real name. His true name is Fekkai, Henri Fekkai, I understand. One man told me Fekkai appeared to be involved with Hezbollah and had played a role in their military operations here in France. A terrorist, basically."

"My God," Jayne said.

"And that's not all," he continued. "He's apparently involved in fundraising for Hezbollah too, the same man said."

Jayne sat back in her chair. A sudden buzz of adrenaline rushed through her. She was surprised that Blondel had found out about the Hezbollah connection. But if money was owed to shady people, then perhaps anger levels would be high and lips might be loose. She knew that Hezbollah had widespread fundraising and money laundering networks all over the world, particularly in Europe, North America, and Asia.

"It sounds like you've reported none of this to the police," Jayne said.

Blondel shook his head. "I don't dare report it. This is Hezbollah we're talking about. Their tentacles go far. I'd likely end up at the bottom of the Seine. To be honest, I've been trying to forget about it, brush it under the carpet. And I was doing just that until you turned up." He gave her an expectant look. "But you said you might be able to help me. Your contacts."

"Yes, with more information, with a lead, we can help."

Blondel inclined his head. "Go on, then."

"You said one man gave his name," Jayne said. "Who was that? The same one who told you about the Hezbollah connection?"

Blondel shook his head. "A different one. Now what was his name?" He looked up at the ceiling, as if seeking inspiration, and screwed up his face. "I can't recall the name. Sorry. We had a chat and he said very little, but when I asked him why he needed to reach Monsieur Simenon, he said he was a business associate who supplied him with cloth for his suits. I pressed him a little, and he let slip that he hadn't seen Monsieur Simenon for some time and was worried about him. He was trying to downplay the whole thing, to show it wasn't urgent, but his body language said something different. He said he was only in Paris for one day and seemed quite stressed, and I remember wondering why that was so."

Jayne's phone vibrated in her pocket as a message arrived. She discreetly took the phone from her pocket and glanced at the screen. It was from Dutoit.

Team now at rear.

"Sorry, just to go back to the man's name," Rafael said. "Is there a way of getting it, if it's slipped your mind?"

Blondel thought for a moment. "Well, I did ask him if he had a business card. He hesitated but eventually gave me one, and there were contact details on it—but I don't have it. I told him I'd pass it on to Monsieur Simenon, and I put it under the counter next door."

"You were working next door at the time?" Jayne asked.

"Yes. Finishing off a job."

Jayne glanced across at Rafael. She could see he was trying hard to contain himself.

"Could we go and get the card?" Rafael asked.

Blondel shrugged. "I guess we can." He reached into his pocket and took out a set of keys. "We can use these. I have a spare set for when I need to get in there to do any maintenance and if Simenon is not around."

Jayne tried hard not to show the surprise she was feeling. But it immediately crossed her mind that by using the keys, they could avoid having the surveillance team use their cutting equipment to break in—which, no matter how careful they were, could attract unwanted attention from nearby residents.

"Are the keys for the front or back door?" Jayne asked.

"The front. For the shutter locks and the door. They are the only keys I have."

The big issue in Jayne's mind would be the reaction of Hassan, assuming he was inside the shop, as the phone signal indicated. If he realized they were coming in the front, he might try to run out the back, in which case the surveillance team could nail him.

Jayne exchanged glances with Rafael, who gave a slight nod of his head.

"Okay, let's do it," Jayne said.

She took out her phone and tapped out a rapid note on the secure group messaging facility.

Stop entry at rear. Entering at front with key. Be on standby in case target exits via rear.

Blondel stood. "I've just remembered the name of that

guy. It was Alberto Casartelli. Yes, that's it. Casartelli. I also remember he said his company makes clothing."

"Casartelli?" Jayne asked. "Sounds Italian."

"Ah, yes, sorry, that was the other thing. I remember now —he also mentioned he had traveled from Rome. He must have been Italian, yes."

Rome?

Jayne's eyebrows shot up. "And his contact details are on the card?" she asked.

Blondel nodded. "Yes. If you want them, come, let's go." Then he stepped toward the door.

CHAPTER TWENTY-TWO

Monday, July 4, 2016
    Paris

Pierre hunched over the hotel room windowsill, his finger tapping unconsciously on the painted wooden surface next to his cell phone. He pulled the lace curtains back a little so he could see down Rue de Saint-Simon and scanned the street in both directions.

There were only a few cars and two vans parked there, and only one pedestrian, an old man, making his way somewhat unsteadily past the Hôtel Duc de Saint-Simon, where he and Hassan were encamped in a fourth-floor room that overlooked the street.

On Pierre's cell phone display were three preprogrammed numbers, ready for him to press the green call button.

Hassan, who knew the hotel well from previous trips to Paris to visit Pierre and Henri, had secured the room earlier that day. It was on the top floor of a wing of the hotel to the right of the main hotel entrance. It was perfectly positioned, with an excellent view of the street and the tailor shop and also with a line of sight right down the narrow alley to the left of the shop into the rear courtyard.

At the end of the corridor outside the room was an external fire escape that led down into the hotel gardens, from where it was possible to hop over a low wall into an alleyway that led into the neighboring street, Rue de Grenelle. The Volkswagen van borrowed from Hassan's Unit 910 contact was parked there, ready as a getaway vehicle if necessary.

The room, in a well-maintained and very luxurious boutique hotel, had cost Hassan over 300 euro. It was furnished in an upmarket but understated style, a throwback to the grand era of Parisian hotels, with mustard-colored velvet lampshades and matching curtains, rose-patterned wallpaper, restored antique furniture, and nineteenth-century watercolor landscape prints hanging on the walls.

Pierre's eyes flicked between the door of the tailor shop at the front of the building across the street and the courtyard that was partly visible behind it.

A short while earlier, Pierre and Hassan had seen two men and a woman arrive in the courtyard via the alleyway that led from the rear of the building. One had a chunky backpack slung over his shoulder. The suspicion was that they were security or intelligence officers and were quite likely linked to Jayne Robinson and Rafael Levy.

That in itself was enough to put Pierre's senses on full alert.

Then, a few minutes later, two other people, whom Hassan confidently identified as Robinson and Levy, emerged from a van at the end of the street near the corner with Rue de Grenelle. The pair walked to the tailor's, paused, then went to the neighboring wine store, where they knocked on the front door.

After a short delay, the door had opened, and a man appeared whom Pierre recognized as Sebastian Blondel, the property manager previously employed by his brother to maintain the premises and who also worked for the wine store owner. Following a short conversation, all three had disappeared inside the wine store.

They were still in there.

Pierre glanced sideways at Hassan. "You're completely certain those two are Robinson and Levy?" he asked.

Hassan nodded. "I should know. I sent photographs of both of them to your brother only a few months ago with instructions to terminate them. As it was—" Hassan stopped.

"As it was, Henri got terminated," Pierre muttered to himself. Not that he needed reminding.

Hassan looked embarrassed. "I knew the bastards would turn up. Revenge will be sweet."

Pierre grunted. He agreed it had been highly likely they would turn up at some point. However, he hadn't expected them to appear quite so swiftly.

They lapsed into silence, both of them focused on the wine shop door opposite. Five minutes passed.

"Robinson's coming out," Hassan suddenly said.

Sure enough, through the window there were signs of movement inside the wine merchant's, and seconds later, Robinson and Levy reappeared, followed by Blondel.

"What does Blondel know?" Hassan asked.

"Nothing, as far as I know," Pierre said. "I'm certain my brother would have told him nothing. He's just the maintenance man."

Blondel pulled a set of keys from his pocket, stepped to the roller shutter that covered the frontage of the tailor's, bent down, and unlocked a large padlock that secured it.

Pierre knew that the shutter could be operated electronically from within the store but could also be moved up and down manually once the padlock was removed and a second locking mechanism was undone.

Blondel pulled the padlock from the shutter, selected another key, and inserted it into a second lock at the side of the shutter, then turned the key and removed it. Finally he began to lift the shutter from the bottom.

"The bastard's letting them in," Hassan said. "He can't do that. They must have bribed him. They obviously think I'm in there because of the phone signal."

Pierre glanced at the back courtyard. "Those three at the rear are still standing near the trapdoor." He had sudden moment of realization. "We can take all of them out in one hit, front and back."

He turned to Hassan, who was staring intently at the scene unfolding in front of him.

"Yes, just wait a second until the front shutter's up so they get the full force of it, then blast them," Hassan said.

Sure enough, two of the three people at the rear of the building were visible, standing hands on hips, looking downward, presumably watching the third person who was out of their line of sight.

"I'm going to trigger all three devices now," Pierre said decisively. "This is for Henri."

He moved his finger to the phone.

CHAPTER TWENTY-THREE

Monday, July 4, 2016
Paris

Jayne glanced discreetly up and down the street as Blondel undid the padlock and then another lock before pulling up the shutter.

The last thing she wanted was for any complications with the police and security services.

Out of habit, she pulled a pair of thin rubber gloves from her pocket and put them on. If they were going into the tailor's, she didn't want to leave any fingerprints. Rafael immediately did likewise. She also had her hand positioned on the Walther that she had stuffed into her belt, in case Hassan opened fire as they tried to enter.

There was a definite possibility this was some kind of trap. She and Rafael needed to be ready.

Blondel pushed the shutter up to the top, then pulled a second set of keys from his pocket. He took a step toward the recess that housed the front door.

"Let me go in first," Jayne said. "I'm not sure what—"

But she was interrupted by a massive explosion from somewhere at the rear of the building.

Before Jayne could move, the blast blew out several small glass panes from a side window to the left of the building, only a couple of meters from where she was standing. It also sent a maze of jagged cracks across the main store window and the pane in the door. It was so violent she felt the ground vibrate beneath her feet.

She reacted instantly.

There could be more blasts to come.

"Get out!" she yelled at Blondel. "Booby trap!"

Jayne took two rapid steps sideways and dove headfirst like a swimmer for the open doorway of the Caves de Saint-Germain wine merchant, landing on her knees and elbows on the stone doorstep and then sliding over the threshold.

As she rolled over, she caught a glimpse of Rafael sprawling on the floor behind her and Blondel's hefty body lumbering toward the doorway.

A fraction of a second later, all hell broke loose.

There came a second deafening, pounding blast from the tailor shop next door that blew half of the store out across the street and into the hotel frontage.

The roar of the explosion sent orange flames, clouds of dust and smoke flying at high speed into the street. Fragments of plaster, glass, wood, and concrete were splattered shotgun-style all over the area, smashing several windows of the hotel opposite. Some of it blew back into the wine store entrance, causing Jayne to start coughing uncontrollably.

A devastating tangle of trousers, jackets, and debris littered the pavement.

Jayne tried to cover her face with her arm to avoid being choked by the dust, just as a huge chunk of plaster fell from the wall that separated the two buildings, landing on the shop floor just a meter or two from where she was lying. Another large piece of plaster fell, then another. For a moment, she was concerned that the entire dividing wall was going to cave in.

Then, a moment or two later, came a third blast that was almost a carbon copy of the second. This time it seemed that all the remaining loose wreckage from inside the tailor store was blown outward in one swoop, as if it were all being sucked by the central funnel of a tornado.

By now Jayne's ears were ringing, and although she could see Rafael mouthing, trying to say something to her, she couldn't hear a single word.

But then behind Rafael, she caught sight of a body lying prone on the ground in the store's entrance, blood pouring from both the stump of an arm that had been ripped off and a chunk of flesh and hair torn from his scalp.

Jayne involuntarily clapped one hand to her mouth and felt her stomach twist in a tight knot inside her. She knew instantly that Blondel was dead.

"Bastards," she muttered.

Then she had another thought.

What about the team at the back?

* * *

Monday, July 4, 2016
    Paris

Pierre tapped the first number on his cell phone, hit the call button, and waited for it to ring.

Boom . . .

Then he moved as fast as he could to the next number.

But although he was concentrating on his phone, not on

what was happening across the street, he immediately realized as the first of the three explosions erupted that in his haste, he had somehow triggered the IEDs in a different order than he'd intended.

So did Hassan.

The guttural sounds of Hassan's native Arabic at full volume, coupled with the Lebanese way of using words in a most pointed way, penetrated Pierre's right ear.

"*Kharaye feek*," Hassan growled a split second after the first blast had erupted. "Shit on you. Wrong one. That's the back."

Pierre felt his scalp tighten but didn't respond immediately as he tapped on the next number.

Boom . . .

"Wait, one more," Pierre muttered as he again tapped on the screen.

Boom . . .

"They've gotten away," Hassan said, raising his voice above the din from outside. They're back in the damned wine shop. You blew them in the wrong order, you fool."

"*What?*" Pierre said, as he looked up from his device.

But he knew.

Hassan let rip with another Arabic curse. "You blew the bomb at the back first, you idiot."

"I don't know how—"

"The back one went off first!" Hassan yelled. "Robinson then escaped into the wine store before the front one went off. The Mossad agent too."

Pierre stared across the street, although little was visible because of the clouds of dust, smoke, and debris that were swirling around below.

Then he remembered.

He had been about to put the devices in place in the shop when Hassan had called and distracted him. When he had returned to his task, he must have somehow mixed up the boxes containing the IEDs. That was the only explanation he could think of.

Then, through the clouds of dust, he saw a body lying on the ground right outside the door of the wine store.

"Who's that, then?" Pierre demanded, pointing downward.

"That's your maintenance man."

"At least there's nothing left for them to find," Pierre said. "Not that there ever was." He gazed across the street at the wreckage.

Hassan turned, marched to the back of the room, picked up an apple from a fruit bowl, and flung it against the wall above the bed, where it smashed into pieces all over the rose-patterned wallpaper and velvet eiderdown.

Pierre felt his entire body tense up.

"*Dhasho b teezak*," Hassan spat. "Shove it up your ass. Come on. Let's get out of here. Quick. I knew I should have brought the sniper rifle. Then there would have been no mistake. Screw you and your explosives."

He marched toward the door. Pierre grabbed the phone and his bag that was on the bed and followed.

* * *

Monday, July 4, 2016
    Paris

A cloud of dust rose from Jayne's clothing as she stood and brushed off the plaster particles and debris that had showered over her, coughing nonstop as she did so.

She indicated with her thumb toward the rear of the Caves de Saint-Germain building. "Out the back," she spluttered to Rafael, who to her relief had also stood and appeared to be uninjured, although was also coughing. "Might be a sniper or something out front."

Again Jayne's gaze returned to the corpse of Sebastian Blondel, which lay in the recessed entrance to the store. She exhaled sharply and shut her eyes momentarily.

Yet again . . .

"Go, then," Rafael said, also glancing back at Blondel. "There's nothing we can do for him, Jayne. Nothing."

She grimaced, then turned and strode through the swinging doors, past the table and chairs where they had been sitting earlier, and through to the rear door. A toolbox stood on the floor near the door, and a couple of screwdrivers and a hammer lay next to it, together with a new window fastener and a pack of screws. That was where Blondel had evidently been working.

Jayne opened the door and walked out into a small courtyard, expecting to find a scene of devastation to match that at the front of the store.

To her surprise, there wasn't.

Immediately she heard voices from the other side of a redbrick wall that separated the courtyard from the one next door. She walked to the wall and peered over.

There were Antonin and Patrick over Dominique, who was sitting on the ground, clutching the back of her head with both hands, which Jayne could see were covered in blood.

Behind Dominique was a steel trapdoor that had clearly been blown open by the first explosion. The trapdoor, about a meter square, had been blasted virtually off its hinges and was sticking upward at an angle—it was mangled, twisted, and now completely unusable.

"Is she all right?" Jayne asked.

Antonin turned around. "She got blown backward when it

went off. Smashed her head on the cobbles. In fact it knocked all three of us over. She came off worst. But she'll be okay, I think."

Jayne let out a breath, then hauled herself up the wall, using holes in the brickwork for footholds, and vaulted over the top, with Rafael close behind.

"Do we need to get her to hospital?" Jayne asked.

Patrick nodded. "We'll use the van. Don't want an ambulance coming here and the crew asking questions."

"Looks like you were all lucky to get away with it," Rafael said.

Patrick nodded again. "Sonofabitch. It was booby trapped. We got saved by the trapdoor. Thankfully the blast went off before we'd gotten it open. We saw your message and stopped work on it. Another few seconds or so, if it was open . . . " He let his voice trail away.

"We'd better get moving," Antonin said. "Police will be here any minute. I'll speak to Francine now. She can fetch us from the end of the dead-end street."

He took his phone from his pocket, dialed a number, clamped it to his ear, and began to speak rapidly.

Dominique hauled herself to her feet, looking very disoriented. She wobbled a little, and Jayne reached out and caught her arm. Patrick took her other arm, and together they guided her toward the gate to the alley at the rear of the courtyard.

In the distance, sirens began to wail. This was going to be touch and go. The last thing Jayne wanted was to be caught up in what was certain to be a prolonged and highly complicated police investigation.

She doubted the bomber, who had to be Pierre Fekkai, was now anywhere in the vicinity. He must have been nearby to have timed the explosions just as they arrived at the tailor's door, she assumed, but he would almost certainly have fled as soon as the devices went off.

They made their way to the end of the dead-end street, just as the CIA Citroën Relay van pulled up outside a Pilates studio on Rue Paul-Louis Courier.

Jayne helped Dominique into the rear of the vehicle, where Francine steered her into a seat and fastened her seat belt. Jayne climbed in and collapsed into a seat next to Francine, feeling suddenly exhausted. Rafael took a seat on the other side, as did Antonin and Patrick.

Francine turned to Jayne. "Are you all right? You're not looking great."

"Not feeling great, no." Jayne wiped her brow, which was feeling clammy.

"What the hell happened?"

"Let's go. I'll tell you in a minute," Jayne said. She suddenly felt a little faint.

The street was one-way, and the CIA driver had obviously realized the only route out going forward was down Rue de Saint-Simon, which was now blocked with debris from the explosions.

So he slammed the Citroën into reverse, let out the clutch and, with engine and gearbox whining, reversed at high speed for more than fifty meters to the junction with Rue du Bac, thankfully meeting no traffic coming the other way. There he braked hard, shoved the gear shift into first, and, with a squeal of tires, shot off down Rue du Bac.

As the van set off, Jayne caught a glimpse of flashing blue and red roof lights as a police car entered Rue de Saint-Simon at high speed.

"We need to get Dominique to a hospital," Jayne said. "Although maybe a little farther away, if possible."

"That's where we're headed," Francine said. "Lariboisière

Hospital, north of the river. The embassy people use it. They say the medics are discreet."

Jayne nodded. She took out her phone and sent Vic a secure short message to let him know what had happened and where they were going. He could follow with the station chief, Wilkie, and she and Francine would brief them both when they caught up.

"Now, tell me what the hell happened," Francine said when they had put a safe distance between them and Rue de Saint-Simon.

Jayne quickly ran through the sequence of events that had led to Blondel's death and Dominique's injury.

"The whole thing stinks of a setup," Jayne said. "I had a feeling it might be. Hassan's phone giving away his apparent location inside the tailor's being the centerpiece of it, but him nowhere in sight. If those IEDs had gone off in a different order, Rafael and I would have been gone, as well as Blondel. We're actually very fortunate the entire team wasn't wiped out."

Francine grimaced. "You're right about that. And that man Blondel died for nothing?"

It was then that Jayne realized she hadn't mentioned the one potentially significant piece of information they had culled from Blondel before his awful demise.

"Not quite for nothing," she said. "We actually got one lead. The name of a businessman, Alberto Casartelli, who told Blondel he was a close associate, a supplier, of Henri Fekkai and hadn't seen him for some time and was worried about him."

"He was from here in Paris?"

"No, Rome," Jayne said. "That's the point—he was from Rome. If he's a close associate of Henri Fekkai, a Hezbollah paid killer, and is from Rome, then in the context of the cardinals' killings we should get him thoroughly checked out."

"Makes sense." Francine paused, a thoughtful look on her face. "Let's get the NSA to run traces on that name. It might give us something useful."

"I'll get Vic to speak to the NSA," Jayne said. "Definitely worth a try, I agree."

"But in the meantime, you do seem to have a serious problem, don't you?"

Jayne knew precisely what Francine was talking about. And it was indeed a major problem.

"Yes," she said. "Every time, they know when we're coming and where we are. The question is, how?"

CHAPTER TWENTY-FOUR

Monday, July 4, 2016
   Paris

There was a strained silence around the long oval table in the CIA station meeting room. It was always the same pattern inside intelligence agencies after a fatality during an operation, whether or not it involved one of the service's own people.

Jayne and Rafael had just given an extensive briefing to Vic and Francine about what had happened on Rue de Saint-Simon, supplemented with a full contribution from Antonin, the only one of the three surveillance team members present. His colleagues Patrick and Dominique were still at the hospital, where doctors were stitching up Dominique's head wound.

Even Avi Shiloah, who this time was the one joining by video conference from his office at Glilot Interchange, sat silently. The image on the huge wall-mounted monitor screen showed him with smoke curling in front of his face from his cigarette, making him look like some kind of ghostly overseer.

Incidents such as the death of Blondel were, sadly, all too frequent. It always made Jayne question the value of what she was doing and why, especially when it involved an innocent person caught up in a situation not of their own making. Blondel had simply been trying to help them.

The negative, self-flagellating thoughts revolving around her head had been well rehearsed over the years and decades.

All our fault—again. Yet another collateral casualty. Another body in the morgue. Probably another fatherless child somewhere. A broken, inconsolable widow.

Her stomach tightened, and she could feel her face muscles becoming rigid as her mind wandered. Then she chastised herself and told herself to concentrate on the others in the room and the task at hand.

Already the explosion and the death of Blondel were the lead items on television and radio news programs in Paris and, indeed, across France. Live reports from Rue de Saint-Simon were being broadcast on most channels, with TV reporters interviewing eyewitnesses from the heavily damaged Hôtel Duc de Saint-Simon, including the outraged owner and several guests.

Although a couple of the eyewitnesses described seeing a man and a woman with the dead property manager, Sebastian Blondel, outside the tailor shop, a police major admitted in a brief interview that he did not yet have any further information and said officers had not yet obtained CCTV footage and were unsure if any existed.

Jayne knew that, as was always the case when intelligence services were involved in such incidents on foreign soil where they were not meant to be operating, they would simply have to sit back and watch the subsequent inquiry unfold without being able to provide input. She found it very tough.

"Let's try and look forward," Vic said eventually, his rather dry tones breaking the vacuum. He looked around the room. "We can't do anything about what happened, so let's summarize where we're at. Then we can decide where we're going. What happened on Rue de Saint-Simon was a rather devastating confirmation that what you learned in Ramallah puts us on the right track. But it still doesn't tell us why those cardinals were killed, or why Hezbollah is involved. And frankly, it doesn't help me if I'm trying to reassure the White House that the president should press ahead with his planned visit to the Vatican. The president is determined to do it, but they are getting very nervous—not surprising, given the Iranians have more or less issued a *fatwa* calling for revenge on him and Yitzhak Katz."

"You're also no nearer knowing who's leaking this shit and putting my operative Rafael in the firing line," Shiloah said.

"Thanks for the reminder, Avi," Jayne said, injecting as much sarcasm as she could into her voice. She felt irritated by Shiloah's slightly hostile comment. "There are others in the firing line too, not just Rafael, remember?" *Like me.*

"We know that, Jayne," Vic said. "And yes, yet again, we find ourselves obliged to run an internal audit to check whether the leaks are coming from within our service, though I very much doubt that's the case. Ricardo is heading up that piece of work."

Ricardo Miller was the CIA's deputy director of counterintelligence, a somewhat dogged and dour character who, through his role, had developed an almost paranoid, suspicious view of almost everyone he came across. He had targeted Jayne for scrutiny on more than one occasion and was deeply skeptical about the use of external contractors such as her, viewing them as a high security risk.

"We are also running a mole hunt," Shiloah's voice growled through the loudspeakers.

Vic nodded. "Nothing less than I would expect." His phone vibrated and he picked it up and studied the screen, then flicked his finger across it, scrolling down.

"It's the NSA," Vic said. "They've run some initial traces on this Alberto Casartelli. He's joint owner of a fashion company, a clothing group based in Rome called Sole Nero. It's got a few subsidiary brands and companies."

"Sole Nero?" Jayne asked. "Black Sun in our language?"

"That's the name of the parent group," Vic said. "They're getting the names of the subsidiary companies."

"I recall the Black Sun symbol was linked to the Nazis," Jayne said. "Could there be some kind of connection? Who are the other joint owners?"

"They're working on that."

There were nods of approval around the table.

"Well, at least you got a lead out of it," Shiloah said. "Go follow it up. It's not going to be a coincidence that the clothing company is in Rome, is it?"

"Sure," Jayne said. "Let's go ask this Casartelli what his involvement with a Hezbollah asset and the murder of cardinals is, shall we? I'm sure he'll sit us down, make us a coffee, and tell us."

There was another brief silence, and Jayne immediately regretted her tone of voice. She was now feeling tired and irritable and, frankly, somewhat off balance following the death of Blondel.

"All right, children," Vic said. "You're going to have to get into this company somehow. I suggest we get the NSA on the case, see if they can penetrate its IT."

"I can ask Unit 8200 to do the same," Shiloah said. "I'll give Neta Rosenblum a call, given that she's already been working with you on this operation."

Jayne gave a thin smile. There was nothing wrong with a bit of competition, but it could end up being counterproductive, in her experience, if two services were working on the same operation without being closely coordinated. There was a risk of compromising each other.

"Too many cooks in the kitchen," Jayne said. "Wouldn't it be best if Neta picks this one up, for continuity given the possible Hezbollah linkage? It's more directly Unit 8200's territory. And if they can't make headway, we'll hand it over to the NSA. And if they don't crack it, we'll resort to more old-fashioned methods."

"Bribery or burglary is your usual old-fashioned method, isn't it?" Shiloah asked.

Jayne ignored the comment, unsure if it was meant as a barb or a compliment. It was partly true, she had to admit. Such methods had often proved mightily effective over the years when trying to extract information from otherwise unwilling participants. She wasn't going to mention that the Mossad often took a far more physical approach than that.

"In the meantime, I want to speak to Michael Gray and others at the Vatican," she said. "I want to get to the bottom of these leaks—given that nobody else seems to be doing so. But then nobody else is on the receiving end of the consequences, are they?"

PART THREE

CHAPTER TWENTY-FIVE

Tuesday, July 5, 2016
The Vatican

Behind Jayne, the spire of the Vatican Radio mast spiked upward, almost touching the low-hanging clouds, as she walked around the St. Peter Memorial statue and past the gardener's lodge.

Next to her, Michael Gray walked with his back stooped a little and one hand clutching his chin as they made their way through the green lawns and trees of the Vatican Gardens.

She fingered the security badge, which Gray had obtained for her from the Swiss Guard, that hung on a Vatican lanyard around her neck.

Ahead of them stood the Sistine Chapel, dominated by the towering dome of St. Peter's Basilica to its right.

Some joker had somehow climbed the huge bronze statue and placed a traffic cone on the head of Saint Peter, who was depicted raising his right hand toward the basilica ahead of him while his left hand clutched the keys of Heaven to his chest. Jayne assumed it was a drunken student prank.

A group of three security men were standing at the base of the statue, trying to work out how to retrieve the cone. On the other side, a stonemason was at work with brushes, buckets, and assorted bottles of solutions, cleaning the plinth on which the statue stood.

"I am so sorry I dragged you into this, Jayne," Gray said, his eyes cast down at the ground. "It is not what I foresaw or intended. Please forgive me."

Jayne had just finished giving Gray an account of events in Paris. She had decided that she would come alone to see Gray, while Rafael worked from the Israeli embassy on their lead.

"You asked me to find out whatever confidential information the cardinals were going to disclose to the White House," Jayne said. "It's very clear to me, Michael, that some people are determined to stop us. We know who they are. But the problem we have is that they're ahead of us every step of the way—they know where we are and where we're going."

Gray stopped walking, glanced at his watch, and turned to Jayne. "Yes, I can see that. I need to be with His Holiness at two o'clock in his private office to give him an update. I was going to do it alone, but would you come with me? I think it would be helpful for him to hear it from you."

Meet the pope? Cool.

The suggestion was an intriguing one, particularly given the circumstances, and would be a first for her. "I have a few questions for him, so yes," Jayne said.

Gray nodded and made a quick call to the pope's private secretary , Christophe Despierre, to let him know.

After ending the call, he put his phone back into his pocket. "There is something I wanted to discuss with His Holiness that may be relevant to all this. I bumped into him carrying some papers from the Secret Archives on Saturday, which he said might relate to the investigation. He was with Bishop Galli, the archives prefect, so I didn't want to say any more. We planned to meet today, so I will ask him when we're there."

Jayne pursed her lips. "I'll let you ask the initial questions about that. Let's hope it helps."

Gray led the way through the Square of the Furnace, past the Sistine Chapel and the Borgia Tower, and into the maze of ancient buildings that made up the Apostolic Palace.

Ten minutes later they were walking from the elevators and along the third-floor loggia, with its inlaid marble floor and frescoes on the wall, toward the pope's private apartments. To their right, through glass windows that stretched up to the high ceiling, was a view out over the gardens where they had just been walking.

Near the far end of the long loggia area, next to the tall double doors that led into the private apartments, a coffee table and six chairs had been laid out as a kind of waiting room.

Gray walked past the table and showed his pass to a Swiss Guard in full uniform standing next to the doors. Jayne did likewise and followed Gray along a corridor past the pope's private chapel.

As they passed the chapel, Gray indicated to the entrance. "Since this started, His Holiness has taken to spending an hour in there every morning, praying for a solution."

He continued along the corridor and knocked on a plain wooden door.

It was opened by an old man wearing a white cassock and skullcap.

"Your Holiness," Gray said. "May I introduce Jayne Robinson."

Pope Julius VI extended his hand which Jayne shook. She had met many dignitaries and influential public figures over her long years of service, but she couldn't help feeling a little thrilled at this encounter with the pope. She had been expecting him to be wearing his papal Fisherman's Ring, but he had a small, simple silver ring that looked to have seen long service, judging by its scratches and heavily dulled surface. Behind him was another man, whom Gray introduced as Bishop Christophe Despierre, the pope's personal secretary.

"Ms. Robinson, I hear you are making progress and I'm sorry you have been suffering on the church's account," the pope said, fixing her with a pair of blue eyes that looked slightly watery. "Please, come and tell me about it."

Jayne glanced over her shoulder at a Swiss Guard who was standing a few meters along the corridor and who was the only other person within range.

"Your Holiness," she said. "Please call me Jayne. I would like to give you a full briefing, but I am concerned about security while doing so."

"Ah, yes," the pope said. "Well, these doors are old and solid and very soundproof, but you would like the guard to be a little further away, yes?"

"It would be a sensible precaution, Your Holiness."

The pope took a few steps and spoke in rapid Italian to the guard, who moved ten meters along the corridor, past the entrance to the private chapel, and resumed his sentry-like posture.

"That should be safe," the pope said. "And you can trust Bishop Despierre with your life. I've been very blessed to have him as my assistant for the past fifteen years."

He walked to his chair behind the desk. "Please. Sit. There is nobody else who can hear us. These walls may have ears, but they are very old and very deaf, like me." He chuckled at his own joke and indicated toward a row of four chairs in front of his desk.

Jayne joined in the joke with a short, deliberate laugh and took a seat next to Gray and Despierre. "You may joke about walls having ears, Your Holiness, but in all seriousness, do your security people, I presume the Swiss Guard, check for listening devices, bugs, recording equipment, and that kind of thing?"

The pope nodded. "They do. Cardinal Saraceni takes responsibility for security, and he assures me that this entire apartment was checked less than a week ago by the Swiss Guard and prior to that, in mid-June. There have been very few visitors in the last few days, apart from the Secret Service people who are working with the Swiss Guard ahead of the president's visit. We are safe here, Jayne."

"Thank you," Jayne replied. "Let's hope so." She guessed the Swiss Guard were well equipped and had to trust that they were doing their job properly. She made a mental note to have a more detailed discussion with Saraceni about security as soon as she was able to arrange a meeting. Undoubtedly, he, the Swiss Guard, and the Secret Service team who were at the Vatican all had matters in hand, but maybe there were additional measures that needed to be taken, given the circumstances.

Jayne gave the pope a short summary of the investigation so far, including a sanitized account of the near misses in Ramallah and Paris. She also outlined briefly the critical roles played by Vic and Rafael, and a little about their backgrounds.

The pope listened in silence, shaking his head periodically.

"Do you have any more leads to pursue?" he asked when Jayne had finished.

"Only one. A clothing company here in Rome that has links to the business in Paris run by the brothers who work for Hezbollah."

"What is the name of this business?" the pope asked. "I may know it, or one of our team here may have a contact."

Jayne hesitated. Her initial reaction was that there was no need to disclose the name at this stage, but they currently had no obvious entry point into Sole Nero at this stage. Perhaps the pope was making a good point.

She told him the company name. "It's apparently run by a man named Alberto Casartelli," Jayne added. "Once we've located him and obtained some background information on him, we're planning to put him under the microscope. It seems unlikely his links to the Hezbollah operatives and to Rome are a pure coincidence."

The pope shrugged. "I have never heard of him." He looked at Despierre, who shook his head.

"Nor I," the secretary said. "I hope you find something helpful from this next stage of your inquiry. I understand the American embassy and the Secret Service are rather concerned about the president's visit here while this remains unresolved, just as much as we are."

Jayne leaned back in her chair. "I'm sure you're aware that the Iranian Supreme Leader has called for revenge against the US and Israeli leaders. Would you still go ahead with the event if we don't find the perpetrator of the killings?"

Pope Julius exhaled and narrowed his eyes. "There is something that my archbishop used to say when I first entered the church. *Morto un papa, se ne fa un'altro.* It means, if one pope dies, they just make another. We are not irreplaceable. It is the same with presidents. So, with that in mind, one thing I have in common with President Ferguson is that I don't like to give in to terrorist threats. I have God on my side, and Hezbollah certainly doesn't. So I have no plans to cancel this event. We are planning important announcements, as you doubtless know, relating to the papacy of Pius XII during the Second World War and to the Palestinian issue. President Ferguson stands fully behind us on the first of those announcements, although perhaps not the second. We will be relying on you intelligence experts and on the security teams we have here, the Swiss Guards and others, to ensure it goes smoothly—I have informed them all, including the Secret Service people, that the event will go ahead."

Jayne had expected him to say something like that.

"Are you intending to have private conversations with President Ferguson during his visit?" she asked. "Do you have a rapport?"

The pope smiled. "That is something we need to work on. We don't know each other well, and so, yes, we have a forty-five minute private meeting here in this office at eleven o'clock, immediately prior to the midday public event and announcement. It will just be us two—not even Bishop Despierre will be present for that one."

The pope sat back in his chair. "I am causing my process-driven people here in the Vatican all kinds of turmoil by meeting the president in my office, but I do have a good reason."

Jayne raised her eyebrows. "What do you mean, Your Holiness?"

"Normally we always hold meetings with heads of state in my private library, downstairs on the second floor. It's an age-old tradition. But the president said he wanted to meet here so he could see the window from where I say the Angelus on Sundays and where we could speak in greater privacy. I agreed. The complicated procedure for the library meetings has been thrown out, and my team has had to devise a new protocol." He smiled, a spark in his eye.

"I see," Jayne said, returning the smile. "Sometimes it's good to tear up the rule book."

"Exactly," the pope said. "I hope that the greater informality of meeting in this somewhat untidy office will help us build the foundations of a good relationship. I understand the Secret Service people are comfortable with that. They will have to be. We make the rules here." He waved a hand toward piles of papers and books that stood on his shelves and desk. "He will find me just as I am and see me as human, I hope. We will discuss the Palestinian issue during that time, certainly. Of course, our future relationship does rather depend on President Ferguson remaining in office beyond this year and me remaining alive—and only God knows the answer to both questions, especially at my age." He gave a short laugh.

Jayne found herself warming to this eighty-year-old who had a sparkly, self-deprecating wit to go with his undoubted political abilities, his faith, and his able leadership of the world's estimated 1.3 billion Catholics. He also clearly had nerves of steel. All that might explain his popularity among his fellow cardinals, who had elected him at their conclave eleven years earlier to replace Pope John Paul II.

"That's good," Jayne said. "However, we have only one problem."

The pope raised an inquiring eyebrow.

"The issue is that our adversaries, who are also undoubtedly the people who are murdering your cardinals, seem to know ahead of time exactly what we are doing and where we are going," Jayne said. "Which explains why, since the killings in Washington, they have been able to find and murder Cardinal Baltrami and come so close to wiping out myself and some of my colleagues."

"Do you believe that's the case?" the pope asked.

"I do. In our business, we would describe someone who provides such information as a mole, a traitor."

The pope absentmindedly wiped his cheek with the palm of his hand. "In our business we might describe them as a Judas."

"That is true," Jayne said. She didn't smile and wondered momentarily why the pope was attempting mild humor about such a serious issue.

"Now, as you would expect," Jayne continued, "there are rigorous internal investigations going on within the two intelligence agencies involved to try to identify whether that mole is one of their employees. My question is, if the leak is coming from the Vatican, do you have any idea who this Judas might be?"

The pope looked down. "No, I have no idea."

There was silence for a few seconds.

Gray broke it. "Your Holiness, when we bumped into each other at the Secret Archive on Saturday, you mentioned that the papers you had with you might be helpful with the investigation. Did you make any headway with them?"

Again the pope shook his head. He looked first at Gray, then at Jayne. "I have been through those papers. They may or may not be relevant, but I'm not in a position to discuss them at the moment. I will let you know if that changes."

"Your Holiness," Jayne said, "we have been battling to make progress with this investigation. We have only one lead, which may or may not amount to anything. It seems tenuous. So if you have something that may be material, I hope you could share it with us."

The pope fixed his gaze on Jayne. "As I said, Jayne. I will let you know."

There was a note of finality in his voice, so Jayne decided not to ask any follow-up questions, and neither did Gray.

The pope caught Jayne's eye. "Can I ask, what is your faith?" he asked. "I always like to know when I meet people."

Jayne shifted a little uncomfortably in her seat. "I don't know," she said. "I know I've sometimes felt God's hand on my shoulder when I've had big issues on my mind. But . . ." She let her voice trail away.

"But you struggle with believing?" he asked.

"It's not so much that," Jayne said. "It's the middleman I struggle with."

"The church, you mean?"

Jayne nodded slowly. She didn't want to upset him, but he had asked. "I sometimes think there are too many humans involved, too much man-made doctrine, too many artificial rules and customs and procedures."

The pope inclined his head. "I know what you mean. That's why I often pray by myself."

He hesitated, and Jayne noticed with some relief that Despierre was pointedly looking at his watch.

"We have our next appointment in a couple of minutes, Holiness," Despierre said.

Gray stood and Jayne followed his lead. She stretched out her hand and shook the pope's again.

"It was good to meet you, Your Holiness," Jayne said. "We will keep you updated with our progress, and I'm sure you will do likewise."

The pope nodded. "Of course."

CHAPTER TWENTY-SIX

Tuesday, July 5, 2016
   Tel Aviv

Avi Shiloah followed the athletic figure of Lieutenant Colonel Neta Rosenblum up the stairs of the Unit 8200 headquarters building, cursing as he did so. She was definitely a lot fitter than he was, taking two steps at a time as they ascended to the third floor, where she waited for him to catch up.

"You need to throw out the cigarettes, Avi," she said, the faint trace of a smile on her face. She pushed her dark ponytail back over her shoulder, from where it had flopped forward.

"You need to make use of the elevators," he retorted. He felt like telling her she needed to show him a bit more consideration given he was now the *ramsad* and was nearly twenty years older than her. But he was no fan of hierarchies and didn't want to pull rank, and he also liked her slightly tongue-in-cheek manner, so he said nothing further.

Rosenblum tapped her security badge on the reader next

to the door, entered her code, and pushed it open. They then took a left down a corridor, where she knocked on the third door she came to.

It was opened almost immediately by a young man whom Shiloah had met before, Daniel Shavit, who was dressed in green military uniform.

"What have you got for us?" Shiloah asked, getting right to the point.

"I'll show you," Shavit said. He turned back into the room, where they had set up a small operational headquarters.

Shiloah knew that for more sensitive projects and for those involving only one or two people, the team at Unit 8200 often found it easier to operate in a quiet environment rather than in the communal open-plan office where Shavit and his colleagues normally sat.

On a long desk were four monitor screens and two computer terminals. Two of the screens were turned on.

"I've just received the data back from Urim," Shavit said as he took a seat.

Shiloah accepted the chair that Rosenblum pushed in his direction and sat down next to Shavit. "What's it showing?" he asked.

Unit 8200's Urim intelligence collection facility, about ninety kilometers south of Tel Aviv, sat on Route 2333 near the junction with Route 241. It bristled with rows of satellite dishes, antennae, huge golf ball–style radar domes, and other monitoring equipment that kept checks on phone calls, emails, and other communications from all over the world.

Shiloah occasionally needed to visit the facility, which was manned by youngsters of a similar age to Shavit, almost all of whom were doing their compulsory military service. Urim did much of the heavy lifting in terms of interception of tele-coms, email, and internet traffic, and most of their output was transmitted to headquarters at Glilot Interchange, where Rosenblum and her team carried out the high-level analysis.

"It's interesting," Shavit said. "Urim has analyzed all the email traffic into and out of Sole Nero over the past six months from the corporate servers. It includes the internal emails. All normal. The type of thing you'd expect from an Italian fashion company. Orders, invoices, customer analysis, retail industry sales data. You name it. A few guys sending each other dirty jokes. Likewise with the files stored on the servers."

"And?" Rosenblum asked.

"And so I asked them to get into the personal laptops and phones of the directors."

"Using Pegasus, I assume," Shiloah said.

Pegasus, a powerful hacking software developed by a group of former Unit 8200 employees who had set up a company called NSO, allowed users to infect a target's phone with malware and extract almost any data required, including encrypted messages. Shiloah knew that Rosenblum's team, and the youngsters at Urim, deployed it almost daily, but never spoke about it externally.

Shavit nodded. "They used Pegasus to get into the phones, and the computer passwords were all saved on the phones, so they got them as well. Most of them stupidly connect their personal devices to the corporate Wi-Fi, so Urim got to them very easily."

"What did they get from the personal devices?" Shiloah asked.

"A few anomalies on the accounting side. See, this Sole Nero makes men's shirts and women's blouses, expensive ones, in Italy, that sell for eighty or a hundred euros. Its sales are almost entirely focused within Italy, with some minor activity in Spain, Germany, and France. And all the accounts are on the corporate servers. But look at these." Shavit pointed to two order forms on his monitor screen. "These were on Alberto Casartelli's personal laptop. He's the managing director. There are hundreds more like this from the last few years, all received into his personal email account from the United States. It seems they have one customer there, a top-end, upmarket fashion retail chain called Adelaide that's based in Charleston, South Carolina. But Adelaide isn't in the corporate accounts."

"Off the books, you mean?" Shiloah asked.

"Completely, *totally* off the books," Shavit said, waving his hand to emphasize his point. "And there's more than that. Casartelli is receiving these orders from Adelaide—mainly women's blouses, T-shirts, and skirts. He is then forwarding the emails containing the orders to someone in Los Angeles named Dimitri Margiotta, who runs a family-owned clothing manufacturing business called LA Fashions. Casartelli is also sending invoices requesting payment for the finished clothing to Adelaide. But here's the strange thing: there's no trace of such payments coming into Sole Nero's bank accounts, nor into Casartelli's personal bank accounts, of which he has a few."

Shiloah's mind was now buzzing as he tried to work out what was going on.

"So why is Casartelli forwarding the orders to this Margiotta in Los Angeles? Is LA Fashions making the goods instead of Sole Nero?" Rosenblum asked.

"Seems a possibility."

"And then there's the question of how Adelaide is paying. Is Sole Nero being given cash, then? Or is the money being sent elsewhere?"

"Presumably one of those," Shavit said.

Rosenblum frowned. "What about the manufacturing of the goods? Is Casartelli ordering the raw materials?"

"No trace of that. And just as strange, no trace of payment for any raw materials either."

Shiloah rose, paced to the window of the ops room, and stared out toward nearby Highway 20 and his beloved Mossad campus beyond. He turned and leaned back against the windowsill, his arms folded against his neatly ironed white shirt. He enjoyed this kind of intellectual jigsaw puzzle and using surreptitious, often illegal methods to solve them. Even after so many such operations over the years, it still appealed to the rebel in him.

"Maybe Adelaide is paying LA Fashions directly for the goods, then?" Shiloah asked.

"That's possible, yes." Shavit said.

"Odd. Have you tried getting into Adelaide's systems to check from the other end?" Shiloah asked.

"Urim is trying. No luck so far, though," Shavit said.

"Did Urim get any background information on LA Fashions?"

Shavit picked at a large pimple on his chin with a fingernail and leaned back in his chair, which creaked loudly. "Not much. It sounds like more of a down-market business, quite different than Sole Nero. They sell mainly to mass-market outlets, super-markets, that kind of thing. Urim had a quick look at the payroll. It looks like there are a lot of Hispanic names on there, so they probably pay low wages to people coming across the border into LA. That's my assumption. I've seen no proof as yet."

Shiloah frowned. "Are you both thinking what I'm thinking?"

"Money laundering," Rosenblum confirmed.

Shiloah nodded.

"There's no evidence of that from all the email traffic, though," Shavit said.

"Of course not," Rosenblum said. "There wouldn't be.

Perhaps someone needs to pay a visit to these companies to check out the situation on the ground."

"I agree," Shiloah said. "Let's pass on what we've got to Jayne Robinson and suggest that to them."

"I'm sure they'll find a way," Shavit said. "There's one thing that might persuade them, if they need persuading."

"Which is?"

"I've done some cross-checks between the cell phone number for Casartelli and the one we got for Talal Hassan," Shavit said. "They speak to each other often, usually at least twice a month, sometimes more. Also, Casartelli often called a French cell phone in Paris—which I've discovered belonged to Henri Fekkai."

Shiloah grinned and walked past Shavit, clapping him on the shoulder as he did so. "Good job, well done. I'll give all this information to Jayne."

Rosenblum nodded her agreement. "I liked Jayne. A smart woman, for a Brit."

Shiloah smiled. "Yes, not bad." He turned back to Shavit. "Can you write up a short report with all that information? We'll send it through as well."

"Will do," Shavit said.

"And we need to know how Casartelli is linked to Hezbollah," Shiloah said. "Do some more digging, see what else you can find on him."

He and Rosenblum headed out the door.

* * *

Tuesday, July 5, 2016
Rome

. . .

The Fiat Tipo sedan, driven by Pierre, was heading along Via Celio Vibenna, past the Colosseum, when Hassan's new burner phone rang. He had only given the number earlier that morning to two people, so he knew who was calling. He tapped the green button.

"What do you have?" Hassan said in a low tone.

"I will be brief," CIRRUS said. "Robinson and Levy know about Casartelli. I assume both the CIA and the Mossad are investigating, and I think it will not be long before they get to the facts."

"How the hell?" Hassan muttered.

"I have no idea how they got the details. But they have them. They also know that Casartelli's business has links to Henri's business in Paris. And they know of Henri's Hezbollah involvement."

"*What?* How could they know about the Casartelli link?"

"I do not know that. But I know what the consequences will be if that inquiry makes progress. They are also making new efforts in the hunt for the mole in their midst—for me. I will need to be careful."

Hassan stared out the window at the ancient curved stone facade of the Roman amphitheater as it flashed past to his right. The broad concourse that separated the Colosseum from the road was swarming with tourists, many of whom were taking photographs or lining up at the entrance barriers for their turn to wander around inside.

All of what CIRRUS had said was bad news.

"*Ibn el sharmouta,*" he cursed. "You're certain about all of that?"

"Of course," CIRRUS said. "It came directly from the horse's mouth. A meeting between the pope and Robinson took place. They told him about this."

"So the pope knows for sure?"

"For sure. It seems he has been doing some digging

around himself. He spoke in the meeting about some papers he had got from the Vatican's archives that may prove important to their investigation."

Hassan cursed again under his breath and glanced at Pierre in the driver's seat, who had clearly picked up most of the conversation and was silently shaking his head, his lips pressed tight together.

"Is there anything else I need to know?" Hassan asked.

"Only a confirmation that the pope and Ferguson are going to meet prior to their big announcement on Monday the eleventh. They are going to have a forty-five minute private conference in the pope's study."

Hassan sat up straight in his seat and pressed the phone tighter against his ear.

"Forty-five minutes? Are they really? Interesting," he said. "That will be a first. What time will that happen?"

"The event is starting at noon and the meeting is scheduled immediately beforehand at 11 a.m. That's all I have. Any questions?" CIRRUS asked.

"Was Cardinal Gray at the meeting, too?"

"Yes, he was there. Anything else?"

"Not immediately. Thanks for the information."

Hassan terminated the call, then sank back into his seat, thinking.

CIRRUS was a complex character, but Hassan knew he could rely on the information just received. The man was deeply motivated. It was partly because of the money he was being paid, which was substantial, and he was not well-off. But it was also because CIRRUS, although not part of Hezbollah and not even a Shia Muslim, had some deep-rooted sympathy for their agendas and for Iran, Syria's closest ally. And CIRRUS was originally from Damascus. As far as Hassan had determined, it also had something to do with the influence of his Arab father, who, like many Syrians and Iranians, hated the United States and Israel.

He turned to Pierre. "I guess you heard what that was all about."

"Yes."

"We'll need to make sure they get nothing on Casartelli," Hassan said. "That could cost us hundreds of millions. The Supreme Leader will go crazy. You know how he would react."

"So, what can we do?" Pierre asked.

Hassan said nothing for several seconds as he stared forward out through the windshield.

Pierre was driving toward a large villa he had rented at significant expense for them both in Via di Sant Anselmo, a quiet, upmarket residential street in Ripa, Rome's twelfth *rione*. The two men had spent the previous seventeen hours driving from Paris with only a few brief stops for a nap and to alternate driving duties. Until a few minutes earlier, Hassan had been feeling exhausted and he had struggled to stay awake in the passenger seat. Now he felt reenergized.

"First thing, I'll tell Casartelli to toss his phone and get another," Hassan said. "They'll have his existing number and will be tracing him." He took out the new phone he had bought in Paris and began to tap out a message.

"We need to have another go at Robinson and Levy," Hassan said as he typed. "We can't give up. Maybe we should get someone else to do our dirty work for us and keep ourselves at arm's length. That's always the less risky option— I feel like our luck is going to run out at some point. We need to find out how much they know, and ideally to have them locked up where they can't do us any damage while we concentrate on finishing what we began in Washington."

Pierre gave a guttural and somewhat sardonic laugh. "Lock them up? You mean handcuff them to a radiator in a basement somewhere? Turn them into hostages? We haven't even managed to take them out with IEDs, although I'll take the responsibility for that."

"You certainly will take responsibility for that." Hassan finished his message to Casartelli, tapped the send button, and looked up. "I was thinking of another approach, though."

"What?" Pierre asked. He glanced sideways at Hassan and, in the process, nearly hit a cyclist.

"Concentrate on your driving," Hassan snapped. "I had a call a couple of days ago from one of my friends in the GSD."

The GSD was the Lebanese General Security Directorate, the country's main intelligence agency, with whom Hassan maintained close connections. They often provided him with useful information.

"Saying what?"

"Saying that a huge consignment of Captagon amphetamines, which has been in the pipeline for the past three months, is finally heading into Naples next week from Syria. I've been waiting for that. It started life as an ISIS shipment."

"Started life?"

"It was produced by a factory controlled by ISIS—like many drug shipments. But we stole it."

"Hezbollah *stole* it from ISIS? In Syria?" Pierre asked.

"We had to hide it for a while. Now we're selling it," Hassan said. "The Italian mafia are buying it for more than a billion euros."

"A *billion*?" There was a note of utter disbelief in Pierre's voice.

Hassan grinned. "Tell me about it. It's going to be better than a lottery win for us. It's more than Hezbollah's annual operating budget. There's fifteen tons of the stuff. It's hidden in shipping containers behind rolls of cotton and woolen cloth."

"Not easy to get fifteen tons of pills into a port."

"Precisely," Hassan said. "That's eighty-four million pills.

They need a bit of help. I got Casartelli to loan them two of his trucks—that way you have fashion company trucks collecting a consignment of cloth from the port. Makes it look completely legitimate."

Pierre threw another sideways glance at his colleague. "So you've played a hand in this. Who have you bribed?" There was a slight note of weariness in Pierre's voice. "And what's this got to do with Robinson?"

"This is what I was coming to. I did play a part in it, I have to say, in return for a suitable contribution."

"To your own coffers, no doubt. Go on."

"I've earned it. Anyway, to continue. Several years ago, I needed to run a shipload of weapons into Naples. To do that, I bought off a police chief superintendent in the Carabinieri and a commander in the Guardia di Finanza, the financial police, who between them were running Naples at the time. However, neither of them is in Naples anymore."

"Don't tell me, they're both now in the Italian cabinet."

"Not quite, but the Carabinieri officer is vice commander general for Italy now. Tommaso Porpora's his name. I used his services to ensure the Captagon would get a safe passage through Naples. Which means he gets a massive payoff."

"Which keeps him firmly in your back pocket."

"Correct. And similarly with Carlo Mangano. He's now corps general, number three for the entire Italian financial police service. Also bought off." Hassan rubbed his index finger and thumb together, as if rustling bank bills.

"What about their bosses?"

"They've both got mafia links, as have Porpora and Mangano from their time in Naples—they were both bought out by the Camorra many years ago. You're not going to get a billion euros' worth of drugs into Naples without the mafia giving a few key players their cut."

"Right. So I'll ask again, how do these guys, Porpora and

Mangano, come into the picture with Robinson?" Pierre asked.

"They owe me a few favors. When we get to the apartment, I'm going to put in a couple of calls." Hassan paused. "I'll also need to call Tehran. I need to know from Nasser Khan which way the wind is blowing there and what the Supreme Leader wants from us. I can see that more cardinal blood may need to be spilled, given the number of people who know various details about Operation Prada. And there's another thing."

"What?"

Hassan glanced at Pierre. "If the pope and the American president are going to be together in a room for three-quarters of an hour, that may also interest the Supreme Leader."

CHAPTER TWENTY-SEVEN

Tuesday, July 5, 2016
Trastevere, Rome

It was the sixth restaurant that Jayne and Rafael had tried along Via della Lungaretta, one of many historical cobbled streets that wound their way through the heart of Trastevere like ancient intertwined snakes, all twists and turns and old shuttered buildings from which plaster and paint were peeling. Crowds of tourists were ambling along beneath inefficient streetlights, many of them with the same objective of locating somewhere to eat.

Aristocampo, like all the other restaurants at which they had inquired, had no free tables inside the restaurant, the waiter said apologetically, fingering his bow tie. But they were welcome to sit outside at the only free one of four wooden tables.

Jayne turned to Rafael. "I don't like the idea of sitting out here where we can be seen."

He threw a glance at the table. "Hardly ideal. But we

could be wandering for some time otherwise. There's nothing else left."

The two of them had arrived late at the Rome safe house, a modern four-bedroom apartment in Trastevere that had been hastily arranged by the CIA station. Donald Constanzo, the station chief, could not accommodate anyone at his home annex this time, as his wife's parents were visiting. He had permitted Rafael to also use the CIA safe house along with Jayne, given they were all working on the same operation.

They had traveled to Rome ahead of Vic, who was on a later flight from Paris, as Jayne had wanted to meet with Gray to discuss progress. Vic was due to have supper with Constanzo on arrival and was intending to stay at a hotel near the embassy afterward.

Despite their hunger, Jayne had insisted on carrying out a proper surveillance detection exercise through the backstreets and quieter areas of Trastevere, where trailing coverage would be more obvious than here among the tourists.

There had been nothing that concerned them.

"We'll eat quickly and get out of here as soon as possible," Jayne said.

Rafael nodded. "No starters, no desserts. Let's take it."

The waiter pulled a chair out for Jayne and indicated to Rafael to take the one on the other side.

The table was covered with a red-and-white checkered cloth, and the specials were scribbled in chalk on a board that hung at a crooked angle from a nail that had been hammered into the doorframe. The tables, like those of the restaurant immediately to its right, jutted out into the street, leaving space for only one car to pass, although tonight few did. The traffic consisted almost exclusively of pedestrians.

Jayne ordered a chicken pasta dish and Rafael a pizza,

both accompanied by a glass of house red, which proved satis-
fyingly full-bodied.

While they were waiting for the food, Jayne tapped out a
quick message using her secure link to Joe, at home in Portland, to tell him she and Rafael had rushed out for dinner and
she would call when she was back at the safe house later. She
knew Joe would appreciate that the operation they were
engaged in was running at a very fast pace, making time a
commodity in short supply.

A family passed by, one of its three noisy teenagers almost
colliding with two uniformed Carabinieri officers who were
ambling in the opposite direction. One of the officers did a
smart sidestep and smilingly apologized, despite not being in
the wrong. A canoodling couple paused at the easel with its
printed menu that stood in front of the tables to attract
customers.

Neither Jayne nor Rafael wanted to talk business in such
an environment, despite having much to discuss.

Shortly after their arrival at the safe house earlier, they
had had a briefing via a secure four-way video conference with
Vic, Avi Shiloah, and Neta Rosenblum. During the meeting,
the Israelis had passed on the findings from Unit 8200's
investigations into Sole Nero and Alberto Casartelli.

The amount of detail in the findings had surprised all of
them. Vic's first reaction was to arrange for someone from
the FBI in Los Angeles to check out LA Fashions, which was
also clearly linked in some kind of dubious way to Casartelli.

Jayne had suggested having Joe Johnson also go to Los
Angeles and to cooperate with the Feds, if they were willing
to allow that. Johnson had considerable expertise in company
finances and accounts and extracting key information and
evidence from them. Vic agreed that was a good idea and had
opted to discuss it with Arthur Veltman and think about it
overnight before deciding in the morning.

Less than forty minutes later, Jayne and Rafael had paid the bill, tipped the waiter, and set off eastward along Via della Lungaretta. They again carried out their usual surveillance detection checks. It was easier with two of them, as they could pretend to have a playful conversation during which they could turn around and joke with the other as a cover for checking the route behind and ahead of them.

There was nobody in sight who appeared problematic.

They took the next right past a trattoria. Then, after another right, Jayne glanced over her shoulder and saw two Carabinieri officers turn the corner thirty meters behind and follow them down the street. They seemed engaged in a light-hearted conversation with each other. That was fine, she thought. It looked like the same pair who had walked past the restaurant earlier.

They continued on and turned left onto a deserted narrow street, Via dei Fienaroli, toward the apartment, less than four hundred meters south.

Ahead of them, two more uniformed Carabinieri walked side by side toward them from the end of the cobbled street, which, like many in this area, consisted of ancient four-story stone apartment blocks on either side. The street was narrow and lined down one side with cars and mopeds parked tight up against the wall.

"There are plenty of police out tonight," Rafael commented.

It was only when they came to within a few meters of the approaching officers that Jayne realized they weren't going to let them pass. She felt her scalp tighten and her stomach flipped over inside her.

This was trouble.

The officers, both wearing black uniforms with a red stripe across the front marked CARABINIERI and peaked caps, stopped dead, side by side. They were big guys and blocked their path.

When Jayne stepped to one side to walk around them, one officer took a sidestep to stand in her way.

"You are Jayne Robinson?" the officer asked in heavily accented English.

Jayne cursed to herself.

Are these men genuine?

She glanced over her shoulder again. The other two officers were closing in fast, no more than fifteen meters away. They were definitely the pair who had walked past their table earlier while they were eating dinner.

Jayne looked at Rafael, who had a resigned look on his face.

Four against two on a deserted street. This wasn't going to end well, she could see that.

"I am Jayne Robinson, yes," she said.

The officer turned to Rafael. "And you are Rafael Levy?"

Rafael nodded slowly.

"You are both under arrest on suspicion of carrying out unauthorized espionage activities on Italian soil," the officer said. "You will need to come with us for questioning. Anything you say may be taken as evidence against you. Do you understand?"

The two officers following came to a halt immediately behind Jayne.

She decided she wasn't going to take this unchallenged.

"We have done nothing wrong," Jayne said to the lead officer. "You have no right to arrest us. We have committed no offense and certainly are not engaged in espionage. So please let us go on our way."

As she spoke, the black silhouette of a car, its headlights off and running only on sidelights, turned the corner ahead of them and crawled in their direction. There was no missing the white Carabinieri insignia across the hood or the blue-and-white light bar on the roof. A couple of seconds later, an identical car, also with headlights off, turned the corner and followed.

Suddenly, Jayne's wrists were grabbed from behind and pulled sharply to the small of her back, causing a sharp pain to run through her shoulder joint and upper arm.

Click.

In less than a second, her wrists were in cuffs. Next to Jayne, Rafael had been similarly handcuffed behind his back by the other officer.

Then the officer behind Jayne shoved her in the small of her back so hard she lost her balance and stumbled forward, only for the officer in front to grab her hard by the shoulders and stand her up straight.

At that point, the red mist descended.

Jayne kicked back hard with the heel of her shoe, straight into the knee joint of the officer who had pushed her from behind, who gave a low-pitched grunt.

Next thing she knew, the officer in front had driven his fist hard into her solar plexus. A knifing pain seared through her stomach and chest and instantly winded her. Jayne doubled up and fell forward onto her knees, hands still cuffed behind her back, which meant she was unable to prevent her forehead from striking the cobbles.

She groaned with her head between her knees for perhaps half a minute, although it felt longer, before she began to get her breath back. Now her head was throbbing too. Eventually, she slowly raised her head to the lead officer in front of her.

"That was stupid," he said. "Don't try that again, *signora*. Very foolish."

The pain began to subside a little and Jayne tried to focus her thoughts.

"This is appalling," Rafael said. "You're going to pay for this, you bastard."

"I suggest you shut up," the officer snarled. "Or else you'll get the same treatment."

"I want to see your bloody identity card," Jayne groaned to the lead officer. She was now battling hard to contain her anger, which she could feel surging up inside her.

He took out a photo identity card from his pocket and flashed it in front of Jayne, too quickly for her to read his name or anything else on it. He then pocketed it again, grabbed Jayne beneath her armpits, and hauled her back to her feet.

The officer who had cuffed Jayne roughly inserted his hand into her right trouser pocket, searched around for an unnecessarily long time, and after a delay, grabbed her phone and pulled it out.

"Get your hands off me!" Jayne yelled. "That's disgusting, you're a disgrace. And you've no right to take that phone. Give it back."

The officer ignored her, searched her other trouser pocket only slightly more swiftly, and removed the key to the apartment.

"Leave the lady alone," Rafael said. "I saw what you did. Do you have an arrest warrant?"

"We don't need a warrant," the lead officer spat.

The officer who had searched Jayne moved to Rafael, delved into his pockets rather more quickly than he had Jayne's, and removed his belongings too before patting him down to ensure he had nothing else concealed on him.

The officer placed both phones in a small padded bag that Jayne recognized as a lead-lined Faraday pouch, ensuring that the phones couldn't be tracked.

He glanced over his shoulder at the oncoming police vehicles. "Get these two in the back of the cars."

"Where are you taking us?" Rafael asked.

"Not far. In fact, very little distance from here," the officer said. "Somewhere where we can ask you more questions without any chance of interference from your service."

Shit.

The officer behind Jayne grabbed her arm, put his other hand on her shoulder, and pushed her firmly toward the first car.

"You will go in the second car," the officer said to Rafael.

Here we go. Divide and conquer.

The officer holding Jayne pushed her to the now open rear door of the first car, shoved her in, and climbed in next to her. He pulled the door shut.

"As my colleague advised you, do not try anything stupid," the officer said, his tone level and unemotive. "Otherwise you will regret it." Jayne caught a strong smell of garlic and coffee on his breath. It looked like he hadn't shaved that morning.

Jayne could see out of the corner of her eye that Rafael was being pushed into the car behind hers.

The officer who had done the talking climbed into the passenger seat in front of Jayne. "Let's go," he said.

The driver, also in Carabinieri uniform, slipped the gear shift into first and let out the clutch.

* * *

The cell door clanged shut and Jayne let out a grunt of frustration.

The cell had high ceilings and no windows. There was a metal double bunk bed in the corner, painted a dull orange, although she was the only person there. There was a small plastic wash basin with a tap, a radiator, and a stainless-steel toilet in the corner next to the door. That was it.

The room reeked of urine and had brown stains on the

walls near the toilet, which Jayne did not doubt were smears of excrement. The square red clay tiles that formed the floor were heavily worn near the door and cracked and chipped in several places. This was an old prison building.

She sat on the lower bunk, her back bent double to avoid banging her head on the upper bed frame, and thumped the thin mattress with a clenched fist.

Unbelievable.

Jayne knew exactly where they were. The journey in the Carabinieri car had taken only five minutes, and she guessed they had traveled little more than a kilometer. She had caught a glimpse through the darkness of the River Tiber to their right as they neared their destination.

This was Regina Coeli, the notorious prison located roughly halfway between Trastevere and the Vatican, not far from the river to the east.

Jayne had walked past the frontage of the old building on a couple of occasions en route between Trastevere and the Vatican and knew what it was. She had even wondered whether conditions inside were better than the impression created by the somewhat dilapidated stone frontage with its peeling mustard-color paint. But she had never expected to end up in a cell here. She recalled reading somewhere in a city guide that the prison's name, which meant 'Queen of Heaven' in Latin, was due to the fact that it had originally been a convent. There was little heavenly about the cell in which she was now incarcerated.

The cell was in a basement. She knew that because after arrival in some internal courtyard, she had been frog-marched through a series of security doors and down a flight of stairs. It was located in a long corridor with many identical ancient steel doors, all painted a rust-brown color, with heavy metal bolts and locks, and with grilles that allowed the warders to open a flap and look in.

All the doors were closed, and there were no signs of other prisoners—no noise, no conversations, in fact no other audible sounds. Jayne immediately found that odd. She had been in several prisons before as a visitor and to interview inmates, and they had all been rowdy, noisy places, with people shouting, doors banging, footsteps thumping, and so on. There were also very few lightbulbs switched on in the corridors and other communal areas.

The handcuffs had been removed only when she was inside the cell.

Jayne's assumption was that this was some kind of holding area, not part of the main cell blocks where the convicted prisoners were confined.

But to have arrested her and Rafael on some trumped-up pretext of espionage was outrageous. And to have taken them to a prison, not even a Carabinieri police station, for questioning was doubly offensive and without a doubt illegal.

True, she was working here on behalf of Langley and Rafael was a Mossad employee, and they hadn't cleared that with Italy's foreign intelligence service, the Agenzia Informazioni e Sicurezza Esterna. They were staying in a CIA safe house in Rome, and had been on the scene of the killing of Cardinal Baltrami near another Rome safe house. But there was nothing they had done that ran against the Italian state. Their focus was entirely on the Vatican. There was no way their activities on Italian soil could be categorized as espionage.

This had to be some kind of setup; she knew that.

Money had likely changed hands to have triggered this.

No surprise there, she couldn't help thinking.

Welcome to Italy.

In the car, Jayne had demanded the right to make a phone call to the British embassy and to have an attorney present. She was certain she had the right to do both of those things, or at least that the police should call the embassy and an attorney on her behalf.

But the lead officer who had made the arrest had simply ignored her.

Bastard.

She did not know which cell Rafael was in, because they had been processed separately on arrival, but she assumed he was in similar accommodation to hers.

Jayne stood and paced up and down the tiny cell. Once again, the other side had known where they were and when and had planned to ensure that their investigation was at the very least disrupted.

How the hell had that happened?

Her mind started to think the unthinkable.

Was Michael Gray all that he seemed?

Was the pope's long-standing private secretary the bastion of faithfulness he appeared?

And was His Holiness . . . no. Don't go there, she told herself. She could feel herself being sucked into a spiral of paranoia. Her strong instinct was that the pope wasn't the corrupted link in the chain.

Instead, Jayne forced herself to think about something productive. Once she was out of here—and she was certain that would happen soon once Vic and Avi Shiloah realized what had happened and started to create merry hell—what would be the next step?

The conclusion they had come to earlier—that given their failures so far to get to Hassan and Pierre Fekkai, they should also target Casartelli—seemed the correct one. Hopefully Vic would send Joe Johnson to Los Angeles alongside the FBI and not be distracted by this.

Jayne suddenly realized that the water she had drunk during dinner, combined with the glass of wine, had left her needing the loo.

She stared at the toilet in the corner, then at the hatch in the door and tried to calculate the angle and whether a warder would be able to see her.

It was touch and go, she thought.

Then, from somewhere in the distance, she heard a woman scream. It was a long, piercing, agonized scream that echoed around the building and made Jayne's scalp prickle. There was a pause, then another shorter scream, followed by another even louder one.

Then came a metallic bang, followed by abrupt silence.

This was all too much.

The screams triggered a series of increasingly black thoughts. She suddenly realized she was very vulnerable in here, as a woman locked up by a bunch of clearly corrupt and unethical police officers.

What was next on the agenda?

Torture?

Rape?

It was obvious the woman she could hear was on the wrong end of something extremely painful.

Jayne found herself fighting back tears and wasn't sure whether they were in anger or self-pity.

CHAPTER TWENTY-EIGHT

Wednesday, July 6, 2016
Rome

By the time Vic Walter walked into the lobby of the Palazzo Margherita at 7:40 a.m., his level of concern was mounting. He ignored the Venus statue ahead of him and took the stone stairs two at a time to the CIA station on the top floor. The elevator in this elegant old building was just too slow when one was in a hurry.

He had already tried Jayne's phone three times that morning in an attempt to get her into the station for a meeting at eight o'clock, but she had answered none of his calls. Furthermore, he had received a message from Avi in Tel Aviv asking if he had seen Rafael, as he could not reach him for his normal 7:30 conference call.

This seemed uncharacteristic of both of them.

Now out of breath, Vic tapped the electronic pad with his security card and entered his PIN before opening the heavy steel door and going into the offices. Several of the station staff were already at their desks, sipping espressos and munching croissants.

He made his way through the open-plan area to Donald Constanzo's office in the corner of the building. The station chief was also drinking an espresso.

"Not sure if something's wrong, but I can't get hold of Jayne this morning," Vic began. "I wanted her to come in for eight. And Rafael Levy has also gone off the grid, according to Avi Shiloah."

Constanzo scratched his gray hair. "That's odd. There is a landline at the safe house. I can give it a try if you like."

Vic nodded. "Yes please."

Constanzo reached for his desk phone, checked a number on his PC, and dialed.

The phone rang for at least thirty seconds before Constanzo put the receiver down. "You don't think she and Rafael are . . ." He let his sentence drift into the ether.

"No," Vic replied, although the same thought had fleetingly crossed his mind before he had dismissed it. Flings were not uncommon in their profession, but he was fairly sure that wasn't the case here. "Definitely not. Jayne's happily entwined with Joe Johnson. She wouldn't. Something's not right."

Constanzo leaned back in his chair, his hands clasped behind his head. "Get the NSA to track her phone. That'll be the quickest way."

Vic nodded. It was approaching two in the morning in Fort Meade, Maryland, where the National Security Agency was based, but that didn't matter. They worked around the clock. He knew they would pinpoint the phone's last known location, as well as its previous movements.

He took out his phone, logged on to the secure messaging service he used to communicate with the NSA, and dispatched a short note outlining what he needed to their operations desk. He also copied it to Alex Goode, one of the sharpest minds in the signals intelligence business, who was his go-to port of call at the agency. With any luck, Alex would be on the night shift and could deal with this directly.

Vic then replied to Shiloah, suggesting he get Unit 8200 to do the same with Rafael, but he replied immediately saying he had already done that and was now waiting for a result.

"If we don't get anywhere, can you put in a call to your Carabinieri contact—what was his name, Porpora?" Vic asked Constanzo after sending the messages. "Perhaps he's picked up something."

"Can do, but let's wait until we hear from the NSA," Constanzo said. "I don't want to set the hares running externally around here if it turns out she's just out buying breakfast or something."

Vic shook his head. "I doubt that's the case, but let's see."

He found himself reflecting that sometimes it was easier just to sit in his seventh-floor office in Langley's old headquarters building and not know minute by minute what was going on out in the field. Operatives had to just get on and fend for themselves and extricate themselves from situations —that was their job, just as it had been his for several decades before he was tapped on the shoulder for a promotion. However, given that he was in this case out in the field himself—an unusual occurrence these days—he felt compelled to act immediately to help his people.

Vic moved to the vacant office next to Constanzo's, set up his laptop, and grabbed a coffee.

Then he waited. That was all he could do.

CHAPTER TWENTY-NINE

Wednesday, July 6, 2016
  Rome

The call from Alex Goode at the NSA didn't come until after nine o'clock, by which time Vic had consumed two large coffees and could feel his blood pressure rising. The veins standing out on the back of his hands and around his temples were the giveaway.

"The bad news is, Jayne's phone is dead," Goode said after they had finally been connected via the speakerphone in Constanzo's office and Vic had thanked him for calling in the middle of the night, Maryland time. "It's either switched off or underground, or it's been put in a pouch or box or something. I'm getting nothing from it."

"Did you get a last signal from her?" Vic asked. He glanced across the desk at Constanzo, who sat, arms folded, now looking just as worried as Vic was feeling. "I need good news, not bad."

"I was just coming to that," said Goode, a geek in his early forties who, whenever Vic met him, invariably had his sandy hair combed over the top of his balding head in a vain attempt to disguise it.

Vic sat up straight. "Where?"

"In a street in Trastevere, Via dei Fienaroli."

"The last signal came in the street?"

"Then it went out like a light. And there's been nothing from that phone since."

"Thanks, Alex," Vic said. "If the phone resurfaces, I want to know immediately." He reached across and pushed the red button to end the call

Vic swore ferociously, his mind now in overdrive, and glanced up at Constanzo.

"This has to be Hezbollah," Vic said.

Constanzo shrugged. "It's likely. In which case I don't give much hope for their chances."

Vic grimaced. He was right about that. "Or could they have been pulled in by the Carabinieri, if they don't like us operating on their turf?" he asked. He knew he was clutching at straws. "Or the state police."

"That's also a possibility, although unlikely. Porpora has seemed onside with what we're doing."

"Can you get hold of him and see what he knows? We need him to help find her."

Constanzo nodded. "If it's the Carabinieri, they'd likely take her to Viale Romania. If it's Hezbollah . . . " He let his sentence drift.

Vic knew what he was referring to. He had twice previously been to the enormous Carabinieri headquarters complex at Viale Romania, a couple of kilometers north of the US embassy. If they wanted to question Jayne, that was the logical place to take her. Hezbollah would likely dump her body in the River Tiber.

"All right. You call Porpora, I'll speak to Avi. Maybe he's had more luck tracking down Rafael."

Vic returned to his temporary office next door and dialed Shiloah on a secure connection.

"Vic, any luck?" Shiloah began as he answered the call.

"We've got a last known location, but that's all. You?"

"Trastevere, yes. After that, off the grid. Disappeared."

"Likewise with Jayne. This is unbelievable," Vic said. "I'm guessing they've been picked up by Hezbollah, unless it's the Carabinieri playing games with us."

"The Italians certainly don't like us operating on their soil, but then again, who does?" Shiloah said. "But I agree, most likely Hezbollah. And we'll need to act fast if that's the case. But to do so, unless we send in your special forces or our Sayeret Matkal—which might not go down too well—we need to get the Italians to help with this. We're having discussions here about how we can pull some levers at government level to get them back."

"We're running out of time," Vic said. "It's only five days until the president's visit to the Vatican. I'm seriously worried, not just about Jayne and Rafael, but also about the security implications for that event. We're facing a possible threat and we've got very few leads. If Jayne and Rafael are out of action, I need to deploy others to get those leads chased down in time. Especially that LA Fashions business."

"Who can you send?" Shiloah asked.

"Feds and Joe Johnson." Vic knew that Shiloah was well acquainted with Johnson's abilities. "I'd prefer just to use Johnson, but I keep getting myself into trouble by bypassing the FBI. Better not repeat the offense."

"I'd activate them immediately, then," Shiloah said. "And in terms of getting the Italians to help, there is something I have in mind."

There was a pause, and Vic heard a noise that was unmistakably a lighter being struck, followed by a faint sucking sound down the line. Vic pictured his Israeli counterpart sitting at his office desk, lighting up a Camel cigarette.

"What's that?" Vic asked, to break the silence.

"Two things at this end," Shiloah said. "First, we picked up from a source in Beirut that a massive drug shipment was leaving Latakia port in Syria on a freighter, bound for Naples. It's fifteen tons of amphetamines—Captagon pills. Originally, it was all produced by some drug factory to raise funds for ISIS, but the shipment was stolen a year ago by Hezbollah."

"Hezbollah stole an ISIS drug cache?" There was a note of incredulity in Vic's voice as he grappled with the sheer audacity of such a maneuver. "Presumably to help fund their operations in support of Assad?"

Hezbollah had long been supporters of President Assad of Syria in his fight against ISIS.

"Probably just general funds. It could go on either pro-Assad or pro-Iran operations," Shiloah said. "We have been told the drugs are worth more than a billion euros. Eighty million pills of Captagon, apparently. ISIS sells this stuff frequently—shipments have gone to places like Egypt, Libya, Greece, Saudi Arabia. Since Hezbollah stole it, they have been trying to sell it, and finally have a buyer, we have been told—the Naples mafia, the Camorra."

"Right, and the second thing?"

"Now, the second thing concerns one of the people involved in this huge drug sale on the Italian side—it's a man you are interested in regarding the Vatican investigation, Alberto Casartelli. Unit 8200 has picked up intercepts that point to him using some of his trucks to pick up the Captagon shipment from the Naples port. You can imagine what his cut will be on a one-billion-euro shipment—Casartelli is apparently a Camorra member."

"Does the Italian government know?" Vic asked, his mind now spinning with possible uses for this information.

"That's the key question. We're fairly sure not."

"Could we use this information as leverage to get the Italians to pull out all the stops to get Jayne and Rafael back? An exchange. If they're still alive, that is."

There was a pause, followed by a barely audible chuckle down the line from Tel Aviv. Vic pictured Shiloah leaning back in his chair and exhaling a trail of smoke vigorously toward the ceiling.

"You're thinking along the same lines as I am," Shiloah said. "It so happens that there might be a way of doing just that."

Shiloah started to explain what he had in mind.

* * *

Wednesday, July 6, 2016
Rome

The bowl of porridge that the prison guard brought for Jayne's breakfast arrived very late—her watch had been confiscated, but her body clock told her it was likely at least ten o'clock. It also tasted disgusting. Her suspicion was that it was made with zero-fat milk, which she hated, and it was too cold. The black coffee wasn't much better. It certainly didn't cheer her up after a night with little sleep on a very uncomfortable bunk.

Jayne hadn't bothered to change into the gray cotton nightgown that the guards had thrown into her cell the previous evening and instead had just pulled the sheet and blanket over her.

Her mood and her level of anxiety had not been helped by

the fact that she couldn't deliver on her promise to call Joe as soon as she had returned to the safe house after dinner the previous evening. She knew he would now be worried.

Half an hour after her breakfast tray had been collected, two guards came into the cell without knocking and took her upstairs to a small room furnished only with a metal table and four chairs in the center and a bright fluorescent strip light that hung from the ceiling. The white walls were all bare and there were no windows.

Seated at the table were the Carabinieri officer who had arrested her the previous night and another man who was older and looked more senior. Both just looked at her as she entered but said nothing.

"Sit," one of the guards ordered Jayne, as if she were a dog. He pointed to the two vacant chairs at the table.

Jayne's stomach flipped over, but she folded her arms and remained standing. "You have no reason to have arrested me. I want to speak to the British embassy and to have an attorney present if you are going to question me. Otherwise, I'm not talking."

The lead officer from the previous night stood and walked to Jayne, pushed his face into hers, then roared at the top of his voice, "Sit, you British bitch! Sit!"

Jayne didn't move.

The officer nodded at the guard who was standing immediately behind Jayne.

The next thing she knew, he grabbed her arms from behind and manhandled her toward the chairs at the table.

Jayne reacted instinctively, as she had done the previous evening. She kicked back, and this time the heel of her shoe made hard contact with the center of the guard's shin.

He groaned, jerked back a little, and removed his left hand from her arm.

Before she could move, she was struck with a tremendous

blow on her left temple. The sheer force of it sent her flying across the room and to the gray-painted concrete floor, where she landed painfully on her right rib cage. Immediately she felt a little dizzy, and a white light flashed repeatedly in her left eye, as if she'd looked directly into the sun.

Jayne tried to haul herself up, but the pain in her ribs and in her temple was too much.

Instead she sat on the hard floor for several seconds, blinking. She rubbed the side of her head where the blow had landed, trying to process what was happening.

Are these really police? Or is this some kind of sting operation?

"Who the hell are you?" she said eventually. "What are your names? Show me your identity cards if you are police officers."

The senior officer leaned forward at the table, his arms folded, and stared at Jayne from beneath bushy blond eyebrows that matched his short, slightly spiky hair. "Are you going to talk?"

Jayne had no intention of saying anything much without an attorney present, but on the other hand, perhaps she could find out what they wanted and who they were if she engaged them a little.

The man's face rang a bell in her mind, but through the fog of pain, she couldn't work out why.

"You need to explain who you are," she said, doing her best to keep the emotion and pain out of her voice. "What do you want me to talk about?"

"Sit at the table like I asked you originally," the senior officer said. "Then we can talk."

Jayne could see she was up against a brick wall. She hauled herself to her feet, triggering another sharp, stabbing pain in her ribs, and immediately felt dizzy again. The flashing white light in her left eye intensified. She paused for a second, then stumbled to the table and sat on one of the chairs.

"That's better," the officer said. He clasped his hands on the table in front of him. "Now. I'm not going to waste time. I'm a busy man. We know who you are, Jayne Robinson. What I want to know is, why are you working illegally on espionage-related activities in Italy, and why are you chasing after one of our industrialists?"

Jayne shook her head. "There's no espionage going on, and I am not going to talk to you unless I know who you are. If you are bona fide police officers, show me your identity cards and give me your names."

She eyeballed the senior officer, who wore a white shirt, black tie, and black epaulets on his shoulders. There were three white stars on the epaulets, all of which were bordered in red. His gray eyes were hard and expressionless. The others wore similar dress, but with fewer stars on their epaulets and without the red borders.

This man's superconfident manner suggested to Jayne that he might be very high up the ladder indeed.

It was at that point, despite the throbbing in her head from the blow she had received, that she remembered. They hadn't met, but she'd seen the man's face before on television.

It was Tommaso Porpora, the man who had provided the DNA results from the Beretta used to kill Baltrami that had falsely framed Rafael Levy. She was certain of it.

"You are Tommaso Porpora, aren't you?" she asked. "You're a Carabinieri commander. You're the one who tried to frame my colleague for the killing of a cardinal. You fixed the DNA test results." She pointed to the other officer who had arrested her. "And who is this?"

Porpora blinked and flinched just enough to confirm in Jayne's mind that she was correct. "I'm the one asking the questions. You don't need to know who I am," he said. "And I don't know what you're talking about, DNA test results and framing. Lies, all of it. Now, tell me, why are you working

here without permission on our soil and investigating one of
our citizens, Alberto Casartelli? What are you up to?"

Jayne rocked back in her chair.

This was outrageous. Another high-level leak.

Was all of this coming from Constanzo?

It now certainly looked like it to her.

And why was the Carabinieri concerned about the CIA
looking into a businessman who certainly seemed to have
strong connections with highly dangerous Hezbollah assassins and operated his fashion business in a very odd way?

"Is this Casartelli someone of interest to the Carabinieri,
Commander Porpora?" Jayne asked.

Porpora hesitated slightly before replying. "He is an
Italian citizen. So if a foreign intelligence agency is poking its
nose into one of our citizen's affairs, we should know about it.
Now, tell me why you're investigating him."

Jayne decided this was the point where she zipped up. She
had learned enough and doubted she would get anything
more of value.

"I told you, I'm not going to talk to you about anything
until you've done what I asked, and given me what I'm entitled to," she snapped. "Get me the British embassy on the
phone, and let me call an attorney."

Porpora turned to the guard who had hit Jayne on the
temple. "All right, if that's how she wants to play it. Take her
back to her cell. She can stew in there for a few days until she
decides she wants to be more cooperative. Then fetch her
colleague. We'll have a go at him instead. Maybe he'll talk."

A few days. He can't be serious.

Jayne's only thought at that moment was of the president's upcoming meeting with the pope and the urgent need
to resolve the problems facing them before that happened. A
few days in here would torpedo her chances of doing that,
without a doubt.

She stood, cursing inwardly as the guard approached. She realized too late, only as he lifted his knee and crashed it into the top of her thigh near her hip joint, what he was doing. A searing pain shot through her leg, and once again, she fell to the ground in agony, her left leg now feeling completely numb.

The guard stood above her, hands on hips, a scowl on his face, and watched as she battled the pain from her dead leg.

At least a minute passed before Jayne felt able to attempt to get to her feet once again.

"Keep your hands off me, you animal," she said.

This time the guard bent down and, using a short but extremely powerful backhand, delivered a slap to the left side of Jayne's face, despite her attempt to deflect it by raising her forearm.

The pain was sharp and immediate.

Jayne spat a mouthful of blood onto the floor.

She could feel a sizable cut on the inside of her mouth, and she knew she had to get up—she wasn't going to stay down and take any more of this. She clung on to the back of the chair as she stood.

The guard turned to Porpora. "You want me to finish the job properly?" he muttered in rapid Italian.

Jayne felt her stomach turn over yet again. The black thoughts of the previous night returned.

What the hell does he mean by that?

Kill me?

Rape me?

Porpora gave an almost imperceptible shake of the head. "Not yet."

Jayne stood still for a couple of seconds, then took a step toward Porpora. She couldn't help herself. She wasn't going to just meekly surrender. "You're going to regret this in a major way, you bastard," she said.

"I don't think so," Porpora said, a wolfish grin curling up from the corners of his thin mouth. "You're the one who's going to regret ever coming here. There are no cameras in here, by the way, no recordings, no evidence. Nobody to see anything. Officially, I haven't been in here, and neither have these others. Now, get back to your cell and stew. We're keeping you out of trouble, doing you a favor."

The guard grabbed Jayne by one arm, the other guard, who had until now stood silently near the door, took her other arm, and they pulled her out of the room.

CHAPTER THIRTY

Wednesday, July 6, 2016
Portland, Maine

Joe Johnson opened his front door and held the lead firmly as Cocoa attempted to rush out, eager to get his walk underway.

It was only five thirty in the morning, but Joe had just come off a phone call with his old friend and former boss Vic Walter, the contents of which had left him in a state of some turmoil.

After finishing the call, he needed to simmer down and collect his thoughts, so he decided to take Cocoa for an early lap around Back Cove, an inlet off Casco Bay north of Portland's city center, where he lived. The circular route was about three and a half miles, and he often either ran or walked around it, sometimes with his dog, sometimes without.

At the back of his mind, the one thing Joe had always feared about Jayne operating on her own, rather than in tandem with him, was that if something went wrong and she needed backup, there might not be any on hand.

He knew she was damned good at her job and was without a doubt tough enough to look after herself in most circumstances. But it was the possibility of some event coming at her from left field that always concerned him.

Now that seemed to have happened.

Worried about Jayne, Joe had woken before five o'clock after less than four hours of fitful sleep, wondering whether to give Vic a call to check what was happening.

Jayne had promised the previous evening to call him after she had finished dinner in Rome. But not only had she not called, neither had she sent a message to explain why.

That was most unlike her. They hadn't spoken for several days, and he hadn't expected to do so, given that she was up to her eyeballs on a seriously demanding operation where unnecessary communications might be a real security risk.

But always, if she said she would do something, she could be relied upon to do it.

And what's more, her phone was dead.

Five minutes after Joe had woken, his phone had vibrated on his bedside table—Vic had called him instead. He broke the news that Jayne had disappeared and her phone had indeed gone off the grid.

Joe's gut instinct had proved correct.

He closed the front door and left the house, a large two-story Cape Cod–style property with green shutters, a double garage, and a white picket fence at the front. He walked with Cocoa to the end of his street, Parsons Road, crossed over Baxter Boulevard, and joined Back Cove Trail, a broad path popular with runners and walkers that ran through the grassy area between the street and the expanse of seawater beyond.

There he stopped, took out his phone, and dialed Jayne yet again.

The number you are calling is unobtainable. Please try again later.

He put it back into his pocket and broke into a gentle jog. Cocoa was used to this and loped along beside him. The ten-foot extendable leash gave him plenty of leeway.

Now what to do?

Joe's overwhelming instinct was to get on a plane to Rome to go and help track Jayne down. But while his heart said go, his head told him that was unlikely to help, based on the conversation he'd had with Vic.

He could see that Jayne's fate was going to be decided at a higher level, probably by trying to involve the Italian government. If Hezbollah had taken Jayne and Rafael, which seemed the most likely explanation, he knew a truth he hated to face: they would both likely be found dead by some rural roadside early tomorrow morning, if not before, their bodies having been bundled out of a car.

But if the Italians mobilized their security forces, then there might be a faint glimmer of hope.

Vic had said he and Avi Shiloah were working on that.

Joe decided not to hold his breath. There was nothing he could do to change things; it was all out of his control.

Instead he focused on Vic's other proposal—that Joe could best help by getting involved with a part of the ongoing investigation that Jayne was certainly no longer going to be able to handle.

He had asked Joe to fly to Los Angeles and work with the FBI to delve into a clothing company that apparently had curious links with a Rome-based fashion firm. In turn, that firm was connected to a Hezbollah assassin who might have been behind the murder of several cardinals.

Joe had agreed that Vic had to involve the FBI if there was potentially some serious criminal activity taking place. But Vic, typically, wanted to retain some control over matters. He couldn't easily deploy his own CIA team within the United States, so his view was that Joe, as always, was a good alternative to join forces with the Feds.

Joe agreed to think it over while running around Back Cove. In any case, he would make contact in an hour or two with the FBI's executive assistant director Simon Dover, who headed up the Criminal, Cyber, Response, and Services branch and whom he knew well from previous operations.

One thing that Dover had in common with Vic was that he occasionally liked to get involved in operations in a more hands-on manner than he probably should for a senior executive, particularly if another agency, such as the CIA, also happened to be interested. Johnson assumed that might be partly due to him wanting to protect his turf, but it might also have been because he enjoyed working on cases with a global reach. It was a change from his usual domestic focus. Either way, his approach seemed to work. He was good at his job and was well regarded at the White House and on Capitol Hill, like his boss, FBI Director Robert Bonfield.

During the next hour, Vic would brief Dover too, and between them they could hopefully devise a plan that could be executed swiftly. There was no time to waste.

Joe ran on, past the supermarket, the park, and the brewery.

By the time he and Cocoa had crossed Tukey's Bridge, which spanned the channel through which seawater flowed into and out of Back Cove, he was feeling slightly less desperate. Having a plan of some kind always helped.

Joe's children, Carrie and Peter, were now aged nineteen and eighteen respectively. Carrie was home on summer vacation from her studies at Boston University, while Peter had recently graduated from high school and was waiting to start at the same college, with a plan to major in economics. At their age, both could cope by themselves at home for a few days. Previously when he had gone away on operations, he had asked his sister, Amy, to move into the house and look after his children. But that was no longer necessary.

He decided that if Jayne's investigation required some work in Los Angeles, he would do it. It wouldn't bring her back, but working on the assumption that she would come back—because he couldn't face contemplating any other outcome—it would do her a favor and help her case along. It would also help out his old friend Vic, and it would keep his hand in the game.

* * *

Wednesday, July 6, 2016
    Jerusalem

Two policemen opened the heavy gray steel security gates in front of the entrance to Prime Minister Yitzhak Katz's official residence, Beit Aghion, and another officer pulled back the enormous black fabric curtain that prevented prying eyes from seeing what was happening beyond.

Avi Shiloah's driver eased the black BMW through the gates and the goalpost-style metal frame that contained the curtain and continued to the parking space reserved for his regular briefing with Katz. Behind Shiloah's car, the policemen swiftly closed both the curtain and the gates.

Beit Aghion, built from Jerusalem sandstone in a modern-looking square block style, stood at 9 Smolenskin Street, on the corner with Balfour Street. It was surrounded by a wall, also built from sandstone and capped with a fence. The perimeter was bristling with security cameras, giant mirrors, and listening devices, and the approaches to it were blocked with double or triple barricades on both streets.

It was the normal location for Shiloah's briefings with the PM. He climbed out of the car, threw the stub of the cigarette he had been smoking on the ground, and made his way to security. After the usual checks, from which he wasn't immune, he continued to the upstairs main conference room. There, he took a seat in one of the brown leather swivel chairs at the long, narrow oak table.

The room was too brightly lit for Shiloah's liking, with an array of dozens of lightbulbs hanging from the ceiling in an enclosure that was shaped to match the table below. Katz sometimes held his private meetings here and sometimes in his smaller private office next door. The detritus of previous meetings stood on the table—dirty coffee cups, milk jugs, half-eaten sandwiches on plates, and crumpled napkins. Paintings of Israeli landscapes hung on the walls.

Shiloah knew from their many private conversations, usually late into the night over a glass or two of Katz's favorite Courvoisier French cognac, that the prime minister didn't particularly like his relatively modest official residence at Beit Aghion. The property dated back to the 1930s and had been used by a series of Israeli prime ministers ever since Katz's namesake, Yitzhak Rabin, moved there in 1974.

Although located in the upmarket Rehavia neighborhood, it was in the middle of a residential area, which caused security issues. Katz didn't consider it large enough for a premier, and to be fair, it was certainly a far cry from the White House or the British prime minister's grand residence at 10 Downing Street in London.

However, the prime minister often qualified his complaints with the comment that Beit Aghion was a significant improvement on the conditions endured by his Polish mother and father, both of whom barely survived Auschwitz by some miracle. The rest of his family, including his cousins, aunts, uncles, and grandparents, were murdered by the Nazis in 1943.

A few minutes later, Katz walked in alone and closed the soundproofed door behind him.

"I hear we may have a problem with our Italian friends?" Katz said.

"You've talked with Ehud, I presume?" Shiloah had briefed the new foreign minister, Ehud Biham, earlier in the day about events in Rome, and he knew that Biham had met with Katz after that.

"He'd like to send in the Sayeret Matkal to extract your man Rafael Levy," Katz said. "I'm assuming you have a more subtle approach in mind."

Shiloah always had a more subtle approach in mind than Ehud, a notorious hawk whose first instinct was always aggressive.

"Is your call with Romano Leone still happening later?" Shiloah asked cautiously. He knew that Katz was due to have a scheduled phone call with the Italian prime minister that evening.

Katz nodded. "I will have to suffer his arrogant utterances for half an hour, yes."

"That helps. Now, as we all know, Leone has been under fire over a resurgence of corruption and badly needs to show he's on top of it ahead of the referendum on the constitution in a couple of months. I'm going to suggest you offer an opportunity for him to earn himself some serious credit on law-and-order issues."

Shiloah went on to outline the details of the enormous shipment of Captagon pills that was en route from Syria to Naples and the deal that Katz might propose to Leone.

When he had finished, the prime minister allowed himself a thin smile. "A viable suggestion, Avi. I might add a few lines to that script, actually, along the lines of what I might do publicly with the information about his country's stance on terrorism, drug smuggling, and money laundering if he indicates he's not interested in cooperating with our proposals."

"Threats and blackmail are a national currency in Italy."

Katz let out a short, sarcastic cackle. Shiloah knew from the prime minister's occasional throwaway comments that deep down, his view of Italy was still colored by the country's alignment with Hitler's Germany during World War II. He seemed to do little to hide it.

"If it goes well," Katz said, "this will also earn us some serious credit with the Americans and the British, given that their operative will also be a beneficiary of what we're planning."

Shiloah nodded. "Let's hope so. We could certainly use it as a bargaining chip in the future." He fingered his chin. "Of course, there is one possible hurdle to overcome."

Katz gave him a look. "Which is?"

"We have absolutely no idea where either Rafael or Jayne Robinson are. We don't even know, let's be honest, whether they are alive or dead in a ditch somewhere. We don't know who's got them—Hezbollah has to be the main suspect, although it could be mafia or even the Italian security forces. And I have to assume that at this stage the Italian government may not know either."

"Well, we'll have to hope that the possible consequences of failing to find that out will concentrate their minds. The potential for international embarrassment usually does."

"And if it doesn't work?"

Katz shrugged, all traces of his smile now gone. "We're playing high-stakes, international poker here, Avi. Just as we've played it for many years in the past and no doubt will play it in the future. Sometimes our bluffs, our truths, half-truths, lies, and our distortions succeed, and sometimes they fail. When they succeed, we walk out of the casino with a smile on our face and our wallets stuffed full. When the game goes against us, as the law of averages dictates it sometimes must, we lose the shirts from our backs—and worse."

CHAPTER THIRTY-ONE

Thursday, July 7, 2016
  Los Angeles

The special agent in charge of the FBI's Los Angeles office, Frank Merlin, stood in front of the reception desk, talking to Dimitri Margiotta, the manager of the somewhat run-down LA Fashions factory unit in which they were standing.

Joe stood well back, near the entrance with Simon Dover, and let Merlin go through the process of showing Margiotta his FBI badge and the search warrant he had obtained from a judge that morning.

The factory was in an industrial park off Amar Road in the La Puente neighborhood. It had gray corrugated steel walls and looked as though it had seen better days. The asphalt parking lot outside was cracked and had weeds poking through in places. It was also very hot inside. Although there were fans and air-conditioning units, they seemed to have little impact on the baking temperatures caused by the hot sun outside.

Joe had been impressed with the speed with which Dover had mobilized his teams following the initial call from Vic in Rome the previous morning. As a result, he had taken a flight that same afternoon from Portland to Washington, DC, where he had joined Dover and other agents on an FBI Gulfstream V twin-engine jet to Los Angeles. Dover said he was well overdue a visit to the LA field office and would combine the two objectives.

Five other agents, all dressed in khaki trousers and navy polo shirts with FBI imprinted in large yellow letters on the back, stood behind Merlin. Two of them carried boxes loaded with computer scanning equipment.

Margiotta, an unshaven Latino with long gray hair, had an air of resignation about him. He stared at the floor and seemed to quickly accept the inevitable. He walked to a door behind the reception desk, held it open for Merlin and the rest of them to go through, and showed them into a small conference room.

Joe suspected he wanted to get the FBI team out of sight of the reception desk as quickly as possible. There were several other visitors waiting there, and an FBI raid didn't look good.

"We'll need access to everywhere," Merlin told Margiotta. "Manufacturing facilities, equipment, products, materials. All computers too, as listed in my warrant. Storage rooms, safes, all offices." He waved the document he was carrying.

Merlin turned to Joe and Dover. "Where do you want to start?"

Joe stepped forward and looked at Margiotta, who again cast his eyes to the floor. "We are particularly interested in the manufacturing work you do for Sole Nero, in Italy. Can we see where that work is done and the products made, please? Also, the materials used and where they are stored."

Margiotta hesitated. "Sole Nero? Never heard of them."

"Don't bullshit me," Joe said. "We have emails, orders, invoices. Everything. The communications between you and Alberto Casartelli. I can show you all of those if you like, but that would simply be wasting your time as well as ours."

Margiotta's gaze dropped to the floor again. Eventually, he nodded. "That work is done on one production line at the far end of the building."

"Show us."

There was another hesitation. "Follow me."

Margiotta led the way out the door, along a corridor that was badly in need of painting, and opened another door.

As the door swung open, the noise struck Joe like a thunderclap.

In front of him was a scene of utter chaos. There was an enormous factory floor filled with lines of individual wooden tables. On each table stood a sewing machine, reels of yarn, and piles of cloth and garments. Joe guessed there were about two hundred tables, of which at least 90 percent were occupied by Hispanic women aged in their fifties or sixties. The clattering noise from the sewing machines was deafening.

All the women were working away on garments.

Margiotta beckoned the FBI team and made his way along a gangway that led through the forest of tables until he came to a section of about forty tables at the far end of the building that was separated by portable dividers. As they walked, several of the women glanced up at the team of agents accompanying their manager, surprise and concern written over their faces.

"Is this the section where you make Sole Nero garments?" Joe asked the manager.

"Yes. Mainly shirts, blazers, and trousers," Margiotta said.

Sure enough, most of the workers in that section appeared to be stitching those items together. Despite the noise, Joe could hear that most of them were speaking with each other in Spanish.

"I know you receive your orders for Sole Nero by email from Alberto Casartelli," Joe said. "Can you just confirm that?"

His question earned a curt nod from Margiotta.

"How much do you sell those items for? Specifically, the ones for Sole Nero that are sold to Adelaide shops?" Joe asked.

Margiotta shrugged. "We sell blazers for sixty dollars, shirts for nine dollars, trousers twenty dollars."

"And what's the usual retail price?" Joe persisted.

"Prices vary. Blazers maybe three hundred fifty, shirts sixty or seventy. Trousers are perhaps a hundred. They're top-end items. Sole Nero is a big Italian brand."

Johnson didn't need to spend long doing the math in his head.

"A huge margin on those items," he said.

It was too big. It didn't make any sense. He guessed the workers in this factory were on sweatshop wages. There had been several scandals relating to extremely low wages paid to textile industry workers in California. This looked like another one.

"Where is the cloth, the raw material?" Joe asked.

The manager pointed to a recess with double doors at the rear of the building. "Through those doors."

"Take us," Joe said.

Margiotta led them through the door into a large, but far quieter, warehouse with racks up to the ceiling filled with rolls of cloth. A couple of forklifts were busy taking down pallets from the higher shelves. He pointed to a shelving section to his right. "That is the cloth for Sole Nero."

"Where does the material for all this come from?" Joe asked.

The manager shook his head and said nothing.

"Come on, we need to know," Joe said.

"I can't say that."

Joe pursed his lips and turned to Dover, who took a step toward Margiotta.

"It is going to be far, far better for you if you cooperate," Dover said. "The owners of this factory are in trouble, and this business is finished now, anyway. You do not want to be implicated in their mess. Now tell us where the material comes from."

Margiotta stared at the floor. "It's from a few different sources. Mexico, mainly."

Dover caught Joe's eye and raised an eyebrow.

"And how are payments made for it?" Dover asked.

Joe somehow knew what the answer to this question was going to be.

"We pay in cash," the manager said.

Dover nodded. "Where does the cash come from? Does the bank deliver it?"

Margiotta shook his head. "I'm going to be fired for telling you all this information," he said. "No, it doesn't come from the bank. We receive a delivery in a truck when we need it."

"Who sends it?" Joe asked.

"I don't know who sends it. Someone connected to Sole Nero."

"Is it kept in a safe?"

Margiotta nodded. "In the office."

"Which office?" Joe demanded.

Margiotta didn't reply but silently beckoned Joe, Dover, and Merlin to follow him. They retraced their steps back toward the reception area, but then turned right through a door with a keypad security lock, where Margiotta swiftly tapped in a code.

The office was almost as chaotic and untidy as the factory floor. There were piles of papers, books, magazines, and brochures on every surface, along with dirty coffee cups and chocolate bar wrappers among the computers and monitors.

"Open the safe," Merlin said. "It's included in the warrant."

Margiotta exhaled, then took a set of keys from his pocket, unlocked a cupboard, and opened the door, and there inside was a large gray steel safe. He tapped a code into a keypad on the front, pressed another button, and silently swung the door open.

Joe, Dover, and Merlin stood staring. Inside the safe was a clear plastic box stuffed full of bundles of used twenty- and fifty-dollar bills. There were also smaller packages of cash in plastic bags, along with a series of cardboard document folders, files, and other items.

"We'll take this lot away for analysis," Merlin said. He glanced at Dover. "I'll take a guess where this is coming from."

"Don't touch any of the notes," Dover said. "You'll get high. It'll all be rich kids' drugs money."

Merlin instructed two of his agents to remove the box and bags of cash and all the document files. They put on latex gloves and lifted the money out of the safe first.

He turned back to Margiotta. "We'll need samples of every item of clothing you're making for Sole Nero and all contact details you've got for suppliers, the people who deliver and collect the money, and anyone else connected to the operation, including your workers here. I'm assuming that the orders to Sole Nero from Adelaide are all actually manufactured here, not by Italian craftsmen in Rome."

Margiotta said nothing, but again stared at the floor. The answer was clearly yes. Buyers in Adelaide stores who thought they were getting genuine Italian-made items of clothing were being sadly deceived.

"How long have you been making the clothing for Sole Nero?" Joe asked.

Margiotta shrugged. "About ten years."

"How did that begin?"

"I don't know," the manager said. "We were just told to start."

Joe glanced around the office and wandered along the aisle between the rows of desks. He picked up a few documents from one of the desks. Most were sales orders and invoices, which he replaced. There was a large bound volume of cloth samples, all of which looked to be made from high-quality wool of the type used for expensive suits.

Stacked on the floor in a corner against a wall were several picture frames. Joe picked them up and glanced at the photos. Most looked like professional individual portrait photographs, with the subjects all dressed in suits against a white background. One was of Margiotta, taken several years ago. Joe guessed they were the senior management team.

The last photo was of what looked like some kind of family group, taken a long time ago, judging by the slightly faded print. There were three men, two women, and three children. Two of the men were wearing suits and the women were in smart dresses.

The third man, however, was wearing a red cassock, a red skullcap, and a chain around his neck with a large wooden cross attached.

Joe stared at it, his mind now fizzing.

A cardinal.

He took the photograph over to Margiotta, who was still standing near the safe, looking somewhat shell-shocked.

"Who is this in the photo?" Joe asked.

Margiotta looked and grimaced, then shook his head fractionally. "It's the family."

"The family? Which family?"

"Do you really need to know all this detail?"

Joe nodded. "We do."

"The family that owns this factory. The Sweeney family."

Joe raised his eyebrows. He knew from the research he'd done, and from the initial work done by the FBI, that LA Fashions was owned through a slightly complicated structure involving three trusts, all of which were linked to a Sweeney family, but that was all. He hadn't had time to dig into the ownership of the respective trusts and the individuals behind them. The plan was to pressure Margiotta to give full details of the ownership and the management structure once they had raided the site, including all relevant share certificates. All of those items had been specifically included in the FBI warrant so they could force the issue with the manager.

Joe pointed. "This guy in the cardinal's cassock. Who's he? What's he doing in the photo?"

Margiotta looked at him. "That's Cardinal Sweeney. Louis Sweeney. He's the archbishop of New Orleans. He's one of the three brothers who own this place."

Joe stood still for a few seconds, digesting what Margiotta was saying.

"So who set up the contract with Sole Nero?" Joe asked, eventually. "Was it Cardinal Sweeney, or was it one of the other brothers, or someone else?"

Margiotta visibly blanched. "I believe it was Cardinal Sweeney who was responsible initially," he muttered. "But that was a long time ago. We never see him here. He never comes."

Joe tried to stop himself from doing a double take. "Why would a cardinal set up an arrangement like this?"

Margiotta shook his head. "I don't know."

Joe paused for a moment. He didn't know whether the guy was telling the truth or not, although his gut instinct said he probably was. "If that's the case, just to let you know, I'll be staying here in Los Angeles until either you remember or we find out some other way."

CHAPTER THIRTY-TWO

Friday, July 8, 2016
    The Vatican

CIRRUS used his left hand to clamp the phone to his ear
and, with his right hand, scribbled notes in his book as his
source rattled through the latest information he had
picked up.

He was sitting in his usual spot on a plain canvas-covered
sofa in his small two-room apartment.

"So Cardinal Sweeney constantly addressed the pope as
'my confessor' during this meeting," the source told CIRRUS.
"He then started spilling out all the details of his sins relating
to LA Fashions."

"Everything?"

"Most of it."

CIRRUS grimaced. This was bad news. "What did he
say?"

There were so many sins on the list that it took
CIRRUS's informant quite some time to go through them all.

The pitifully low wages paid to the workers, all well below the legal minimum, the awful working conditions, the stressful daily targets. That was just a starting point. Sweeney had apparently admitted he had often been able to insist that these conditions be improved but didn't do what he should have done.

Then Sweeney spilled out details of the financial fiddling. The cash payments to suppliers and workers so that there was no record and no taxes paid. There was the fraud perpetrated on the main customer, Adelaide, who thought it was getting blazers and shirts hand-made by craftsmen in Rome. And in turn, the fraud suffered by Adelaide's customers, who bought in good faith at prices ten times higher than cost and at a quality quite different from that advertised.

And the biggest sin that Sweeney asked forgiveness for was in allowing all this to happen in order to line the pockets of one of the world's largest terrorist groups—Hezbollah—and their Iranian masters.

Not that Sweeney had had much choice in the matter, CIRRUS thought as he listened. But that was entirely the fault of the cardinal himself and was another story. CIRRUS didn't have any sympathy for him.

To him, Sweeney was just another American who had become rich on ill-gotten gains at the expense of his impoverished immigrant workers. It reinforced the anti-American views expressed by many people, including his father, back in Syria, where—as in so many countries of the Middle East—everyday life for millions of people was a battle for survival in the face of poverty, disease, never-ending wars, and political upheaval. CIRRUS's heart went out to such people every day.

Clearly, Sweeney had abused his position of trust as a high-ranking clergyman to avoid scrutiny and criticism. CIRRUS had no time for such people. As a younger man, his father had often told him in forceful terms that America was the cradle of evil and that the likes of presidents Reagan, Bush, and Clinton needed to die very painful deaths. He had to agree. Over the years since, CIRRUS had tried to put such prejudices aside, but now aged sixty-one, he had to admit his views were too deeply ingrained. These days, such views helped him to justify both what he was now doing and the large amounts of money he was receiving from Hezbollah coffers for his services.

Finally the informant finished his account.

"Did Sweeney tell the pope why he was confessing all this now rather than years ago?" CIRRUS asked.

"He asked forgiveness for the delay, said he had made a big mistake, and should have drawn a line at what was happening a long time ago. He told the pope that recent events had forced him into the confession."

Cardinal Sweeney had then gone on to describe to the pope how the premises of his family's factory in Los Angeles had received a visit the previous day from a group of FBI agents, including one who was very senior, Simon Dover, and a private investigator, Joe Johnson, the source continued.

"He told the pope that all the detail would become public knowledge at some point, with the potential to seriously embarrass the Catholic Church and the Vatican," the source said.

Apparently the pope had listened to the confession and said little but evidently felt surprised and shocked.

There had obviously been prior discussions and confessions between Cardinal Sweeney and the pope because there were several somewhat vague references in their conversation to past unnamed sins having led to these latest ones.

Neither Sweeney nor the pope went into any detail about what these other sins were, but CIRRUS knew exactly what they were referring to.

At the end of the confession, the pope had of course given

Cardinal Sweeney absolution and forgiven him for his sins, the source reported.

"Did Sweeney mention either of us to the pope?" CIRRUS asked.

"No," the source said. "So I'm hoping we weren't mentioned to the FBI either."

"But do you think the FBI might find out how this all started, and what we did?" CIRRUS asked.

"If they decide to interview Sweeney, and maybe the pope, then it's quite likely."

CIRRUS felt his stomach tighten into a knot.

This seriously complicated things.

It now seemed to him a virtual certainty that Hassan's entire highly lucrative, well-oiled, hitherto successful scheme was going to be completely blown apart. The considerable and risky steps that Hassan and his colleague Pierre Fekkai had taken to protect their positions seemed to have failed, thanks to some unexpectedly dogged and insightful work by the investigator Jayne Robinson and her group. There was no doubting that this FBI raid stemmed from their work.

Hassan and Pierre were in considerable jeopardy, it seemed.

But even worse than that, if Sweeney and the pope gave away what they knew, it could lead to the discovery and arrest of CIRRUS and his source at the Vatican. Their reputations would be trashed and their way of life destroyed.

CIRRUS wasn't about to let that happen.

There was only one way to resolve this, as far as he could see.

"Have you picked up any details about what the pope's and Sweeney's movements are going to be ahead of this event with the American president?" CIRRUS asked.

"Some, yes," the source said. "The pope has little in his diary from now until the event takes place. He's preparing carefully. There are a few meetings. Then, on the morning of the event, just his usual routine—his hairdresser, his tailor, his speechwriter. That's it."

"How do you know this?"

"From conversations between the pope and Despierre."

"What about Sweeney?" CIRRUS asked. "What's he doing?"

"Sweeney I know less about, but I believe he's expecting to remain in the Vatican until after the event with the president."

CIRRUS sat silently for a few seconds, thinking. He then thanked his source, ended the call, and sat back.

It took him a short while to clarify his thoughts. But he quickly realized there was no way around it.

Sweeney and the pope would both have to go.

He picked up his phone and called Hassan.

* * *

Friday, July 8, 2016
Tehran

It was the first time that Nasser Khan had seen the Supreme Leader get up and walk around the room during one of his briefings. Normally he sat almost motionless, virtually unblinking, and stared at Khan while he explained the progress or otherwise of whatever operation was on the agenda that week.

But the news that Khan imparted had appeared to suddenly galvanize Ayatollah Hashemi.

"You are telling me they are going to be in the same room for three quarters of an hour?" Hashemi asked. He paused in mid-stride and stood, staring at Khan and tugging at his neatly clipped white beard so firmly that a few hairs came loose in his hand.

"That is what I am led to believe," Khan said. "I am not able to confirm it with complete certainty, but that is the briefing I have received."

"From Talal Hassan?"

"It was he, yes. His view also is that given the way this operation is proceeding, there may be a need to terminate more cardinals if it becomes clear they have knowledge of Hezbollah's activities and if there is a risk they will make that public. Of course, that would seriously threaten Hezbollah's flow of income, were it to happen."

The Supreme Leader walked to the door, turned, and made his way back to his chair, where he sat once again.

"If he needs to terminate them, then he must do so," Hashemi said. "There is no value lost to this planet by terminating a cardinal. In fact, it is a major gain. But I am interested in the even greater opportunity—this meeting between the pope and president to which you referred."

This time the Supreme Leader reverted to his usual motionless mode and stared at Khan, clearly expecting some kind of response.

"You mean you would like us to take advantage of the situation if that is possible, sir?"

For the first time since Khan had taken command of the Quds Force four years ago, he saw the corners of the Supreme Leader's mouth turn up. It was the closest Hashemi had ever come to a smile in his company.

But he knew what was coming next, and counterintuitively, his heart sank.

"Do you believe there might be an opportunity to remove both of them from the field of battle?" Hashemi asked. "Our battle against Christianity is real. Taking down the pope would strike a huge blow. And if we could do likewise to the leader of the western world at the same time . . . "

The Supreme Leader left his sentence unfinished.

It was obvious what Hashemi was thinking—such a triumph would seal his place in history.

Khan swallowed hard. There was no doubt such a challenge appealed to the soldier in him. He had spent thirty-one years as a Quds Force officer, and of those, twenty-two had been in the field conducting a variety of lethal operations against Iran's enemies.

But his thoughts turned not to how he and Hassan might plot such a maneuver, but what the consequences might be if they failed. He knew he would have to choose his words carefully now and at least attempt to manage expectations.

"Sir, I mentioned this meeting because there is a possibility, however remote, that it may present an opportunity," Khan said. "But I do not want to raise your hopes. The obstacles to success are great and the overwhelming likelihood is that an opportunity will not exist. This meeting will be conducted in the heart of the Vatican, in the pope's private office. It is guarded even more securely than your residence here and will be doubly so when the American president is there. It will never be possible to devise a normal operation involving our usual top officers. I believe that some kind of subterfuge will be the only way—and I know not what that might be. However, if it is your wish, I can issue instructions that an attempt be made, if workable."

The Supreme Leader's eyes, already the hardest, most unyielding that Khan had ever come across, took on a new intensity.

His head remained motionless as his lips moved. "Get it done."

CHAPTER THIRTY-THREE

Friday, July 8, 2016
   Rome

"There's an old British saying that a friend of mine in London taught me many years ago when we were working on a bombing campaign," Talal Hassan said from his seat on the sofa.

He leaned forward and replaced his phone on the coffee table in front of him, having just finished a call with CIRRUS. The news he had been given had left him feeling irritated and angry.

"What's that?" Pierre asked.

Hassan pulled out a pack of Futura cigarettes, the brand he always smoked when in Italy. "It was a wartime saying. Careless talk costs lives."

He removed a cigarette from the pack and lit it. "It was very appropriate. I've never forgotten it. Obviously, our friends at the Vatican never knew this saying—especially Cardinal Louis Sweeney."

Hassan glanced at Pierre, who was perched on the edge of a chair on the other side of the living room in the rented safe house on Via di Sant'Anselmo. The villa, a smart two-story terracotta building, was close to the Pontifical University of Saint Anselmo and less than four hundred meters east of the River Tiber, near the Ponte Sublicio, the most ancient bridge in Rome that linked Ripa to Trastevere.

"Unfortunately, cardinals are paid to talk," Pierre said, his face contorted into a grimace. "Not to stay silent."

Hassan swore out loud. "They are not learning from their mistakes either. We have no choice. We will need to continue teaching them until they do learn. Our American friend Cardinal Sweeney is apparently now singing like a canary. He's already confessed his many sins to the pope. Who will he confide in next? The FBI or the CIA? Maybe he has already, for all we know."

Hassan stood and walked to the window, took a deep drag from his cigarette, and glanced up and down the street, which was lined with similarly large and expensive villas. He turned, tipped his head back a little, and blew a stream of smoke toward the ceiling.

His phone vibrated noisily on the table. He strode back over to it, picked it up, sat down on the sofa again, and read the message. It was from Alberto Casartelli.

Operation Prada is blown. FBI raid in LA. Have pulled strings to muddy waters in short term, but need to leave country immediately. Suggest you act now re Sweeney. Will be in touch ASAP.

Hassan swore again, tossed his phone to the far end of the sofa, and forcibly stubbed out his cigarette in the ashtray on the table.

"This is getting out of control," he said. "Operation Prada is blown. The FBI has raided the LA Fashions factory and—"

Hassan didn't finish his sentence because his phone rang. He reached over, picked it up, and after seeing who the caller was, caught Pierre's eye and put a finger to his lips to warn him not to talk. He keyed in his code to accept the encrypted call, then pressed the green button.

"This is good timing, sir. I need to speak to you."

"I need to talk to you too," Nasser Khan replied. Hassan immediately caught the intensity in his voice. "But go ahead," Khan said. "Tell me what you know."

Hassan quickly rattled through a summary of what had happened in Rome and the content of the message just received from Casartelli. "It's a financial disaster," he concluded.

Khan's deep tones came down the line. "Not good, Talal. Not good for you. I agree, it's time to act on Sweeney. But I need to tell you, I've just come from a meeting with the Supreme Leader. He has issued some instructions."

Hassan listened with mounting concern as Khan talked without a break for the next few minutes. What Khan was instructing him to do was something he had vaguely considered at the back of his mind but realistically had written off as infeasible. Now he was being told it was an order from the Supreme Leader.

"I don't think this is going to work very—"

"We have no choice, Talal, you and I," Khan interrupted. "You know very well what happened to Abbas."

Hassan said nothing.

"You need to sit down with Pierre and work out a plan," Khan said. "And you need to do it quickly. Let me know when you've done that." He ended the call.

Hassan quietly put his phone down on the sofa next to him.

"I got the general idea of what that was about," Pierre said.

Hassan pursed his lips. "He's not giving us a choice."

"What are we going to do?"

Hassan pointed at him. "It's more about what *you* are going to do. Now, listen to me."

He began to outline his plan.

CHAPTER THIRTY-FOUR

Friday, July 8, 2016
Rome

"I assume you're providing the usual new cassock and skullcap for the pope's meeting with the president?" Pierre asked. He took a sip from the steaming cup of double espresso that had just arrived.

"Of course," Vincenzo Zeffirelli said. "And not just for the pope, but for several other cardinals in the Holy See. They all want to look good. These meetings with international leaders are always huge moneymakers for us, as you know." He gave a slight chuckle.

The two men were sitting in Vincenzo's somewhat cramped wood-paneled office at the rear of the Fratelli Zeffirelli tailor shop on Borgio Pio street, near to St. Peter's Square. Pierre had arrived just as Zeffirelli was closing up the store, and now almost all the staff had gone home.

An old-fashioned desktop computer with a large, chunky monitor sat on the dark oak desk next to piles of invoices and bills. On a shelf behind Vincenzo were stacked bulky fabric swatch books filled with cloth samples from various suppliers.

Pierre put his blue porcelain cup back on the saucer that Vincenzo's secretary had provided. "I suppose it's the usual round of last-minute fittings and adjustments with all of them, too?"

He knew that supplying new outfits for big occasions, when the eyes of the world would be on the pope and his cardinals through the lenses of multiple TV cameras, was always a slightly fraught affair.

"Of course," Vincenzo replied. "We're always last on the list, and they expect miracles at short notice. They don't realize we can't walk on water like they seem to think." He gave a cracked, wheezy laugh at his own clerical joke.

Pierre also laughed. He knew from his own occasional visits to the Vatican alongside Vincenzo how things usually worked with the pope and his cardinals. They were all such busy people that the tailor's meetings and fittings were repeatedly postponed and delayed to make room for other commitments and meetings until whatever event was about to take place was right upon them. They then expected the tailor to fit their cassock and accessories and make the necessary adjustments at the last minute.

"It makes your job difficult," Pierre said. "It's been a few years since I was there, but I guess nothing changes."

"Correct. Nothing changes." Vincenzo shook his head in mock despair.

"So when are you fitting the pope?" Pierre asked, as casually as he could.

Vincenzo creased his forehead. "As usual with the pope, it's all very rushed. Final fitting is about two hours before the event. It's tight timing. That was the only slot in his diary, I was told. He has appointments with his hairdresser, his speechwriter, and others to fit in." He shrugged. "I just hope he doesn't need any major changes, otherwise I'll be in trouble."

Pierre nodded. It was tight timing indeed. But on this occasion, that might help.

"What are you fitting the pope for this time?" Pierre asked. "Just a cassock, or all the trimmings?"

"He likes his trimmings," Vincenzo said. "So yes, the lot—the *mozzettas*, the lace rochets, and the biretta caps. They are all ready. I just hope the fit is to his liking. We also need to take some cloth samples. He wants us to make some extra shirts he can wear when he's not on duty. He doesn't like the material for those he got from the other tailor he uses, so he wants us to provide his shirts as well as his cassocks and formal wear."

"How long will you have for this meeting?" Pierre asked.

Vincenzo shrugged. "Not long enough. Maybe half an hour. He's always in a rush."

"Are you going alone or taking someone with you?" Pierre asked, trying to keep his voice level and conversational.

"Just me and Massimo. The usual team. Why do you ask?"

"Well, I thought that with so much to be done, you might need some additional help. I would like to offer my help. I'll come along too."

"You know that Massimo and I always handle it well," Vincenzo said. "The pope only wants two there at most."

Pierre leaned back in his chair and folded his arms. "Listen, would you mind if I came along with you instead of Massimo this time? It's been a while since my last visit with you."

Vincenzo narrowed his eyes and scrutinized Pierre. He didn't speak for several seconds.

"That's just not going to be possible," he said eventually. "Massimo and I have been doing all the work on the garments. We know precisely what they need and what adjustments are going to be likely." He stroked his chin and stared at Pierre. "What is your game here?"

Pierre had been expecting pushback.

"I need access to the pope's private office on that morning, but I can't tell you precisely why," Pierre said. He paused and looked at Vincenzo from beneath his spiky eyebrows. "Listen, you've sold your business, haven't you? You're heading into the sunset, retiring from all this, and taking a well-deserved rest."

Vincenzo put his coffee cup down with a slight clatter, his eyes now only dark slits. "How the hell did you know that? I've told virtually nobody."

"I have my sources."

Pierre knew from CIRRUS that Vincenzo and his brother had indeed sold their business and were preparing to retire once a proper handover had been completed. He also knew that the company, as a small niche tailoring business, was profitable but certainly wasn't earning its owners a fortune. A buyer was unlikely to pay a high price for it. Doing business with the Vatican was not particularly a route to great riches, and the selling price of the business would reflect that. Furthermore, although the Zeffirelli brothers had mafia connections, they generated little additional income. So, while comfortably off, Vincenzo and Luigi were unlikely to spend their last years in the lap of luxury.

"What's that got to do with the pope, anyway?" Vincenzo asked.

"It crossed my mind that you might like the idea of a more affluent retirement than you might otherwise have anticipated. A lot more affluent."

"You have no idea how affluent or otherwise our retirement is going to be," Vincenzo said.

"I'm a tailor too, remember. I know what businesses are

worth. It's hardly a license to print money—even if the pope is your customer. Who have you sold to?"

Vincenzo exhaled. He got up, walked to the door, and opened it, checked the corridor outside, then closed it again. Then he returned to his seat, placed his hands behind his head, and stared at Pierre. "Confidentially, I've sold to someone you know—Alberto Casartelli. We agreed to continue running the store for a short period until he installs his own management team."

"Casartelli? *Really?* Have you got the money yet?"

Vincenzo nodded. "A few days ago."

Pierre had to suppress a grin. "Just as well, as I don't think he'll be spending much time in Italy in the future."

Vincenzo looked confused. "What do you mean?"

"Never mind. You'll find out in due course." He wasn't going to go into detail about Operation Prada being blown and the implications for Casartelli.

"And explain what you mean by a more affluent retirement," Vincenzo said in a lowered voice. "What sort of affluence are you talking about?"

Pierre paused, then gave the figure supplied by Hassan, who had been given instructions by Nasser Khan in Tehran.

"Seven figures."

Vincenzo's eyebrows rose in a reflexive action he was unable to prevent.

"Seven figures?" he asked, his tone skeptical. "How far into seven figures?"

"Two million."

Vincenzo sat up in his chair. "And what are you proposing to do with this access to the pope you're asking for?"

Then a light dawned across Vincenzo's face as he put two and two together. "Don't tell me you're planning a hit on His Holiness and the president? Is this one of your Hezbollah operations?"

Pierre inclined his head a little but said nothing. Vincenzo was well aware of his activities on behalf of Hezbollah and how far into the distant past those activities stretched. However, in true Italian mafia fashion, he had always kept his mouth shut, which was why Pierre had felt comfortable approaching him. A kind of mutual trust had evolved between them over the years stemming from their respective allegiances to Hezbollah and the Naples mafia. Both had much to lose, and both had significant firepower to call upon if required.

"Are you crazy?" Vincenzo said. "Do you want to put me in Regina Coeli for the rest of my days? Why are you doing this? You won't get a gun into the Vatican, anyway. They have metal detectors. You get shaken down by the Swiss Guard."

"Who said anything about guns?" Pierre said. "Nobody will know about your involvement, and you'll have complete deniability, anyway. There'll be no fingerprints, and nothing will happen while we're actually in the Vatican. We'll be long gone by then. And our arrangement will include a very generous resettlement fee, besides the two million. You and your wife won't need to set foot in the Vatican or in Italy again."

"Explosives, then? Is that what you're planning?" Vincenzo said. He knew where Pierre's expertise lay.

Pierre evaded the veteran Italian tailor's stare. "You mentioned you were taking some fabric samples in for the pope. I presume you'll be using one of these," he said, indicating toward the pile of sturdy swatch books with rigid wood and plastic bindings that stood on the shelf. "I will need the book you want to take before we go in there."

"What do you want to do with the book?" Vincenzo asked, now visibly agitated.

"You'll see. Have the Swiss Guard confiscated cell phones

when you've gone in there recently? I know they never used to."

Vincenzo shook his head. "Mine has never been taken."

"That's good," Pierre said. "One other thing. I was last in the Vatican with you about five years ago, under my Philippe Simenon identity. Will that still be in their visitor logs?"

Vincenzo groaned and stared at the floor. "Most likely, yes," he said in a flat monotone. "They don't delete people, in my experience."

"That will make things easier."

Pierre felt a spark of energy fire up inside his chest.

The pieces were falling into place. The endgame was about to begin.

* * *

Friday, July 8, 2016
    Rome

Jayne jerked awake, then groaned and winced as the metal bed spring dug into her bruised rib cage through the thin mattress. She had hardly slept the previous night after her beating at the hands of the Carabinieri thugs in the interrogation room upstairs. Based on meal deliveries by the guards, she estimated it was now early evening, and she kept half dozing as her body tried to catch up.

But it was a losing battle. Even when she managed to nod off, every time she shifted in her sleep she caused some damaged nerve ending to jar her back to consciousness again.

Furthermore, her jaw ached where the guard had hit her, and the cut on the inside of her mouth kept bleeding every time she moved her face muscles. It was impossible to eat without causing another bout of bleeding, and there was no way she could get her teeth to close together to chew.

Jayne had been expecting to be hauled back for another grilling and probably another beating, and she wondered whether Rafael had been enduring a similar experience and if he responded somehow. Would he have fought back more than she had, landed a few blows in return? And if so, what would they have done to him? She decided not to catastrophize too much about that, as it was making her feel even worse.

One thing was for certain: Tomasso Porpora and his men were wasting their time. Did they really imagine that giving her such a beating was going to result in a productive outcome for them? She hoped that locking her up here at Regina Coeli prison wouldn't slow down the investigation much and that Vic Walter and Avi Shiloah would make alternative arrangements to keep the momentum moving.

She was also certain they were trying to locate her and engineer a way to have her and Rafael released. How that would happen, though, she had no idea.

Jayne turned onto her side to give herself some relief. There was no chance of getting any painkillers in here, that was for sure.

She had just dozed off again when the cell door rattled. There was a metallic clang as the steel security latch on the outside was released, followed by the familiar sound of a key being turned and a squeak of hinges before a man in Carabinieri uniform appeared, complete with a peaked cap. Jayne hadn't seen him before.

"Get ready to go," the officer said in a flat voice devoid of any emotion.

Jayne gingerly climbed off the bed and stood, her ribs throbbing. "To go where?" she asked.

"Upstairs, first. Turn, put your wrists behind your back."

Jayne complied without arguing.

Click. On went a set of handcuffs.

"Walk in front of me," the officer instructed.

Jayne cursed under her breath.

Here we go again.

She walked ahead of the officer, taking rights and lefts as instructed.

"Where are we going after upstairs?" Jayne asked.

The officer replied in a level, icelike monotone. "To somewhere you won't be coming back from."

Jayne felt her heart rate soar, and it wasn't because she was climbing a flight of stairs to ground level. She battled to calm herself, telling herself that whatever happened now was out of her control, but she knew she needed to be clearheaded in case an opportunity came up to extricate herself

They emerged in a corridor down which Jayne could feel a breeze blowing. They turned right, and just outside a set of double doors was a Carabinieri van, its twin rear doors both open.

To Jayne's surprise, inside the van, sitting on a bench seat, was Rafael, hands cuffed behind his back, alongside another Carabinieri guard who was holding a pistol.

Jayne could see immediately that Rafael had been roughed up even worse than she had been. His lower lip was cut, black-and-blue, and swollen, and there was another cut on his right cheek. His left eye was black, with a purple bruise spreading down across his cheek, and there were several smaller bruises visible around his temple and lower jaw. He looked a mess.

"Get in," the guard instructed.

"Where are we going?" Jayne asked, her level of alarm rising. Were they going to take them somewhere, shoot them dead, and abandon them? They certainly wouldn't have given both of them such a beating if the intention was to let them go—she knew that.

"I said get in."

Jayne did as instructed, and the Carabinieri officer climbed in after her, pulled the twin doors shut behind him, and sat next to her. He pulled out his pistol and racked the slide.

"Go," he instructed the driver.

With no blindfold, Jayne could see precisely where they were headed. They drove across a small courtyard, through two archways, and up to a heavily guarded entrance to the prison. The gate opened, a barrier went up, and then they were out in the streets of Trastevere.

The van headed south at a sedate pace, then cut right onto Via Garibaldi. Jayne knew where they were, near to the CIA safe house where Baltrami had been shot dead.

She assumed they were headed to the Carabinieri regional headquarters at the far end of Via Garibaldi.

But the van shot straight past the headquarters building and continued south.

Jayne jumped as a cell phone belonging to the officer next to Rafael rang loudly. He glanced at the screen, answered it in a respectful tone, and then listened carefully. Jayne guessed it was one of his superiors.

As the van climbed Janiculum Hill, the officer turned and instructed the driver to pull over to the side of the street. When the van had stopped, directly opposite the Garibaldi Ossuary Mausoleum, the officer pulled open the side door, climbed out, and slammed the door shut again. Jayne could just about hear him outside the van, continuing his phone conversation, but couldn't make out what it was about.

What the hell?

About a minute later, the rear doors of the van were flung open by the officer outside.

He pointed to Jayne, then Rafael. "Both of you, get out," he ordered.

Jayne's stomach flipped over.

Surely they weren't going to execute them here, right opposite the mausoleum.

Slowly Jayne climbed out of the van, followed by Rafael.

"Stand against that wall," the officer ordered. He pointed toward a four-meter-high wall that ran alongside the side of the street and flicked off the safety on his pistol.

Jayne looked at the wall.

"If you shoot us, you'll pay," she said. "You won't live past the end of the week."

"I said stand there," the officer repeated, ignoring her. He raised his pistol.

"You do realize you'll have the CIA, the Mossad, and MI6 chasing you until you're wild dog food," Rafael said.

"Shut up. Move," the officer said.

Jayne felt there was no option.

She walked to the wall, hands cuffed behind her back, and stood there facing the officer.

Rafael did likewise.

The officer turned to his colleague and nodded once.

The other man walked to the Carabinieri van and climbed in.

The first officer stood in front of the van, his pistol leveled at Jayne.

Shit. This is it.

PART FOUR

CHAPTER THIRTY-FIVE

Saturday, July 9, 2016
The Vatican

Cardinal Louis Sweeney walked to the living room window of his two-room apartment on the fourth floor of St. Martha's House, the guesthouse where he normally stayed while working at the Vatican. He placed his large hands on the window ledge and leaned forward until his forehead was pressed hard up against the glass pane.

The Vatican's financial chief gazed down on the parking lot in the St. Martha Piazza ahead of him, dwarfed by the enormous dome of St. Peter's Basilica that stood only a hundred meters beyond, as it had done for almost four hundred years.

Once again, he had that strange sensation of watching himself from outside his own body, observing his own behavior and emotions as if he were an onlooker. He felt detached from himself.

Recently, Sweeney had frequently thought seriously about

opening his window and jumping out. The pressure that had built up over recent months, driven by wrongdoing and guilt, felt as though it were squeezing his head in a vise. It had stopped him from sleeping properly, seriously hampered his work inside the church, and had left his entire body feeling stressed and rigid.

Death often seemed like the best option.

Why was it that most outsiders always imagined clergymen to be immune from this kind of thing?

But so far, each time Sweeney had found himself in that headspace, he had instead sunk to his knees, ignoring the growing pain from his arthritic right hip, bowed his head to the floor, and prayed.

Each time he had done so, he received the same message from God: a clear instruction to confess his sins and seek forgiveness.

Well, he had done that twice—once at his home office with the now sadly deceased Cardinal Daniel Berg, archbishop of Galveston-Houston, and once with the pope. Indeed, he had felt better afterward, though not hugely so. He had promised to rectify the sins he had committed and had received absolution.

But saying he would fix it and actually doing it were two quite different matters. It was far from easy to untangle himself from the mess he was in—not least regarding the family clothing factory in Los Angeles. After finding himself forced to initiate a despicable contract with Sole Nero and to recommend it to his brothers, despite not having day-to-day involvement in the business, it was now backfiring on him badly.

He had heard just yesterday morning from one of his brothers that the factory had been raided by the FBI, which was focused on the Sole Nero arrangement. The net was closing in on him. He was certain it was only a matter of time before someone from the FBI office in Rome turned up to interview him. That would bring disgrace on him, his family, the Catholic Church, and the pope.

Sweeney was also certain that his first confession to Cardinal Berg, an old friend, had somehow led to the horrific murder soon afterward in Washington of Berg, two other American cardinals, and the papal nuncio.

Quite how and why it had resulted in that awful outcome, he didn't know. But he was sure that the Hezbollah terrorists who had entangled him so firmly in their net were behind it, and that he had confessed to Berg had somehow been the trigger.

Had Hezbollah become aware that Berg knew of their involvement? He doubted Berg would break the seal of confession—or would he? But perhaps Berg had somehow inadvertently let it slip to someone else. Or was there a mole in the camp?

And if Berg and the others had been killed, then who was next?

Would it be him?

He had a gut feeling that he might have been saved in the short term by being out of reach on a church trip to South Africa, Zimbabwe, and Zambia when Berg and the others had been killed. Otherwise, there was a distinct possibility he might have been included in the delegation that had been heading to the White House that fateful morning.

Since returning from southern Africa, his depression had been worsened by the other gut feeling that Hezbollah might now target him too. And yet he couldn't go to the Vatican police or the FBI at home about it without opening a massive can of worms.

As he stared out the window, a group of tourists stopped outside the guesthouse, which was one of the newest buildings in the Vatican, constructed in 1996 to provide accommodation for visiting cardinals, especially during the rare conclaves when they gathered to elect a new pope. Like thousands of others every day, the tourists took out their phones and took selfies. First, they used the guesthouse as their backdrop, including the two Swiss Guards in full, colorful uniform who stood outside the imposing front door. Then they turned around and repeated the performance, this time with the basilica as the focal point behind them. They joked and laughed as they did so. Clearly they had little weighing on their shoulders, unlike him, Sweeney couldn't help thinking.

He turned and glanced at the clock on the wall of his living room. Twenty minutes until his scheduled meeting with the pope, who had kindly agreed to a further confessional, despite being under severe time pressures with the imminent visit of the United States president and major announcements to make. It would soon be time to get moving.

He sat on the two-seat sofa and gazed around the room.

The stone-clad St. Martha's House comprised 106 apartments with two rooms, twenty-six that had just one room, and one larger apartment.

Sweeney was fortunate, as a senior member of the Roman Curia—the administrative body through which the Catholic Church's affairs were governed—to have access to a two-room apartment. But like all the others, it was sparsely furnished in quite a basic fashion. Apart from the sofa on which he was sitting, there were two other padded chairs in the living room, along with an old-fashioned wooden desk, a large closet, and a storage cabinet, on top of which stood a flat-screen TV with a satellite box and Wi-Fi hub. The bedroom had a sturdy iron-framed bed, a dresser, a small bedside table and lamp, and a clothes stand. The adjoining private bathroom had a shower but not a bath. Apart from the TV and the Wi-Fi, the entire accommodation could easily have dated from the 1950s, not the twenty-first century.

Sweeney always described his apartment to others as comfortable but a long way from luxurious. It was certainly very much more modest than the grand two-story redbrick archbishop's residence he occupied on the nine-acre Notre Dame Seminary campus in New Orleans. The house, just off Walmsley Avenue, stood about three miles west of his workplace for the previous three decades, St. Louis Cathedral, a short distance from the Mississippi River.

After putting on his clerical collar, Sweeney drank a glass of water, said another prayer for guidance in his meeting with the pope, and headed out the door, which he locked behind him.

The corridor, with its plain cream-painted walls and dim uplighters, always reminded Sweeney of a hospital. He made his way past the elevators and, as always, pushed open the squeaking door to the concrete stairwell. At the age of sixty-eight, aware that his fitness was fading fast, he tried to take what exercise he could to stave off the inevitable. His knees groaned when going up and down stairs since there wasn't much cartilage left to absorb the pressure on his joints, but he nevertheless persisted.

His footsteps echoed down the stairwell as he made his way down the first flight.

As he reached the landing for the third floor, the door above through which he had come squeaked open again.

He paused, turned his head, and looked up. Another clergyman, dressed in a black shirt, black jacket and trousers, and a white clerical Roman collar, emerged from the recess and began to walk quickly down the stairs, his footsteps also echoing loudly. A large wooden cross hung around his neck.

Sweeney didn't recognize him, so he turned and continued down the next flight of stairs toward the second floor.

"Cardinal Sweeney?" came a deep bass voice from behind

him, in a heavy accent that Sweeney couldn't immediately place.

He stopped and turned. "Yes, that's me. How can I help?"

The man, tall, well muscled, with a generous mustache and black hair, was now standing on the landing, looking down at him through dark glasses. "You can't help me. In fact, quite the opposite."

Sweeney's stomach flipped over inside him as the man reached swiftly inside his jacket pocket and took out a handgun. It had a long tube on the barrel that he instantly recognized as a silencer.

The man lifted the weapon and leveled it.

"No!" Sweeney squawked, his voice strained and cracked. He wanted to scream but found his voice was paralyzed, and he couldn't say another word.

He raised a hand in a reflexive attempt to protect himself but felt the impact of the first round in his chest and staggered backward.

The second round smashed straight into his skull.

CHAPTER THIRTY-SIX

Saturday, July 9, 2016
Rome

There was no mistaking the look of shock on the face of
President Ferguson. The clarity of the secure video link from
the White House ensured that his reaction was very clear to
Jayne and the others assembled in Donald Constanzo's corner
office on the top floor of the Palazzo Margherita building.

"I don't know what to say," the president said, his head
bowed. "This is appalling. I can't believe what's been happening. I don't get it. Sweeney should have been in custody
anyway. We all know now what he was doing, the clothing
factory stuff, but nobody deserves that. How did this happen?
How did an assassin get past Vatican security—what were
they all doing?"

Nobody replied.

Nobody had the answer.

Jayne could physically feel the despair in the room.

The president's reaction was due to the news that had

been delivered to him by his aide, Charles Deacon, less than twenty minutes earlier of the horrific killing of the archbishop of New Orleans, Cardinal Louis Sweeney, while on his way to meet with the pope at the Vatican.

Ferguson was now seated at the conference table in the White House's Situation Room, along with the familiar figure of Deacon and his national security advisor, Phil Anstee, the director of the Secret Service, David Bhatia, and the Secret Service special agent in charge of the president's security detail, Ronald O'Toole.

The president looked back into his camera. "I assume you're taking the view that it was the Hezbollah pair who are responsible for the hit?" the president said. "Fekkai and Hassan?"

"We are, sir," Vic said.

The president paused. "Jayne, I've heard from Charles that you've also had an ordeal. I can see the bastards roughed you up. How are you doing? What happened?"

"I'm okay, thank you, Mr. President, given the circumstances," Jayne said. In truth, she wasn't okay, but she wasn't going to admit that on a call with the president. She knew she would feel the aftereffects of what had happened for some considerable time, not just physically but mentally, too. But for now, there was too much to do. The internal processing would have to wait.

She gave the president a very brief account of her incarceration, including the drama when she and Rafael had been released.

"They stood us up against a wall," she said. "I was convinced we were going to be shot. But the Carabinieri removed our handcuffs, threw us our phones and wallets in a plastic bag, drove off, and left us on the street. I gather I need to thank the Israelis for pulling a few strings with Romano Leone to get us out."

"Yitzhak Katz pulled the strings," the president said. "Look, don't take this the wrong way, but you look as though you've just come out of ten rounds in a boxing ring. I'm sorry you've had such a beating. It's outrageous. I will be making my feelings known to Leone in no uncertain terms when I meet him after my Vatican visit. I will be demanding a full inquiry into this Carabinieri commander, Porpora, and a proper prosecution."

Jayne fingered her cheek where the deep cut inside her mouth was still causing her considerable discomfort. She looked up at the president's image, which loomed large on the giant monitor screen on the rear wall of Constanzo's office. She appreciated that he always remembered her name. Not all political figures of his rank would do so, regardless of how many interactions they had with someone. Next to her were Vic and Constanzo, the latter with a look of intense embarrassment on his face as the discussion about Porpora continued.

Bloody hell, Jayne thought. Was the president still planning to travel to the Vatican, then, despite what had just happened?

The Italian prime minister had appeared live on television at a press conference a couple of hours earlier, claiming the credit for seizing a freighter as it entered the Port of Naples with a huge cargo of drugs from Syria estimated to be worth more than one billion euros. It was "a victory for law and order in Italy," Leone trumpeted.

Leone didn't mention the Israeli intelligence that had informed the seizure, and made no reference to two foreign intelligence operatives having been held, beaten up, and then released in controversial fashion by a very senior officer in the Carabinieri. Jayne hoped that Leone's idea of law and order extended to clamping down on corruption inside his own police services.

"Mr. President, the biggest question we have right now is whether you're still committed to this Vatican visit on Monday," Vic said, voicing the question that was on everyone's lips. "It sounds, from what you just said, that you still are."

The president sat up straight in his chair and patted down his neatly coiffured iron-gray hair. "We had a call from the Vatican just a short while ago confirming that the pope is definitely continuing with the event on Monday, despite what happened to Cardinal Sweeney and the others. He is still planning to make the announcements on the Secret Archives material relating to Pope Pius XII and the Nazis and on recognizing the Palestinian state," he said. "The pope is eighty years old, and I am a mere sixty-six. If he can stand up and show solidarity against these Hezbollah terrorists, then I certainly can. I've discussed it with David and Ronald, and I think it can be managed securely, although they have doubts. We have been urging the Vatican to release the Nazi papers for many years, in line with our friends in Israel. So when the pope actually does as we've been requesting, we need to be there to show support. Apart from that, three cardinals and an archbishop have been violently murdered on US soil, and two other cardinals in Rome—it's critically important we stand by the pope."

There was a brief pause. The president went up a couple of notches in Jayne's estimation. He certainly had some backbone. It would have been quite easy, and understandable, and probably sensible, for him to have withdrawn from the Vatican visit on security grounds, she thought.

Deacon leaned forward. "The plan currently is for the president to fly to Rome tomorrow morning."

"All right," Vic said. "Can I ask David and Ronald to clarify what their advice to the president is?"

"We've both advised him not to go," Bhatia said in a flat

voice. "As usual, we've had a team in Rome and the Vatican for the past few weeks preparing for this, and they and I and Ron are unanimous that it's just not a good idea at all." Next to him, O'Toole was nodding in agreement.

Jayne hadn't had any contact with the Secret Service team in Rome, but knew it was standard procedure for them to send their best people to carry out a thorough advance security exercise to ensure everything was set up in line with their usual protocols.

"I have heard what they had to say," the president said, "but I have overruled them." His tone left little room for argument.

"We respect that, sir," Vic said. "Phil, David, and Ronald, will you three be able to coordinate effectively with the Vatican and wrap a ring of steel around the president and the pope? It sounds like the Swiss Guard may need some considerable assistance from us—getting them to accept it might be easier said than done, especially on their own turf."

Anstee, a tall, lank man who Jayne had always thought had the air of a policeman about him, nodded. "Look, I can't say I'm not anxious by what's just happened. Of course I am. But we have worked with the Swiss Guard in the past, and we've already had several detailed discussions with them this time, albeit before the latest killing there. I hear David and Ronald's concerns, but I'm a little more pragmatic. I do think we can manage the situation. There will be very few visitors to the Apostolic Palace between now and Monday anyway. We will all travel to Rome later today, ahead of the president, and begin work tomorrow. I would like to meet the pope and see the Apostolic Palace, particularly his private apartments, at that time. It would be good if you, Vic, and whoever you think appropriate could join me. My team will go through the building with a fine-tooth comb later in the day, after which it will hopefully be off-limits, apart from essential personnel.

There will be the usual precautions, including blocking of cell phone signals during the time the president is on-site."

I think we can manage the situation. Jayne had to stop herself from making some kind of sarcastic comment. That was hardly the voice of confidence. But she didn't know Anstee and he was well regarded, so who was she to take a negative view.

"Thank you, Phil," Constanzo said. "Will any of your team accompany the president for the meeting with the pope?"

Anstee glanced sideways at Charles Deacon, who leaned forward.

"The pope has insisted on this being a private meeting," Deacon said. "No other attendees."

"And in any case, the Vatican technically doesn't allow Secret Service officers into the Apostolic Palace," Anstee said. "It's their rules. They insist on the Swiss Guard running security. It's their job."

"I notice you said technically. I assume you usually manage to sneak one or two of your agents into the presidential group?" Jayne asked. She recalled that had been the case on a couple of presidential visits to London that she had been tangentially involved in.

"We try," Anstee said. "But it might be a little difficult this time given that it's a one-to-one meeting." He gave a thin, sarcastic smile and shrugged.

"We will have to respect the pope's wishes," Constanzo said. "I will go through the schedule for Monday and ensure you all continue to receive updated copies if anything changes."

Constanzo ran through a detailed description of how the president would travel from the US embassy by armored car as part of a large motorcade and arrive at the Vatican at 10:40 a.m. There was a backup plan to fly him by helicopter to the Vatican's helipad if traffic was especially heavy or in case of a security risk, such as anti-Palestinian protesters outside the Vatican.

The pope and the president would meet in the pope's private office for forty-five minutes, beginning at eleven o'clock, and then walk the short distance from the Apostolic Palace to St. Peter's Square. At noon, the pope would address a select gathering in front of the international press corps and television cameras for about ten minutes. The president would then make a shorter response of about five minutes.

There were no plans for a question-and-answer session by the media, Constanzo continued. Journalists would need to rely on the Vatican's press office and their counterparts in the White House press office for more details of the pope's announcement and the speeches. The square would be closed to the general public all day.

"All areas will be tightly secured during this period," Constanzo said. "All guests will be accounted for by the Swiss Guard and searched on entry to the Vatican."

President Ferguson listened carefully, and then nodded as Constanzo wrapped up. "That sounds like an excellent arrangement. Thanks."

The president leaned forward, picked up a sheet of paper that was lying on the table in front of him, and waved it in the air for emphasis. "I have read the summary update you sent through earlier, Vic. Robert's too, on the FBI end. I am up to speed on everything. I also note your report on what Sweeney had been up to. We need to know more about this clothing scam he and his family were involved in."

"Yes, sir," Vic said. "Work has been underway for a little while on that. We're talking to the Vatican, and I know the Feds are chasing down his family in the States, I know that."

"Good," the president continued. "You and your team need to do all you can to track down Fekkai and Hassan so they can be brought to justice in the US and Italian courts for these horrific killings—before they do any more damage."

Jayne tried not to roll her eyes. What did the president think they'd been doing?

There was a pause as the president took a sip of water. "I want you to find them before I get to the Vatican." He looked into the camera from beneath his bushy eyebrows. "Understood?"

There was no mistaking the body language nor the tone of voice.

"Yes, Mr. President," Vic said. "Understood."

* * *

Saturday, July 9, 2016
  Rome

The black clerical shirt and white Roman collar lay where Pierre Fekkai had thrown them, on the kitchen floor of the house on Via di Sant'Anselmo. Next to them lay a false mustache, a pair of black plastic glasses, and a dark wig.

Since returning from the successful elimination of Cardinal Louis Sweeney, he had no further use for the items. The instructions from CIRRUS on the location of Sweeney's apartment and how to enter St. Martha's House without scrutiny had been spot-on, just as they had been ten days earlier on the whereabouts of Cardinal Baltrami when Pierre had carried out the hit on him.

Now it was time to focus on the things that lay in front of him on the table.

There was a thick fabric swatch book, about forty centimeters long and thirty wide, containing dozens of samples of cloth of different colors, weights, and textures. It was bound at one end by two solid slats of wood, each half a centimeter thick and the same length as the cloth samples that were clamped firmly between them.

Two long vertical screws penetrated the wooden slats at each end and pierced all of the samples of cloth. They held the book together so that a user could flick through the different swatches, a little like reading an ordinary book.

Pierre undid the screws, removed the wooden slats and the long screws, and made some careful measurements. He then used a ruler to draw faint pencil lines on the top piece of cloth in a rectangular shape that fitted neatly between the two screws. The shape would be concealed by the wooden slats when they were put back in place.

Next he took a new scalpel and, using the ruler as a guide, cut out the rectangle shape from the piece of cloth. After double-checking that the wooden slats would indeed cover the fresh hole in the material, he spent the next half hour carefully cutting identically sized holes in all of the cloth samples apart from two at the front of the swatch book and two at the back.

Pierre then reassembled the book, including the bottom slat and long screws, but he left the top slat and top two pieces of fabric off. Now there was a rectangular hole about twenty centimeters long, six centimeters wide and about six centimeters deep that, when fully assembled, would be well concealed beneath the slats.

He picked up a rectangular plastic container, the same size as the hole he had made in the fabric book, and slotted it into the void. Inside the container was a deadly mixture of ground ammonium nitrate pellets and diesel fuel oil. Buried in the pellets was a small nonmetallic detonator, incorporating a portion of lead azide, from which two very thin wires emerged out of the plastic container.

Pierre knew the wires were so thin and short they would

almost certainly never be picked up by a standard magnetometer of the type used in airport metal detectors, and so those deployed by the Swiss Guard likely had no chance.

He then picked up an old cell phone, a Nokia 105, identical to the type he used to own in the days before smartphones, and checked that the wires emerging from the explosive could be slotted quickly and properly into a small adaptor that he could then click into the charging socket. Once he was happy they did, he placed the phone on top of the plastic container and covered it with the top two pieces of cloth and the wooden slat.

It all fit together just as he had intended.

Having completed his check, Pierre then removed the phone again and detached the wires. The phone would remain in his pocket until he was safely inside the pope's private apartments. Once there, it would be the work of a few seconds to access the void and reconnect the wires. That could be done during a swift restroom visit or any other opportunistic moment. The Nokia, which had an anonymous pay-as-you-go SIM inserted, worked as any other phone did. He was ready with an explanation of why he preferred it to the newfangled smartphones that, he would argue, were far too complicated for an old-fashioned tailor like him to come to terms with.

The detonator would not be triggered in this case by calling the phone. That was too risky, because Pierre knew the Secret Service might well deploy cell phone signal blocking technology during the time the president was in the Vatican. Instead, it would be set off by an electrical signal generated by the phone's alarm, which would be set to go off at 11:25 a.m., midway through the scheduled private meeting between the pope and the president.

When fully assembled, the fabric swatch book looked like nothing more than a perfectly normal book of cloth samples of the type used by tailors all over the world to show their customers.

It was perfect, Pierre thought. Even Nasser Khan would surely be impressed with it. And he knew it would work, as he had deployed similar devices twice in the past with dramatic results, including the assassination of a German intelligence officer in Berlin.

He turned and called through to Hassan, who was working on his laptop in the living room. "Talal, come and have a look at this beauty."

Hassan appeared in the doorway, holding his phone and looking distracted.

"What do you think?" Pierre asked, pointing to his creation.

"What? Oh, yes, looks good," Hassan muttered. "But I've just had another message from Casartelli." He held up his phone.

"Saying what?"

"Saying he's heard that Robinson and Levy have been released after the Italian PM apparently did a deal with the Israelis. The Italians have also confiscated the drugs shipment from Syria. This is a disaster."

Pierre stared at him. "The Italians have confiscated the Captagon? So much for the Robinson arrangement that Porpora made. What happened to that?"

"I don't know," Hassan said. "But it means that Robinson is presumably back on the investigation."

CHAPTER THIRTY-SEVEN

Sunday, July 10, 2016
   The Vatican

The view out of the third-floor window of the pope's private office in the Apostolic Palace was spectacular. Jayne gazed out over the expanse of St. Peter's Square below, with its soaring Egyptian obelisk and the grand curves of the twin Doric stone colonnades that framed the northern and southern sides of the elliptical cobbled area.

At the western end, in front of the basilica's facade, workmen were busy putting the final touches to a large covered raised platform from which the pope and the United States president would make their speeches the following day.

Jayne tried to imagine being the pope and standing at this window every Sunday at noon to deliver the Angelus prayer and blessing to the massed crowds gathered in the piazza below.

After a few moments, she turned to find Pope Julius VI's

pink face looking a little quizzically at her from his seat behind his desk. The pope, who was wearing his usual white cassock, looked a little flushed, his eyes moist.

On the other side of the desk sat Michael Gray wearing a black cassock and scarlet sash. His face too reflected the stress and tension that was now running through Vatican City like red, hot lava, seeping into every nook and crevice, tearing the fabric of the holy city apart.

Jayne and Gray had arrived for a discussion with the pope about what had been discovered by Joe Johnson and the FBI at the clothing factory in Los Angeles. She had left Rafael working on his laptop in the CIA safe apartment in Trastevere, as it didn't seem necessary for him to attend.

However, before they could start, they had to wait while the three men responsible for the pope's and the president's security during the event the following day oversaw a thorough check of the Holy Father's office.

The trio were now standing behind Gray: the ramrod-backed commander of the Pontifical Swiss Guard, Heinrich Altishofen, together with one of his senior lieutenants and the Secret Service special agent in charge of the president's security detail, Ronald O'Toole. They had all been busy for the previous fifteen minutes watching as two technical officers systematically swept the room with handheld detectors that would reveal any hidden listening devices, unauthorized electronic devices, or explosives.

An officer from Altishofen's team finished his sweep by running his detector across the items on the pope's desk, including his books, piles of papers, and two crucifixes. When he had finished, he turned and nodded at Altishofen. "All done, sir. It's clean," he said.

Altishofen turned to the pope. "We'll bring in the sniffer dogs tonight, Holiness, just to make doubly certain. Then it will be good for your meeting tomorrow."

"Thank you, Heinrich," the pope said. He nodded at O'Toole. "I see you were given special consent to come up here. Thank you."

O'Toole glanced sideways at Altishofen. "Yes, Your Holiness. I'm grateful to Heinrich for allowing this. It means I can inform the president I have personally supervised the final checks, as well as Heinrich. It will help reassure him. It's a difficult time for all of us. I sympathize with you."

"I apologize that the Secret Service are not allowed in this building for the head of state meeting tomorrow," the pope said. "But our Swiss Guard will ensure there are no issues."

"No apology necessary, your Holiness," O'Toole said. "I understand you have your protocols."

"We'll go now," Altishofen said. "You can finish your meeting in peace, your Holiness. I apologize for the disruption."

The security men made their way out of the office and closed the door behind them.

Jayne returned to her chair in front of the pope's desk, alongside Gray.

"The security teams are very professional," the pope said. "We must be thankful to have them." He scrutinized Jayne's face. "I didn't want to comment while the others were here, but I hope your injuries heal quickly. You have a lot of bruising. I hope those who did it are brought to account."

Jayne inclined her head. She was still feeling very sore, particularly her ribs, which had meant she again hadn't slept well.

"Thank you, Holiness," she said. "It wasn't the first time. I'll be fine. Now, let me tell you about what the FBI team found in Los Angeles."

She ran through the details of how Cardinal Sweeney and his family had been involved in a deception and a fraud, and the involvement of Sole Nero in that.

The pope listened in silence.

When she finished, he sat motionless for a few seconds, his lips pressed together. "This is all very sad," he said eventually.

"What is your feeling about what's going on here, your Holiness?" Jayne asked. She sat up straight in her chair, watching his face carefully.

The pope averted his gaze and lowered his eyes to the floor. "Cardinal Sweeney got into something he shouldn't have. I am still looking into that and I do know a few things. We can discuss it further once the president's visit is out of the way and I can think more clearly about it. Perhaps later in the week. But not now." He looked up again. "I'm sorry, but I need to focus on tomorrow's event. One step at a time. When you get to my age, multitasking does not come so easily, you understand. I need to fine-tune my speech for tomorrow and consider how I should reference the tragedies we have suffered, because I will of course need to say something. I will also need to say a prayer for those we have lost and for peace."

Jayne felt an immediate sense of impatience at his answer. It was obvious that he wasn't telling her everything he knew. But why? She was finding the old man was not easy to read.

"Your Holiness, I do understand," she said. "However, we need to progress our investigation as quickly as we can. If what you are hesitating over could put other lives at risk, please consider telling me now."

"Let's do it after the event. I would prefer it that way," the pope said. "The things I know I were given in complete confidence. It was a confessional. That is the issue."

Now Jayne was feeling irritated. She paused for a couple of seconds before continuing. "Are you completely sure you want to continue with the event tomorrow, Holiness? Given what happened to Cardinal Sweeney, you would be entitled to postpone. In fact, it might be a sensible option."

The pope pushed himself up in his chair and looked Jayne straight in the eye.

"I don't know you very well, and you don't know me very well," he said. "But let me tell you a little about my background. When I was a young man, growing up in Sicily, my family was poor. In fact, we occasionally resorted to crime to survive. I did jobs like barman and taxi driver to get by. I had to be tough, you understand me?"

Jayne nodded.

"If I didn't scrap and stand up for myself, I'd have been sunk. Then I joined the church at twenty-nine. You know why?"

"No, your Holiness," Jayne said.

"A close friend was shot dead by a householder during a burglary that I was involved in as a getaway driver. I realized it had only happened because we had chosen to follow the path of evil. It could easily have been me. It made me question everything—the meaning of life, why we are here, the existence of God. I decided to change, to follow a different path. I ended up as archbishop of Naples, where I came under a lot of pressure from the mafia and received a lot of threats to turn a blind eye to what they were doing, to let them continue without challenge. I refused to do that. I said what I thought from the pulpit. And today, I still continue to refuse to bow to evil. Hezbollah might have shot Cardinal Sweeney and the others, but that will not stop me. It will not stop my colleagues." He turned his glance to Gray. "We'll all be there tomorrow, won't we, Eminence?"

"Of course, Holiness," Gray said.

"So that's the answer to my question, I guess," Jayne said.

"I'm not backing down," the pope said. "And I've sent a

message saying that to President Ferguson. He intends to be there tomorrow too."

Jayne folded her arms. "I understand. But I had to ask. What is your schedule tomorrow, Holiness?"

"I need to see my hairdresser, Pedro, at nine. My tailor, Vincenzo, is here at nine thirty to make sure my cassock and accessories are all in order, and my speechwriter, Alfonso, at ten so we can make any final changes to the text before the president arrives. That is always my routine for visits by heads of state or other important guests. It doesn't change. The Swiss Guard know that, and they know all those people very well. They've worked for me for many years. I am an old man of habit, despite all the horrific incidents that have been occurring around me. Alongside my faith, my routine gives me something unchanging in my life. Perhaps the only thing."

Jayne nodded. "Do those three always come on such occasions?" she asked.

"Always. I'm incapable of making my hair look neat. And I'm incapable of adjusting my cassocks correctly, especially since my valet is on sick leave at the moment, having a hip replaced. The tailor and his assistant will do it instead. And I always fail to spot errors in my own scripts, so the speechwriter is essential."

"Okay. And these people are known to and are thoroughly checked by your Swiss Guard."

"Of course they are."

Jayne leaned back, feeling only partly reassured.

"The problem is, Holiness, the people we are pursuing seem to have inside knowledge of our movements, our plans, and our discussions," she said. She looked around the office. "I know the security team has just checked this office and given it the all-clear, but I have to say, some of the confidential things discussed here seem to have somehow become known to our opponents."

Jayne felt a sense of unease even mentioning this in the pope's presence, feeling it was somehow going to come across as accusatory, but it had to be said.

Gray, sitting next to her, leaned forward. "I too was thinking the same thing, Holiness. I am particularly thinking of the events in Ramallah, where I disclosed to you Jayne's plans to hold discussions with Cardinal Baltrami's siblings. We all know what happened there."

The pope's face drained of color. The pink tone that had been there vanished and he went visibly white. He glanced first at Gray, then at Jayne, his eyes now wide.

"Surely you can't possibly think that I am passing on information discussed here in deepest confidence?" he asked, his voice faltering in such a way that Jayne knew he wasn't putting on an act. "I can assure you that I wouldn't consider breaking even the smallest confidence."

The pope pressed his hands together in front of him, as if praying that his two visitors would understand what he was saying.

"I know, Your Holiness," Jayne said. "I'm sure you haven't done anything deliberately. My question was more aimed at any inadvertent disclosure you might have made to anyone else here in the Vatican or elsewhere."

The pope shook his head. "Without a doubt, that has not happened."

Jayne nodded. "That's very good to hear, Holiness."

She fingered her chin. "But the information is nonetheless leaking from somewhere. Are there any anomalies, changes, to your equipment, your computer, your phone? Anything here in this office, or in your apartment in St. Martha's House, that you have noticed that has made you think there's something not right, or has caused you concern?"

The pope pursed his lips, his face still pallid. "I don't

think so." He shook his head. Then he suddenly grasped the edge of his desk. "Wait. There was something."

He pointed to a small wooden crucifix, about fifteen centimeters high, that stood on the edge of his desk, close to Jayne. "That crucifix. There was something that confused me recently. An old friend gave it to me many years ago when I was a lowly priest, and I've kept it on my desk since then. I use it as a paperweight. But I dropped it on the floor one day, a few months ago, and it knocked a small chip out of the bottom of the base."

The pope picked up the crucifix and showed it to Jayne. "There, that's the chip."

Sure enough, there was a small chip at the bottom of the clay base, no more than a few millimeters long.

"So what did you notice about it?" Jayne asked, wondering where this was heading.

"One day, I think about a week or ten days ago, I noticed that the chip had disappeared. I couldn't work out how that could have happened. I just assumed somebody, probably my secretary Christophe, had replaced the crucifix and not said anything—they sell them in the Vatican souvenir shop, and so they're easily available. They only cost ten euros each. Then, yesterday, I noticed the chip had reappeared."

Jayne shot up in her chair. "*What?*"

The pope stared at her. "Yes, that's what happened. Very odd. Obviously someone had put back the old crucifix. I was going to mention it to Christophe, but I forgot. There has been so much going on that it slipped my mind."

"Where's Christophe?" Jayne asked.

"He's down the corridor, in my dining room, doing some paperwork."

"Can you get him in here?" she asked.

The pope picked up his phone, dialed a number, and spoke in rapid Italian.

Shortly afterward, the door opened and in walked Bishop Christophe Despierre, the pope's private secretary.

"Christophe, can you help me?" the pope said. He held up the crucifix. "Did you replace this at some point recently with a new one? And then put the old one back again?"

Despierre frowned. "No, definitely not. I didn't even realize it had been replaced."

"Do you know who might have done so?"

Despierre shook his head. "I have no idea."

"All right, thank you. You can go."

Despierre turned and exited the room.

There was silence for several seconds.

"This is a terrible thing to say, your Holiness," Jayne said. "But again I have to ask: do you trust your secretary implicitly?"

"Absolutely," the pope said, his voice firm and decisive. "I would trust him with my life."

Gray leaned forward. "I've just remembered something, Holiness," he said to the pope. "It happened when I arrived here for the meeting when we had to watch that horrible video of the shootings in Washington. It must have been the Thursday, the day after the killings."

Jayne turned to look at Gray. "What happened?"

"One of our group was here in the office when I arrived, holding that crucifix in his hand. When I walked in he put it down on the desk."

"Who was it?" asked the pope.

"Cardinal Saraceni."

A jolt went through Jayne.

Is this the breakthrough?

"Can I have a look at that crucifix?" she asked.

The pope nodded and Jayne picked it up. She turned it upside down and examined the molded clay base. It was covered with a chunky, circular piece of green baize that was glued to the bottom. Jayne pushed a finger into the baize and it gave way a little under the pressure of her fingertip.

"Is this base hollow?" she asked.

The pope shrugged. "I have no idea."

"Do you mind if I remove this piece of baize to look?" Jayne asked.

The pope nodded his approval.

Jayne pulled at one edge until the baize slowly peeled away from the base. Sure enough, there was an empty cavity about two centimeters across and of similar depth in the center of the base.

She knew instantly what had likely happened.

"I think it's possible your crucifix was replaced with another that was bugged," Jayne said. "I suspect a microphone transmitter might have been hidden in there. Now it's gone. You've got the old one back."

The pope stared at her. "You know what? When I noticed that the crucifix with the chip in it had somehow reappeared, it was not long after a meeting I had yesterday morning."

"Who with?" Gray asked.

Jayne knew already what the pope's answer was going to be.

"It was with Cardinal Saraceni. And I had to visit the bathroom halfway through the meeting for several minutes."

Jayne felt like swearing heavily, but decided it was better to hold back, given the company she was in. Her mind flashed back a few days to when she had made a mental note to meet with Saraceni to discuss security but had never gotten around to doing so.

She also instantly felt a sharp spike of guilt for having suspected others of potentially being the mole, including Constanzo, and for inadvertently sending the CIA's counter-intelligence chief Ricardo Miller on a wild goose chase to find a mole in the CIA. No wonder he had unearthed nothing.

Another thing crossed Jayne's mind. She turned to the pope. "Can I ask, Your Holiness . . . prior to my visit to Paris a week ago, did you discuss it with anyone in this office?"

The pope creased his brow and then looked a little embarrassed. "I think I may have referred to it here briefly with Bishop Galli after Cardinal Gray mentioned it to me outside the archives building."

Jayne nodded. That accounted for everything that had happened at the tailor shop on Rue de Saint-Simon and how that detail had reached Pierre Fekkai and Talal Hassan.

"I seem to remember you telling me last week that Cardinal Saraceni takes responsibility for security here, Your Holiness," Jayne said.

The pope nodded.

"And you also said that he had assured you that the Swiss Guard had checked this apartment regularly and had done so less than a week ago."

He inclined his head. "Yes, he did." His lips were now pressed tightly together.

"Where is Cardinal Saraceni now?" Jayne asked.

"He's working on the event for tomorrow," the pope said. "He's extremely busy."

"I bet he is," Jayne said. She got up, walked to the window, and looked down. There, on the newly erected platform down below in St. Peter's Square, was the figure of Saraceni. It looked like he was giving some instructions to two men in suits who were standing in front of him.

What to do next? She could call the commander of the Swiss Guard, Heinrich Altishofen, back in and arrange to have Saraceni questioned. But at this stage they had no proof he had done what they suspected. What if he had already disposed of the bugged substitute crucifix and simply denied all knowledge? It would be difficult to prove his involvement. Or having him questioned would simply alert him and enable him to warn whomever else he had been working with. One thing was for sure: he wouldn't have been working single-handedly. And there were certainly no clear grounds for arrest at this stage. She needed evidence.

"What do you want to do?" the pope asked.

"I'm just thinking it through," Jayne replied.

"Should we call Heinrich?" he asked, as if he had been reading her mind.

She shook her head. "I think not at this stage, Holiness. We have no proof. It might be awkward for you and us. I'm going to have some checks done. We might be able to find out by another means exactly what he has been up to and get something more concrete that we can confront him with at the right time."

Jayne paused. "Your Holiness, is it possible that someone else might have planted a listening device here, not Cardinal Saraceni? I don't want to start chasing a red herring. Can you think of any other possibilities, anything else that has struck you as being odd over the past few weeks?"

"I have a lot of visitors," the pope said. "But I can think of no other person who might have done that. With the other visitors, I was here constantly and I was aware of nothing like that. I might be getting ancient now, but I do still have my faculties."

"I'm sure you do," Jayne said. "Where are Cardinal Saraceni's apartment and offices?"

The pope pointed down at the floor with his index finger. "His offices are two stories down, on the first floor. His apartment is on the top floor of Saint Charles Palace—the Palazzo San Carlo—next to St. Martha's House."

Jayne turned to Gray. "Do you have Cardinal Saraceni's phone number?"

Gray nodded and reached for his cell phone.

Jayne knew exactly what she needed to do next.

* * *

Sunday, July 10, 2016
   Rome

Jayne gave Rafael a brief explanation of events in the pope's private office as soon as she returned to the safe house.

The heavy bruising around Rafael's face following his ordeal at Regina Coeli prison, particularly his left eye and down his cheek, had gone from purple to crimson and was starting to turn yellow around the edges. His injuries were now definitely even more colorful than Jayne's, but there were no broken bones and his mood was much improved.

"We need to get Unit 8200 to run traces on all Saraceni's calls, emails, everything," she said. "Personally, I can't see him getting his hands dirty too much, given his position, but maybe there's a chain of other people involved."

Rafael nodded. "Such as the Italian contact in Ghassan Nafi's phone, perhaps," he said.

That had also crossed Jayne's mind. She recalled that the Hezbollah Unit 133 leader's call register, recovered by Unit 8200, had included an incoming call from a burner phone using a now inactive Italian SIM card from the Rome area.

Could that have been Saraceni?

"Can't they just postpone the president's visit and the announcement?" Rafael asked. "That's the logical thing to do."

Jayne spread her hands wide. "That's what I suggested, but neither the pope nor the president want to do that. They're not going to give ground to terrorists—that's just not in their DNA." She shrugged.

"Then let's find a way to get Saraceni taken into custody," Rafael said.

"We can once we have proof that he's doing something he shouldn't. That's what I want from Unit 8200. Then we can act."

A few minutes later, Rafael had used his laptop to get Lieutenant Colonel Neta Rosenblum on a secure video call from Unit 8200's headquarters in Tel Aviv. The lighting in her office was poor and her olive face appeared even darker than usual.

Jayne gave Neta the cell phone number she had got for Saraceni and requested that she try to pull out all his phone records over the previous two months, which she thought should be more than enough to cover any activity relating to the Vatican killings.

"We need this urgently," Jayne said. She told Neta about the pope and President Ferguson's refusal to call off their meeting the next day. "We might also need to chase down the records of some of those he's calling, if they trigger red flags. There could be a chain involved."

"This is going to be an overnight job for Daniel," Neta said. "I'll give him the bad news as soon as we've finished here." She paused, and then continued, a distinct note of uncertainty in her voice. "I don't want to get your hopes up. It's going to be tricky to get the data so quickly, especially if it means getting into the phones of others on Saraceni's call register. I suspect someone in his position is going to have a very long list of calls every month. We'll do our best to get it to you in the morning, though."

"Thank you," Jayne said. "Tell Daniel if he can do it, we'll owe him and you dinner at the best restaurant we can find next time we're in Tel Aviv."

Rafael ended the call and sighed. "This is going to be touch and go." He closed his laptop. "There may be only one way to prove Saraceni's involvement in any bugging activity, of course."

"That's to find the bug," Jayne said. "Yes, I know. I'm thinking I'll need to get Michael Gray to help sneak us into Saraceni's office. And maybe his apartment too, if necessary."

A trace of a smile crossed Rafael's heavily blotched face. "Your father's old friend Gray is proving to be something of a human master key. Access all areas."

Jayne nodded and tapped her fingers against the Vatican security pass, provided by Gray, that hung around her neck. "Let's hope he's got one final key left on his keyring, then." She reached for her phone. "I need to brief Vic and Constanzo next."

CHAPTER THIRTY-EIGHT

Monday, July 11, 2016
  The Vatican

Pierre stood watching, arms folded, as Vincenzo carefully checked the ornate white cassock that the pope was now wearing. To Vincenzo's visible relief, the garment appeared to fit correctly in most respects, but he was nevertheless going through his usual routine of systematically checking it over.

Pope Julius stood a couple of meters in front of his desk, next to the chair that was doubtless ready for the United States president when he arrived later that morning.

He had his back to Pierre. Now was probably the best time to do what was needed.

"Hold your arms out horizontally, please, Your Holiness," Vincenzo instructed the pope, who complied with the request.

At that point, Pierre turned and swiftly opened the fabric swatch book that he had placed on the pope's desk behind him. It lay next to three books, all written by Pope Julius, all wrapped in clear cellophane with a red bow tied around them. There was also a large medallion in a velvet case and bearing some kind of inscription. Pierre guessed they were all to be presented to the president.

He carefully stood in such a position that even if the pope turned his head, he wouldn't easily see what Pierre was doing.

With the ease of long practice, he loosened the long screws that held the top wooden slat tightly in place and moved the slat to one side, along with the top two fabric samples that covered the cavity behind.

He then reached into his pocket and took out the Nokia 105. From his other pocket he took the small charging socket adaptor, into which he slotted the two thin wires that protruded from the plastic case inside the cavity. He then connected the adaptor to the base of the phone and placed the device into the cavity on top of the container. The alarm on the phone was already set to 11:25 a.m.

Finally, Pierre covered the cavity once again with the cloth swatches and screwed the wooden slat back into position.

The entire maneuver had taken only a minute or two, during which the pope was engaged in conversation with Vincenzo. His focus was on the fit of his cassock, which felt a little tight beneath the arms. He understandably seemed anxious to get the fitting completed so he could focus on his main task for the day.

Pierre then placed the book of samples on a shelf behind the pope's desk at about chest height, where it would do maximum damage. He turned and watched as Vincenzo finished his fitting process.

The pope had seemed a little distracted and had only spoken a couple of times to Pierre the whole time he was in the office.

When they had walked in, the pope had given an effusive greeting to Vincenzo, then looked at Pierre. "No Massimo today? Don't I remember you from a previous visit?"

"Massimo is away. And yes, I was here with Vincenzo a few years ago," Pierre had told the pope as they shook hands. "You have a good memory, Your Holiness."

"It's nice to see you again," the pope said.

After that, the pope had focused his attention almost exclusively on Vincenzo and his cassock. Pierre assumed, correctly, that they would not be disturbed by anyone bursting into the room. Nobody, not even the pope's secretary, Christophe Despierre, would want to come in and risk seeing the Holy Father in a state of partial undress while his tailors worked away.

The security process on entry to the Vatican had also gone smoothly. Vincenzo had sent the Swiss Guard details of Pierre's attendance, under his Philippe Simenon identity, in place of his chief tailor, Massimo Valli, so his presence triggered no red flags.

As Pierre knew would be the case, the security scanners at Santa Anna Gate didn't pick up the two short, fine wires concealed in the cavity of the fabric swatch book. The rest of the nonmetallic explosive materials also went undetected. And the Nokia 105 merited only a very quick glance by one of the Swiss Guard, as did his Philippe Simenon French passport.

As he and Vincenzo got ready to depart, Pierre spoke up again.

"Holy Father, I have put the fabric samples for your shirts on the shelf there behind your desk for you to examine when you have more time. I hope the meeting with the president goes well, sir."

"Thank you," the pope said absentmindedly. "Have a good day, both of you."

With that, Pierre and Vincenzo left the office, and a Swiss Guard who had been waiting for them outside the door accompanied them to the elevators.

All Pierre had to hope for now was that nobody moved the book of swatches. But he knew that was highly unlikely. It was the last thing on anyone's mind in the Apostolic Palace that morning.

Now he needed to get back to the safe house, where he would lie low for a few hours and watch the drama unfold on satellite TV. Then he would get out of Rome under cover of darkness in the cab of a long-distance truck, arranged by Hassan, that was bound for Slovenia. From there, he planned to catch an indirect flight from Ljubljana to Bangkok, where he aimed to take a long break.

Hassan, for his part, had left early that morning in a car that he was planning to drive to Marseille, where he had another safe house.

Vincenzo, meanwhile, had now done his final day's work for the company he had founded. His brother, Luigi, had left on a flight for Lisbon the previous afternoon, and Vincenzo would follow as soon as he could get to the airport. Both men would then head for Brazil on the next available flight.

Job done.

* * *

Monday, July 11, 2016
The Vatican

At ten o'clock, the Santa Anna Gate into the Vatican was bristling with a battalion of unsmiling, hard-eyed Swiss Guards in full dress uniform. Jayne and Rafael made their way through the series of temporary checkpoints set up there, in line with Gray's instructions.

They were given thorough, and quite personal, searches by the guards and were directed through airport-style metal detectors. Jayne's bag, containing a laptop and a few other items, was put through a scanner, along with Rafael's laptop case. The Swiss Guard was taking no chances, it seemed. Quite rightly so. It would be impossible for unscheduled visitors to get in with anything that could do any damage.

Gray met them at Santa Anna Gate, which was closed to normal traffic today. From there, he led them along Via Santa Anna, through the Belvedere Courtyard, and left past the museums, the Sistine Chapel, and the Basilica to St. Martha's House.

They were stopped five times by Swiss Guards en route to St. Martha's House and another three times at the door and inside the building before they made it to Gray's two-room apartment on the second floor. On every occasion, they faced demands for their identification passes.

With each stop, Jayne's level of anxiety rose a little. Not so much because of the Swiss Guards, but more because she and Rafael still had heard nothing from Neta Rosenblum in Tel Aviv. She had gotten Rafael to message Neta twice, but there had so far been no response. Time was running out if they were to get anything actionable on Saraceni. At the forefront of Jayne's mind was that he might somehow be involved in something monstrous at the pope's meeting with the president, and as yet she had no evidence of anything and could do nothing about it.

On the upside, there had been no word of disaster during Pope Julius's scheduled meetings with his hairdresser, tailor, and speechwriter, for which she was extremely thankful.

Once inside the apartment, the plainness of which struck Jayne immediately, Gray shut the door and walked to the dark wooden desk that stood against a wall in his living room. He picked up a piece of paper and waved it at Jayne and Rafael.

"I have got this, and I have made a plan," Gray said. "It's the new protocols that the pope's team and the Swiss Guard have devised for the president's arrival and meeting with His Holiness today. It's been signed off by the Secret Service."

He had a somewhat guilty look on his face, so Jayne didn't ask how he had obtained the sheet.

"I hope it's going to get us into Saraceni's office," Jayne said.

Gray motioned to his guests to sit on a pair of old-fashioned padded chairs next to a coffee table and took a seat himself on a two-person sofa next to them.

"I have got you both onto the list to attend the initial greetings given to the presidential delegation in the Sala Clementina room and the Sala di Sant'Ambrogio on the second floor," Gray said. "I arranged it on security grounds with Altishofen and Christophe Despierre."

"Thank you, but how does that help?" Jayne asked. "We don't want to be stuck in the delegation, surely. We need to be sneaking into the secretary of state's offices instead."

"You'll see, don't worry. You don't know how Vatican protocols work, but I'll hopefully be able to give you a lesson. This is the only way we can get in today."

The conspiratorial nature of what she was planning with Gray—the leading Catholic churchman in England—suddenly struck her and left her biting back a grin, despite the gravity of the situation.

Gray glanced at a clock on the wall that read 10:29 a.m. "His Holiness will be finished with the speechwriter by now. We need to move down to the San Damaso Courtyard, next to the Apostolic Palace, to join the reception party. The president will be here soon."

Jayne nodded. "I assume the pope and the Swiss Guards have been happy with events so far this morning?"

"I had a message from Despierre saying the appointments with the hairdresser and the tailor had gone well," Gray said. "They have left the Vatican grounds."

"That's a relief."

"The decks are clear for the president. Follow me."

CHAPTER THIRTY-NINE

Monday, July 11, 2016
   The Vatican

The number of people waiting in the magnificent San Damaso Courtyard, a sixty-meter-long rectangular space, surprised Jayne. There were about a hundred from the Vatican, she estimated, mainly consisting of cardinals and other clergy. But there were also dozens of journalists, photographers, and TV cameramen gathered behind a low barrier.

Gray led her and Rafael to the rear of the waiting group, where they mingled with the others, all of whom were now awaiting the imminent arrival of President Ferguson.

The grandiose courtyard, enclosed on four sides, was dominated on its northeastern side by the Apostolic Palace with its elevated arched full-length windows and by other buildings to the southeast.

There were two squads of eight Swiss Guards. Gray pointed out their ornate Grand Gala uniforms, with blue and yellow stripes, red vest and pants, and red feathers topping their helmets. They were led by their commander, Heinrich Altishofen, who was in full uniform, including white feathers on his helmet. Behind the Swiss Guard was a group of officials that Gray explained included the prefect of the papal household. Saraceni was also there.

Jayne kept checking her phone to see if there had been a response from Neta Rosenblum, but there had not been. She caught Rafael's eye.

"Neta?" she asked.

"Nothing," he replied.

Five minutes later, a huge motorcade of at least thirty vehicles wound its way at a snail's pace into the courtyard from beneath the entrance arch, led by a squad of Swiss Guards on foot. At the center was the president's black armored Cadillac limousine, which came to a halt near the entrance to the palace.

Immediately an American flag was hoisted up a flagpole beneath a clock mounted on the facade of the Apostolic Palace, and a band that was standing to the right of the entrance played "The Star-Spangled Banner."

President Ferguson emerged from the presidential limo to the almost deafening sound of clicking press cameras and journalists yelling questions, which he ignored apart from giving a wave and a smile for the benefit of the TV cameras.

The rest of his delegation emerged simultaneously from some of the other vehicles. Jayne guessed from the bearing and urgent body language of a few of them they included at least a couple of Secret Service officers, despite the official instruction that they should not enter the palace.

After the president had been introduced to the papal group, they filed up a short flight of steps beneath an open porch and into the palace.

"We go last," Gray murmured to Jayne and Rafael. "You'll see why."

Inside, the group went up to the second floor, using both the elevators and the stairs. Jayne and Rafael followed Gray up the stairs and into the Sala Clementina, a long hall whose walls and high ceilings were covered with intricate Renaissance fresco paintings. Hardly a square foot was left undecorated.

"Sixteenth century," Gray muttered as he noticed Jayne gazing up at the arched ceiling. At the front, a squad of the Swiss Guard were paying some kind of tribute to the president.

"Come this way," Gray said. He steered Jayne and Rafael to the rear of the group just as it began to process in a synchronized fashion through a door at the far end of the hall.

They joined a bunch of people at the tail end of the line. Jayne noticed that a number of the party had peeled off from the group and had headed for the exit rather than joining the procession.

"That's our cover," murmured Gray. "People gradually leave the party, until there's just the core top level left, plus the president."

They continued along a corridor into another equally lavishly decorated room, the Sala dei Sediari.

Just before they reached a third room, the Sala di Sant'Ambrogio, Jayne felt Gray's hand tug her forearm. She glanced over her shoulder. Nobody was behind them. Then she followed him down a narrow passage that led off to the left, Rafael close behind her.

Gray glanced over his shoulder, then pushed open a paneled door ten meters farther along the corridor, revealing a narrow staircase. He led the way down the wooden stairs, which they were forced to descend in single file and which creaked loudly underfoot in places.

"An old servants' staircase," Gray said. "Nobody uses it much. But it comes out next to Saraceni's office. And with any luck, the office will be empty, because the said secretary of state and all his staff are upstairs with the president for at least the next fifteen minutes until the president goes to join the pope on the third floor. After that, they could come back anytime."

Sure enough, when Gray clicked open a narrow door at the bottom of the staircase, they emerged at one end of an ornately decorated corridor.

Gray pointed. "Four doors down there on the right." He walked on down the deserted corridor.

They came to a grand set of double oak doors with a large brass doorknob in the center. Gray glanced in both directions up and down the corridor, then twisted the knob. The door clicked open.

Saraceni's office was in reality a suite of rooms, with a luxurious main office containing a large mahogany desk, on which stood a large silver crucifix, and a sitting area with padded chairs and a coffee table. There was a secretary's office adjoining, along with what looked like a soundproofed conference room, and another set up with video equipment.

It was scrupulously tidy and modern looking, unlike the pope's office on the third floor.

More to the point, it was deserted, as Gray had predicted.

Gray went sharply up in Jayne's estimation.

"Now all we need to do is find that crucifix," Rafael said.

"If it's here," Jayne said.

She took out a pair of thin rubber gloves from her pocket and put them on, as did Rafael.

Gray stared at them. "What are you doing?"

"Fingerprints," Jayne said. "I don't like leaving them. Do you want some gloves?"

Gray shook his head, a look of slight distaste on his face. "You can do the searching. I will direct you. Try his desk first, but be quick. They'll be back in ten minutes. Then the storage cupboards and the secretary's room."

Jayne strode to the large desk while Rafael headed to the secretary's office.

She went through three large drawers beneath the desk, but none of them contained what they were looking for. There were only pens, ink, a stapler, and other stationery items. Next, Jayne turned to the storage cupboards against the wall behind the desk. But again she drew a blank. The cupboards were full of files, books, and boxes. One of the boxes contained a wooden crucifix, but it wasn't the type they were seeking.

"Nothing," Jayne said to Gray, who stood near the door, his face taut and tense. Clearly he wasn't enjoying the prospect of one of the secretary of state's team, or Saraceni himself, returning and finding him there overseeing an attempted theft, no matter how justified the circumstances.

"Try the bookcases," Gray said. "But be quick, please."

Jayne nodded and went through the bookcases, one of which had opaque frosted glass doors. But yet again, she found nothing.

Jayne could feel her level of irritation rising. She walked through to the secretary's room just in time to meet Rafael walking out.

He shook his head. "Nothing there."

"Shit," Jayne said. She turned and realized that Gray had heard her. "Sorry, I'm getting frustrated."

Gray ignored the comment and glanced at his watch. "We need to go. Or else we'll be in trouble."

Jayne and Rafael looked at each other. With a nod, they

stripped off their rubber gloves and stuffed them into their pockets. Time was up.

Gray stepped to the office door, turned the doorknob, and pulled it open.

Standing there were two tall Swiss Guards in full dress uniform.

Jayne felt the skin on her scalp tighten.

CHAPTER FORTY

Monday, July 11, 2016
    The Vatican

Jayne cursed under her breath. Was this just a routine check, or did they know?

"What are you doing in the secretary of state's office?" one of the Swiss Guards asked. His deep bass voice boomed into the room.

"We need to see Cardinal Saraceni extremely urgently," Gray said, jumping in before Jayne could speak. "There is an issue, an investigation, we have been trying to resolve on His Holiness's behalf, and it's critical that we speak to the secretary of state as soon as he returns from the presidential reception. We thought best to wait for him here."

Jayne could see Gray almost cringing at the half-truth he was speaking.

As he spoke, Jayne heard Rafael's phone ping three times in succession as messages arrived. Simultaneously, her own phone, which she had turned to silent, vibrated in her pocket.

She pulled it out just as the Swiss Guard who had done the talking took a step into the room.

"Who are these people?" the guard asked, pointing at Jayne and Rafael.

Jayne felt pulled in two directions simultaneously.

She knew instinctively that she and Rafael receiving messages at the same time likely meant only one thing: it was Neta with some information.

She glanced at Rafael, who was already reading his screen. He caught her glance, his face suddenly animated.

Jayne decided the guard had to come first; otherwise, she might not even get the chance to read the messages. She turned back to the guard. "I am Jayne Robinson and this is Rafael Levy. We are working with Cardinal Gray on a confidential investigation on behalf of His Holiness, as you have just been told. It relates to the recent deaths of the cardinals. You really will have to excuse us. While we are waiting for Cardinal Saraceni to return, we have urgent calls to deal with." She held up her phone and seized her identity card, hanging around her neck, and raised it for the guard to see.

The guard looked extremely suspicious. He folded his arms and scrutinized all three of them, his mind clearly working overtime as he decided what to do. He turned to his colleague, who was still standing at the door. The other guard gave a slight nod.

"All right," the first guard said, his attention now turned back to Gray. "Cardinal, I suggest you wait outside the office. Not inside. There's nobody else here. It doesn't look good."

"Of course," Gray said. "I apologize. We didn't think it through. We'll wait outside in the corridor. Thank you."

Jayne followed Gray out of the office and immediately focused on her phone messages as the two Swiss Guards retreated back down the corridor.

Rafael was also reading his messages.

Sure enough, they were all from Neta.

URGENT. Apologies for delay. Needed to break encryption. Cell phone records for Saraceni show multiple calls to Lebanese cell phone belonging to Cardinal Filippo Martelli, code-named CIRRUS.

Jayne looked up at Gray. "Saraceni's been calling Cardinal Martelli."

"*Martelli?*"

"Is he here today?" Jayne asked.

Gray shook his head. "I think he's in Lebanon."

Jayne clicked onto the next message.

Saraceni call timings consistent with hits on cardinals in US and Rome and with attempt on you in Ramallah. Martelli's phone shows similarly timed calls to Talal Hassan's French cell phone—we got Pegasus onto that phone. Three calls yesterday. Location details following.

Jayne was instantly impressed. She knew Pegasus could be installed without needing to lure the target into clicking on a phishing email or message, but to have embedded it on a phone owned by someone like Hassan, a streetwise operator who would have a heavily protected Hezbollah device, in such a short space of time showed remarkable skill. Clearly Hassan didn't realize that his French phone had been compromised—Jayne certainly owed Abu Alami in Ramallah, who had given her that number.

She turned to Gray and Rafael. "So, Saraceni has been calling Martelli, and Martelli's been calling Talal Hassan," she said.

As she spoke, the linkage between Martelli and Hassan struck her and sent her internal alarm system flashing red. Now her mind was spinning faster than the reels on a slot machine.

Saraceni. Martelli. Hassan. Hassan's *French* phone.

The same thoughts were obviously going through Rafael's mind. "Shit."

"Pierre Fekkai—the *tailor*," Jayne said.

Jayne looked again at Gray, whose face was a little blank.

Sometimes Jayne just worked off her gut instinct. Over the years, more often than not, this happened at moments of crisis when decisions needed to be made immediately.

She knew she was looking at an assassination plot, and her mind flashed straight back to the attempt on her own life at the tailor shop on Rue de Saint-Michel in Paris.

Jayne knew right then how this attempt would be done.

"Did you say the tailors visiting the pope this morning have gone?" she asked, her voice now tense.

"Yes, Zeffirelli," Gray said. "And an assistant. They went some time ago. Why do—"

"Can we get to the pope's office from here—fast?"

"But the president will be in there now. We can't go in and—"

Again Jayne interrupted. "That's why we need to. There's something going on. I don't know what," she snapped. "Quick —how can we get there?"

Gray nodded. "Follow me." He turned decisively and led the way at a fast walk down the corridor in the direction the guards had gone.

They turned a corner and there in front of them was a small elevator door.

"Service lift," Gray said as he pushed the button. The doors creaked open to reveal an ancient-looking wood-paneled elevator. "The main lifts will be closed off for the president. We can use this. Get in."

The elevator, which had an open wire mesh window at one end through which the shaft wall and electrical cables and connections could be seen, grumbled and whined its way upward.

While the elevator was rising, Jayne's phone vibrated

twice with two more messages from Neta. Rafael's phone also pinged twice.

Pegasus traced Hassan's calls to Martelli. They were made at following address, read the first message.

The second message contained a house number in Via di Sant'Anselmo, Rome, and an attachment showing a satellite map with the location marked in the Ripa neighborhood, east of the River Tiber.

Eventually, the elevator ground to a halt with a shriek of metal on metal.

The door opened, and they emerged into a corridor lined with portraits of what looked like previous popes.

"This way," Gray said. He headed toward a narrow doorway at the end of the corridor. "Takes us to the third loggia. I will need to talk to the Swiss Guard. Hopefully Heinrich will be there, waiting for the president to finish."

Jayne glanced at her watch. It was now 11:16 a.m. The meeting between the pope and the president, if it went to schedule, still had almost half an hour to run.

She felt her stomach churn.

They emerged halfway along the long, fresco-painted loggia. There were four Swiss Guards stationed against the wall at intervals along the length of the walkway. One guard immediately headed toward them at a fast pace.

"Eminence, what are you doing here?" the guard said to Gray, his tone of voice rapid and urgent. "You can't be here while the presidential meeting is in progress. I must ask you to leave immediately."

"There's an urgent security issue affecting the pope," Gray said. "Is Commander Altishofen here? We need to speak to him—it's extremely urgent."

"You can't, Eminence. I'm sorry. The commandant is outside the pope's study, waiting for the president."

Jayne stepped forward. "Sir, we're intelligence officers

working for the Holy Father. We have reason to believe he and the president are in potentially serious danger. Know one thing: we are not trying to interrupt such a meeting lightly. Several cardinals have died in recent weeks. We don't want to add a pope and a president to the list. Now, can we go, please? Right now."

The guard hesitated, clearly taken aback by the forcefulness with which Jayne spoke.

"Quickly," Gray said. "We need your commandant right now. We can explain to him, not you. This is serious."

Finally the guard nodded. "Come this way, Eminence."

The guard led them across the marble floor to the end of the loggia, where he spoke rapidly to a colleague standing guard at the double doors that led left into the papal apartments.

The guard turned back to them. "You can come and speak to Commander Altishofen."

He pushed open the double doors and continued into the papal apartments and along the corridor with which Jayne was now familiar. Standing outside the pope's private chapel was Altishofen, who turned upon hearing footsteps. He looked hot and sweaty beneath his heavy uniform and helmet.

There was no sign of any Secret Service officers, just as there hadn't been outside in the loggia. Jayne assumed that they had been unable to get around the protocols laid down by the Prefecture of the Papal Household. She saw only Swiss Guards here.

"What are you doing here?" Altishofen hissed. "How did you get in?"

"I'm sorry, sir," the guard accompanying them said. "There is apparently an urgent security issue and—"

"We have very strong reason to think the pope and the president are in danger in there," Jayne interrupted. She put her hands on her hips and raised herself to her full five feet nine inches. "We need to get in there—and probably get them out immediately."

"The room has been checked," Altishofen said. "I supervised it myself, with the Secret Service." He pointed at Jayne. "You were there. You know that was done. You saw me do it."

"Since then, two tailors have been in," Jayne said. "We believe they might have links to a Hezbollah terrorist."

Rafael stepped forward. "Sir, intelligence from Tel Aviv this morning, from the Mossad, has shown clear links. Phone records. There's something going on. We *must* interrupt them."

Smart move by Rafael, Jayne thought. She presumed he had thought that invoking the Mossad's name would carry more weight than mentioning Unit 8200, with which Altishofen might be less familiar.

"I'll lose my job if this is wrong," Altishofen said.

"You might lose your pope if you don't move," Jayne shot back.

She glanced at her watch again. "The meeting is about halfway through. Well?"

Altishofen grimaced. "Let's go in."

He turned and paced swiftly toward the wooden door to the pope's office, knocked sharply twice, then turned the doorknob and walked straight in. Jayne and Rafael were one step behind, followed by Gray.

Pope Julius and President Ferguson were sitting on either side of the desk, clearly in midconversation. They stopped and stared as the four people walked in.

"What is happening?" the pope said. "Why are you interrupting? And who is this?" He pointed at Rafael.

"Holiness, this is Rafael Levy, of the Mossad, working with Ms. Robinson," Altishofen said. "They say they have information that you both might be at risk right now. It came from the Mossad this morning."

Jayne marched up to the pope's desk. "Your Holiness, did the tailors who were here this morning do anything unusual? Did they interfere with any of your books, touch your cabinets, leave anything unexpected behind?"

"What is this?" the president said. "Jayne. What are you doing here? What's going on?"

"Sorry, Mr. President," she said abruptly. "We need to get an answer from His Holiness."

The pope shook his head. "No, they touched nothing. They fixed my cassock, my skullcap."

"So they left nothing odd behind?" Jayne persisted.

"No. Nothing. Oh, there was a book of samples, of material, for my shirts." The pope turned his head toward his bookshelf behind him. "That. The fabric samples." He pointed toward a large, chunky fabric swatch book that lay in a space on a bookshelf directly behind his desk.

Jayne stared at the swatch book.

"*Shit*," she said out loud.

"Get them out," Rafael said. "Right now."

"We need to get you out of here," Jayne snapped. "Both of you. Mr. President, leave. Now."

Neither man moved.

"You need to get up and get out," Jayne said, her voice rising rapidly. "I mean what I say. If I'm wrong, you can hang me out to dry afterward. Come on. Move."

Altishofen stepped forward. "Come, Holiness, I will help you."

The pope, his face now looking shaken, rose to his feet. He walked around from his side of the desk and joined President Ferguson, who had also stood.

"I think we should go, Mr. President," the pope said. "These people know something we don't."

The president exhaled. "Let's go, then." He glared at Jayne. "You better be—"

"I am," Jayne said. "Please go."

"You heard what they said, Holiness," Gray said. "There's no time. Go."

Gray opened the door and Pope Julius, followed by President Ferguson, filed through into the corridor. Gray and Altishofen went after them, then Rafael, and finally Jayne at the rear.

"Get out into the loggia," Jayne called. "Quick as you can. Then go downstairs."

They had just passed the entrance to the pope's private chapel and were heading toward the tall double doors to the loggia when from behind them came a deafening explosion, followed immediately by a second bang.

The next thing Jayne knew, she had been catapulted forward onto the floor, half on top of Rafael, half on top of Gray. Although she threw out her arms to break her fall, she banged her chin hard on the marble surface and felt a sharp pain at the back of her jawbone.

A cloud of dust and debris was blasted into the corridor and splattered all over her. All the lights went out with an extended electrical fizz, and the corridor was plunged into darkness, just as something hard hit Jayne on the back of the head.

She immediately felt as though her head was spinning.

From behind came an enormous crash of falling masonry, which she guessed was likely the ceiling of the pope's office caving in.

Jayne coughed violently. She could feel her lungs filling with dust and instinctively reached for her pocket, where she carried a handkerchief. She pulled it out, opened it, and held it over her nose and mouth.

At that point, the double doors to the loggia were flung open and light came streaming in.

Jayne lifted her head.

The first thing she saw was the dark silhouetted figure of a Swiss Guard standing in the doorway against a bright white backdrop of light.

As her eyes adjusted, the second thing visible was the pope, lying motionless on his stomach, his arms flung out in front of him, where presumably he had tried in vain to break his fall. A trickle of blood coming from his head was visible on the white marble floor and splattered over the white arm of his cassock.

Behind him lay the president and Altishofen. Neither of them was moving.

CHAPTER FORTY-ONE

Monday, July 11, 2016
    The Vatican

The president of the United States, having arrived at the Vatican by limousine in a huge motorcade, left in the second of two ambulances, the first of which contained the pope. Jayne watched as the two vehicles, accompanied by a posse of Vatican and Italian state police cars and motorcycle outriders, headed slowly beneath the archway that led out of the San Damaso Courtyard.

Both were heading for the Gemelli University Hospital, the enormous Rome teaching hospital seven kilometers to the north, where the pope had a special suite permanently reserved for his use on the tenth floor.

There were still a large number of journalists and camera crews in the courtyard when the bomb went off upstairs, guaranteeing that the entire drama made instant headline news around the world.

The paramedics who had been on standby at the Vatican

had acted swiftly after the explosion in the papal apartments —Jayne had to concede that. They had rushed to the third floor and stabilized the pope, who had suffered a concussion, a broken nose, a badly split chin, and a suspected fracture and cut to the cheek from where he had fallen headfirst onto the marble floor. The bleeding from his wounds had been so great that they had not managed to fully stop it before the ambulance departed.

Although the pope had just about regained consciousness, he was fading in and out and had to be taken away on a stretcher, wearing an oxygen mask to help his breathing. The worry was that when he banged his head on the hard floor, it caused some internal damage or bleeding.

The president had also been knocked out when his temple struck the floor and had broken his right forearm while attempting to brace himself as he was propelled off his feet by the force of the explosion. His right eye was almost completely closed up, and he had massive bruising down that side of his face.

The blast had blown out both windows in the pope's private office as well as the doors to his bedroom and the corridor. It had set the office ablaze, destroyed the ceiling, and sent clouds of smoke billowing out over the Vatican, which had made for dramatic television footage. After fire crews had put out the inferno, it was clear the entire apartment was destroyed.

Jayne herself was feeling a little dizzy, and her jawbone felt sore and painful on both sides at the back around the hinge with her skull. But she declined the strong advice from the paramedics to go to the hospital for checks and possibly overnight supervision. She knew they would likely stuff her full of drugs and forbid her to discharge herself, which she couldn't allow—their investigation would be left miles behind.

Rafael had also gone against the paramedics' orders and declined a hospital visit, as had Michael Gray and Heinrich Altishofen. All seemed to have found a way to cushion their falls and had not suffered seriously, although the explosion had left both Gray and Altishofen with persistent ringing in their ears.

There was much that was confusing Jayne, and through the persistent brain fog, she retreated back into the lobby of the palace, where she held a quick discussion with Rafael and tried to prioritize their tasks.

It was virtually certain that the bomb had been planted by Pierre Fekkai, working in tandem with Talal Hassan, and that he had come into the Vatican with the official tailor, Vincenzo Zeffirelli. The big issue now was how to track them down and capture them so they could be brought to justice.

She knew she also needed to urgently understand precisely why the killings and attempted killings had taken place. They surely couldn't just be opportunistic. There had to be a reason. Was this linked to what the pope had held back from disclosing? she wondered?

There still seemed more questions than answers.

Jayne and Rafael decided their best option now was to persuade Altishofen to help them. The Swiss Guard commander appeared to be rapidly recovering his faculties after the blast, despite his lavish uniform being smothered in white dust and debris. He was standing a few meters away from them, directing operations.

Jayne walked up to him and showed him the messages received from Unit 8200 and asked him to ensure that the Swiss Guard took the Vatican secretary of state, Cardinal Alfredo Saraceni, archbishop of Turin, into custody immediately, before he could flee.

Although visibly stunned by the messages and by what Jayne told him, he immediately delegated his deputy to bring

Saraceni in for questioning and to search his office, as well as his apartment on the top floor of the Palazzo San Carlo. Specifically, Jayne told him, it was suspected that the secretary of state might have hidden a crucifix adapted as a listening device somewhere.

We should have had Saraceni taken into custody yesterday, even without evidence, Jayne thought.

"The other key thing is, we need to track down the two men we are certain did this, Pierre Fekkai and Talal Hassan," Jayne told Altishofen and a stunned-looking Ronald O'Toole, who had joined them. "We have an address in the Ripa district from where Hassan called Cardinal Martelli. I would like to go there. My guess is that both of them are long gone, but they will have no idea we know the location, so there might be a chance."

"Do you want me to involve the Italian state police?" Altishofen asked. "I have a direct line to its *capo*. Or the Carabinieri?"

Jayne shook her head. "I would prefer not to. Certainly not the Carabinieri, based on my experience with them on this trip. They locked me and Rafael up and beat us up in Regina Coeli." She pointed to the bruises still showing across her face. "However, if you think the state police are best placed to handle this, I will bow to your judgment."

"I don't like to tread on the Italians' toes," Altishofen said. "But I do have a squad of highly skilled plainclothes operatives I can call on. It's the closest we have to a special force. They guard the pope on overseas trips. I used to work in that unit myself, years ago, and at one time I was in the Swiss Army's special forces command. I sometimes get involved in their work. It may cause some trouble if I deploy them outside the Vatican, but let's cross that bridge if we get to it. I think we have some justification for using them."

The existence of such a unit was news to Jayne.

Altishofen, just like Michael Gray, was proving to be far more helpful than she had expected.

"Yes, please," she said immediately. His approach would yield swifter results at this juncture than by involving the Italian police.

She glanced at O'Toole who gave a nod of agreement. "Do it," he said.

"Can we go immediately?" Jayne asked. "I'm assuming they are armed?"

"They are better with their guns than anyone in the state police, put it that way. Since the assassination attempt on Pope John Paul II in 1981, we have always made that a priority. Our men get their basic weapons training with the Swiss Army, and we then raise them to a different level. They are more skilled and less corrupt than the Italians."

Jayne gave a thin smile, as did Rafael, also visibly reassured.

"Do you have a couple of handguns that Jayne and I could borrow?" Rafael asked.

Altishofen sucked in air. "I will check. We should have SIG Sauer P220s you could use, yes."

He took his radio from his waist, flicked a switch, waited for a loud squelch break to clear, then issued a series of instructions in rapid Italian.

When Altishofen had finished, he replaced the radio on his waist. "The plainclothes squad will be ready in ten minutes. There's six of them. We can go immediately in two vehicles. I will change my clothes now and come with you."

"One other thing," Jayne said. "What about CIRRUS? Cardinal Martelli?"

"Good question," Altishofen said. "I believe he's in Beirut. I have to be honest—I've had doubts about him for some time. We don't allow him to be alone with His Holiness. You won't know this, but he was once caught smuggling weapons

into the West Bank in the trunk of a Mercedes. He's originally from Syria. Grew up in Damascus. So in some ways I'm
not surprised by this. Cardinal Martelli has an interesting
history. We will need to work out a plan to deal with him
later."

* * *

Monday, July 11, 2016
    Rome

The two black vans departed Vatican City through the Santa
Anna Gate at an interval of two minutes. The gap was standard practice on the rare occasions that the Swiss Guard's
plainclothes special forces team had to operate outside
Vatican territory, Altishofen explained to Jayne.

"It looks more casual, less operational, than if we have
vans going out in convoy," he said. "We don't want Italian
police surveillance following us."

Jayne, Rafael, and Altishofen were in the first van, which
had one-way windows so passengers could see out, but
nobody could see in. Also in the van were three plainclothes
Swiss Guard officers, all dressed in dark suits and wearing
ties. They could easily have been businessmen, were it not for
the SIG Sauers tucked into holsters at their hips and neatly
hidden beneath their carefully cut jackets.

Three more officers were in the second van, which
followed on behind.

The van cruised at a sedate pace southward along
Lungotevere Gianicolense, the street that ran along the west
bank of the River Tiber, before crossing the water at the
Ponte Palatino bridge and into the Ripa neighborhood.

As they drove, one officer, who introduced himself as

Franz, pulled out an iPad and explained to Jayne and Rafael in fluent but heavily accented English their proposed operational strategy.

Jayne had to admit, the Swiss Guard had wasted little time and was clearly well used to preparing such operations at extremely short notice and with no time for discussion.

Franz showed a close-up high-resolution satellite photograph of the house on Via di Sant'Anselmo. It certainly had a large footprint, including an outbuilding, and looked as though it must have extensive accommodation, likely at least four or five bedrooms, he said.

He pointed to a roof terrace at the top of the building, typical of some of the larger houses in Rome. Four loungers, a large sun umbrella, a table and chairs, and potted plants were clearly visible.

"Weak point," Franz said. "That terrace gives us an entry option. We will look for a way to scale the wall and get in from the top—always best to clear a house from the top down. If Fekkai is in there, we could take him by surprise that way. Nobody expects entry from the roof. They expect people coming up the stairs, usually, not down."

Jayne nodded. That was in line with her operational experience at MI6, too. "You have someone who can climb?" She felt slightly surprised that the Swiss Guard would need such a skill set.

"Of course. It's part of our training, though we don't broadcast it widely," Franz said. "Every building has drainpipes. Or if not, then gutters for J-hooks and ropes. If he's in there, he will surrender, fight, or run. If he runs, we will have our people strategically stationed outside the property, ready to grab him. If he fights, we're confident we're better equipped than he is to prevail." He stabbed a fleshy index finger on the iPad's screen, pointing out key positions. "The garage, the driveway, the front and back doors will all be covered. You understand me?"

She did. "You can deploy me and Rafael wherever you need us. We are used to these scenarios."

Franz glanced at Altishofen to gauge his reaction.

"Thank you," Altishofen said. "We might well do that, if needed."

Altishofen's phone beeped. He scrutinized the screen. "His Holiness is being stabilized in hospital. Still in and out of consciousness," he said.

Nobody responded. Jayne could imagine the reaction among these men, who were charged with the pope's safety, if the worst happened.

Franz removed six earpieces with embedded microphones from a bag, switched them all on, and handed them around.

"These will keep us connected. It's a secure, encrypted dedicated network. The three men in the other van are also in the group. Keep silent on it unless spoken to, or it's absolutely necessary. "

"Got it," Jayne said. She inserted the tiny device in her right ear and hooked the silicone loop designed to keep it in place over the top of her lobe.

Franz went back to his iPad and began a discussion with Altishofen and his other colleagues about tactics. A few minutes later, Altishofen turned to Jayne and Rafael. "We would like to use you in this operation. We'd like you to approach the house from the street, pretend to be a couple walking along. The rest of us will come from the rear."

He showed Jayne and Rafael the aerial photograph again and pointed. "You both enter the garden through this hedge from the neighboring property. Jayne, you take this outbuilding." He indicated to a rectangular building several meters from the main house with a smaller square one behind it. "Get in these bushes next to the door to make sure he doesn't try to run in there or escape through the garden next door. Rafael likewise with this smaller one, which looks like a garden shed. Okay? We will man the main house and the roof."

Jayne and Rafael both nodded.

"I doubt he'll be there," Jayne said. "But I appreciate all this. Definitely worth trying, given we have no other leads."

The van pulled up in a small square, Piazza di Sant'Anselmo, next to a crumbling stone wall that marked the boundary of the nearby university, only a hundred meters from the target property.

"We walk from here," Franz said. "This is where we part company." He pointed through the window to one street that led off the southeast corner of the square. "That's where the house is. You two go that way. We will go the other, down that street and come in from the rear, down a neighboring driveway." He pointed toward another street leading off the northeast corner and a long driveway branching off it.

The other Swiss Guard van drove past them and parked up on the northeast corner of the square, near the exit Franz had indicated.

"We're not going to waste any time," Franz said. "You two go now. We'll follow. We're in touch on the radio. If you see anything that causes concern, let us know. We'll do likewise. Otherwise, radio silence."

Jayne glanced out the van windows. There was nobody around. She looked at Rafael.

"Let's go," he said. He slid open the van's side door and climbed out, followed by Jayne.

They both walked casually away from the van without looking back, but took the opportunity to check out the rest of the square. Immediately they fell into the role of a couple, chatting about their favorite European cities and using the conversation to turn and face each other, thus giving them an opportunity to scan their surroundings.

As they walked out of the square and onto Via di Sant'Anselmo, Jayne caught sight of the three Swiss Guards climbing out of the other van. Two of them had black backpacks slung over their shoulders, which looked a little incongruous with their suits. She guessed they contained climbing ropes and other gear.

The target street was lined with large, elegant detached villas.

"Jayne, Rafael, can you slow a little so we coordinate our arrival?" crackled Franz's voice in Jayne's earpiece. "Our ETA is two minutes. Over."

"Roger, will do. Over," Jayne responded.

This type of operation took Jayne back many years to her days in Bosnia and Serbia, and beyond that to Pakistan and Afghanistan, when she on several occasions worked alongside British special forces to trace and capture terrorists and suspected war criminals.

Now walking at only an amble, they timed their arrival at the neighboring property on the left side of the street almost to the second. To Jayne's dismay, the driveway at the side of the house was blocked by a tall gray double metal gate. A similar gate guarded the vehicle entrance to the target house.

After checking they remained unobserved, Jayne turned the handle of the gate to the neighboring property. It was unlocked, so she opened it a little. Now she could see the driveway would indeed allow them access to a low wall that marked the boundary between the two properties. It would be easy enough for them to climb over.

They slipped through the gate, which Rafael closed behind him. Then they crossed a narrow strip of lawn to the wall and climbed over.

There they were shielded from the target house by several

shrubs that were about head high. However, through the bushes, Jayne saw a movement from the end of the garden, perhaps thirty meters away. She figured it was the Swiss Guards entering the rear of the property.

Jayne took out the SIG Sauer that Altishofen had provided, racked the slide, and flicked off the safety. Rafael did likewise.

She just hoped that if the property had motion detectors, they were not activated during daylight hours. This operation would not be easy to execute without being spotted.

Rafael pointed out the outbuilding that Jayne had been designated to cover, and they made their way cautiously toward it alongside the boundary wall, still concealed by shrubs.

The garden shed, designated for Rafael, was on the far side of the outbuilding. When they reached Jayne's designated spot, they parted. She remained a meter from a green wooden door that formed the entrance to the single-story shed. From there, she had a slightly obscured line of sight to the front door of the house, which was inside a large open porch with a timber frame.

The outbuilding structure was a little run-down, and it looked as though it might be for storage. Rafael continued along the side of the building to the shed at the far end.

Jayne slowly pushed down on the door handle to the outbuilding. It was locked. She peered through a small window next to the door, but although she only had a narrow field of vision, she could see there were no lights on and no sign of life.

She turned her attention back to the house and garden. Two men sprinted from the bushes farther up the garden to a pair of drainpipes that ran down the western side of the house from gutters at the top to a drain at the bottom.

Within seconds, it seemed, the men were scrambling up

the drainpipes, using the brackets and fittings to provide their foot- and handholds. Neither bothered with safety ropes, not that there was time for that. Jayne had at one time had sufficient upper-body strength to climb like that, but she doubted whether she would have made it a quarter of the way up these days.

Both men completed their two-story climb and disappeared over the top of the roof.

Through the bushes, Jayne spotted another Swiss Guard crouching at the side of the single-story garage that was joined to the front of the property. These men had moved swiftly and decisively.

"On the terrace. We'll be inside in a few seconds," came a voice in German over the radio. "Someone has been up here very recently. Cigarette butts in ashtray."

Ten seconds later, the voice came again. "We're in. Stand by."

Jayne edged backward a little, so she could get a better view of the front door through the bushes.

As she did so, she heard a faint noise from behind her. She half turned her head, realizing that the door of the outbuilding behind her had opened.

But before she could react further, a black gloved hand clamped itself over her mouth and yanked her head back hard, twisting her neck and causing a sharp pain to jag down her spine. Another hand grabbed her right wrist, where she was holding the SIG Sauer, and bent it back.

Caught off balance, she could not stop herself from being pulled hard backward into the outbuilding. The door was kicked shut with a sharp click.

CHAPTER FORTY-TWO

Monday, July 11, 2016
   Rome

The man flattened Jayne to the floor while she was still unbalanced. He continued to hold her right wrist in an iron grip and pinned her to the ground, holding her legs down with his thighs and her left wrist with his right hand.

"Drop that gun," he hissed in a low voice with an accent that sounded half French, half Middle Eastern. "Let it go. Now."

He tightened his grip even further on her right wrist until she could feel her tendons being crushed. A spike of agony shot up her arm and she let the pistol go.

"Sensible," he muttered, his face looming close to hers. "Okay, you bitch. Now you pay for my brother's death, one way or another. If I go down, you go down."

She knew it was Pierre Fekkai.

It was at that point he spotted the earpiece. He let go of his grip on her left arm and, with lightning speed, ripped it out of her ear. Then he resumed his grip on her wrist and, while still holding her, bashed the earpiece repeatedly on the floor until it broke into pieces.

This guy was strong.

"Who are you with?" he demanded, his voice still no more than a hiss. "How many people?"

Jayne hesitated for only a couple of seconds. What should she tell him?

"Answer," he said. "Who are you with?"

"Two others are going to the back of the house," she said. She knew it was risky to say that, but she didn't want to let him know there was a squad of Swiss Guards and a Mossad agent involved.

Jayne could now see the room was set up as an office, with two desks, monitor screens, and a couple of filing cabinets. A TV in the corner was switched on and showing what looked like Italian satellite news, but it had been muted.

She cursed herself. After checking the door, she had assumed the outbuilding was unoccupied and had been too focused on watching the main house. Now she was likely going to pay heavily for that.

Her only chance was to try to buy herself a bit of time and hope the others would realize what had happened and swiftly regroup.

"I didn't kill your brother," she said. "I had nothing to do with that. It was a British security services team who did it because he had tried to kill me by putting an IED through the letterbox where I was. I wished that had never happened."

She was certain he would not believe her, but it was worth a try.

"Bullshit," he said. "I see that now you're trying to have me killed too—or you were going to do it yourself." He glanced at her SIG Sauer lying nearby. "Well, that's not going to happen. First, you're going to be my ticket out of here. Then you'll be the one doing the dying, not me. I might have gotten it wrong in Paris, but I won't make that mistake again."

Jayne's stomach turned over inside her.

Hostage.

That's what he's planning.

Suddenly, Fekkai flipped Jayne over, wrenching her left arm over and causing another spike of agony, this time in her shoulder joint. Now she was facedown and Fekkai had hold of both her wrists behind her back.

Using his right hand, he picked up the gun she had dropped.

Jayne knew that given the opportunity, she could try a few things to get loose, but he was far stronger than she and wasn't giving her an inch. And he was now doubly armed. She could see his own pistol, a Beretta, on a table within a meter or so, quite apart from now having hers.

Fekkai reached to his right and, through her peripheral vision, Jayne saw him grab a length of electrical cable from a toolbox on the floor. While keeping her tightly pinned to the floor with his legs, body, and left hand, he used the cable to lash her wrists tightly together behind her back.

Then he hauled her to her feet, put down the SIG Sauer, and picked up his Beretta. He quickly racked the slide, turned off the safety, and held the barrel against the back of her head.

Please, God, don't twitch that trigger finger.

"Right, we are going to take a walk to the garage. I have a car there. We will then drive out of here. If anything happens, if your people do anything foolish, the back of your head disappears. Understood?"

"I guess you were the one who took down all the cardinals. In Washington? In Rome?"

Fekkai gave a sardonic half laugh. "Do they pay you to come up with such insights? Genius. Who else do you think did it?"

"But why? And why take out the pope? I don't understand. What has he ever done against you? What has he ever done against Hezbollah?"

Delay. She had to delay. The more she could slow him down, the better her chances.

"He knew. Too many of them knew," Fekkai muttered.

"What did they know?" Jayne asked.

"It doesn't matter."

Despite her situation, Jayne now felt utterly intrigued.

"What is this all about?" she asked again.

"What do you think it's about? Money, of course. Like everything in this world. How do you think Hezbollah could survive without money? How could we carry out the Supreme Leader's work without money? How could we do our work in Lebanon without money? Are you really so stupid you can't see all that? And all of it is Allah's work. That's what it's about."

"So killing the cardinals in Washington was solely about protecting the money that was coming from the Sole Nero arrangement? You knew they were going to tell the White House about that and about the cash being pumped into LA Fashions, which I guess came from drug sales or something. Is that it?"

"Isn't that reason enough?" Fekkai muttered. He pushed the barrel of his gun harder into the back of Jayne's head. "We need to go."

"But how did you blackmail Cardinal Sweeney to involve his family company in that scam?" Jayne persisted. "And what's the pope's got to do with it? And what's your connection to Cardinal Martelli in Beirut?"

Now she could hear herself gabbling, talking far too fast,

speaking rubbish. She was feeling more than a little panicked. Her gut feeling was that once outside the door, anything could happen—most likely with extremely negative consequences for her.

"Martelli's heart is in the right place. Now, we need to go," Fekkai growled. "Stop talking."

He pushed Jayne toward the door, then wrapped his heavily muscled left forearm tight around her windpipe, pinning her to him. He leaned forward, moved his right hand with the Beretta sharply away from her head, and used it to reach out and grab the door handle.

Just as he pushed the handle down, there was an explosion of semiautomatic gunfire and the sound of shattering glass. A plume of red blood and brains splattered in Jayne's face and over the door as Fekkai's head, only a few inches from hers, was blown apart.

Fekkai's grip on Jayne's neck loosened, and his body slowly crumpled to the floor.

Jayne sank to her haunches and closed her eyes momentarily before turning her head.

The side window of the outbuilding was shattered, and there, holding his gun up behind the remaining shards of glass, was Rafael, his mouth set taut in a grim line.

"Are you okay?" he asked. "Sorry, I had to wait until he moved that gun away from your head. Didn't want to risk it."

Jayne nodded. "I'm okay, I think," she said in a slightly croaky voice. "Just come and untie me."

Rafael emerged through the door a few seconds later and used a penknife to release her hands.

She wiped her hand across her face, leaving it smeared with red. "The bastard crushed my windpipe."

"We need to get out of here. I told Altishofen what was happening on the radio link. He doesn't want to be caught here with a dead body—and I definitely don't. There was nobody else in the main house."

Jayne stood. "You're right. Let's go."

She bent down, checked Fekkai's pockets, and removed a smartphone and a wallet. She left a set of car keys. Then she retrieved her SIG Sauer and walked out the door.

CHAPTER FORTY-THREE

Tuesday, July 12, 2016
Gemelli University Hospital, Rome

Jayne climbed out of the rear door of the unmarked CIA
sedan and stood for a moment in the tree-lined parking lot of
Gemelli University Hospital. She shielded her eyes from the
sun and stared up at the modular building, all concrete, glass,
and steel. In particular she was looking at a row of five
windows on the tenth floor. All had white blinds that were
pulled fully down.

That was where Pope Julius VI and President Ferguson
were being treated in a special suite of rooms reserved for the
pope and his entourage of Vatican staff, including several
nuns and Swiss Guards.

There were at least a dozen television vans and associated
camera crews in the parking lot, along with journalists
waiting for updates on the pope's and the president's
condition.

Media coverage of the blast in the pope's private apartments had been intense and continuous. There were also a large number of Catholic faithful, at least two hundred by Jayne's reckoning, camped out in another corner of the lot. Many had been there all night, carrying out a prayer vigil for the pope's swift recovery. Italian state police officers were keeping a close watch on all of them. No Carabinieri were to be seen.

The Italian state police had wasted no time in finding and identifying the body of Pierre Fekkai following reports of gunshots by other residents on Via di Sant'Anselmo, and this too was being widely reported. Fekkai was immediately linked to the bombing at the Apostolic Palace through false ID documents found in the house under the Philippe Simenon name.

Jayne had been keeping an anxious eye on media coverage, although as far as she could tell, there had been no witnesses in the vicinity to see her and the Swiss Guard team leave the Hezbollah safe house via the neighboring garden.

Police had so far failed to work out who had killed Fekkai and were operating on the premise that it might have been the result of some kind of internal Hezbollah dispute after the pope and the president survived the bombing. Despite some minor damage done to the property where he was found, there had been no useful forensic evidence, journalists were reporting.

Jayne herself had only been discharged from the hospital that morning after an overnight stay, mainly as a precaution given her various injuries from the explosion in the pope's office and her brief stay in Regina Coeli prison.

Heinrich Altishofen and his team had persuaded her and Rafael that a hospital checkup would be a good idea and had taken them to the Gemelli after she had showered and changed the bloodstained clothes she had been wearing.

Although Jayne had removed Fekkai's phone, the contents

of which had been uploaded to the tech team at Langley for analysis, and his wallet, there must have been other documents in the house that the Swiss Guard had not had time to remove.

If she was honest, her overnight hospital stay was a sensible move, and she had thankfully been given the all-clear. She also felt that some kind of justice, albeit very unsatisfactory, had been served on Pierre Fekkai, and so the pressure was off a little—she could afford a few hours in a hospital ward.

She hadn't been accommodated on the tenth floor, of course, but rather in a somewhat drab room on the third floor, in the same ward as Rafael.

Now Vic and Rafael got out of the CIA vehicle and both stood next to Jayne in the parking lot. Vic and Donald Constanzo had fetched her and Rafael from the hospital that morning and taken them back to the CIA station at the Palazzo Margherita for a debriefing.

The meeting had been interrupted by a call from Gray, who had remained at the hospital and was on the tenth floor with the pope's entourage.

Gray reported that Pope Julius had made excellent progress overnight and, although in pain, was now talking, eating, and drinking. The pope also wanted to speak to Gray, Jayne, Vic, and Rafael as soon as possible, he reported, not least to thank them.

Vic had received a similar message from Charles Deacon to tell him that the president was also fully conscious and had eaten a small breakfast, and he also wanted a debrief at his bedside as soon as possible.

"No rest for the wicked," Jayne said.

"That probably explains my state of permanent exhaustion, then," Vic said.

"Shall we go to the pope first?" Jayne asked. "I have unanswered questions I need to ask him before we see the president."

Vic nodded.

Ten minutes later, Vic, Rafael, and Jayne emerged from the elevators on the tenth floor of the Gemelli, where Michael Gray was waiting. Constanzo had remained at the CIA station, where he had a long list of formalities to deal with.

Gray stepped forward and gave Jayne a hug, the first time she could recall such a public display of affection from him. She could tell it was a gesture born largely of relief that she was alive—and probably of the fact that the pope was apparently recovering too.

"His Holiness is improving quickly and is eager to speak to you," Gray said. "He said he feels bad that you have been put in this position as a result of his request to investigate, as indeed do I—it's been awful. But he would also like to discuss things further."

Jayne nodded. "Good. Let's speak to him before he changes his mind."

Gray led them past a battery of Swiss Guards who were on duty next to the elevators and stairwell, through a set of double doors, and along a brightly lit corridor with wooden doors leading off either side at regular intervals. The Gemelli, named after an Italian Franciscan friar and physician, was one of the largest private hospitals in Europe, and the corridors seemed to go on forever.

Eventually they came to another double door, also manned by Swiss Guards. Gray showed his Vatican identification badge and explained why they were there, and they were eventually allowed through.

They emerged into a large reception area with a central

desk at which four white-coated doctors were conferring. One of them peeled off and walked over. Gray introduced him as the papal physician, Dr. Paolo Bravi.

"Can we see His Holiness now?" Gray asked.

Bravi nodded. "Come with me."

He took them to a door leading off the reception area, where he knocked. The door was opened by another Swiss Guard, who stood aside as they entered.

Pope Julius was sitting up in a standard hospital bed in a large but somewhat plain room with the usual vital signs monitors and screens behind the bed. It had a small sitting area at one end, a vase of flowers on the table, and a television on a stand that was showing a live report from a journalist outside the hospital.

Jayne was shocked by the pope's appearance. He was wearing a white plastic nose splint, a bandage on his chin, and a row of wound closure strips over a cut on his left cheek. One eye was a purple-black color, and he had more large bruises elsewhere on his face. He was almost unrecognizable. Rather than his usual cassock, the pope was wearing what looked like a standard hospital gown over purple pajamas. At his age, it was going to take some time for the wounds and bruises to heal properly.

The sight of him gave Jayne a sudden and vivid flashback to another man whom she had often visited in the hospital: her father. She had spent a lot of time at his hospital bedside in 1994. Even now she often found herself missing doing things with him: the games of chess, which he had taught her to a high standard as a youngster and which they continued to play, the long walks, and the occasional runs.

"Can you leave us to speak in private?" Gray asked Dr. Bravi and the Swiss Guard. They assented and withdrew, and Gray closed the door behind them. Jayne was relieved that the pope's personal secretary, Christophe Despierre, was nowhere in sight. She didn't know who could be trusted and who couldn't.

The pope attempted a smile as his visitors gathered around the bed. "I apologize for all this trouble," he said in a voice that sounded faint and distinctly shaky compared to the last time Jayne had heard him speak. "It is all my fault. I hope none of you were injured too badly."

"We are all doing well, thank you, Holiness," Gray told him. "We have a few cuts and bruises, but nothing that won't mend. It is you we are worried about."

The pope winced. "I will recover. Don't underestimate me. It is all superficial. Nothing too major. It can be repaired by nature—just as the damage to my office can be repaired in time. Maybe it's an opportunity to modernize a little." He caught Jayne's eye. "I need to thank you, Jayne, and your colleague Mr. Levy for forcibly persuading an old man that he needed to do as he was told and get out of his own study."

He turned to Rafael. "I apologize if I was a little abrupt when you were trying to save my skin."

"Not at all, Your Holiness," Rafael said. "And, please, call me Rafael."

The pope nodded. "We were only just in time. You both saved President Ferguson and me from a very messy end. I am blessed by you and indebted to you."

"We were all just doing our jobs, Your Holiness," Jayne said. "I certainly couldn't have done it without Cardinal Gray and my colleagues, who all provided superb support, not least my boss Vic, one of the global legends of our industry." She introduced Vic to the pope and outlined the vital role he had played behind the scenes during the operation.

The pope apologized for not being able to shake Vic's hand. "I am indebted to you too," he said. "Your people are a credit to you. I will tell your president that when I can speak with him again."

He paused for a second. "I see that the man who apparently planted the bomb in my office, while masquerading as a tailor, is now deceased. I do not intend to ask you all, or the Swiss Guard, exactly how or why that happened."

Does he somehow know?

"And what happened to my tailor, Vincenzo?" the pope asked. "He must have somehow been involved in what happened."

Jayne glanced at Rafael, whose face remained impassive, and at Vic, who stepped forward.

"We've heard that Vincenzo Zeffirelli and his brother were detained by police at Lisbon Airport, Your Holiness," Vic said. "They were about to board a flight to Rio de Janeiro. They will be brought back here and dealt with."

The pope shook his head. "Unbelievable," he said.

Jayne and Vic left unspoken the obvious truth that it was certain the pope's longtime tailor knew of Fekkai's plan.

She also wanted to tell the pope that although it was in many ways a good thing that Pierre Fekkai was no more, his ringmaster, the Hezbollah Unit 910 commander, Talal Hassan, almost certainly was still at large. But she didn't want to cause more alarm, and so instead she changed the conversation.

"We don't want to keep you talking for too long, as I'm sure you are exhausted," Jayne said. "But I have a few quick questions, if I may."

The pope exhaled heavily and paused for a couple of seconds before replying. "Jayne. There are things I need to tell you and Cardinal Gray. Things that perhaps I should have said before."

He paused again and looked at Gray and then back at Jayne again, his eyes watery.

"We're listening, Your Holiness," Jayne said.

"In fact, there have been wrongdoings," the pope continued. "I actually need to make a confession. I know you're not a Catholic, but will you be my confessor this time?"

CHAPTER FORTY-FOUR

Tuesday, July 12, 2016
    Gemelli University Hospital, Rome

Jayne stared at the pope silently for a few moments.

His confessor?

What's coming now?

"I'm not really used to listening to confessions other than those from terrorists and foreign spies and war criminals," she said, a note of uncertainty in her voice. "Wouldn't Cardinal Gray be a better choice?"

"Not this time," the pope said.

Jayne looked sideways at Gray, who just stared at her, clearly as surprised as she was, but not wanting to interfere.

"I will try, in that case," she said.

The pope indicated toward a row of chairs against the wall. "Pull those chairs up near the bed and take a seat, all of you."

They did as he asked. As she collected her chair, Jayne

fished out her phone and surreptitiously switched on the voice recorder so the pope didn't see. She felt guilty about doing so, but she had a gut instinct that she might need a record of whatever he was about to tell them, even if only for her personal reference later.

Then Jayne, Gray, Rafael, and Vic sat silently as Pope Julius began to speak in a voice that often faltered but was nevertheless clear enough.

"I was extremely distressed and very confused by the terrible murders of my Catholic brothers in the United States and here in Italy," the pope said. "I could not understand why this was happening, and that is why I asked for an investigation, particularly to find out what the men shot in Washington had been intending to tell the White House and me."

The pope paused and winced, pain written across his face. "But with your help, and with the help of what few brain cells I have that are still active, I have worked out a few things."

Jayne gave a slight smile at the pope's self-deprecating sense of humor, which clearly remained intact despite his obvious discomfort. She really was starting to feel some affinity for this old man.

"It sounds like you might have worked out more than we have," she said, a dry tone in her voice. "I feel like we have only completed half a jigsaw puzzle, despite all our efforts and progress."

"Perhaps between us we can complete the picture," the pope said. He closed his eyes and gritted his teeth as another wave of pain visibly went through him.

Nobody spoke as they watched him struggling.

Eventually Gray, who was nearest, reached out and placed his hand on the pope's hand. "Take your time, Holiness. Take your time."

The pope opened his eyes again. "I have to say, it is not a

pretty picture, so prepare yourselves—and I must ask you to promise secrecy regarding what I am about to tell you. You may inform the president, and as soon as we can meet again face-to-face, I realize I have to discuss it with him. But please do not tell anyone else yet."

"We give you our word," Jayne said, glancing at the others, who all nodded their assent.

Gray, to her left, was sitting with his mouth slightly open, clearly intrigued. To her right, Vic was also visibly astonished at the way the pope's conversation was unfolding.

The pope clasped his hands together. "As we all now know, Hezbollah was using in a fraudulent way the clothing company that was part-owned by our late brother Cardinal Sweeney and his family. It was linked to the Sole Nero company here in Italy."

Jayne leaned forward. "Yes, and my question has been how that link happened and developed—why Cardinal Sweeney allowed it to occur," she said. "It's what I was trying to ask you two days ago, but you didn't want to answer."

"That is what I'm coming to," the pope said. He shifted slightly in his bed and winced heavily. "I learned the truth through a combination of confession, when Cardinal Sweeney spoke to me, and through somehow having my wits about me to locate certain documents in the Vatican Secret Archive that helped to fill in the blank spaces. And I'm not talking about those relating to Pope Pius and the wartime papers."

Jayne caught sight of Gray shifting in his chair, and she recalled him telling her that last week he had bumped into the pope emerging from the Secret Archive with some documents.

"Cardinal Sweeney made a confession to you?" Jayne asked.

"Yes. The great issue with this," the pope said, "is that we have something called the seal of confession, which you will probably know about—it means that anything said during a confession is completely confidential. That was why I hesitated over telling you these things two days ago. However, because what Cardinal Sweeney told me is also largely included in the documents from the archive, and because it has led to such tremendous loss of life, including Cardinal Sweeney's, I feel I should disclose that material now, at least to you here if not in public. I know I have to—there is no choice."

Pope Julius pressed his lips together. "In retrospect, I should not have hesitated. I should have acted sooner. That is a sin I need to confess."

"And what was in those documents?" asked Gray, who apparently couldn't contain himself.

"Just wait, Eminence, I'm getting to it," the pope said, a clear note of impatience in his voice. Again he closed his eyes and screwed up his face as another shard of pain shot through him.

Everyone in the room waited.

Eventually, he opened his eyes again and continued. "The documents were deposited in the archive by Cardinal Sweeney in a sealed envelope some time ago. What emerged from them explains how Hezbollah persuaded, or shall we say blackmailed, him into entering an arrangement that must have benefited Hezbollah by many, many tens of millions of dollars, if not hundreds of millions. It must have been paying for their terrorist operations all over Europe, all over the world. That money came partly from the clothing fraud, which we know about, and from the laundering of cash received from large-scale drug transactions in the United States."

The pope paused again, his chest rising and falling. From outside came the distant wail of an ambulance siren and the faint roar of Rome's traffic, all mingling with the intermittent beeping of the vital signs equipment behind the pope's bed.

"I am sorry to tell you that I have now realized Hezbollah must have somehow managed to find out about a cover-up involving Cardinal Sweeney," the pope said.

"A *cover-up?*" Jayne asked.

The pope nodded. "And they must have used that information to blackmail him into entering into the arrangement between LA Fashions and Sole Nero. The cover-up related to something that Cardinal Sweeney knew about but neither addressed nor disclosed until he finally and belatedly spoke to me about it under seal of confession."

There was another pause.

"And this all related to Cardinal Sweeney's diocese in New Orleans?" Gray asked.

The pope glared at Gray, who shrank back a little in his seat.

"The cover-up related to a saga of abuse by several Roman Catholic priests who worked in Cardinal Sweeney's diocese," the pope said, visibly struggling to get his words out.

There was an audible gasp from Gray.

"It was what you might call systematic abuse of both girls and boys, from what I can gather," the pope continued.

"Do you mean Sweeney—" Jayne began.

The pope shook his head as he interrupted. "He wasn't involved in it himself, but he completely failed to deal with the issue and instead swept it under the carpet, apparently fearful of the consequences. He simply moved the priests involved to different positions. He didn't get rid of them, and he didn't report them to the police or any other authority. Unfortunately, I am ashamed to say there have been many such cover-ups in our church worldwide, of which this was the latest. A small minority is involved in these things, but that is too many—it stains the reputation of the church in irreparable ways. It is not God's work—quite the opposite. And it is something I am determined to tackle and resolve. However, that will not help us here. The point is, the Hezbollah people discovered this cover-up and capitalized on it."

Jayne heard Gray give a slight gasp.

She rocked back in her chair. Nothing related to such an abuse scandal had appeared publicly so far, to the best of her knowledge.

This was going to be like a nuclear explosion once it surfaced.

She had not been expecting this.

But it explained everything.

Pope Julius looked at Jayne from beneath lowered eyebrows. "We have an old proverb in Italy," he said. "*Vecchi peccati hanno le ombre lunghe*. The best translation of it is, 'Old sins have long shadows.'"

He was right about that, Jayne thought. "How could they discover the cover-up?" she asked. "There's a mole somewhere, presumably."

"A mole, yes. A mole in our midst who provided them with the necessary information," the pope said. His anger now seemed to have surpassed his pain, and his tone of voice grew stronger.

"And that is who?" Jayne asked. "Cardinal Martelli, the Beirut-based bishop I assume. Or Cardinal Saraceni?"

"You assume correctly," the pope said. "Yes, Martelli, the Maronite Catholic Patriarch of Antioch and head of the Maronite Church. He obtained his information, I suspect, from Cardinal Saraceni, who spends a lot of his time in the Secret Archive looking at documents. It is something I had noticed but always assumed he was doing necessary research for his role as secretary of state. He is very friendly with the prefect in charge of the Vatican's Secret Archives, Bishop

Galli, who I am sure doesn't question him too closely about what he is doing, if at all. The papers that Cardinal Sweeney deposited in the archives, all originally sealed, were unsealed by the time I located them. You might notice, if you visit Cardinal Saraceni's apartment, that he likes his material possessions, his comforts. His apartment is significantly more luxurious than mine, that is for sure. I am sure his motive would have been financial. Hezbollah were doubtless rewarding him handsomely."

That would account for the multiple calls between Saraceni and Martelli that Unit 8200 had picked up, Jayne reflected to herself.

"Why would Martelli do this?" she asked.

The pope looked at her. "I suspect partly for money, but I believe it may be more than that, knowing his background and his history. He is an Arab, deeply rooted in Syria, Lebanon, and the Middle East. I think he has some considerable sympathy for Iran and the ayatollah, and probably therefore Hezbollah. He doesn't express it in public, but in private I have heard the odd comment."

There was a short silence.

"Even the Vatican is not exempt from corruption," Jayne said.

The pope gave a sarcastic laugh, then uttered a loud groan as the action clearly triggered another spike of pain. "The Vatican has been a corrupt place throughout its history, sadly. Just like with the abuse scandals, it is a small minority who get involved in that kind of thing, but nevertheless often a high-profile minority, made up of those who should know better and set an example to others."

But there was one other element that didn't make sense to Jayne.

"The cardinals who were shot dead in Washington—what was the reason for that?" she asked. "They presumably found out what was going on, but how? And what were they going to do about it?"

"Of course they knew," the pope said. "They were killed to silence them. Just as the bomb in my office was no doubt an attempt to silence me because I too now, finally, know what is going on. As to how they knew, I believe from my conversations with Cardinal Sweeney that before confessing to me, he also made a confession to Cardinal Berg, who was the archbishop of Galveston-Houston. He was one of the four shot in Washington. I suspect that Cardinal Berg and his colleagues were going to inform the White House, and then me, about what was happening with LA Fashions and the role Cardinal Sweeney was playing, and so on. Hezbollah became aware of that, I strongly believe."

"How?"

The pope shrugged. "I have no idea. Maybe they bugged Cardinal Sweeney's office in New Orleans to protect their operation, just as you think my office was bugged. He told me he used to meet Cardinal Berg there and in his home quite often to talk over things. They were on friendly terms with each other. Perhaps the bug picked up any such conversation or the confession. I don't know. I am guessing."

Jayne sat up. The pope was too smart. No wonder he had risen to become leader of the entire Roman Catholic Church. What he was suggesting made total sense. She made a mental note to discuss it with Vic afterward and to get Joe to have Sweeney's office checked for bugs and to involve the FBI in that search.

There was one other element of the scam involving LA Fashions and Sole Nero that she didn't quite get. "Your Holiness, I can see now how LA Fashions was dragged into this scam. But I'm less clear about Sole Nero and their boss, Alberto Casartelli."

The pope exhaled. "Ah, yes. After you mentioned them

before, I asked a few questions and got Christophe to inquire if anyone in the Secretariat of State knew anything about them—they are the ones who handle all the Vatican's investments and dealings with companies. It's Saraceni's responsibility. Christophe was given a tip-off by one of his friends there. As a result, he obtained another document from the Secret Archive for me that showed the Secretariat of State's list of investments in the textiles sector."

Jayne leaned forward. "Don't tell me, Your Holiness. Saraceni had bought shares in Sole Nero?"

The pope pressed his lips together. "Not Saraceni personally, but I found that the Vatican owns fifty-one percent of Sole Nero—through some obscure holding company that gives no clue of the Vatican's involvement. I had no idea. I don't get involved in day-to-day investment decisions. It's owned those shares for many years. They were bought from the owner, Casartelli." The pope shook his head. "Our inquiry into Saraceni needs to be wide ranging and thorough. I am wondering what other deals he has done without my knowledge. It is worrying."

"So Saraceni must have engineered the deal at the Sole Nero end with Casartelli?" Gray asked.

"It seems so. We will get more detail once Saraceni is questioned on all this. But just for your ears, confidentially, I am thinking of stripping the Secretariat of State of its responsibility for investments and having all those shares and investments transferred to the treasury office instead. I want them supervised with more expertise and more accountability in the future. Saraceni's office is now too tainted."

Gray was nodding his approval. "I would strongly support that," he said.

"So what's your solution to these scandals, the abuse particularly, given that was the root cause of all this?" Jayne asked.

The pope eyed her carefully. "How to stop the abuse? You want my private opinion or the church's official position?" he asked.

"Your private one," Jayne said.

"Don't tell anyone this, because it does not align with the official church position." He glanced questioningly at Rafael, Vic, and Gray, as well as Jayne. "Do you all promise?"

Everyone nodded.

"Put it this way: if priests were allowed to marry, that might solve a lot of these problems, in my personal opinion. We could learn something from your Anglican church, the Church of England, in that respect. But that will never happen, as it would reverse two thousand years of Catholic doctrine."

Jayne couldn't prevent her eyebrows from rocketing up. "But you're the pope," she said. "You can't suggest such things —it's against the church's teaching."

"You asked me what my solution might be. I have told you. But you're right. I can't suggest it publicly. If I did, I would likely be forced to resign. There would be another conclave, another pope. Now, don't tell anyone I said it. As you intelligence service people doubtless say to your sources, this conversation never happened."

Jayne smiled at the trust the pope was putting in them. She suspected he rarely, if ever, let his guard down this much. Perhaps his injuries and the shock of what had happened had loosened his tongue. It was interesting he thought that way, though—it was a sentiment she had held for some time.

"The Swiss Guard is holding Cardinal Saraceni," Jayne said. "We need to do the same with Cardinal Martelli. I mentioned it to Commander Altishofen, who is also speaking to the Carabinieri to try and arrange the arrest of Alberto Casartelli, if he hasn't already fled the country. Interpol may get involved if so."

She knew that Altishofen had undertaken to deal with the Carabinieri, which he strongly disliked, only because there were no other options to have Casartelli held.

The pope nodded slowly. "I am sure Commander Altishofen will find a solution for Martelli. I tend not to delve too closely into his methodology."

"What about the announcement you and the president were due to deliver?" Rafael asked. "The recognition of Palestine and the release of the Secret Archives papers on the Nazi era?"

The pope pressed his lips together. "That will happen as soon as I and the president are physically able to do it. We will rearrange as soon as possible. Our staffs have exchanged messages this morning."

He scrutinized Jayne's face, his still-watery eyes flicking over her. Then he turned to Vic, who had remained silent during the pope's confession. "You must find Jayne a useful asset," he said. "She has a way of working that I suspect doesn't fit into your normal pattern."

"She has a unique skill set," Vic said. "Like you with your Swiss Guard, I generally like to let her do what she does best and not ask too many questions."

A thin smile spread across the pope's face. "Maybe I need to ask more questions of my people, though. I'm not sure my approach is necessarily a healthy one, based on what we have seen in the past few weeks."

He was right about that, Jayne thought. "Cultivating a culture of openness might be more productive in your line of work than in Vic's and mine," she suggested. "To be honest, it might bring about more trust in the Catholic Church. Perhaps if any good is to come out of what has happened, it could come from that lesson."

"Everything happens for a reason," the pope said. "You make a very good point—one that I need to take on board.

But perhaps the most important point of all concerns the way in which one sin often leads to another. The Bible has something to say about that. Take a look at Ephesians 4:27, where it says, 'Do not give the devil a foothold.' Unfortunately, Cardinal Sweeney did just that when he failed to deal with the abuse in his diocese. There is a lesson there for all of us."

He bowed his head.

CHAPTER FORTY-FIVE

Tuesday, July 12, 2016
  Gemelli University Hospital, Rome

President Ferguson, who was in a room three doors down the corridor from the pope, seemed to Jayne to be in no better shape than the Holy Father. He too had suffered enormous facial bruising and could not yet see out of his right eye because of the swelling around it. His right forearm was in a cast. However, his nose had somehow escaped unscathed, and he was in bullish mood despite his injuries.

Vic had spent ten minutes negotiating with the president's Secret Service detail outside his suite of rooms before he managed to secure entrance for Jayne and himself. They had been forced to leave Rafael and Gray waiting outside.

"I'm going to kill those Hezbollah bastards," were the president's first somewhat croaky words from his hospital bed when Jayne finally walked in with Vic.

"No need for that, sir," muttered Vic as he took a seat next to Jayne at the bedside. "At least in one case."

"*What?* You mean you've—" Ferguson turned his head so he could see Vic properly with his good left eye.

"Not me," Vic said. "For your ears only, sir, our Israeli friend did the honors and thankfully ensured that Jayne didn't have her head blown off in the process."

Jayne explained briefly what had happened at the Hezbollah safe house.

"We got the killer, Mr. President," Jayne said. "But the head of their Unit 910, Talal Hassan, wasn't there, unfortunately. He's still on the loose."

Ferguson squinted at her through his left eye. "Well, between you, you've dealt them a major blow and gotten some justice of a sort for those cardinals. Most of all, I need to thank you for saving my skin, as well as the pope's."

The sheer act of speaking was taking a visible toll on him.

"Thank you, Mr. President," Jayne said. She went on to detail what had been discovered about the fundraising operation involving LA Fashions as well as the abuse cover-up that had allowed Hezbollah to blackmail their way into Cardinal Sweeney's family business.

Vic then went on to explain the news that had emerged only that morning at their briefing. Following a dawn FBI visit to the headquarters of the retail chain Adelaide, they learned that the payments for the clothing that Adelaide had been buying from Sole Nero were going into a Swiss private bank, Banco del Lago di Lugano, based in Ticino, an Italian canton of Switzerland. Adelaide's finance director thought the account, denominated in US dollars, was operated by Sole Nero, but in fact it was under the control of Hezbollah, and Talal Hassan was one signatory. That explained the final element of how the money laundering operation had been functioning.

The president looked visibly shocked at all the disclosures about the money laundering and especially the abuse cover-up. "We must ensure justice is done in those cases. I will speak to the pope to ensure we get cooperation from Sweeney's diocese over that."

"The pope wants that discussion with you," Jayne said.

The president attempted another weak smile. "I'd also like to congratulate you, Jayne, on a well-executed operation. Please pass that on to your Mossad friend, Rafael, too. I have frankly been ashamed of the extent to which Hezbollah has been running these money laundering scams in the United States during my watch—we have suspected them of operating on our territory, but we hadn't pinned down any details, and I didn't think it was such a large or damaging arrangement."

The president leaned back on his pillow. "Now you need to make sure you watch your back, Jayne. They'll be gunning for you after this."

She knew he was right. The dismantling of one of Hezbollah's major fundraising and money laundering operations at LA Fashions and the loss of a billion-dollar drug deal were enough for Hassan to paint a target on her back. Yet on top of that was the loss three months ago of one of Hassan's key lieutenants and operational assassins in Europe, Henri Fekkai, followed now by the death of a second, his twin brother Pierre. Taken all together, Jayne had dealt the organization several serious blows.

"Don't worry, Mr. President. I'm used to watching my back," she said. "Thank you for your concern."

Ferguson nodded and closed his eyes.

Jayne glanced at Vic.

"I think we'd better leave the president to rest," he said.

They stood and looked down at the leader of the United States.

"I hope you recover quickly, sir," Jayne said. "The pope

has unfinished business he needs some help with. He wants to go ahead with his announcements."

"He's not the only one," the president said, his left eye open once again. "Make no mistake, I am staying here in Rome until I have completed what I came to do. I will join the pope for the planned announcement in St. Peter's Square just as soon as we can drag ourselves onto that platform—I don't care if we're bruised and battered. I hope you will both be staying for that event."

The president looked inquiringly at Jayne and Vic.

"I will be here, sir," Vic said. "Our embassy food is magnificent."

"I would like to stay, Mr. President," Jayne said. "However, I do have a little unfinished business relating to Cardinal Sweeney's office in New Orleans. I was discussing with the pope how the killer, whom we know to have been Pierre Fekkai, knew that the cardinals who were murdered in DC had uncovered details of the clothing company scam and were going to pass those details to you and your team at the White House. His Holiness speculated that perhaps there was a bug hidden in Cardinal Sweeney's office. I would like to go and check myself whether that is the case. Joe Johnson has already gone to New Orleans with the Feds to look into it. It would complete our jigsaw puzzle, more or less. I also need a break—and it is a long time since I was in Louisiana. I was planning to kill two birds with one stone, so to speak."

The president nodded. "That makes sense. You deserve it. Find a good jazz bar," he said. "You know, the pope is a smart man. Perhaps he chose the wrong profession."

Jayne smiled. "Indeed. I think he's somehow managed to pull off a neat bit of intelligence gathering that puts us to shame. Maybe we should try and cultivate a few sources of our own in that Secret Archive building rather than leave it to an eighty-year-old clergyman—who knows what else we might find?"

She exchanged a grin with Vic.

There was more than a little truth in what she had said. The volume of hidden secrets within the Secret Archive was almost certainly huge and largely untapped. She had filed it away as something to place on her to-do list for the future.

"I have heard worse ideas," the president said. "But it strikes me you have somehow developed the best source of all inside the Vatican—the Holy Father himself. I don't quite know how you've done it. Did he have a twinkle in his eye when he saw you for the first time?"

Jayne looked at Vic, who was still smiling.

"I think it's all about chemistry, Mr. President," Vic said. "Perhaps Jayne has a hidden ingredient that we, as men, somehow lack."

* * *

Tuesday, July 12, 2016
    Beirut

The layer of dust on Talal Hassan's desk seemed to have grown deeper just in the couple of weeks since he had been away. He wiped a finger through it and gazed at his visitor, who had turned up unannounced just a few minutes earlier.

"I am sorry, sir," he said. "Our plan was proceeding as intended but was thrown offtrack as soon as the British woman, Robinson, got involved along with her Israeli colleague. The bitch had so many strokes of good fortune, I found it difficult to believe, frankly."

The visitor, Nasser Khan, the head of Iran's Quds Force special operations group, did not appear impressed. He had arrived that morning less than an hour after Hassan himself, who had only returned from Italy via Marseille and Tunis late the previous night. It meant that Hassan had had no warning, no time to prepare a briefing on the ill-fated operation in Rome, and no time to properly rehearse his excuses.

Khan, whom Hassan had always found to be a ruthlessly calm character, was now sitting in a plain wooden chair on the other side of Hassan's desk. He appeared unusually stressed.

"The Supreme Leader had asked, or rather demanded, that we take advantage of the opportunity to eradicate the United States president and the pope during that meeting," Khan said. "I had told him about it. He told me to get it done. Now I face explaining to him yet another failure."

From outside in the corridor, there came the crack of a neighboring office door being slammed by someone. The vibration caused a few fragments of plaster to fall from the ceiling onto Hassan's desk.

The Unit 910 offices were in the second basement of a high-rise office building in Dahiya, a southern suburb of Beirut, near to Hezbollah's main headquarters. The building above was still unusable ten years after a series of devastating bombing raids by Israeli forces during a month-long war between them and Hezbollah.

Most of the other buildings in the suburb that were destroyed during that short conflict—the Second Lebanon War—had since been rebuilt and restored, but not yet this one. Hassan had been waiting for months for his smart new office, located in another nearby underground bunker, to be finished, but that had been delayed. So he had been forced to continue working in these dilapidated surroundings.

Hassan knew it had been a smart move on his part to have exited Rome when he did, given what had happened to Pierre Fekkai. But that was only a slight consolation. Losing yet another highly skilled lieutenant in Europe was a devastating blow. Quite how the safe house on Via di Sant'Anselmo had been discovered remained a mystery, as Hassan had been convinced their security and surveillance detection precautions had been very thorough. But these days, the ability of Western intelligence services to trace and track targets was so advanced, it was difficult to remain a step ahead.

"The failure to eliminate the president and pope had nothing to do with Pierre Fekkai's operational planning," Hassan said. "In fact, he had done remarkably well to gain the access he did. It showed great ingenuity. We were simply outdone by a combination of a smart opponent and pure bad luck. Another few seconds and it would have worked perfectly. Both the pope and the president were badly injured, as we have seen on television. We were that close."

"I suspect the Supreme Leader will not see it that way," Khan said.

The two men had similar backgrounds. Both had spent much of their careers out in the field on operations, culling Iran's and Hezbollah's many enemies across Europe and beyond. But now, they both spent most of their time behind their desks.

An imposing physical specimen, only a few centimeters shorter than Hassan and with close-cropped graying hair atop a bulletlike head, Khan appeared a little fragile for the first time that Hassan could recall.

"And what of Robinson?" Khan continued. "I am not sure I want to admit to the Supreme Leader that she has again managed to get the better of us. It might not do much for my life expectancy."

"I know. Well, you can tell him I'm not going to surrender to her," Hassan said. "These things go in cycles. We've come very close to taking her down a couple of times. Third time lucky, perhaps. I'm not giving up. I don't have to tell you about the fine margins between success and failure in this business. The wheel of fortune turns. We'll have our day, believe me. Then we can deliver her head to the Supreme Leader in a box."

"But you need to find yourself another operator to do that."

Hassan nodded. "I have others. Pierre and Henri Fekkai were top class over many years. Multiskilled and brave, who did a lot of high-value work for us. A tremendous loss. But they are not irreplaceable."

He knew he could find others, although they definitely wouldn't be of the same caliber as the Fekkai brothers, who had served Hezbollah with great distinction for a very long time. They had both been unfortunate, particularly Pierre.

"What about your asset inside the Vatican?" Khan asked.

Hassan grimaced. "Cardinal Martelli will be less easy to replace. I received a short message from him this morning. He's left Beirut and returned to his old home in Damascus. His plan is to lie low for a while, out of reach of the Swiss Guard and the Vatican police."

Martelli's career at the Vatican was certainly over, and Hassan guessed the same would surely apply to his tenure as Maronite Catholic Patriarch of Antioch and head of the Maronite Church.

Maybe he might be useful to Hassan again in the future, though. His contacts across the Middle East spread far and wide and reached right up to the heads of government in some countries. Martelli was something of an enigma to Hassan. A man of deep compassion for his people, and of deep convictions and faith, he nevertheless operated in ways that never ceased to surprise Hassan. If Martelli thought the outcome was morally justified, he never seemed bothered about the ethics involved in achieving it.

Martelli was unusual, that was for sure. Maybe he could

help Hassan to identify another source within the Vatican when the dust had settled.

It also seemed that the Carabinieri commander, Tommaso Porpora, a useful ally, had been decommissioned following his detention of Robinson and the Mossad agent. Hassan had tried to contact him several times but had failed to get a response. He had heard from another source inside the Carabinieri that Porpora, suffering from stress, had gone on indefinite sick leave. He hadn't been able to verify that, but if true, it seemed likely that rather than suffering stress, Porpora was being ousted from his position and would probably leave the service under a cloud.

More bad news had been forthcoming regarding Alberto Casartelli, who according to one of Hassan's sources, had been detained by airport police at Sarajevo the previous evening while waiting to board a Turkish Airlines flight to Manila, via Istanbul. He was now in custody in Sarajevo, awaiting extradition back to Rome, and Hassan knew he likely faced a long spell in jail.

"And what about the funding operation?" Khan asked. "Your main cash-generation source in the US has also gone. The Supreme Leader will be angry about that too. Oil prices are falling, and he doesn't want to give Hezbollah more money to offset what you've just lost—he'll say that's your fault, not Iran's."

Hassan leaned back and glanced up at the flaked plaster on the ceiling. "There are many other opportunities. Western institutions, governments, politicians, companies, and bosses are so corrupt, so laden with cash, their leaders so greedy. Many of them are sitting ducks. Take the Vatican—it is rich and there are many opportunities for blackmail. I'm not saying we will return there so soon, but it is an option. We will find a way. Leave it to me."

Khan nodded. "Just make sure you move quickly. I need

something positive to present to the Supreme Leader." He placed his hands behind his head and exhaled. "There's perhaps only one thing we can do in the circumstances, then. I can't drink alcohol in Tehran, but I can here. It's been a terrible week. I feel like I need a beer."

Having spent blocks of time in Tehran at different points of his career, Hassan sympathized. Alcohol had been banned there since the revolution in 1979—although it didn't stop the wealthy and powerful from obtaining it and drinking it behind closed doors.

"Me too," Hassan said. "But I need something stronger than beer."

EPILOGUE

Thursday, July 14, 2016
   New Orleans

The heady cocktail of jazz, alcohol, and smoke from a variety
of cigarettes that swirled around Bourbon Street as darkness
descended was starting to finally infect Jayne. She had the
same slightly euphoric feeling she often got when her more
successful investigations drew to a close. It was a mixture of
relief and achievement, seasoned—as often seemed to be the
case—with more than a few regrets for what might have been
and for collateral casualties suffered.

   She glanced across the balcony table she and Joe had
somehow secured at Felix's Restaurant and Oyster Bar, which
provided a vantage point from which they could view the
street scene below. The balcony, with its elegant black
wrought-iron fence, was one of several in that part of the
most famous street in the historic old city.

   While they waited for their oysters, Joe had ordered a Po-
Boy cocktail, which he reported contained significantly more

than the usual volume of Bacardi dark rum. Jayne had a Bloody Mary in front of her, which was also rapidly taking effect.

They were awaiting the return of Simon Dover, the FBI's executive assistant director in charge of the Criminal, Cyber, Response, and Services branch, who had flown with Joe from Los Angeles to New Orleans following the LA Fashions factory raid. Dover and one of his agents from the New Orleans field office had gone to carry out a search of Cardinal Sweeney's office and home to check for evidence and any clues how Hezbollah knew Sweeney had confessed his wrong-doings to his friend Cardinal Berg.

"How are Carrie and Peter getting on without you?" Jayne asked. She had been wondering about Joe's children, given that he had been away from home for more than a week.

"They seem to be doing better without me than with," Joe said. "At least that's what they tell me. No doubt they've had parties every night and the wine cellar will be empty. Maybe I'll just stay here."

Jayne smiled and raised her glass. She knew he was joking about his children. "That's good. They're growing up. Anyway, here's to your part in this investigation," she said. "Getting that information out of the LA Fashions factory was the key to unlocking the whole thing. I owe you."

"Hardly," Joe said. He scrutinized her face as they gently clinked glasses. "Looking at those bruises, I think I've had a walk in the park by comparison. Remind me not to rush to Rome next vacation."

The pain from the bruises incurred at the hands of the Carabinieri had faded, but Jayne's face remained a colorful patchwork quilt of purple, green, and yellow. It had provoked more than the occasional stare from strangers as they walked down Bourbon Street earlier.

Down in the street below, a conga of scantily clad girls

passed by, all singing some Taylor Swift song, all very obviously drunk. The throbbing music and neon lights that pulsed from outside most of the bars and restaurants created a real party atmosphere.

"Since I was here last time, I think in 1995, the music seems louder, the street busier, the lights brighter, and the people more drunk," Jayne said. "Or is it just that I'm getting older?"

Joe laughed and placed a hand on her thigh. "Probably all of those things. But I'm looking forward to making you feel young again later."

He gave her an exaggerated wink, which made her smile.

"Hmm. I'm looking forward to feeling young again too, in that case," Jayne said, lowering her already whisky-low voice by another tone or two, which she knew he found a turn-on.

Joe took a sip of his Po-Boy. "So, you hit it off with the pope, then? A useful inside contact to have cultivated, I have to say. How did you manage that?"

She struggled to keep a straight face. "The president asked me the same question. Vic said it was chemistry. But seriously, the pope's a very bright, insightful man. The information he sourced from the Secret Archive was also crucial. You'd like him. The only time he really threw me was when he asked me to be his confessor."

"His *confessor*? He wanted you to be his confessor?" Joe had a grin on his face.

"I'll tell you about it later, after I swear you to secrecy."

"Were you a good confessor?" Joe asked. "Did you give the pope absolution?"

"I don't think I'm qualified for that."

They both laughed.

"Well, I guess if you've saved someone's life, then you have a kind of bond with them for the rest of your days," Joe said. "And you've just done that with both pope and president. A double jackpot."

Jayne shrugged. "I'd rather I didn't have to do that to build my contacts book, frankly. I'd have been history alongside them had we been a minute later moving out of the study. But it wasn't just me saving lives. I'd probably have been history if Rafael hadn't saved my skin at the safe house. And if Avi Shiloah hadn't pulled strings with his prime minister, Rafael and I would likely still be in Regina Coeli prison—or dead. At the end of the day, we all owe each other. It's teamwork."

As she spoke, the familiar white-haired figure of Dover appeared through the door leading to the inside of the restaurant. Wearing his trademark black slacks and blue shirt, he strode up to them, took a seat, and placed a plastic evidence bag containing a small black box, half the size of a matchbox, on the table.

"We found this in Sweeney's study in his house," Dover said. "A transmitter. Hidden in a bookshelf. His staff said he never locks the office door. Easy for someone to have planted it."

Jayne examined it. "That looks similar to the one that the Swiss Guard found in the Vatican secretary of state's apartment."

She fished out her phone and located an email she had received from Heinrich Altishofen a couple of hours earlier. Sure enough, the attached photograph showed an identical transmitter found in a crucifix in Saraceni's top-floor apartment in the Palazzo San Carlo building.

Jayne showed the photo to Dover and Joe. "I have to say, Hezbollah leaves little to chance," she said. "I'm guessing it's all under the direction of Talal Hassan. A pity he wasn't in the Rome safe house along with Pierre Fekkai."

"People like that have the survival instinct of rats," Joe said. "You'll need to be doubly careful in the future, Jayne."

"The president also told me to watch my back," Jayne said. "Neither of you is wrong."

Dover leaned back and surveyed Jayne, then Joe, with a pair of laser-blue eyes. "I think I'm going to leave you two to enjoy a romantic evening," he said. "You probably don't want to talk business. I need to shower and call my wife. Let's catch up in the morning."

"Is there anything else significant to report from the Sweeney house?" Jayne asked.

"A few things. Not as important as the bug. But let's leave it until tomorrow." Dover stood, nodded to both of them, and left.

Jayne felt a sense of relief flood through her, partly driven by the final main missing piece of the puzzle having been found, partly because her Bloody Mary was now taking effect.

"They say oysters are a great aphrodisiac," Joe said. He carefully chewed his bottom lip.

"Good thing we ordered a lot of them, then," Jayne said. She reached across the table and took Joe's hand. "But do you really like oysters that much? I didn't know."

Joe paused. "Is the pope Catholic?" he asked.

They burst out laughing.

* * *

PRE-ORDER THE NEXT BOOK:
Book 4 in the **Jayne Robinson** series

The Queen's Pawn

If you enjoyed *The Confessor*, you may like to pre-order the next book I am writing. It will be Book 4 in this **Jayne**

Robinson series, entitled *The Queen's Pawn*. It is scheduled to be published in late 2022, depending on progress. It is available to pre-order in Kindle format on Amazon—unfortunately, Amazon does not allow pre-orders for paperbacks. If you make a pre-order, the book will be automatically delivered to your reading device as soon as it is published. You will only be charged on delivery.

To pre-order *The Queen's Pawn* just type "Andrew Turpin The Queen's Pawn" in the search box at the top of the Amazon page and you'll find it.

I should mention here that if you like **paperbacks**, you can buy copies of all of my books at my website shop. I can deliver to anywhere in the US and UK, although not currently other countries. That may change in future. You will find generous discounts if you are buying multiple books or series bundles, which makes them significantly cheaper than using Amazon. Buying this way also means I do not have to give Amazon their usual large portion of the sale price—so it helps me as well as you. Go to:

https://www.andrewturpin.com/shop/

To give you a flavor of *The Queen's Pawn*, here's the blurb:

> *CIA checkmated* . . . **A defecting oligarch meets a grisly death in London over a game of chess. CIA investigator Jayne Robinson is sent to Moscow on a high-risk mission to find out why. And the US president prepares for a crisis summit as Russia grabs a chunk of Ukraine.**
> The dead oligarch is apparently ready to pass on top secret information about the Kremlin's increasingly

hostile plans and strategy. But he never gets the chance.

Jayne Robinson is dispatched to Moscow to extract information from a highly-placed asset in Russia's foreign intelligence service.

But the operation does not go to plan, and Robinson is left in a desperate battle not just to get what she needs, but for her personal survival.

The ensuing game of diplomatic chess becomes highly personal for Robinson as she swiftly learns it's impossible to know who to trust—either on the other side, or on her own.

She ends up delving deep for answers into the dirtiest and most dangerous corners of Russian and western European capital cities—as the US president fights to save his career.

***The Queen's Pawn*, book number four in the best-selling Jayne Robinson series, is a nail-biting spy thriller with throwbacks to the Cold War and twists that will shock the reader.**

* * *

ANDREW'S READERS GROUP

If you enjoyed this book, I would like to keep in touch. This is not always easy, as I usually only publish a couple of books a year and there are many authors and books out there. So the best way is for you to be on my Readers Group email list. I can then send you updates on the next book, plus occasional special offers. There's no spam and you can unsubscribe at any time.

If you would like to join my Readers Group and receive

the email updates, I will send you, **FREE**, the ebook version of another thriller, *The Afghan*, which forms a prequel to both the **Jayne Robinson** series and my **Joe Johnson** series and normally sells at $4.99/£3.99 (paperback $11.99/£9.99).

The Afghan is set in 1988 when Jayne was with Britain's Secret Intelligence Service and Joe Johnson was with the CIA —both of them based in Pakistan and Afghanistan. Most of the action takes place in Afghanistan, then occupied by the Soviet Union, and in Washington, DC. Some of the characters and story lines that emerge in my other books have their roots in this period. I think you will enjoy it!

The Afghan can be downloaded **FREE** from the following link:

https://bookhip.com/RJGFPAW

The **Jayne Robinson** thriller series so far comprises the following:

1. The Kremlin's Vote
2. The Dark Shah
3. The Confessor
4. The Queen's Pawn (due to be published in late 2022)

If you have enjoyed the Robinson series, you will probably also like the **Joe Johnson series**, if you haven't read them yet. In order, they are as follows:

Prequel: *The Afghan*
1. The Last Nazi
2. The Old Bridge
3. Bandit Country

To find my books on Amazon just type "Andrew Turpin" in the search box at the top of the Amazon page — you can't miss them!

* * *

IF YOU ENJOYED THIS BOOK PLEASE WRITE A REVIEW

As an independently published author, through my own imprint The Write Direction Publishing, I find that honest reviews of my books are the most powerful way for me to bring them to the attention of other potential readers.

As you'll appreciate, unlike the big international publishers, I can't take out full-page advertisements in the newspapers.

So I am committed to producing books of the best quality I can in order to attract a loyal group of readers who are happy to recommend my work to others.

Therefore, if you enjoyed reading this novel, then I would very much appreciate it if you would spend five minutes and leave a review—which can be as short as you like—preferably on the page or website where you bought it.

You can find the book by going to the Amazon website and typing "Andrew Turpin The Confessor" in the search box.

Once you have clicked on the page, scroll down to "Customer Reviews," then click on "Leave a Review."

Reviews are also a great encouragement to me to write more!

Many thanks.

THANKS AND ACKNOWLEDGEMENTS

I would like to thank everyone who reads my books. You are the reason I began to write in the first place, and I hope I can provide you with entertainment and interest for a long time into the future.

Every time I get an encouraging email from a reader, or a positive comment on my Facebook page, or a nice review on Amazon, it spurs me on to press ahead with my research and writing for the next book. So keep them coming!

Specifically with regard to **_The Confessor_**, there are several people who have helped me during the long process of research, writing, and editing.

In particular, I have two editors who consistently provide helpful advice, food for thought, great ideas, and constructive criticism, and between them have enabled me to considerably improve the initial draft. Katrina Diaz Arnold, owner of Refine Editing, again gave me a lot of valuable feedback at the structural and line levels, and Jon Ford, as ever, helped me to maintain the authenticity of the story in many areas through his great eye for detail. I would like to thank both of them—the responsibility for any remaining mistakes lies solely with me.

As always, my brother, Adrian Turpin, was a very helpful reader of my early drafts and highlighted areas where I need to improve. I also had very valuable input from my small but dedicated Advance Readers Group team, who went through the final version prior to proofreading and also highlighted a number of issues that required changes and improvements—a big thank-you to them all.

I would also like to thank the team at Damonza for what I think is a great cover design.

AUTHOR'S NOTE

Over the centuries, Vatican City, the world's smallest state, has been at the center of endless fascination and intrigue out of all proportion to its tiny 121-acre size, tucked away in the center of Rome. The reason, of course, is that it houses the headquarters of the Catholic Church and is the home of its leader, the pope.

For many, the story of the Vatican really is a case of truth being stranger than fiction. That has not stopped many fiction authors from building stories around it, however, and I was inspired to join their number after a visit to Rome and the Vatican in the summer of 2019. *The Confessor* results from that, and I hope you enjoy it.

At this point, I should once again remind readers that, as ever, my books are fictional, designed for entertainment, so the characters and the plots are all either from my imagination or used in a fictional sense. *The Confessor* is not an exception, and you should not read anything more into its contents, particularly when it comes to the political and religious figures and plots, and ideas I have depicted. I'm definitely not aiming to take sides or express my own views in any way—only to entertain.

My real fascination as a fiction writer lies in the big picture conflicts that exist in our world—the ongoing battles between the leaders of democratic nations on one hand and the dictators and autocrats on the other. These are fights that we in the West tend to portray in black and white terms and often in a very personalized way, given the larger-than-life nature of many of the characters who run the countries involved. It's Good vs. Evil, Light vs. Dark.

In the dark corner are the most notorious and powerful dictatorships operating in the world today, namely Vladimir

Putin's Russia, Ayatollah Ali Khamenei's Iran, Xi Jinping's China, and Kim Jong Un's North Korea. Even as I type these words, atrocities, mass murders, and war crimes on a large scale are being committed by Russian troops who have been sent into neighboring Ukraine by Putin as part of an invasion designed to subjugate the entire country.

For thriller writers, these regimes are unfortunately the gift that keeps on giving—they provide a real life backdrop for our fictional stories. Indeed, it's sometimes a challenge to avoid portraying the entire country as the villain, rather than just the leadership.

These dictators see it as their role to not just disrupt and interfere with Western democratic nations, but ultimately to supplant them—to weaken them to the extent that they can effectively take their place. They are looking for all opportunities and methods to undermine Western political, religious, business, and cultural institutions as part of this battle. It is an existential fight, in all senses of the word, because these dictators don't simply have powerful cyber and battlefield weapons at their disposal, they have the nuclear warheads that could potentially wipe out all of us, or in the case of Iran are working to develop them.

For Western leaders, to fight successfully against this onslaught requires strong, moral, and brave leadership—and I'm not talking just about those operating in political institutions but others too, ranging from the church, to businesses, to universities, sports teams, media, and cultural entities. If the dictators see a weakness, they will seek to exploit it.

My heroes, the likes of Jayne Robinson, Joe Johnson, and their colleagues, are at the coalface of the battle against such attempts to corrupt and destroy. In **The Confessor**, we see a fictional plot to achieve exactly that. But the plot mirrors and draws on many of the maneuverings and tactics that we see happening in real life every day across multiple continents, and illustrates why we need to be on our guard.

In terms of the locations and buildings featured in **The Confessor**, most are real but are used in a completely fictional sense. A few are completely fictional, but may resemble real-life places. The same applies to many of the organizations and institutions described in the book—I have written a fictional story set against a realistic backdrop.

You will search in vain for Pope Julius or any of the cardinals or other clergymen named in this book. They are all figments of my imagination, and although the dioceses they come from do exist in real life, the events attributed to them did not happen as described. For example, although there have been claims in real life of abuse relating to the Catholic Church in New Orleans and in many other US dioceses, I have not used these as the basis for my story and they certainly have no linkage to a clothing manufacturer.

As far as I know, there are no such clothing companies as my fictional LA Fashions or Sole Nero, and neither is there a clothing retail chain named Adelaide.

In Rome, readers will have no luck looking for my fictional Vatican tailor shop, Fratelli Zeffirelli, although there are other similar outfitters who do supply garments to cardinals.

Similarly, there is no tailor shop on Rue de Saint-Simon in Paris, although there is a lovely hotel in that street named Hôtel Duc de Saint-Simon, where I stayed in 2009 during a family trip. I would thoroughly recommend it, and I apologize to the owners for staging my fictional bomb explosion in the street outside and for allowing Hezbollah terrorists to trigger that explosion from one of their hotel suites.

The buildings described within Vatican City all exist and can be viewed on a tour of the site, although I have, on occasions slightly fictionalized elements of their interiors and their layouts to suit my plot.

The Vatican Secret Archive, renamed in 2019 as the Vatican Apostolic Archive, very much exists. Within its fifty-three miles of shelving lie documents dating back to the eighth century, including numerous letters and documents written by popes. As well as the historical documents, there are also many relating to more recent times, many of which are effectively classified and inaccessible to outsiders.

These include papers finally released in 2020 after much delay that related to Pius XII, who was pope from 1939 to 1958 and who has been under scrutiny in the decades since over his stance during the Holocaust. He stood accused of failing to denounce and act against Hitler and the Nazis during that period and of doing less than was practically possible to help Jews to escape.

For details of further reading relating to the plot of **The Confessor**, see the next section, which covers some of the sources I used during my research prior to and during the writing of this book.

All the best,
   Andrew

RESEARCH AND BIBLIOGRAPHY

The decision to involve the Vatican in my plot for ***The Confessor*** brought me significant challenges. The Vatican and the Catholic Church is a complex institution and the volume of reading and research required to get to grips with its structure and character was significant. The same could be said for Hezbollah's global fundraising operations through its Unit 910, which incorporates its Business Affairs Component.

In terms of the physical layout and descriptions of the Vatican and its history, I drew heavily on my own experience while visiting it and the wider Rome area, particularly Trastevere, during the summer of 2019. Indeed, it was that visit that inspired me to write this book.

But I needed far more than that, of course. Below is just a flavor of the books, websites, and other publications I consulted during the writing of this thriller. While trying to fit the Vatican's complicated structures, processes, people, and hierarchies into the fast-moving flow of a thriller story, I have done my best to make my characterizations as true to life as possible. Inevitably, there have been some distortions. The responsibility for that is mine alone.

The germ of this story came from a Congressional Testimony for the Homeland Security Committee, written by Dr. Emanuele Ottolenghi and entitled State Sponsors of Terrorism: An Examination of Iran's Global Terrorism Network. The testimony detailed Hezbollah's fundraising operations globally and described some of the ways in which the organization corrupts and blackmails its way into some of the key pillars of society in the United States and many other countries.

It made me wonder how far Hezbollah's tentacles really spread, and what might happen if they infiltrated and corrupted other organizations that might have left themselves vulnerable to such actions, including the Catholic Church. You can find the Ottolenghi testimony here: https://docs.house.gov/meetings/HM/HM05/20180417/108155/HHRG-115-HM05-Wstate-OttolenghiE-20180417.pdf

There have been several in-depth publications from The Washington Institute for Near East Policy about Hezbollah and its operational strategies and tactics globally, most of which have proved useful. For example, Matthew Levitt wrote an article entitled Breaking Hezbollah's Golden Rule, which detailed some of the activities of Unit 910, the organization's external terrorist operations wing and responsible for its fundraising arm, the Business Affairs Component. You can find it here: https://www.washingtoninstitute.org/media/367

Another helpful article from the institute, detailing Hezbollah's fundraising and organized crime activities, is entitled Hezbollah as a Criminal Organization, and can be found here: https://www.washingtoninstitute.org/policy-analysis/hezbollah-criminal-organisation

Grey Dynamics has also published an interesting account of Hezbollah's Business Affairs Component, responsible for global fundraising, which can be found here: https://www.greydynamics.com/hezbollahs-stock-market/

I refer in The Confessor to a huge haul of Captagon amphetamines worth $1.1 billion that was intercepted on its way into Naples from Syria. This is based on an actual drugs seizure by the Italian authorities during 2020. The prime suspect for the smuggling operation, though not proven, was Hezbollah. There are several articles available about this case, including this one in *The Washington Post*: https://www.washingtonpost.com/national-security/hezbollah-operatives-seen-behind-spike-in-drug-trafficking-analysts-say/2020/08/03/fa286b1a-d36a-11ea-8c55-61e7fa5e82ab_story.html

For those interested in learning more about Hezbollah's

Unit 133, which operates primarily in the West Bank and which features in *The Confessor*, there are a number of articles available. A starting point is this piece in FDD's Long War Journal: https://www.longwarjournal.org/archives/2016/02/hezbollah-tries-to-shift-attention-to-the-west-bank.php

There is another article in Israel Defence about Unit 133 here: https://www.israeldefense.co.il/en/content/hezbollahs-unit-133-exposed

The Vatican has long been the center of numerous scandals of all kinds, from financial to sexual abuse. A number of books have been published in recent years detailing these and the efforts by Pope Francis to try and implement reforms.

Of these, one of the most enlightening is by Italian journalist Gianluigi Nuzzi, entitled Merchants in the Temple. It details Pope Francis's battle against corruption and the obstacles he has faced in trying to bring about change. It can be found on Amazon or at other bookshops: My Book

It was Nuzzi, of course, who was pivotal to the "Vatileaks" scandal in 2011-12, when confidential documents were removed from Pope Benedict XVI's office by his butler, Paolo Gabriele, and leaked to Nuzzi. The documents were the subject of one of Nuzzi's other books, His Holiness: The Secret Papers of Benedict XVI. The book, republished in English as Ratzinger Was Afraid, revealed corruption that cost the Vatican many millions of euro in higher contract prices, as well as details of the vicious factional fighting, bribery, and intrigue that was ongoing within the Vatican. It can be found here: My Book

Pope Francis's attempts to reform the Catholic Church and the Vatican have predictably met with intense opposition from conservative elements and vested interests. A good account of this conflict can be found in The Guardian here: https://www.theguardian.com/news/2017/oct/27/the-war-against-pope-francis

The recent opening of the Vatican Secret Archive papers on Pius XII, pope from 1939 to 1958, triggered a wave of speculation about what might be found. Academic researchers are continuing to plough through the mountain of papers in search of a "smoking gun" that might reveal something Pius had done to indicate alignment with Hitler. But it was probably more about what he didn't say or do that is the key issue. He failed to publicly condemn the Holocaust or Hitler's regime, and this failure has been the basis of works such as John Cornwell's book Hitler's Pope: The Secret History of Pius XII, published in 1999. It can be found here: My Book

However, the recently released papers have confirmed that behind the scenes, Pius XII did considerable work to help protect Jews fleeing the Nazi regime, and saved an estimated 15,000 through various means. The chief archivist of the *Bundestag* (German parliament), Michael Feldkamp has been extensively quoted on this work, including this article in Vatican News: https://www.vaticannews.va/en/church/news/2022-02/feldkamp-pope-pius-xii-holocaust-history-archives.html

And also this article by Feldkamp, published on LinkedIn, which argues that Pius XII did more for the Jews and to promote European peace than his previous reputation suggests: https://www.linkedin.com/pulse/pius-xii-diplomat-pope-peace-michael-f-feldkamp/

The Confessor describes how my fictional Pope Julius is taken to Rome's Gemelli hospital after the bomb blast that injured him. Indeed, the 1,575-bed Gemelli, opened in 1964, really does have a suite on its tenth floor reserved for papal medical emergencies. For example, in 2021, Pope Francis underwent colon surgery there. For more, see the following article: https://thetablet.org/gemelli-hospital-is-known-as-go-to-health-facility-for-popes/

Within the Vatican and elsewhere, some cardinals choose to live in very simple accommodation, such as Pope Francis, who has a small apartment in St. Martha's House, while others choose much more lavish quarters.

This article in National Geographic describes Pope Francis's apartment: https://www.nationalgeographic.com/culture/article/130328-pope-francis-vatican-casa-santa-marta-apartment-rome-catholic

And these describe the large, lavish apartment occupied by the Vatican's former secretary of state Cardinal Bertrone on the top floor of the Palazzo San Carlo: https://www.telegraph.co.uk/news/worldnews/europe/italy/10777482/Cardinals-vast-luxury-apartment-in-Vatican-angers-Pope.html

And: https://www.huffingtonpost.co.uk/entry/cardinal-tarcisio-bertone-pope_n_6699464

Other cardinals located elsewhere are also sometimes to be found occupying grand properties: https://edition.cnn.com/interactive/2014/08/us/american-archbishops-lavish-homes/index.html

For those interested in the layout of the pope's private apartments at the Vatican, including his chapel and office, on the third floor of the Apostolic Palace, further details can be found at the following links:

https://www.theeponymousflower.com/2013/03/the-pope-lives-in-hotel-pope-and-papal.html

https://www.pinterest.co.uk/pin/338684834468239359/

The above details give you at least a flavor of some of the sources and locations I have used in this book. There are, of course, many more, too numerous to mention. I hope it is helpful—I am quite willing to exchange emails if readers have questions about any others not detailed here.

ABOUT THE AUTHOR AND CONTACT DETAILS

I have always had a love of writing and a passion for reading good thrillers. I also had a long-standing dream of writing my own novels, and eventually, I got around to achieving that objective.

The Confessor is the third in the **Jayne Robinson** series of thrillers, which follows on from my **Joe Johnson** series (currently comprising six books plus a prequel). These books pull together some of my other interests, particularly history, world news, and travel.

I studied history at Loughborough University and worked for many years as a business and financial journalist before becoming a corporate and financial communications adviser with several large energy companies, specializing in media relations. I am now a full-time writer.

Originally I came from Grantham, Lincolnshire, and I now live with my family in St. Albans, Hertfordshire, UK.

You can connect with me via these routes:
E-mail: andrew@andrewturpin.com
Website: www.andrewturpin.com.
Facebook: @AndrewTurpinAuthor
Facebook Readers Group: https://www.facebook.com/groups/1202837536552219
Twitter: @AndrewTurpin
Instagram: @andrewturpin.author

Please also follow me on Bookbub and Amazon!
https://www.bookbub.com/authors/andrew-turpin
https://www.amazon.com/Andrew-Turpin/e/B074V87WWL/

Do get in touch with your comments and views on the books, or anything else for that matter. I enjoy hearing from readers and promise to reply.